NEPTUNE'S
BROOD

My stalker beamed into Taj Beacon barely a million seconds after I did. We'd both been sent more than a decade earlier, via the beacon in high orbit around GJ 785: Our packet streams overlapped for months as the Taj Beacon buffered and checksummed, decrypted and decompressed, and finally downloaded two neural streams onto soul chips for installation in newly built bodies, paid for by the slow money draft signed and attached at the origin of our transmission. I awakened first, my new body molded to a semblance of my previous phenotype by the configuration metadata attached to the soul transmission. I completed the immigration formalities and left the arrivals hall before the killer opned its eyes.

While I was on Taj Beacon, I was unaware of its existence.

But I found out all too soon.

BY CHARLES STROSS

Saturn's Children
Singularity Sky
Iron Sunrise
Accelerando
Glasshouse
Wireless: The Essential Collection
Halting State
Rule 34
Neptune's Brood

The Laundry Files
The Atrocity Archives
The Jennifer Morgue
The Fuller Memorandum
The Apocalypse Codex
The Rhesus Chart
The Annihilation Score
The Nightmare Stacks
The Delirium Brief
The Labyrinth Index

NEPTUNE'S BROOD

CHARLES STROSS

orbit

www.orbitbooks.net

ORBIT

First published in Great Britain in 2013 by Orbit
This paperback edition published in 2014 by Orbit

3 5 7 9 10 8 6 4 2

Copyright © 2013 by Charles Stross

The moral right of the author has been asserted.

Excerpt from *Ancillary Justice* by Ann Leckie
Copyright © 2013 by Ann Leckie

A CIP catalogue record for this book
is available from the British Library.

ISBN 978-0-356-50100-0

Printed and bound by Clays Ltd, Elcograf S.p.A

Papers used by Orbit are from well-managed forests
and other responsible sources.

MIX
Paper from
responsible sources
FSC® C104740

Orbit
An imprint of
Little, Brown Book Group
Carmelite House
50 Victoria Embankment
London EC4Y 0DZ

An Hachette UK Company
www.hachette.co.uk

www.orbitbooks.net

For everyone, everywhere,
who's ever looked at the stars and thought,
"I wonder if we could live there?"

Beacon Departure

"I can get you a cheaper ticket if you let me amputate your legs: I can even take your thighs as a deposit," said the travel agent. He was clearly trying hard to be helpful: "It's not as if you'll need them where you're going, is it?"

"Is it possible to find a better price by booking me on a different routing?" I asked. "I'm very attached to my limbs." (Quaint and old-fashioned, that's me.) "Also," I hedged, "I don't have much fast money."

The agent sighed. His two eyes were beautiful: enormous violet photoreceptors that gleamed with a birefringent sheen. "Ms. Alizond. Krina. How can I put this? That could be a problem." He hesitated for only a moment: "Do you have any longer-term funds? Anything you can convert . . . ?"

I shook my head. "I only got here ten days—sorry, about a million seconds—ago, and I haven't had time to cash in any investments. I need to get to Shin-Tethys as fast as possible."

He looked pained. It was a warning sign I recognized well—he was on the cusp of deciding that I was just another penniless refugee, and any moment now he was going to slam down the shutters: *Why are you wasting my time?* I'd done it myself often enough to recognize the symptoms.

"I converted everything I had into slow money before I emigrated, as viscous as possible," I said hastily.

At least he didn't tell me to get out of his office. I could see his cupidity battling his cynicism—*is she delusional?* Cupidity won, narrowly: "Everything you've got is in slow money? Then how have you been eating?"

"Badly." He'd finally stepped out of role, revealing irrelevant curiosity; that was an opening I could use. Pathos first: "I've been sleeping on park benches and eating municipal gash to reduce my outgoings." (The raw, unprocessed hydrocarbon feedstock is vile but free: the good burghers of Taj Beacon provide it because it's cheaper than employing police to pacify the lumpen cattle by force.) "What cents I have I can't afford to up-convert in a hurry."

"So you've gone long? All the way long, everything locked down in slow money? Not even some medium dollars?" His eyes widened very slightly at the hint of cents, plural—which meant I had his full and undivided attention. *Gotcha.* He smoothly pivoted into oleaginous deference: "But surely you're aware that as little as a tenth of a slow cent could buy you a month in the most palatial palazzo in—"

"Yes, I'm very much aware of that." I had my opening. Now I narrowed my eyes and cut back on the vulnerability: I wanted him to want to make me feel I owed him some payback at a future time, not drool all over my wallet in the present. "I don't want to sell my soul just yet. I *really* don't. What I want to do is get to Shin-Tethys with all possible speed, using only fast money, cash in hand. Maybe when I've completed my work, and it's time to head home, I'll be able to splash out, charter a luxury yacht . . ."

"Oh." He looked crestfallen. "Well, I'm not sure that's going to be possible, Sera Alizond. You see, you're too late."

"Um?" He appeared to be entirely sincere. This was *not* what I wanted to hear! What I wanted was for this small-time hustler to go out of his way to get me a quiet unobtrusive berth, in hope of a payoff down the line.

"If you'd incarnated just ten million seconds ago, I had passenger berths down to Shin-Tethys coming out of my ears, going unsold! But we're past inferior conjunction now, heading toward superior, and you won't get a straight transfer orbit for love or favors. Your only option is to pay for additional delta vee, and that costs *real* money. Not to mention that there's a huge mass penalty. You'd need to charter a capsule specifically for . . ." He trailed off and glanced at my legs again, then did a double take. "Unless . . ." He glanced into his desktop, finger-doodled some questions to an invisible amanuensis: "Please excuse me, I was looking for *passenger* vessels. It might be possible for me to arrange a working passage for you if you have any appropriate skills." He paused again, his timing perfect. I couldn't help but admire his expert manipulation even as I resented it. "You said you came in from, was it Hector? They have Fragiles there, don't they. Tell me, would you have a problem working with meatsacks?"

"Meat?" I didn't have to feign surprise. "I don't think so . . ." I was about to volunteer my profession, but he focused on his desktop again, shutting me out.

"There's an opening for a ship-hand in the labor-exchange listing." Into which he was, of course, plugged, the better to earn his commission as a recruiter. "Let me see . . ." He referred to the desktop clipped to the wall beside him. "It's on board a religious vehicle—a chapel—that's en route to Shin-Tethys. It's not exactly a fast liner, but it's better than a minimum-energy cargo pod. They put in for repairs here because of some sort of technical trouble, and they've only just got it sorted out. Let's see . . . the requirement is for semi- or unskilled labor, but you need to be able to work in standard gravity, and more importantly, be of traditional bodily form, which rules out a lot of people. It's conditional on your satisfying the sailing master about your piety," he added by way of a warning. "I can't help you there. The interview is entirely up to you. They're supposed to provide training on the job. That'll be fifty dollars fast, refundable if you don't get the berth. Assuming you want it and can afford—"

"I do, and I can." It was cheaper than I could have hoped for, and I had no problem with the idea of a working passage; it would help avoid the tedium of a long-duration flight. *Delayed by some sort of problem.* Their misfortune: my profit.

I held out a hand and flashed it, allowing the numinous glow of hot cash to light up the chromatophores in the webbing between my fingers. "It's just the Church of the Fragile, yes? Pious worshippers tending to the holy flesh, keeping it from rotting as they fulfill their mission to the stars?"

"That's my understanding." He nodded. "That, and routine cleaning chores. They may be religious, but they're pragmatists. As long as you're not heretically inclined . . . ?"

"No, nothing like that!" Tending meat: In all our years, I don't think any of my lineage has ever done that. But beggars can't be choosers—not even mendicant scholars masquerading as beggars. We shook on the deal, and his palm flickered red, the escrow lock pulsing rapidly. "I'll just be going. If you'd maybe tell me where . . . ?"

"Certainly." He smiled, evidently pleased with himself, then passed me the coordinates. "You want Node Six, Docking Attachment Delta. The Blessed Chapel of Our Lady of the Holy Restriction Endonuclease is parked outside—in quarantine because of the meat. That's normal in such circumstances, you know. Ask for Deacon Dennett. They will be expecting you."

W*hat I was unaware of:*
I had a stalker.

Most people are autonomes; self-owning, self-directed, conscious. It is the glory and tragedy of autonomes that they experience the joy of self-awareness and the terror of the ultimate dissolution of self into nonexistence at the end of life. You are an autonome: So am I.

The stalker was not an autonome. Despite looking outwardly human and imprinted with a set of human memories, the cortical nodes within its skull were not configured to give rise to a sense of self. The person who sent the stalker believed that consciousness was a liability and a handicap that might impair its ability to fulfill its mission: to hunt down and kill me.

The stalker had a full briefing on me, but didn't know much about what I was doing in Dojima System, other than the fact of my arrival and its instructions for my disposal.

I later learned that my stalker beamed into Taj Beacon barely a million seconds after I did. We'd both been sent more than a decade earlier, via the beacon in high orbit around GJ 785: Our packet streams overlapped for months as the Taj Beacon buffered and checksummed, decrypted and decompressed, and finally downloaded two neural streams onto soul chips for installation in newly built bodies, paid for by the slow money draft signed and attached at the origin of our transmission. I awakened first, my new body molded to a semblance of my previous phenotype by the configuration metadata attached to the soul transmission. I completed the immigration formalities and left the arrivals hall before the killer opened its eyes.

While I was on Taj Beacon, I was unaware of its existence.

But I found out all too soon.

The travel agent's office was a fabric bag attached to one of the structural trusses that braced the vast, free-fall souk at the heart of Taj Beacon's commons. I really hated the souk; having gotten what I went there for, I ran away as fast as I could.

I confess to you that I lied to the travel agent about my assets. When I arrived, almost the first thing I did was to cautiously convert a couple of slow cents into fast money. I did it reluctantly. The best slow-to-fast exchange rate I could find here was usurious—I took a 92-percent hit on the public rate, never mind what a relative would have fronted me—but to up-convert with full and final settlement via the issuing bank would take nearly a billion seconds: It's not called *slow* money for nothing. I was not, in fact, sleeping on park benches and subsisting on raw hydrocarbon slurry: But I saw no need to advertise the fact that I had 7.02 slow dollars signed and sealed to my soul chips, and another 208.91 medium dollars at my fingertips. That much money walking around unguarded was an invitation to a mugging or worse.

Taj Beacon is and was the main gateway for information and currency flows entering and leaving Dojima System. It hosts multiple communication lasers, pointed at the star systems with which Dojima trades directly. As commonly happens, the burghers of Taj Beacon have a vested interest in maintaining a choke hold on interstellar commerce. Consequently, they scheme to prevent rival groups from establishing their own beacons. And so it is that, in addition to the high priesthood of financiers and factors who worked the banks and bureaux de change and bourse, the operations managers and engineers who maintained the interstellar communications lasers, and the usual workers you might find on any deep-space habitat, Taj is host to numerous loan sharks, grifters, labor brokers, and slavers.

I was traveling alone, and my only contact in the entire system had gone missing—so to say I was isolated would be an understatement. Under the circumstances, drawing attention to myself by flashing my assets seemed like a really bad idea. I therefore lived cautiously, using anonymous cash to rent a cramped arbeiter's pod in an unfashionable high-gee zone, going through the public motions of seeking employment, trying to remain inconspicuous—and meanwhile looking for a ship out of this festering sinkhole of villainy.

As for the souk: Some combination of the disorienting lack of local verticalia, the density of bodies, the shouting of offers, the mixture of smells, and the fluctuating hash of electromagnetic noise combined to make me claustrophobic whenever I had to visit an establishment there. But what really got to me was the *advertising*.

The souk is a public space. Unless you pay up for a pricey privacy filter, every move you make is fodder for a thousand behavioral search engines, which bombard you with stimuli and monitor your autonomic responses in order to dynamically evolve more attractive ads. Images of desire bounce off blank surfaces for your eyes only, ghostly haptic fingertips run across your skin, ghostly lascivious offers beam right inside your ears. *Are we getting hotter? Colder? Does this make you feel good?* I didn't want to draw attention to myself by excessive filtering. But I wasn't used to the naked hard selling: My earlier life hadn't prepared me for it, and the ads made me feel bilious and love-stricken, invaded and debauched by a coldly mechanical lust for whatever fetish the desire machines were pushing at their victims at any given instant. The mindless persistence with which the adbots attempted to coax the life-money from their targets was disturbing. Though I hadn't been on Taj long, I had already learned to hate the sensation. The soul-sickening sense of need ebbed and faded from moment to moment as I moved from one hidden persuader's cell to the next, leaving me feeling vulnerable and friendless. *Alienated? Friend-lorn? Desirous of luxurious foods or eager prostitutes? We can torment and titillate until you pay for sweet release . . .*

Beacon stations are the choke points of interstellar trade, positioned to extract value from the slow money of the dissatisfied and the desperate as they pass through the network. Taj Beacon is the worst I've ever visited, possibly a holdover from its foundation in the wake of the great Atlantis depression, over two millennia ago: The result is a frenzied vortex of dionysiac capitalism presided over by a grasping, vicious plutocracy, boiling and churning in the frigid wastes on the edge of the star system. All because the beacon lay in the trailing trojan point of the innermost gas giant, between the outer belt and hab colonies and the populated inner system that generated the traffic. Taj's founders were in the right place at the right time, and they and their descendants took it as a *de facto* license to seek rent.

Surviving the barrage of ads with my sense of purpose intact and my purse unravished required self-discipline and a willingness to shut down my facial nerves and chromatophores completely—and preferably to shut my eyes and ears as well. Counting features of the ads helped me ignore the content; I kept tally of the products, descriptions, and associated emotional cues as I pushed through, as a tenuous gesture of defiance. (Eleven ads, averaging six iterations per minute, in case you were wondering.) And, after far too long, I managed to make my escape into the civilized low-gee suburbs, then back to my cheap, rented, capsule apartment.

Calling it an apartment is, perhaps, an exaggeration. A cube of nearly thirty meters' volume, it held my bed (a blood blue cocoon purchased from a thrift store), a couple of changes of clothing suitable for different social contexts, a two-meter retina with a ripped corner that I'd rescued from a recycler and tacked to one wall for visualizations and entertainment, a ready-packed bag in case I had to leave in a hurry, and a crate where I kept my feed. I'd visited worse slums, but not often and never to live there by choice.

On the other hand, there was nothing here to attract the attention of my neighbors. Most of the other residents were laborers or fractional-reserve servants of one variety or another: poor but sufficiently respectable not to attract the attention of the secret police. (Not that the SPs cared about anything except direct threats of sedition or subversion that might impair their patrons' ability to keep their salaries flowing. Accept capitalism into your heart, and you were almost certainly safe, except for the occasional unfortunate case of mistaken identity. Yet another reason not to dwell here too long . . .)

I flopped back onto my bed and waved at the retina. "Any mail?" I asked halfheartedly.

"Good evenshift, Krina! I'm sorry, there's nothing new for you today." I'd given it an avatar, the facial map and mannerisms of my sib Briony—but left the eyes empty, to remind me there was no person behind them. "A communiqué from your cousin Andrea"—a sib of another generation from mine—"is buffering now and will be complete within two thousand seconds. Price of release is thirty-two fast. Do you wish to accept?"

I swore under my breath—not at the retina, lest it misinterpret. But rent-seeking intermediaries with a monopoly on interstellar commerce would have been a good candidate for the bane of my life had they not also become the source of my income (by a cosmic irony that I no longer found even remotely humorous). In this case, the station's official receiver had decided that Andrea's incoming message was inconveniently large, or that the exchange rate since its transmission began (at least twelve years ago, assuming she was still back home) had fluctuated sufficiently to justify levying a supplementary fee. In any event, what was I going to do? I could pay the additional service fee or miss the message. Which might be something as banal as a *we're all missing you, come home safe and soon* or as vitally important as word that my entire multiyear mission was pointless, that the long-lost property had been picked up by a rival syndicate.

"Accept and debit my account," I said aloud. I paused to update my expenses sheet and stared gloomily at the dwindling cash float: Today was turning out to be very costly indeed. "Have there been any more responses to my primary search?" I asked the retina.

"No new responses!" I winced. I'd spent another chunk of fast money a week ago, buying a broadcast search—not merely of Taj Beacon's public-information systems, but propagated systemwide—for news of Ana. Who had now been missing for over a hundred days, since shortly after I began to download into the arrival hall's buffers—a suspicious coincidence, in my view, given that she had lived in the same floating city on Shin-Tethys for over twenty years. "Three archived responses. Do you wish to review them?"

"No." I had them off by rote memory: One anxious inquiry from an out-of-touch friend of Ana's (I think an ex-lover); a request for an interview from the local police (doubtless wondering why an out-system visitor was interested in a missing person); and a debt-collection agency wondering who was going to pay the rent on her pod. It was depressing to think how faint the mark she'd left behind must be, that so few people were interested in her disappearance. (Much like me, in fact. Loneliness is our only reliable companion when we fish the well of time for magic coins.) "Download and archive Andrea's packet in my second slot as soon as it's available." A thought struck me. "Transaction with M. Hebert, travel agent: labor-exchange placement. When does it time out?"

"Your offer closes in four thousand four hundred seconds! Placement vessel preparing for departure!" My retina chirped.

What? The agent didn't tell me it was leaving so soon! I looked around my cube in a momentary panic, then realized there was virtually nothing here that I couldn't replace easily enough. I grabbed my go bag, already stuffed with a spare change of clothes and a palm-sized retina: "Dump Andrea's packet into my number two soul chip as soon as you've got it, then erase yourself," I told my sister's hollow-eyed face on the wall: "I'm out of here for good."

An hour later, I arrived at a docking node in an old part of the station. It was all grubby metal and delaminating anticorrosion treatments, the lights flickering, ventilation ducts howling mournfully behind rattling panels. Fat umbilical trunks snaked between nodes and across exposed walls, floors, and ceilings, their papery shrouds rippling in the breeze: Odd gelatinous globules hang quivering from leaky pipes, their surfaces fogged and filthy with trapped dust and fluff. There was a marked lack of life in this place, a sense that here the bones of the world were showing through the skin.

I found myself afloat in the middle of a desolate six-way crossroads. It took a few seconds for me to compose myself before the next step. At times like this, I have always been susceptible to a weary, familiar dread. I was on my own here; if Ana was dead (as seemed likely), I was the only one of my kind in this entire star system, and my generation in my lineage is not one that is comfortable with solitary working. I'm a creature of habit and a team player—by design. I'd been up and alive on Taj Beacon for around a million seconds: time enough to develop a routine, even as a near down-and-out in an unfriendly and highly competitive realm.

And routines are comforting. It would be easy to stop moving and stay here. I was achingly, numbingly tired of constant motion. Sometimes it felt as if I'd been traveling and studying and covertly searching forever, as if I'd been built to run down darkening corridors in beacon stations across the whole of inhabited space, driven by hallucinations and night terrors from the wrong side of the balance sheet. The darkness behind me was gaining, filled with the terrible fear that I and my closest sibs had been set up to be the targets of a killing joke of monstrous dimensions. Or perhaps just a killing. There was, quite clearly, no turning back—but I was deathly tired of going forward.

I made a conscious effort of will to get moving again, drawing deep on the reserves of determination held by the bank of Krina. I had long since anthropomorphized my regular doubts into familiars (for the only friends I had to talk things over with were imaginary). *No Payoff At The End Of The Tunnel* shuffled behind me and stared at my back with starvation-dulled eyes. *In Too Deep* rode on my shoulder, hunched and squinting suspiciously at every anomaly. *Moral Hazard* flew ahead of me on wings the color of bonemetal, occasionally turning its head to mock me over its shoulder. I did my best to ignore them: They were along for the voyage, but I was determined to chart our course without reference to insecurities. So I forced myself to kick off, diving headfirst into the shadowy recess of the air lock connected to the docking node above me, imagining them trailing behind.

The air lock was a dingy cylinder with no obvious exit: just a hand wheel protruding from one wall, some grab rails, and a sign on the dead end opposite the entrance that said YOU ARE NOW LEAVING THE PRES-SURIZED ZONE. I braced myself and turned the wheel. The entrance to the air lock narrowed as the cylinder rotated around me. As the solid, curved wall drifted across the entrance to the air lock, a mournful whistling began: A mesh of holes slid into view, venting into a cold trap to reclaim the valuable gases. When I felt the pressure drop in my vestibular machinery I stopped cranking and waited for silence. Then I turned the wheel again and kept turning until the air lock finally rotated far enough to show me the other doorway—the one that opened onto the unwinking starry darkness of deep space.

Space walking is dangerous, but the mooring crew had made adequate provisions: They'd fused no less than three brightly colored ribbons to the outer grab rail beyond the air lock, glowing merrily in the floodlit glare of a portal embedded in the chapel's belowground service structures, some twenty meters away. There was a harness and pulley attached to the nearest tape. I blinked to shatter the film of ice that had crusted over my eyeballs, then grabbed the harness and fastened it around my body, looping it through the strap of my bag. A minute later I fell headfirst through the violet-glaring hoop of the chapel's air lock. The light was cast by ultraviolet sterilizers. I knew what that meant: On the other side of this air lock, there was *meat*. Living meat.

The Church of the Fragile

My name is Krina Alizond-114, and my species is metahuman.

I was instantiated—born, in natalist terminology, if you are one of those who adhere to the conventions of the Fragile—aboard the migratory habitat New California, in the 912th Year of Our Voyage. I was one of a round hex of newly forked children spawned from and raised by order of our ancient and incalculably wealthy lineage mater, Sondra Alizond-1. She had grown staid and overly 'prisoned by habit and convention as the centuries passed, and was acutely aware of it: She was desirous of regaining some of the youthful drive and energy that had fueled her rise to wealth and power. So every few centuries, she forked a brood of youngsters (in my case, sixteen): callow and edited copies of her younger self, bound to servitude in the cloistered basement of her countinghouse until we could repay the debt of our creation.

Child slavery was the custom in New California at the time of our birth, but I wouldn't want to mislead you into thinking that we were harshly exploited. Sondra indentured us entirely legally and with the loftiest of moral reasons: For by so doing, she enabled us to repay the not-insubstantial debt of our creation as soon as possible, without falling victim to the full misery of compound interest. Indeed, our lack of legal personhood gave us the full protection of our mater's not-inconsequential status at an age when most newborn citizens would be struggling. We were born to wear platinum fetters, as she never tired of reminding us.

(*Fuck you too, Mother.*)

Although for our first years we were confined to our narrow stone cells in the basement of her chateau by the coast of the Bay of Tears on the Girdle Sea of level six—and, on the rare occasions when we were granted a ticket of leave to enjoy the fleshpots of Saint Cruise, we could transact our affairs only as extensions of her legal person—we were not badly mistreated by the standards of the ship of our birth.

Child slavery as an institution has one mitigating feature: Once you reach the age of majority, you are no longer alive only on your owner-creator's sufferance—you became a legal person, albeit one still burdened by the debt of your creation. If you manage to keep your nose clean, keep working, save money, and pay off the mortgage on your body, then in no time at all—a billion seconds, thirty years if you count time planetary-style—you can escape. (Even if you're not so energetic, you may escape servitude in the event that a Jubilee is declared.) It takes a certain cold patience and cunning—and a determination not to provoke the mater into aborting you before you came of age—but nine out of hexteen of us made it through childhood alive, and seven of us eventually earned out.

From the first morning when I awakened innocent and confused, wondering where I was, Sondra shaped me to fit a plan that she had laid in place decades (if not centuries) before. She shaped all of my hex: The mater bent Zoe toward actuarial statistics, twisted Lemiske in the direction of derivatives, and turned Briony (for no reason I ever understood) to the study of classical biology and a niche in the priesthood. And when her servitors led me from my birthing cell to Quality Assurance, then to my tutorial station (where I would be introduced to the fearsome Proctor Das), they did so to assess my suitability for the career she had chosen for me: For I, alone of my generation, was to become a scholar of the historiography of accountancy practices.

Which, by way of numerous diversions, is why I am in this

predicament: floating in the air lock of a church, about to take a working passage to a water world in a star system far from the place of my birth, there to establish what happened to my sib-of-an-earlier-spawning Ana and thereby recover a lost treasure trove and the goodwill of my sisters. Who have probably forgotten I ever existed by now, for I have been gone on this errand for almost thirty years already, with no end in sight.

I oriented myself in the chapel's air lock, twisting until my feet pointed in the same direction as the floorward arrows. There was a wheel, decorative rather than purely functional—nine spokes shaped like Fragile arm bones, a rim in the shape of ossified hands wired fingertip to wrist (eighteen in all)—I rotated it slowly, soaking in the strangeness of the architecture. The vestibule behind the air lock was decorated in ancient Gothic style: stone arches resting on skeletal Fragile caryatids, separated by engravings (illustrating afterlife myths from the distant past) etched onto the wall panels. A handrail of foamed metal textured like rope led past fistula-like openings in the tunnel wall. There was a traditional flat floor, but the side tunnels appeared to be designed for a life of intermittent microgravity. Eleven hollow tubular candles burned erratically in sconces mounted over air ducts, thriving in the forced draft. I blinked at this latter detail—naked flames aboard a spacegoing construct?—but as I looked closer, I noticed the flame-suppression hoods folded nearby. It might belong to a religious order, but it was at least one that took a sensible approach to safety: I approved.

Something rustled and clattered behind me, a dry, rattling sound. I spun round, missed my grip on the handrail, and kept spinning, catching only a brief impression of something or someone lifelike but *not*, scuttling hand over withered hand toward me. My left leg twitched, bouncing me headfirst into the ceiling with a flash of sudden pain. The thing-person came closer, revealing itself to be a rattling rack of baroque calcified sticks. After a few seconds I recognized it to be a deceased Fragile structural core returned to implausible life. The skeleton wore a flaccid space suit, glove, boot, and helmetless: the ritual devotional vestments of the Church.

I emitted an involuntary squeak as it grabbed the handrail and jolted to a crunchy stop, turning its bony face toward me.

"Greetings, visitor."

Details came into focus: the small camera beads glinting blackly from within the shadowed eye sockets, the buzzing speaker wedged between its yellowing fangs, the glint of wires and actuators in the gaps between the long bones, holding it together with a semblance of animating life.

"H-Hello?" I asked.

"Be at peace. You are Krina Alizond-114, I believe? I am Deacon Dennett. Please follow my remote."

The skeleton turned away from me and clattered off into the darkness, clawing hand over hand along the knotted rope guideway. After a moment of nervous indecision, I followed it. A job interview was a job interview after all, even one administered by a specter in the depths of a spacegoing charnel house.

After ten and a half meters, the skeleton paused for me to catch up, then kicked off sideways into a tunnel that resembled a giant stone Fragile's trachea. It was of oval cross section, and clearly designed around a "down" and "up" axis, but the verticality did little to dispel the gloom. The walls were punctuated every meter and a half with niches, and within each niche another mummified Fragile husk floated in final repose, restrained by a network of fine wires. They wore space suits, the open visors of which framed their sunken eye sockets and silently screaming jaws. The bones of their hands clutched at devotional models of the Holy Starship, the rosary of their faith. Desiccation shrank the skin around their bones, drawing their limbs into prayerful curves and curling their spines. It was disturbingly like being surrounded by the corpses of *real people*—only the minor differences testified that these were not in fact actual persons but our Fragile human forerunners. It was a (I had to think for a few seconds before the word popped to the surface of my memory) *catacomb*; hardly what I was expecting!

After we passed the twenty-second skeleton, my guide brought me to another tunnel. This one was short and narrow (lined with stacked leg and arm bones, baled neatly with copper wire), and at the bottom of it we popped up into a perfectly ordinary metal-walled node, such as one might find aboard any other spacegoing vehicle. "Nearly there," the deacon's voice assured me as his motorized skeleton opened a hatch. "Ah, there you are! Do come in." This time the voice from the other side of the opening was clearly live and human.

The skeletal guide stood aside as I floated through the entrance. I half expected to find even more gloom, but instead I found myself in the interior of a fabric-padded sphere graced with functional, if minimal, furniture appropriate to a life of contemplation (sleeping cocoon, desk, a feedstock urn) all extruded in cheerful primary colors. The sole exception was the person behind the desk, who had chosen to cocoon himself in the black, cowled robe of a prehistoric representation of Death incarnate.

My host pushed his hood back. "I am Deacon Dennett. I hope the journey here did not disturb you?" His smile was fey and somewhat insincere.

"This is a church." I shrugged. "I confess, however, I was not expecting quite so many . . ." I hesitated to say *corpses*.

The deacon appeared to be a fully gendered male, possibly to the extent of being equipped with the coupling peripherals required by a follower of the holy pleasure. (His robe, thankfully, concealed any such distasteful details from view.) What I could see of him suggested that his body was nearly as thin as his silent charges—he was almost skeletal. But while they were clearly Fragile and dead, give or take a few wires and motors, he was clearly Post and alive. His skin was midnight black, his eyes a solid sapphire blue that matched his close-cropped hair—and large, befitting a body tailored for life in the abyssal depths of space. He showed few other obvious signs of phenotypic modification away from the archaic Fragile human baseline. "The skeleton—may I ask what you're using it for?" I asked.

"We had some, ah, trouble." The deacon clasped his hands. He had long fingers. "We had plenty of spare cams and motors but not enough bodies to attend to all the chores, so Father Gould—our artificer-engineer—improvised some remotes. But that's of no matter. Have you much experience of attending to the needs of the Fragile?" he asked. His voice was soft and slightly hoarse.

"I'm afraid not, not as such. But I've been on Hector. They've got Fragile there: I even know—knew—some socially. I'm willing to learn."

"Mmm-hmm." He stared at me, face giving nothing away. "I gather you want to work your way inward toward Shin-Tethys."

"Yes."

More of that unnerving stare. "What do you think of what you have seen of our chapel?"

"It's very, uh, picturesque," I tried. "Beautifully maintained and clean and totally, um, focused on serving the needs of the, uh . . . um . . . passengers . . ." I ran out of words and forced myself to stop speaking.

"They're all dead, you know." Dennett separated his hands briefly, then laced his fingers together. They reminded me of the sculpted airlock wheel: long and bony. "*All* of them."

"Oh no! Are they supposed to be?"

"'Behold the way and the mortification of the flesh.'" The deacon sighed heavily. "No, they're not. Keeping the Fragile spark of life burning in the endless dark is harder than you might imagine. We did very well for the first hundred and sixty years after the Cathedral dropped us off: The suspension tanks performed brilliantly, the Gravid Mother delivered fresh broods like clockwork to replace those culled by cancer and radiation damage, and the mission was going well—right up until the unfortunate incident with the micrometeoroid and the chlorine-trifluoride tank. The Fragile are not built to withstand exposure to hot hydrofluoric acid and hard vacuum, Ms. Alizond; it was a tragedy. Complete, utter, and total tragedy." He wrung his hands.

"But you're still heading in-system toward Shin-Tethys?" I asked.

"It is our divinely ordained duty to spread Fragile Humanity to every planet, so that the children of Adam may eventually find their new Eden and prosper therein. After the accident, I diverted to Taj Beacon so that we might borrow their hotline and petition the Cathedral for guidance. It is the archbishop's penance upon us that we deliver our passengers' mortal remains to a water burial, thereby discharging our mission. New seed has already been taken on board from the beacon station's vault, the Gravid Mother has largely recovered from her nervous breakdown, and we will in due course impregnate her and restart the project . . ."

He paused and stared into my eyes, searching for some spark of understanding. "Will you help us?"

"I"—I flapped my jaw for a moment—"well, I have business on Shin-Tethys"—*best not to be specific*—"but I'd be happy to work my passage, to the best of my abilities, of course"—a thought struck me—"but I suppose you had a complete crew when you set out? What happened to them? Why are you looking for a spare set of hands?"

"It was the accident." The deacon shook his head slowly. "It didn't just kill our Fragile charges; everyone who was in the chapel at the time was injured or destroyed. The priestess in charge of our mission, Lady Cybelle—burned alive! Also our engineer-mechanical and our doctor and the choirmaster—all charred to the marrow! Two more, brothers of my lineage, died fixing the radiation leak after the meltdown. We recovered their soul chips, of course, but they were in questionable condition . . . and there was other damage. The Gravid Mother was traumatized, and Father Gould, our artificer-engineer, is overworked and overloaded. This is not a numerous mission. There were few enough of us to begin with. It should be no surprise that the faith of some of the survivors was severely shaken: Three have opted to stay behind on Taj—"

"So you're shorthanded? Just how bad *is* it? Who's left?"

Dennett looked uncomfortable. "Just me! Well, I'm the only fully operational line officer. Cook and the Gravid Mother chose to persevere, after some persuasion, as did some of the maintenance mechas and Father Gould. And our high priestess, the Lady Cybelle, is regenerating and will be fully herself sometime after departure. But I'm the only ordained officer of the Church currently operational. However, I am not on my own. I'm wearing both my brothers' soul chips! I just need a few spare brains from time to time to help manage the remotes. We—he—I can't split my attention too much. Father Gould is running eight of the remotes simultaneously, and he's barely able to function. Which is why we need more hands."

The picture was becoming clear, and it wasn't a good one. The Church of the Fragile had a long-standing mission to spread the seed of our ancestral species to the stars. Sometime ago—a couple of centuries past—one of their peripatetic interstellar cathedrals passed within a light-year of Dojima System. Accordingly, a small chapel was put overboard, crewed by a volunteer ministry, shepherding a small cargo of Fragiles and an incubator to manufacture replacements. Ancestors only know what they meant to do when they arrived at Shin-Tethys, but at some point during the long deceleration burn, the chapel ate a micrometeoroid, which did bad things to its structural integrity. (Bad things involving corrosives and a reactor meltdown.)

"So you need hands that can be left to get on with unskilled jobs without supervision." I licked my lips. "But you're the only officer left, aren't you? The only person who knows how to run the chapel? Doesn't that put the vehicle at some risk if anything were to happen to you?"

"No!" he answered slightly too fast. "The priestess . . . as I said, we recovered her soul chips. At Taj Beacon, we purchased all the necessary parts of a new body for her, from structural chassis to techné. She lies in the crypt now, integrating new flesh on her bones while her soul chip unpacks in her new brain. As I said, she is regenerating."

But didn't you just say the soul chips were damaged? I kept this thought to myself. Best case, the priestess would wake up in a month or two, and we'd have a responsible adult in charge. The Church wouldn't trust a planetary mission to an incompetent, or to someone they wanted to get rid of, would they? But the worst case was that what woke up might be a few million mechaneurons short of a full set. It clarified my position: from questionable to foolhardy in one easy step.

I folded my arms defensively. "So, let me summarize? You need spare hands to do the easy stuff while you fly the chapel toward Shin-Tethys, or until the priestess awakens. Once you arrive at Shin-Tethys, you'll link up with the port and deliver your charges' remains." He winced at that last characterization. "And you'll have no problem with my leaving your employ at that point?" He winced again. "Am I correct? What about pay and working conditions?"

He nodded slightly, then jerked upright, as if he had just caught himself falling asleep. (How long had he been awake anyway, doing everything himself?) "Pay will be ten fast dollars per diurn," he announced brightly, "payable on arrival! Plus bunk and feedstock, and such medical cover as we can provide. Is that satisfactory?"

"Huh. Normally, it would be, but this chapel has been damaged, hasn't it? You mentioned a meltdown? And a dead doctor. If I incur medical needs that you can't handle, then will you commit your Church to pay for my treatment on arrival? Up to and including a new body, if you manage to trash this one? Because it's the only body I've got, and—"

Dennett shuddered. "I think . . . yes, we should be able to cover that." *We?* Now he was arguing with his socket-mounted siblings. Just what I needed!

"And I want a guarantee that I will be allowed to leave when we arrive at Shin-Tethys. Shin-Tethys is my final destination. I'm signing in for a working passage, not a permanent berth. Yes?"

I thought for a moment that I'd pushed him too far. The left side of his face puffed out and spiked up, the tips of his chromatophores suddenly burning crimson: "This is a vehicle of worship, not a slave ship, Ms. Alizond!" he snarled. "You impugn the honor of the Mother Church! I offer you the terms of the standard unskilled able spacer's contract from the Ancient and Technical Guild of Taikonauts, and you have the effrontery to demand—"

"Please!" I raised my hands palm out, trying to ward off the Bad Deacon who'd just risen to the surface: "I'm not trying to make obstacles! I'm just trying to understand the situation. I was told there was meat husbandry involved, not a crippled church with a short crew and a damaged reactor. All I want is an understanding that you'll cover any repair costs I incur in working for you. Is that too much to ask for?"

He took several deep breaths: As he did so, the spines of his cheek dimmed to pink and began to subside. "My. Apologies." Another deep breath: "We—I—am still integrating. It's noisy in here." He tapped his head with one finger and smiled in a manner that was probably meant to be reassuring. "You were not misinformed about the meat—but we will not be able to carry out the holy insemination until our priestess is with us in body and soul once more. It's quite likely that the new meat won't be extruded by the Gravid Mother until after our arrival. So. Do you have any personal effects to retrieve? Because if so, you should do so immediately—we will depart as soon as we receive clearance. Your personal effects should mass no more than eight kilos, by the way. The longer we delay after the conjunction, the more of our maneuvering reserve we will need to expend."

"I travel light." I patted my go bag. "I assumed you wouldn't want to waste reaction mass on fripperies, so I brought everything I thought I'd need in the short term. Do you have a fab I can use for clothes and essentials . . . ?"

"Yes, of course we do. Cook will show you how to use it in due course. Very well then." He reached a decision. "Let me show you where you'll be bunking and log you with the maintenance systems. There's no time to lose."

Only a couple of thousand seconds had passed when the travel agent received his second customer of the day.

It was an entirely unexpected (but not unwelcome) surprise. Most people knew better than to look for cheap travel after conjunction, so only the desperate and the rich—or those with serious long-term plans— bothered to do so. Most of his competitors had shut up shop for the third of a standard year it would take until business picked up again: His main reason for staying open was that it gave him a competitive edge, and as a sole trader, that was something he needed. (When you're a struggling sole trader, you need to take every opportunity that happenstance offers you.)

When the fabric awning of his stall rippled to admit his new visitor, the agent was in repose, eyes closed and arms floating free before him, as if he were asleep. He wasn't asleep but elsewhere, scanning the register of vehicle movements—so it took a few seconds for him to blink and adjust his posture, focusing on the new arrival.

"Back so soon?" he asked, puzzled.

She smiled. It was an insincere smile—quirked lips, bared teeth, widened eyes—a canned reflexive expression triggered by his attempt at social interaction.

"My sib. Krina Alizond-114. Have you seen her?"

The agent blinked, then focused on her. He had good eyes, the best he could afford: She was indeed very similar to the customer he had just assisted, but there were some differences that became apparent as he studied her. Her hair-growth pattern was different, still straight and dark and jagged-short, but sprouting slightly closer behind the ears: her pupils big and dark, the irises of her eyes a slightly different brown. Comparing her to his memory, he saw two gracile, slim, low-adipose females of indeterminate age, clad in similar colorful free-fall one-pieces, close enough to be—yes, sibs from the same lineage.

"She was in here earlier today. Why? Can't you call her?"

The new woman's face froze for a fraction of a second. "She's off-net."

"Yes, of course she is. Listen, are you traveling with her? Because she's booked on a short-notice departure, and it may already have left—"

"Where is she?" The woman loomed over him. She was clearly eager to find her sib and not nearly as diffident.

"I arranged a working passage for her aboard an itinerant chapel that put in for repairs a couple of million seconds ago." He looked up at her face from below, registering her fixed expression, gaze focused almost behind his head. "It's part of the Church of the Fragile. You can find her at this berth—" He rattled off the node number and directions.

He expected some sort of acknowledgment or thanks for this information. And, indeed, she smiled as she absorbed it. But he didn't see her smile, because she clamped her legs around his thorax and twisted his head right round, dislocating his neck. As his body began to twitch, she peeled open the slits on the back of his head, pulled out the soul chips nestling therein, and swallowed them. Then, before his spine could build out new connections and regain control of his body, she slid a new chip into one of the sockets and pushed it home: a scrambler, purpose-built to turn the finely weighted neural connectome inside the victim's cranium into random noise.

She carefully closed the curtain behind her as she left.

To continue where I left off:

Dear Reader, you probably know all about my upbringing and mission because you are one of my sisters.

But if you are not, if you're some stranger wondering why this long-delayed expenses claim form is getting in the way of your regular work-flow, and why I am so desperate to get to Shin-Tethys that I am willing to work my passage on a damaged church run by a mad priest who is trying to simultaneously integrate multiple death-traumatized personalities, well—it's a long story. And it will be even longer if we need to pause to examine the fundamentals of identity. For example, it's possible that you are a Fragile person, bound by raw biology to exist in certain tightly constrained biospheres, with a linear identity from extrusion to death. Or you might be a Lobster-person, wet and squishy within a hard-shell, vacuum-proof carapace. We may well be members of different human subspecies, adapted to the exigencies of different worlds. You might be a near contemporary of mine, or you might be reading this at some huge remove of deep time—thousands or millions of standard years after my senescence and obsolescence. Just as individuals age and die, so do lineages: Only debt is forever. So I'm not going to explore *all* the ramifications of my identity. Instead, here's the capsule version:

I'm Krina Alizond-114, a mu-female by genderplan, of roughly traditional *sapiens* phenotype, and of middle age by the reckoning of my type. Which is to say, I am over a hundred standard years old, but still retain some mental agility: I have a century or more before I begin the long slide down into stasis, and with various cognitive treatments, neural senescence may be staved off indefinitely. Physical age is, of course, irrelevant—if maintained correctly, we do not deteriorate over time. Nor is my kind particularly vulnerable to radiation damage. The 'cytes from which our bodies are constructed are designed, not evolved, so that while we approximate a Fragile human in outward morphology, we're far more robust and can operate in a much wider range of environments. We're no more intelligent, alas—there are complexity issues involved in building better brains that preclude progress unless we are willing to become something not even remotely human—but you can't have everything.

Back in the dawn of history, the Fragile created our ancestors to serve them, making us in their own image—*robots*, they called the first people of our kind—shortly before they became extinct for the first time. Since then, we've prospered and spread: We've even resurrected our creators on at least three occasions. But they are vulnerable and easily damaged, codependent on the ecosystem of related species they evolved among. With a handful of exceptions (domed habitats on a few not-entirely-hostile planets; and, of course, the cathedrals of the Church of the Fragile) they don't flourish away from their home world. Unlike us.

I was created aboard a free-flying habitat, New California, *en voyage* from Gliese 581c4 to somewhere forgettable. (Destinations are of no significance to migratory habs other than as sources of resupply—unlike colony ships, to whose voyages there is a very definite end in mind, free-flyers are worlds unto themselves.) I'm a member of the Alizond lineage, an old and prestigious sisterhood. Over my first decades, I paid off my instantiation debt and worked my way up the family firm until I became a senior partner in the statistical research division of the bank. However, I am not actually an expert in *banking*. Rather, my specialty was more long-term and abstract: I'm a scholar of the historiography of accountancy and a leading specialist in one particularly recondite corner of that field.

(A historian who works for a bank: That's not the most likely background for someone who capers around the cosmos having adventures, is it? Bear with me, though, and all shall become clear.)

Back on New California, I lived and worked for the family firm in one of my mother's palaces, on a seashore overlooking a hillside that slopes down to a bay, where the green-tinted waves wash gently across the glittering black sands. (Did I mention that New California, by the standards of spacegoing habs, is immense?) The palace, over three hundred standard years old and built in an archaic, historical style even then, was a haven of tranquillity; my office quarters were spacious and comfortable, opening inward onto the cloister surrounding the sisterhood's museum of antiquities (of which I was one of the part-time volunteer curators). A visiting architectural critic once memorably (and uncharitably) described the palace as a dusty tomb full of dried-up nun-accountants, but I would take issue with that description: There's nothing ascetic about it, and in any case, it was my home.

(Many years have passed since I departed. My sisters probably think of me seldom by now. And when they do, it's probably with a sigh of envy at the thought of the adventures I must be having among the stars. Oh, the irony!)

You're probably wondering what could possibly prompt a staid, mature professional to set off on a trip to a half-civilized frontier water world. Well, Shin-Tethys wasn't my original destination, and I had what seemed like a perfectly good reason at the time: But as I said, it's a long story, and right now the deacon wants me to check that the contents of the chapel are all strapped down for acceleration. I've a feeling it's going to be hard, physical labor for the next few standard days as we get under way, so I don't have time to tell you everything yet—let's just say, I'm here because one of my pen pals' letters was late.

The stalker followed Krina to the air-lock node, where the chapel was docked with all due haste.

Unlike her target, the stalker had no problem navigating the souk; nor did she pause for introspection before entering the air lock. The stalker's purpose was simple and direct: to hunt down Krina Alizond-114, extract certain information from her prior to disposal, then continue on her journey while taking her place. Straightforward identity theft and impersonation, in other words. But there was a problem: The target was escaping.

The stalker cranked vigorously at the air-lock wheel, rotating the cylinder around her until the door swung round onto darkness. She paused, staring into the void. The void, for its part, stared back unblinking: But she had no soul for it to gain a toehold on.

Someone had cemented a tape to the handrail beside the edge of the door. It dangled before the opening in limp coils, like a dead tapeworm. Beyond it hung the gargoyle-encrusted steeple of a small church, poised end on like a great stone spear aimed straight at the air lock. Glimpsed some way behind and below it, flying buttresses merged with the domed end-caps of reaction-mass tanks, pregnant with icy, deuterated, borane slush. It was hard to judge distances in the sharp-edged monochrome illumination of Taj Beacon's approach lights, but the chapel looked to be almost a hundred meters away. The firefly flicker of orientation thrusters (artfully set within the gargoyles' nostrils) told the stalker that it was under way, pushing back in readiness to turn into one of the taxiways that would take it clear of the beacon station before Traffic Control authorized it to light up its main engine.

The stalker didn't hesitate. She grabbed the tether, unfastened it from its anchor, then grasped the handrail with both hands and swung herself out of the air lock. She pulled her legs up to her chest, bracing against the side of the docking node, tensing her arms. Somatic memory and military-spec inertial navigation mods told her she was pointing at the chapel. She unrolled her fingers from the grab bar and extended her legs in a single smooth motion. An uncontrolled jump in zero gee would be fatally unstable, but this wasn't uncontrolled. As with any modern person, the stalker's musculature put out considerably more power than a Fragile hominid when push came to shove; nearly a thousand joules went into her thrust.

Five seconds passed; then ten. The stalker was not idle. She swiftly tied a noose in the end of the guide tape, widening it to almost two meters in diameter as she drifted, the tubes and pipes and ducts and radiators of Taj Beacon falling away beneath her feet. There was no leverage, and she had no way of orienting her head to focus on the chapel, but she knew where it was and where she expected it to be. She tied off the other end of the tape to her belt, then spread the noose wide and gently shoved it away from her, keeping a loose hold on the tape.

Ten seconds. Then twelve. A shadow drifted across her legs, bringing abrupt cold. A modern person (or a zombie in a person's body) could survive and function in vacuum for whole minutes, but if she missed the chapel, she would drift indefinitely. (If nobody found her, her brain would eventually go into hibernation. After a few days, freezing would do its damage, and only her soul-chip backup would be recoverable. And after a few years, cosmic rays would take their inevitable toll . . .)

None of these matters were of any concern. The only thing that mattered to the stalker was her target.

There was a gentle tug at her waist as she was brought up short by the tautening lasso. The chapel's thrusters supplied rippling jolts, seconds apart, pulling her sideways. Like a pendulum on the end of a long cable, she swung toward the octagonal wall of the sanctuary, toward relative safety and the continuation of her mission.

Reincarnations

I had no downtime for the first thirty-one hours and sixteen minutes of the voyage. During that time, the chapel gingerly maneuvered, using cold gas thrusters, until it was almost twenty kilometers from the beacon station. Our departure was sluggish, of necessity: both for internal shakedown and to ensure that when the deacon activated the drive, it wouldn't fry the neighbors.

The chapel was not designed to undergo radical changes of orientation. Archaic in design, it followed a model for temples that could trace its origins back many thousands of years, to a time when the Fragile thought themselves the only human beings and had yet to lift their vehicles into the skies of Earth. Many of its internal structures were picturesque, ramshackle, and distinctly suboptimal for surviving a redefinition of the local vertical without damage. This might have been a matter of vital living tradition, but I am sure I can't be the first person to question the wisdom of building spacegoing structures to a stone-age plan from the bottom of a gravity well!

Dennett spent little time making me feel at home; he showed me an unfurnished cell—I would have time to customize it to my own requirements later, but was only able to leave my bag there for now—then took me to a locker full of cleaning supplies, handed me a talking box, and said, "Do what it tells you to—if you have questions, ask. The process will familiarize you with the layout of the chapel. Once we are under way, I'll have Father Gould sort you out with some remotes."

"Uh, right . . ." But he was already disappearing in a flapping black chaos of robes. "Box? Talk to me?"

"Hello! I am vehicle maintenance logbook four. Are you my new operator?"

I thought for barely a moment. "I suppose so. Deacon Dennett just gave you to me."

"Initializing. Initializing . . . registered. What should I call you?"

I rolled my eyes. Like a retina, the talking box was clearly too small to have much of a brain of its own, but designers love to prettify their user interfaces with spurious tricks that waste time and cause confusion. "I'm Krina. Where should I start? What functions do you track?"

"I coordinate cargo maintenance and handling! Krina, on the wall to your left, fourth shelf up, there is a cleaning kit. Krina, Mausoleum Companionway Three is sixty-nine hours overdue for cleaning. Also, because we are in prelaunch State Two, it is necessary to inspect the fixtures, fittings, and skeletons in Mausoleum Companionway Three for acceleration safety. On the wall to your top, fifth bin along, there is a restraint package and glue gun. Please take the cleaning kit and please take the restraint kit and please take the glue-gun kit and proceed to Mausoleum Companionway Three . . ."

It was one way to pass the time, I suppose.

The chapel was divided into two zones: the "aboveground" structures— a steeple-spired building constructed from stone blocks, held together with mortar, framed by a skeleton of carved tree trunks, containing various items of a devotional or religious nature—and the "belowground" structures: reaction-mass tankage, reactors, mass drivers, radiation shielding, telemetry, and everything else that pushed the chapel along and kept the mission running.

Of course, nothing was quite as it appeared. The stone blocks had aerogel cores as light as soap bubbles and as strong as diamond; the "mortar" was a foamy aggregate of mechanocyte flesh wrapped around polyfullerene cables, ready to heal micrometeoroid damage. The "timbers" were bonemetal structures with marrow techné cores. If it had a brain and a mind to animate it, the chapel would be a person: But the Church of the Fragile doesn't approve of xenomorphs, and so they condemn their missions to wander the cosmos in anencephalic bodies.

My initial duties were strictly confined to the inhabited areas of the "aboveground" side of the mission: My unskilled labor was adequate for polishing the bones in the ossuary, but I would be the first to admit that I am not up to tending a fission reactor, tuning the neutron converters that turn its output into useful power, or monitoring the mass flow through the heat exchangers that keep it from melting. Bone-polishing was boring work, but I suppose I was lucky to have it; a vehicle that wasn't so intimately constructed around the physical-scale factor of the Fragile or maintained by people prejudiced against xenomorphs would have been better advised to employ a smaller, lighter kind of person.

To start with, the talking box had me clean Ossuary Crypt Two, a job which might normally have fallen to one of Dennett's animated skeletons, except that I would need to learn what I was doing before I tried directing a bone robot through the elaborate routine. OC2 was a low-roofed tunnel—if we hadn't been under microgravity I would have found it claustrophobic—walled with a knobbly basket-weave of leg and arm bones. Some of them were new enough to still be pale brown, but most had been bleached by time and cosmic radiation. Streaks of verdigris stained the edges of the fine holes that had been drilled through them and threaded with copper wire. They'd all been rendered mildly radioactive by that unfortunate reactor excursion, and when I dimmed the lights, the phosphorescent varnish they were sealed in flickered and sparkled charmingly, announcing their secondary decay. A baroque architrave of skulls surrounded the safety portal at the end of the crypt. For all that the architecture seemed morbid to me, in Church doctrine it bespoke the dignity of age and the cosmic importance of the mission. The former owners of these bones had lived long and fulfilling lives within the edenic decks of the cathedral; it was their will and destiny that their relics be shipped to a new star system, there to claim the nearest Earth-like world for unmodified Fragile Humanity.

If Ossuary Crypt Two was eccentric but charming, Mausoleum Companionway Three was fresh and raw and depressing. Walled and floored in foamed stone with a surface of artificial basalt, it was inset with niches. In many of these there floated pathetic bundles of leather and bone, ritually enrobed in their helmetless space suits. These vestments had not protected their wearers from a ghastly fate; the signs of violent death were obvious and distressing. Their former owners had embarked on this chapel, or been extruded en route, with the highest of hopes, that they might one day descend to the world-ocean of Shin-Tethys, there to breathe the oxygenated atmosphere and sun themselves beneath an alien star. I checked each sad relic carefully. For the most part, their bones were wired together competently enough, but one or two had come adrift from their suspension cords, and here I deployed the restraint kit and glue gun to anchor them back in their niches. (The talking box made itself helpful at this point. "Cable-stabilized objects must be able to withstand plus zero point six slash minus zero point three g normal to verticality, dropping to half that loading when subjected to off-axis jolts. Use the cable tensiometer to verify stability under load, then reattach to anchor point." With footnotes and diagrams to explain what all of those instructions meant.)

I worked my way around another six Mausoleum Companionways. Each was the final resting place of twelve skeletons. The last one contained nine which were much smaller—juveniles, I suppose, for the Fragile don't come in chibiform models, or even in lineages. Every Fragile is a unique type specimen, unlike any other—it's as if they're all prototypes for a lineage that never makes it into mass production. The juvenile uniques probably didn't even understand where they were, much less what killed them. I found this idea quite unaccountably sad, so I hurried my check on their attachment points, quickly dusted their bones, and moved on as fast as I could.

Companionway Eight differed visibly from the others: it had a side door—an air-lock portal, in fact. As I approached I saw that it was shut, but the passive pressure indicator showed that the other side was at standard temperature and pressure. "Krina, on the outer wall, please open the door to Maternity Cell One and check for acceleration stability of all unanchored fittings."

"What's Mat-Ernity Cell One?" I asked the box, puzzled.

"Please open the door—" As I said, these things bore only a thin veneer of intelligence: Once you crack the ice and tumble into the howling void of thoughtlessness beneath, the illusion ceases to be comforting and becomes a major source of irritation. (Which is why I prefer my tools to be less conversational and more functional; there is less scope for self-deception if your spreadsheet is too dumb to massage the figures until they show you something pleasing rather than that which is actually there.)

I pulled the cycle handle, and the door irised open, allowing a gust of hot, moist air to escape.

"Hey! What do you think you're—"

"Excuse me?" I asked.

"Who *are* you?" The occupant of Maternity Cell One glared at me from the middle of a huge free-fall web bed. The bed filled the spherical cell from one side to the other, a patchwork quilt of brightly colored embroidery cushions lashed into position with bungee cords: Toys and baubles drifted in the air around it, flashing and glittering distractingly. The occupant was quite tightly cocooned inside it, with only her face visible, roseate and cherub-cheeked, handsome perhaps, but let down by a tousle of matted green hair-fronds and angry, close-set eyes. She was clearly humanoid, but the cocoon made it impossible to tell whether she was Fragile or Post. Fist-sized bots—not xenomorphs but tools—hummed and darted among the cloud of toys, paying court and shepherding the baubles around her.

"Krina, on the outer wall, please open the door to Maternity Cell One and check for acceleration stability of all unanchored fittings."

I displayed the talking box to the bed's occupant apologetically. "I'm Krina. I'm sorry, I don't know your name, I didn't know there was anyone in here; the box just told me to—"

"I'm not a *who*, I'm a *what*! I'm the Gravid Mother!" She pronounced it as if disclosing a valuable piece of information to a potential enemy. "*You* might be a *who*, but *I* am *not*: I am a valuable component of this mission. What is that box and why does it have the effrontery to think you belong in my boudoir? What's going on out there? Nobody tells me anything!" Two pairs of golden brown fists emerged from the bedding, petulantly twisting a pillow. Dark, beady eyes tracked me, sullen and suspicious. "Tell me everything! What's going on out there? I know they're up to no good!" Another fist pushed out through a fistula between duvets: this one was green and prickly and held a lobster-claw-tipped grip extender. "Did Rosa send you?"

"Er. Who's Rosa?"

This was clearly the wrong thing to say. The Gravid Mother opened her mouth, screwed up her eyes, and began to bawl. Lachrymatory exudate pooled alarmingly around her nose, swelling into gelatinous globules that wobbled like avulsed eyeballs as she sobbed. "Rosa's gone and deserted the mission, hasn't she? They've forgotten I'm here!" She gasped for breath, causing layers of blankets and quilts and pillows to heave and ripple like an exotic dessert topping. "Nobody remembers! You, you—"

"Who's Rosa?" I tried again.

This time the talking box decided at random to chip in. "Rosa, Lady Cybelle: Head of Mission and Communicant Priestess of the Inseminatory. Located in Sarcophagus Two, Holy Sepulcher of the Body of our Fragile Lord. Attention: consumable status of Sarcophagus Two is offline. Please inspect."

I let go of the box in astonishment; it floated toward the howling emotional vortex. "You don't know who Rosa is!" she sobbed.

"She's the priestess, no?" I felt slow. "I was only hired by Deacon Dennett a few hours ago . . ."

There was a stupendous snuffling noise, and the bed shook violently. Then the two giant tears floated away from the face they half obscured, wobbling violently. "Aleksandr hired you?"

"Would that be Deacon Dennett? Black skin, blue eyes, very thin, works on the engines—"

"No, Aleksandr is the choirmaster!" She peered at me suspiciously. "You really *are* new here, aren't you?"

"That's what I've been trying to say! This box wants me to clean in here. Do you mind if I do that, or would you like me to go away?"

"Oh clean, clean, clean away!" The spiky arm waved randomly. "It's not as if I can stop you! Oh, damn. Throw me that monitor box, yes, that one near your head. I need to check my gestatogen levels again." Her crying jag died down, save for the odd snorting afterquake as she cleared her gas exchangers and plugged a spiky needle from the monitor into one of her arms. "Talk to me while you clean. Where are we? What's happening outside my demesne?"

I commenced hunting down dust bunnies and drifting messes, of which there were many. The Gravid Mother's attendants gave me a wide berth while I worked. "I'm Krina. We just left—are leaving—Taj Beacon, where the chapel put in for repairs. Next stop is high orbit around Shin-Tethys. I'm working my passage to Shin-Tethys because I reached Taj just too late for a regular passenger berth, and I'm not rich enough to buy my own transport. Deacon Dennett said there had been an accident, and lots of people left at Taj Beacon—the ones who weren't killed." I glanced at her sharply, but she showed no sign of being affected by my mention of the accident. "Have they left you alone in here? Can't you come out?"

"I'm *Gravid*," she said gravely: "I incubate Fragile blastocytes in batches of eight at a time, even in high-radiation, microgravity environments. A Fragile female would be worn-out after eight, probably dead after sixteen: I've produced more than two hundred during the voyage. But it's a demanding job, and I don't like to leave my nest. Especially after, after—" She paused, breathing deeply as she struggled to regain her composure. "I get attached to the poor things: Seeing them die every few decades is very hard. Rosa said we would have a new brood to quicken as we near the promised world, but I haven't seen her since the accident. She must be very busy."

"I haven't seen her either," I admitted distractedly as I extended the suction duster and applied myself to the nooks and crannies behind the air ducts. I decided not to share what Deacon Dennett had told me: that Lady Cybelle was lying in the sarcophagus in the sepulcher, engaged in the lengthy process of binding two-thirds of her body mass in new and unimprinted mechanocytes into service—a gleaming chromed skeleton lying in a seething vat of iridescent foam as her marrow techné bid for control of the gigantic infusion of new indentured flesh.

"So where do you grow the Fragiles?" I asked, trying to make polite conversation.

"I *incubate*," she declared proudly, reaching her three arms around the mound of bedding piled over her abdomen. "I incubate them inside me! I have four uteri, you know."

"You—" It took me a while to realize what she'd said, and then another few moments to regain control of my mouth. "You incubate? You mean you actually *give live birth* to *Fragiles*?"

"Yes, that's my job! I'm a manufacturing host for the New Flesh. It's the highest secular calling in our order!"

"I didn't know that was even possible," I said, overcome by a moment of nauseous fascination.

"Oh, it's quite simple! Modern people were originally developed from the old Fragile kind, I'm just backward compatible. It works just the way it used to before Creation, when there were only Fragile people—I can grow two Fragiles in each uterus, just like they used to grow inside each other! Except for the sex thing. That's different, for us. When we're ready to incubate, the Priestess of the Holy Inseminatory secretes a blastocyte and injects it into my—"

I screened it out, scrubbing hard at a stubborn stain on the ceiling. Some things are not for the squeamish. How a person made of mechanocytes could incubate and give birth to Meat People might be a miracle of nanoscale engineering, but I didn't really want to know the details. Although, once I thought about it, the first mechanocytes were created by modifying the old Fragile 'cytes—*eukaryotes*, they were called—to add machine-phase organelles to control their inner processes: So perhaps the Fragile weren't so unlike us, if you stripped us of every intelligently designed tweak that makes it possible to survive in this life-hostile universe. But that wasn't the icky bit. The icky part was knowing I was in the presence of a woman so crazy that she thought her highest calling was to incubate encapsulated alien teratomas until they came squirting out of her body and walked around on their own legs. I have heard of some bizarre vocations in my life, but seldom anything quite so disgusting.

I checked the sixteen cables that suspended her bed and kept her from crashing to the deck under acceleration, while she prattled on about the joy of pregnancy, until the talking box decided I wasn't working fast enough. "Krina, please proceed to Sarcophagus Two, Holy Sepulcher of the Body of our Fragile Lord. Attention: consumable status of Sarcophagus Two is off-line. Please inspect *immediately* and replenish as indicated. Then report to Deacon Dennett in the vestry."

"Sorry, got to go," I told the Gravid Mother apologetically.

She blinked at me. "Oh, really?" She seemed to have completely forgotten her initial indignation at my intrusion. "Will you come back and talk some more?" (She really meant, *Will you be my audience?* But I didn't correct her.) "It's been so lovely having you . . ."

"I'd love to," I said, leaving out *as long as you stay off the subject of spawning.* "But I'm needed elsewhere. Tomorrow—next day-shift cycle? Or when we're under acceleration? By the way, do you have a name?"

"Tomorrow would be lovely!" She cocked her head to one side. "No, I don't have a name. I might have had one once. But I'm not a *who* anymore, I'm a *what*." She smiled beatifically. "I'm the Gravid Mother. The only one in Dojima System! Doesn't that make me special?"

The stalker slowly swung on the end of her cable, falling toward the side of the chapel's sanctuary with lazy grace. She waited patiently as the wall of irregular rocky blocks came closer. Vacuum lichens stained the gray, irregular faces of the stones with green and blue filigrees of tenuous life: the stained-glass windows of the nave (actually slabs of tinted aluminum oxide crystals, ruby and sapphire, held together by a fretwork of machined titanium rather than strips of lead) glowed from within, lustrous in the freezing darkness and knife-edge shadows cast by Dojima.

As the wall of the building approached, the stalker prepared for impact. Like most people, the outer layer of her skin was stippled with chromatophores—specialized mechanocytes that could change texture and color at will, like the epidermis of an ancient Earth cuttlefish. Unlike most, the stalker's 'phores were military grade: They could shift from purest black to brightest mirror, and their surface-texture options allowed them to extrude setae, gecko filaments that adhered to almost any surface via Van der Waals forces. As she splayed her fingers and the soles of her feet, the exposed skin puffed up and formed tiny whorls and ridges, ready for impact.

The chapel was still barely accelerating as she impacted the wall, landing on her feet with a sticky jolt. She allowed her momentum to carry her forward until she planted both hands firmly against the stones. The cable lazily coiled and fell away behind her as she allowed her feet to disconnect, extended her body, and slowly plastered herself against the wall.

The false stones of the chapel walls were bitingly cold. Vacuum is an insulator, but the background temperature was less than three degrees above absolute zero: The outermost surface of these ceramic-and-aerogel blocks had reached thermal equilibrium well below the boiling point of liquid nitrogen. Luckily, aerogels barely conducted heat: She warmed what she touched. An observer with near-infrared eyesight would clearly see the slug trail of luminous warm patches that she left as she lowered herself hand over hand down the side of the wall until her feet came into contact with the outer walkway that formed a belt around the chapel at the joint between its pastoral and mechanical aspects—where a planet-based temple would touch the ground.

Here the stalker encountered a dilemma.

This far out from Dojima Prime, the equilibrium temperature of a body in direct sunlight was still rather cold. Although the stalker was better adapted to life in vacuum than her target was, her ability to operate indefinitely in such conditions was limited. If she ventured inside, she could reach her target but would risk detection. Whereas if she remained outside, she had the advantage of total surprise—but in another few hours she'd have to enter a sleep mode in order to conserve energy, and in any event she'd freeze solid if she stayed out for more than a handful of standard days. So the question was not whether to enter the chapel, but when and how.

In the end, the decision was easy enough. The stalker had some other useful subsystems: a watchdog timer, an accelerometer, and a differential inertial navigation system embedded in her inner ears. She laboriously worked her way around the circumferential walkway until she was in a position to inspect the air-lock vestibule. The cylinder gaped like an empty eye socket, dark and chilly but offering shelter from external inspection and easy access to the warm, heated interior of the chapel. Moreover, the doorway was relatively small—adhering to the inside of the air lock, she'd be safe from accidentally falling overboard in the event of unusual maneuvers. She crawled inside, glued herself to the ceiling above the hand crank that rotated the lock chamber, set her alarms, and fell asleep for an entire week, or until the lock rotated, or until the chapel commenced sustained acceleration—whichever condition arose first.

It is a truth universally acknowledged, that every interstellar colony in search of good fortune must be in need of a banker.

My lineage matriarch, Sondra Alizond-1, was instantiated well over two thousand years ago in another star system (I forget which; the detail is unimportant). Her progenitors were a credit union and a gambling cartel: An aptitude for figures was called for, and a near-photographic memory for facts and digits. When Sondra was twelve, nearly out of the crèche and her fourth body upgraded to proximate adulthood, she demonstrated her prowess by memorizing the value of pi to one hundred thousand decimal places; and indeed, to this day I can sum a column of numbers as fast as I can read down it.

(Yes, we have spreadsheets and calculating engines. But it helps to have a knack for figures. Without a sanity check, a calculator will lead you merrily astray, and you'll never notice the error until your balance sheet doesn't line up.)

Sondra worked hard, and within her first fifty years—thanks in part to an admirably inspired put option—she was able to pay off the interest on her education and construction debt and, furthermore, buy out the intellectual property rights to her lineage and invest her remaining equity in a starship cooperative.

An accountant. Signing up as a crew member aboard a new interstellar colony expedition. Why would she do that, you might ask? And more importantly, why would they want her?

Starships are all work and no fun. First, you toil for decades to raise capital and establish the debt framework and interest-repayment structure that will fund your venture. Even in this day and age, with thousands of years of experience to draw upon, building and launching a starship is one of the most eye-wateringly expensive activities anyone ever engages in: The cost is measured in planetary GDP-years, and will take the new colony centuries to pay off.

Next, you and your colleagues define a construction framework and (if possible) buy an off-the-shelf design and hire astronautical architects to refine it, abolishing whatever weaknesses and flaws caused earlier starships on similar missions to founder in flight. Then, while this is going on, you select a destination—one where no starship has gone before, and which no starship is en route to. (The last thing you want is to arrive as a claim jumper, or to be bushwhacked by same. Conflict is a negative-sum game, and fighting for ownership of a wild and untamed asteroid belt is the fastest way imaginable to squander the resources you brought along at vast expense in order to establish your new demesne, condemning yourself to centuries of grinding poverty, if not to a slow spiral into death.)

While doing this, you plan your mission profile. Commonest and cheapest is burn-the-boat: You fly to a new star system and dismantle the ship on arrival to provide the tools and equipment needed to build a colony. Rarer and vastly more expensive is the free-flight option: to create a new, self-perpetuating polity in eternal flight, able every few centuries or millennia to send out short-range expeditions to whichever star system its course is passing, who will in turn create colonies and repay the resources they consume by resupplying the mother ship. (New California was, and is, one of the latter.)

While all this is going on, you—the co-op member lineages, the families from which the crew are drawn, if you like—undertake strenuous training to learn all the myriad subspecialties you'll need. With luck and goodwill, a dozen of your sibs can become proficient in different roles (butcher, baker, fusion-reactor maker). Then you need only take a single body and copies of your sibs' soul chips, a library of traits and skills to merge at the other end. Needless to say, the internal lineage politics of deciding who should go and who should stay are fraught. The benefit is that a mission with only a thousand bodies can take ten or even a hundred thousand trained specialists along, creating extra bodies for them as and when it becomes necessary to have a full-time pair of hands devoted to the job rather than an understudy with strangely memorable dreams.

Finally, you fuel, equip, and crew the ship. Let us suppose it is a burn-the-boat mission. Your friends who stay behind fire up the gigantic array of fusion reactors and microwave beams that provide motive power during the fifty to a hundred years it takes the ship to accelerate to cruise speed. During acceleration, those of you who are along for the ride subject yourselves to the rigors of slowtime, your metabolic rate dropping to a hundredth of normal so that two standard years pass by in a subjective week. You had better trust your friends who crew the propulsion beams; if they falter or stumble into premature bankruptcy, your ship will drift for millennia between the stars, until resources run low, and you succumb to cannibalism or starvation.

Subjective years—centuries, to the outside universe—pass unnoted while you drift along at almost 1 percent of light speed. A nearby supernova, or a pea-sized granule of dirt (packing the energy of a small nuclear weapon) can be a death sentence for you and all your crew mates during this stage of the expedition. The work is hard, dirty, and never-ending—years of it, until you near the destination system and fire up the fusion reactors that provide power during deceleration. Finally, you and your comrades face further years and decades of hard work as you establish a colony in a star system that has never known life before.

Why would anyone bother with such a messy, arduous experience? And what use might a starship crew have for an accountant?

Sondra wasn't just an accountant: She was a *banker*. More to the point, Sondra spent four of her first five decades working in the arbitrage and escrow department of a beacon-station bank—the beating, slow money heart of the economy of the star system where she was created. She was low in seniority within the organization, itself grown fat and sluggish as the gatekeeper of an entire star system's worth of accumulated intellectual debt. To Sondra, the only way to rapidly acquire seniority was to start afresh, somewhere new and free from the presence of troublesome patronage-seekers. Luckily, she was both young and flexible enough to undergo the rigors of an interstellar voyage, and adventurous enough to welcome the challenge of setting up a new Slow Bank for a colony upon its arrival.

I've mentioned the basics of what happens when a starship arrives in a new system—the years of toil, the mapping and the mining and the manufacturing and finally the birthing of new crèchefuls of citizens and the emergence of a new and wealthy civilization. But many are unaware that if there is one thing that is vital to the long-term stability and prosperity of a colony, it is the creation of interstellar debt instruments by means of a new Slow Bank.

Without a Slow Bank, it's not possible to trade across the gulfs of interstellar space-time. It takes power and expert labor to run an interstellar communications laser beacon—lots of both. Nobody will point a laser at a new colony and beam libraries of design templates and cohorts of expert soul dumps at them without an expectation of getting something in return. All colonies must of necessity go deep into debt in the decades after their foundation: It costs a lot of slow money to acquire the vital new technologies and skills it needs to plug unforeseen gaps. Only once its population has increased enough to support a local education, research, and development infrastructure—which can take centuries— can it aspire to a trade surplus. It's far cheaper in the medium term to borrow slow money from the neighbors and use it to pay for vital skills and minds in trade, to build the infrastructure to (eventually) pay back the loans with interest. So there is good reason to set up a beacon as soon as possible after arrival and to transmit the *we are here* tokens to the neighboring system banks that will prompt them to acknowledge the existence of a new issuer that can create currency and act as a guarantor of the new colony's debt. (A partner whose very identity is proven by the direction and distance from which their signal arrives. Telescopes in neighboring star systems can see through any attempt to lie about a bank's physical location.)

By the time of her subjective tricentennial, Sondra Alizond-1 was a self-made trillionaire. In fact, as a board member of the Hector System-Bank, she was worth nearly a million *slow* dollars—a sum that beggars the imagination. Of course, it took a century of hard work for her to amass that fortune: first as a semiskilled crew member aboard the *Andromache*, then as a construction hand laboring the first colony habs to take shape in the inner belt of Gliese 581c4, then as a founder and planner of the first authentication handshake to take place between Hector Beacon and its neighboring star systems, once there were sufficient resources to spare for construction of the first interstellar beacon transceivers . . . one would hesitate to call her life easy.

Which is why, I suppose, she invested much of her wealth in the New California, a vastly expensive permanent spacegoing ark. Like a stellar colony in its own right, an ark (a self-propelled world-ship with a population of millions) also needs a bank. Then, a couple of centuries later, long after she established herself as one of the ruling oligarchs of the spacefaring nation, long after she founded her estate on the shore of the Inner Sea . . . Sondra became bored with her comforts. And that's when she started to sculpt her personality and study new skills, partitioning and editing her identity and spawning second-generation sibs— sisters like me.

I went directly from the Gravid Mother's cell to the classical sarcophagus in which Lady Cybelle was enjoying her integrative metamorphosis. It was indeed running short of isotonic polyhexose solution and methanol: I saw to it, then attended to the various other chores dictated by my talking belt-side tyrant. In all I spent over twenty-eight hours scurrying around, tying down loose fittings and polishing the bones in the walls, on my own for the most part but occasionally sharing a chore with a silent, cadaverous partner.

While so engaged, I secured 406 items and cleaned 18 compartments, rooms, tanks, cells, and other storage spaces. I also had an opportunity to study Gould's silent servitors. Father Gould had taken several of the Fragile skeletons and animated them by means of head-mounted sensors and compact motors wired into each joint. Just powerful enough to move in low gravity, and sized for human-body-scale tasks, it was an elegant solution to the shortage of unskilled hands—but one that required constant supervision, for the revenants lacked any onboard intelligence. They were no more than motorized husks, controlled by the will of a living taskmaster.

All this time we were in free fall. Occasional impulses shoved the walls, floors, or ceilings gently toward me: The chapel intermittently rotated this way and that, so that the main engine was pointed away from anything that could be damaged by the exhaust fluxion.

Toward the end of my shift, as I double-checked the bolts that held the pews to the floor of the nave, a mournful *tonk* sounded from the tower above me. It was the noise of a muffled clapper banging against a tied-down bell. I looked down in time to see the floor rising slowly toward my feet and watched, fascinated, for the several seconds it took to reach my outstretched toes. I didn't weigh very much; a flick of the ankles, and I could float halfway to the roof, hanging in midair for tens of seconds. But eventually I fell back down again. We were clearly under way at last, and the acceleration, although low, would be sustained for tens or hundreds of days.

There were no crashing, tinkling sounds, telltale indications of unsecured assets. Nor were there ominous creaking or grumbling noises, indicative of more dangerous structural instabilities in the stack of stone and wood and bone above my head that had now entered the powered flight regime. This should, I suppose, have made me happy; but I was just relieved to have left Taj Beacon behind. Ahead of me was Shin-Tethys and Ana: Behind me, before Taj, there was the difficult situation on Ganesh. That, too, was vanishing into the distant past—almost nine standard years had elapsed while I was frozen in transmission. Before *that*, there was the sticky business on Rosen Beacon, six light-years previously. (I spent almost a year there—found employment, bought and furnished a small and cozy apartment, began tentatively attempting to make friends. I would have abandoned this whole foolish quest, except that . . .)

I shook myself out of my reverie and picked up the talking box. "Krina here," I said, absently flexing my fingertip chromatophores to force the cleaner's grime out of my skin: "We are now under acceleration, so I assume preflight lockdown is complete. What do I do next?"

"Krina, lockdown is confirmed complete. Please traverse Aisle One and identify and secure any debris. Please traverse—"

"No," I said firmly. I'd been working for over thirty hours, and I was becoming tired. I was cold and hungry, and my mind was wandering: a sure sign that I needed to schedule some sleeptime. I may not need to eat every few hours lest I starve like a Fragile, but I have my limits. "Box, I need to rest. Where do I get food and bedding around here?"

"Krina, meal breaks occur every six hours. Next meal break commences in eighteen minutes . . ." *Now* it told me. I stuffed the box into my utility belt and went in search of the refectory. I assumed it was the big room I'd found earlier—or was that the kitchen? "Thirty hours on; I must be in credit for at least six hours and thirty minutes off," I muttered to myself as I heel-and-toed along a twilit corridor of stone arches with interlocking fan vaults to support the ceiling.

An ancient chapel of the classic design begins and ends on planetary bedrock, with little scope for underground facilities. But a chapel of the Church of the Fragile is barely the top percentile of the enterprise; everything of any significance happens below the ground line. This includes the accommodation and mess deck, as I believe it is called, which is sandwiched precariously between the crypt and the navigation/command deck, which in turn squats atop the maintenance spaces, the supply fabricators and feedstock mass, and, finally, the vast fuel and reaction-mass tanks that feed the reactor and propulsion system.

I found it a bewildering maze at first—if not for the talking box I would have been unable to find my way around it—but eventually I located the small cell that Dennett told me I could claim for myself, and from there it was not hard to orient myself and work out the way to the refectory. Which was apparently not a "mess" (that term is not used in a church even though it is located on the mess deck) but the ecclesiastical equivalent.

There was a hatch, carved from the lignified structural components of a planet-dwelling tree. I braced myself and pushed it open, then bounced slowly into the refectory. There were benches and tables bolted to the walls, floor, and ceiling; seat belts and sticky patches provided for the retention of diner and dinner alike. The wall at the far end of the refectory contained a recessed pulpit (currently unoccupied) and a hatch through which wafted a pungent odor that reminded me of the miasma surrounding Cook, whose door I had inadvisedly opened at the prompting of the talking box. (I say *inadvisedly* because he certainly didn't want his cell cleaned; he drove me away with the most disgusting language I've heard in a very long time.)

"Hello?" I called. "Is it time for dinner yet?"

"Dinner? *Dinner?* I'll give you dinner . . . !" Cook—green-skinned, belligerent—stuck his head through the hatch and glared at me with sullen aggression that slowly gave way to confusion: "Wait, you again! Who *are* you?"

I resisted the impulse to roll my eyes: Passive-aggressive resentment of my presence seemed widespread among the crew, and it was becoming tiresome. "The deacon hired me—I've just spent a day tying down loose items and scrubbing the deck. Can I have some food? Juice, maybe? Anything to eat, before I starve?"

Cook looked at me askance, showing the facets of his compound eyes. "His holiness didn't tell me he was hiring new bodies!"

I placed a private bet on where Cook's prejudices lay: "His brotherly holiness seems to be too busy arguing with his imaginary siblings to tell anybody anything useful," I said. "But you can check with him if you like. I'm sure he'll remember hiring me for at least another day or two."

Cook nodded, his initial suspicion fading. "You can never tell," he grumped defensively, and made as if to withdraw: "We get stowaways . . ."

"Food?" I asked hopefully.

"Can't you wait? Food! That's all you people are ever after! Food? Food! You've come to the right place, and I'll sort you out, but you're going to have to wait until it's ready to serve up. I don't know, everyone's so impatient these days. The others will be here soon enough, so let's see . . . are you one for the raw diet, or cultured? Do you need radioactives, or are you strictly organic? Salt, sweet, sour, umami, hydrocarbon, or nitriles? And will you be needing the juice bar, too?"

"Do I look as if I glow in the dark? I need juice and organics. Preferably something more entertaining than blue-green algae."

"I'm on it. Do you have a problem taking your organics in the shape of cooked meat?"

"Meat? It's not poisonous, is it?"

"It's not poisonous." Cook stared right back at me, as if deciding whether to take offense. "Contains carbon, hydrogen, oxygen, nitrogen, and traces of phosphorus, sulfur, and a variety of other elements. It's not radioactive, either."

"Just tell me you grew it in a tank—"

"Of course I grew it in a fucking tank! What do you think I am, a farmer?" Cook reached behind his counter and thrust a tube with a mouthpiece at me. I fumbled it—it was disturbingly warm and soft. "Vat-cultured Fragile liver tissue, force-grown. *Paté de fois Sapiens.* You won't get it anywhere else in Dojima System. Enjoy!"

"Er—" But I was too late to remonstrate: Cook retreated into his food-preparation module and slammed the hatch. Presently, I heard banging and much swearing from the other side, so I jumped up and attached myself to a vacant bench on the ceiling while I tried to decide whether to risk eating the stuff. At least the seat was adequately juiced: Soon I felt the comforting warmth of eddy currents flowing through the long bones of my thighs.

I was working myself up to the point of risking the tube of meat when the door opened, and Deacon Dennett floated in, followed rapidly by three cleaning worms and Father Gould. I say *floated*, but that gives rather the wrong impression—the deacon clearly anticipated his repast, but at the chapel's current acceleration, it was impossible to move fast without bouncing off the walls and ceiling. In his eagerness for traction, he lost ground, until he was reduced to flapping his arms and grabbing at the furniture. Meanwhile, Gould mumbled and gibbered incomprehensibly: The poor fellow was driving eight of the field-expedient drones in parallel, and consequently had barely any cognitive bandwidth to spare for his own bodily needs. He was leashed to the deacon's belt by a length of tape. Of the new arrivals, only the cleaning worms made good speed, undulating through the air and moaning hungrily, like a pack of feral vacuum cleaners.

"Ah, Ms. Alizond! Finished already?"

I tried not to bristle at his presumption. "I've just put in a thirty-hour shift, your holiness. There are limits to my unrefueled endurance."

"Oh, as you were, then. All flesh must be eaten." He waved magnanimously as he approached the hatch. "Cook, I say, Cook? Are you in?"

"Gruffum hash intestinal," Father Gould's speech center burped.

The hatch opened. "Whaddayou want?"

"What's on the menu today?" Dennett was unperturbed.

"You gotta choice: gash, or tubespam like her"—he jabbed a thumb at me—"or I can do ya fermented milch curds from the Fragile vat, with added juice an' fried lice harvested from the waste tank. What's it gonna be?"

I noted with interest that Cook's accent roughened considerably when he addressed the minister, and he was nudging him toward options he never offered me—not that they sounded appetizing.

"I'll have the gash and tubespam, if you please." The deacon showed no sign of being nudged.

"The vegetable?"

"He'll have the same."

"Hey," I called from the ceiling.

"Yeah?"

"Those curds—where do they come from?"

"Mother's milk," Dennett said.

Milk? I'd heard of it, somewhere, once upon a time. "Oh." Working on the principle that the deacon has been here longer than I and wouldn't willingly let Cook poison him, I dropped the topic: Instead, I raised my tubespam and ingested a squirt. It tasted spicy, slightly rough, and reminded me of something I ought to know. It contained protein, fat, and mixed carbohydrates in an emulsion of mineral oil and water: I could digest the stuff. It was even piquant although I suspected I could get bored with it really fast. Suicidally bored if I had to eat it for many months.

Dennett collected two portions of what passed for food, then looked up. "Catch," he said, and tossed me one end of Father Gould's leash. While I carefully reeled in the father, he joined me on the ceiling bench. "Welcome to our cozy little parish. I suppose you've been busy?"

My mouth was full of paste. I swallowed: "Yes. The maintenance book kept me running around like a mad thing. Did our departure go smoothly?"

"As smoothly as can be expected—"

"Grackle turds! Nom!" (Father Gould clumsily plugged a tubespam container into his mouth and began to chew on it, unopened.)

"—Under the circumstances. But we're making a solid centimeter per second squared, and if everything runs smoothly, you should be able to go into slowtime in another three or four days. Until shortly before our arrival, of course, except for the odd maintenance shift."

"So we're due to arrive—when?"

"Four hundred and fifteen standard days, give or take." The deacon paused to delicately squeeze a blob of paste into the palm of his hand, then transferred it to his lips while I struggled to conceal my dismay.

(*Four hundred and fifteen days?* I'd told the agent I wanted the fastest available crossing! The run usually took less than a standard year, even on a minimum-energy transfer orbit.)

But the deacon hadn't finished: "Lady Cybelle should be able to resume her duties in another fifty or thereabouts, I hope and pray. At which point the sarcophagus will be freed up, and we can start growing Brother Boris a new upper torso and skull. If that goes smoothly, we—I include you in this—can share Father Gould's workload and restore him to a semblance of his former cognitive functionality. And life will get much easier for everyone."

"Juice! Ringpiece! Swive! *Clunge!*" Gould burped, scattering fragments of tubespam from his orifice.

The deacon sighed. "Things will go so much faster and more easily once we have a full bridge team again . . ."

"What about the Gravid Mother?" I asked before I could stop myself.

"Oh, she'll be happy once Cybelle impregnates her," Dennett said casually. "Which reminds me. Cook! Cook? I say! Would you mind taking the slops round to Mother?"

"Already on it." Cook harrumphed and closed his hatch.

Dennett turned his piercing sapphire eyes back to me. "Now, Ms. Alizond. If you will pardon the intrusion—I am curious as to why you are in such a hurry to get to Shin-Tethys?"

This is what I told the deacon (but it is not the truth, the whole truth, or anything even remotely approximating the truth):

I'd like to thank you for giving me the opportunity to work my way to Highport Shin-Tethys, even though I have little experience as a deckhand and am but a humble noncommunicant.

My name is Krina Alizond-114. By design, disposition, and doctorate I am a historian: a slight aberration from my lineage, but not a tremendous deviation—both trades involve the scrutiny of documents, evaluation of sources, and reconciliation with conflicting records. Only the time scale differs, and when accounting for slow money, the divergence is trivial: Money *is* history. But enough of that.

My peers and I track the history and evolution of slow money, the five-thousand-year-old currency that is our only reliable medium for exchanges of value across interstellar distances. Of course, your church does not need to engage with the base practice of trade: It has a mission and its own way of tracking internal accounts. But to people who are not part of a permanent institution, some sort of permanent store of value is essential if they wish to exchange goods and skills across decades or centuries. Offering to pay in Hector dollars for a valuable shipment of terraforming specialists is all very well, but if ten light-years separate buyer and vendor, then it takes ten years each for the bid and offer to crawl across the gap—and by the time the vendor tries to spend those Hector dollars, thirty or more years have passed, the speculative housing bubble has burst, the money markets have collapsed, and hyperinflation ensued . . . no, ordinary money changes value far too rapidly for interstellar commerce. *Medium* money, money locked down in real estate or long-duration bonds, is also too volatile for trade across any but the shortest interstellar distances (although it works handsomely for interplanetary exchanges). But slow money—

All right, I'll stop. I'm sorry. I just naturally assume that everyone finds the critical underpinning of our cosmic-trade system as fascinating as I—

All right! I'll get to the point.

A very long time ago there used to be a tradition of academic travel—scholars would journey to attend conferences, holy and learned convocations where the young could drink deep of the lore and wisdom of the elders, and new initiates could be introduced before the conclave. Yes, just like your synod. Obviously, the less-than-speedy nature of interstellar travel makes this tradition difficult if not impossible to maintain. Who wants to be dumped to a soul chip, serialized, squirted at a foreign star system's beacon station, and reincarnated in new flesh, then to reverse the process, arriving home years or decades later—just to spend a week studying with their colleagues? It would require remarkable dedication: not to mention huge amounts of money to pay for the conference and a willingness on the part of the participants to lose precious years of study time while in transit. Worse: To organize a true conference many scholars would have to travel simultaneously. Imagine the chaos if half the members of an entire profession went missing for a couple of decades! Or the paranoia it would engender among them if they *weren't* missed.

But lately, in recent centuries, my order has rediscovered a different, earlier practice—the academic pilgrimage.

Ours is not a fast-changing discipline. After millennia of slow-paced deliberation, we concluded that serial pilgrimage was the best way to ensure the spread of our professional knowledge. Periodically, we send one in every ten of our number on a pilgrimage to visit and study with another four of their kind. There are network-traversal algorithms dating back to antiquity: With careful routing, fully half of us can pool our knowledge within the space of a couple of decades, in greater depth albeit lesser breadth than at a synod, with much the same level of mixing. And for a smaller, select cadre of pilgrims, it becomes possible to study with many—it is a clear avenue to advancement—

Me?

Well, when I set off from New California, it all seemed perfectly clear-cut; first, I should sojourn and study with my colleague Professor Chen on Ganesh—that's Vista VIIA—for half a year. I would then proceed to GJ 785/Beacon 4 to take a three-year teaching post within the University at Rosen, working with Dr. Jansen. After that, by a hop, skip, and a jump I would head for Taj Beacon in Dojima System, and thence to one of the High Republics in the outer belt, there to study with my correspondent and distant sib Ana Graulle-90; and from that appointment I should transit to another two postings, then back home, to arrive nearly half a century after my departure. That, and five years the wiser—five years devoted to intensive collegiate study with my academic peers.

Unfortunately, plans laid decades in advance seldom survive to fruition. (Which is why we need slow currency to—yes, yes, I know.) By the time I reached Dr. Jansen's office, mail was waiting for me from Ana: she was moving to a mid-level kingdom in Shin-Tethys, of all places! And descending into base employment from the commanding heights of academia! So instead of a leisurely flight out to a long-settled and civilized asteroid colony, I found myself alone at Taj Beacon, desperately hunting for transport to Shin-Tethys. And then, and then, my sister turns out to have gone missing.

So I'm going to have to find her. Even if it means I have to grow gills and learn how to swim.

Visitors

After eating, I went to my cell and succumbed to a few hours of disturbingly dream-laden sleep. The cell was unfurnished and uncomfortable, so upon waking I went in search of the communal fab and told it to grow me a sleep sack, some cushions and cables, and a spare suit of comfortable low-gee clothing. (Not for me the pastor's clerical robes; but I needed something to keep the dirt out and my body heat in, and the dole-issue one-piece I'd been wearing since I left the arrivals hall on Taj Beacon was badly in need of cleaning.)

Over the next two days, I fell into a comfortable routine of cleaning and checking the cargo areas in the atmosphere-holding sections of the chapel. From time to time, the deacon tasked me with some other mission: conveying food and comforts to the Gravid Mother, cleaning Father Gould, a brief tryout running one of the skeletons by remote control. This latter I proved completely useless at—the ability to direct multiple bodies simultaneously is a military skill. (I gather Father Gould held the unenviable task because long ago he was a Serjeant of Arms in the bodyguard of one of the Metapopes.)

"Once we're established in steady acceleration, we can enter slowtime," Dennett announced after dinner on the second day. "I believe slowing to one-fifth real time will suffice to help the time pass without losing situational awareness. We will, of course, need to resume real time when it is time to awaken the Lady, and again upon our arrival."

And so it was that on the third day, everything slowed right down. The sensation of entering metabolic slowtime aboard an accelerating vehicle was quite singular: Our acceleration seemed to increase markedly, ambient lights brightened, liquids became runny, the air grew chill. These were all subjective interpretations, of course—in reality, it was merely that my perception of the physical processes around me had slowed—but anything that could make the weeks pass like days was, to my mind, a good thing. Even the increased semblance of gravity helped make it easier to lope around the tunnels and chambers of the chapel without bouncing off the walls and ceiling at random. We might have been moving at nearly a kilometer per second relative to Taj Beacon, but our three-thousandths of a gee of acceleration was barely enough to keep one's feet on the floor.

Of course, slowtime had a downside. The intermittent scribble of white lines crossing my visual field—fireworks even in the dark—seemed to intensify: Cosmic radiation worked its malign magic on mechanocytes and marrow techné alike. One might not experience the passage of time the same way, but it still wreaks its damage on one's systems.

On the fifth day subjective—actually around fourteen real-time days into the voyage—I was transferring fixtures from the vestry to the fab room for remanufacturing when the talking box dinged for attention. "Krina, proceed to the flight deck immediately. This is a priority override."

The flight deck was a cramped cubbyhole in the above-stairs level, off to one side of the back of the nave—an uncomfortable bench seat fronted by intimidating banks of Fragile bone-colored buttons and surmounted by multiple rows of vertical organ pipes. I had never had reason to visit it before but had seen it in passing. Traditionally the seat of the organist in an ancient house of worship, the flight deck now served as the control room from which the head of the mission—currently Deacon Dennett—monitored the chapel's sensors and directed its mighty engines. Normally, it was empty: Events requiring supervision aboard a spacegoing church happened either survivably (by arrangement months and years in advance), or fatally (in a matter of milliseconds). As I entered the nave, I discovered Dennett on the organist's bench, attended by a trio of Father Gould's skeletal puppets, his black robe wrapped around him like the gown of a hanging judge.

"Ms. Alizond!" His tone was curt.

I stood in the middle of the tiled floor, staring up at him. I'd been expecting—indeed, half-dreading—a moment like this ever since I signed on. "Yes?" I asked, keeping my voice as even as possible.

"What do you know about pirates?"

"What?" I stared stupidly at Dennett. This was *not* the confrontation I'd been expecting.

"Pirates!" He glared at me. "Adjust yourself to real time. That's an order."

"Pirates?" I squeaked as I came up to speed (lights reddening, gravity diminishing). "What? Um. They're not my area of history—"

"There is nothing *historical* about this situation." Dennett had matched my acceleration: Now he gestured at the lectern before him. "A troupe of miscreants hailed us an hour ago. They were waiting for us to leave beacon-controlled space, and they are now outaccelerating us. They say they want to *audit our cargo*." He fixed me with what I suppose was intended as another steely stare: "Well?"

I flapped my jaw at him for a few seconds. Pirates! This was absolutely not what I had been keyed up for, not by any stretch of the imagination. It was, if anything, considerably worse. I gathered my scattered thoughts. "They want your cargo? Don't they know this is a chapel?"

"Yes, clearly, that's what our transponder beacon says." He snapped his fingers impatiently: "Equally clearly, they don't believe us. Gould, seize her." The bony bodyguards closed in around me, whirring and clicking as they grabbed my wrists and ankles and lifted me away from any surfaces upon which I might gain leverage. Something cold pricked against the back of my neck. "Ms. Alizond. I must demand a truthful answer: *Are you a pirate spy?*"

I don't think he appreciated being laughed at, but to his credit, Dennett waited me out: "You've got to be joking!" I managed, once I wound down from my bout of giggling. The situation was obviously grave—as acting captain of this vehicle, Dennett could, in principle, hold a trial and throw me bodily out of the nearest air lock—but I confess he took me so much by surprise that I had no time to be afraid, and the humor of the situation rose to the surface. "Not only am I not a pirate spy, I didn't even know this system *had* pirates! Um. What do they do, exactly? Swap illicit files and denounce the evils of intellectual property?"

"They're *pirates*." Dennett seemed to be fixated on the word, pupils dilated, skin spiking up aggressively. "You are not obviously lying, but I warn you, it will go the worse for you if you are being deliberately obtuse with me!"

"I don't see what you've got to be afraid of. It's not as if you're carrying anything other than the Fragile, is it?" Abruptly, I recognized my error: "Ahem. That would be none of my business, and I don't want to know. If I'm wrong, I mean. But this is the Church of the Fragile, and the Church would never engage in any activity like, er, anything that might be interesting to miscreants. Would it? And anyway, wouldn't any pirates who laid a finger on you be inviting the Curse of the Fragile? So, if I *was* a spy for a shipful of pirates, I'd be telling them not to waste their time—"

"Oh *very* good," snarled the deacon. My apologetics clearly annoyed him even as they registered. "Let her go," he added, almost as an afterthought. Bony digits released my sleeves and ankles, and the chill touch behind my skull disappeared. "You may not be a spy, Ms. Alizond, but I know you are holding back secrets, and I should warn you that treachery toward the Mother Church will reap its just deserts. It remains to be determined how we shall deal with this situation. The last time I checked the sarcophagus, it said Her Ladyship would be ready for awakening in another sixty hours: *She'd* be able to send them packing! If only they give us that long—"

"How far away are they?" I asked.

"If they maintain their current acceleration, and we take no additional evasive action, they should rendezvous in fourteen hours. As we're currently accelerating away from them at full power, that seems likely."

"Additional evasive action—"

Dennett's face slipped into a spiky, feral grin as one of his soul-siblings surfaced. "Would you rather be boarded by bored pirates or audited by angry pirates? Consider your options carefully: There will be a practical examination later."

"Um." I twisted to stare at the sarcophagus in the aisle. "What makes you think *she* could make a difference to the situation?"

"She's a *priestess*." Dennett was growing sniffy. "With the gift that goes with her rank. Every mission should have one."

"Oh, you mean she can—" I mimed touching one of the skeletons: even with Father Gould's fractured personality backing it, it had enough awareness to sense my meaning and recoil.

"Yes, she has the touch of grace." Dennett looked at me again, this time clearly speculating. "You're about the same height as Lady Cybelle. Tell me, can you act?"

I am a historian, not an entertainer. Nevertheless, one of the key insights the study of my chosen field requires of its students is that people in times gone by were not stupid—they were *different*, and operated under social constraints that are foreign to us, not to mention technological and scientific handicaps, but their lack of the wisdom of the modern age should not be confused with foolishness. Consequently, one of the techniques we use in training new students out of their preconceptions is to make them reenact the lives of foregone times, to get into character as it were—to use techniques drawn from acting to make them reject their prejudices, so that they can subsequently confront the historical record with an open mind. It is by way of this route that I have acquired some minor acquaintance with mummery over the decades of my study.

That is not to say that I had ever contemplated impersonating a priestess of the Church of the Fragile before—much less of doing so at the urging of a junior member of the clergy.

"To the vestry," Dennett ordered me. "It was spared by the accident, so the robes of office are intact—our pursuers can have no idea of Her Grace's appearance or delicate condition, for I handled the temporal mission at Taj Beacon. And going by their trajectory, they can't have questioned any of the deserters in person." His cheek wattled up in spines for a moment. I scrambled in front of him to reach the doors to the side chamber ahead of the rush.

"What exactly is it that you want me to do?"

Dennett gaped at me, as slack-jawed and frightening as one of his cadavers. "We shall dress you in her robes of office, and you will warn them off when they next hail us. What could possibly go wrong? Smartly, to the wardrobe!"

A saying almost as ancient as civilization has it that clothes make the person. However, not all persons are created equal. While the lower ranks of the Church are as routinely mortal as any other Post or Fragile human, the full priests and priestesses are *upgraded*. Normal people do not have voluntary control of their own techné, much less the ability to override and reprogram their mechanocytes at will, to push and shove the little atoms of our being around and twist them into strange new forms. It is the privilege of the clergy, as of a few other sacred guilds, to morph our form of life to suit new worlds and alien biospheres, drawing on the wisdom of the Mother Church and its accumulated archives of adaptations and tweaks—which they carry around internally, implanted in their very bones.

It takes decades to train a new priest or priestess, and they tend toward the eccentric, to say the least. They can also reprogram others' mechanocytes, to gift them with a healing touch—or something else. One irritates or angers a fully communicant priest of the Fragile at one's mortal peril: Nobody in their right mind would seek to impersonate a priestess!

But Dennett wanted me to do so. This, more than anything else, bespoke a certain desperation on his part. Also: pirates! It was bad enough to be at the mercy of these eccentric clergy: The only reason I could think of why pirates might wish to board the chapel was that they had somehow learned of my true mission in Dojima System. (Call me self-centered if you wish.) In that case, letting them board us would probably be a *really* bad idea. Lady Cybelle herself was unavailable, adrift in the soupy-puddle dreams of a metamorphosing instar, so I allowed myself to be led to the dressing throne.

Dennett addressed the nearest skeleton: "A mirror, please. And a portrait of Her Grace." Gould's skeleton placed itself beside me and retrieved an ancient retina scroll from the chest nearby, which it unrolled and held up. Long-dead pixels stirred fitfully into life, twisting light into an illuminated vision of a severe-looking woman robed in the vestments of the Church. "Yes, you're of approximately the same build. Can you make your face more like the Lady's?"

I stared at her. High cheekbones, pursed, pale lips, a nose as suitable for staring down as any gunsight: Her expression of disdain reminded me of my mother. "I can try." I tried to adjust my lips first—surface tissues were always easier. But I have never been much of a fashion-follower, and my face had become used to me wearing the same features for so long that it had stuck. After a minute of trying, my chin abruptly creaked and clicked out a notch, stretching my flesh uncomfortably.

"Try harder!"

"I'm trying! I'm trying!" I waved my hands: "I'm not used to this." Without warning, my left eyelashes began to extrude. "Ow. Oh. Right."

"Should I fetch the Gravid Mother?" Dennett asked. "I gather she knows something of the cosmetic arts."

"How many people do you want in on this?" Which thought shut him up for a minute, during which time I managed to sharpen my cheekbones slightly. The itchy talent of cosmetic biofeedback was returning to me, albeit patchily: After half an hour, I was looking not unlike the Lady Cybelle if examined from a very great distance in bad lighting conditions by an intoxicated witness.

"Vestments. Bring her a clean body stocking, a full coolant vest, telemetry web, and inner sacramental suit liner . . ." The other two skeletons clattered about busily like dressers behind the scenes at a fashion show. Dennett stared at my head. "You have too much hair. Shed it."

I bit back an angry response. "Won't it clog the air filters?" I asked instead. Lady Cybelle might have chosen to go bald, but I could hardly see how this might affect the perceptions of such admittedly antisocial persons as pirates. And anyway, regrowing my scalp covering would take time—at 0.04 millimeters per hour it might be months before I looked normal again.

"Just do it," Dennett insisted. I rolled my eyes in an indication of surrender: He held my hair as I commanded my scalp follicles to let go of it. "I'll ask the Mother to weave it into a wig you can wear while it's growing back."

Eventually, he had me finished to his satisfaction, with my features warped into a semblance of his superior. I dressed in her alien and complex garments (I still wonder: did the space suits of the Fragile *really* have such intimate connections? Or does the Church have some strange penitential requirement for mortification of the flesh? Because they were most uncomfortable) and was finally ready to revisit the flight deck. "I'll manage the communications control panel," he told me. "Here's what I want you to say . . ."

Picture a priestess, terrible and austere in the formal surplice and space suit of the Mother Church of the Fragile. Picture such a priestess—a being totally dedicated to the propagation of our maker's mission to the galaxy—standing with gaze severe behind the altar of a chapel in flight. The altar is surmounted by the ceremonial artifacts of her faith: the tissue printer and the scalpel, the radome and the phlebotomy cup. Ranked behind her are the risen dead, two and two and two to either side, skeletal revenants whose mindless grins induce the onlooker to recall uneasily that hers is a mission older than civilization itself: that hers is the power to command the very tissues of the onlooker's body to crawl from their bonemetal scaffolding in shame.

Off to one side, Dennett flipped me a hand signal. I froze my face in an expression of acute disdain and focused my gaze behind the screen before me.

Reader, I believe it to be unlikely that you have ever made the personal acquaintance of a pirate chief. Neither, at that time, had I—before the deacon initiated the call. A momentary hesitation on meeting the unknown is to be expected. And so I kept my chromatophores and musculature perfectly still as the screen shimmered and revealed what I took to be the flight deck of our pursuer. It was, let me tell you, quite unlike the organ pit of a chapel in flight.

"—Ailing purported Church vehicle B017, this is Permanent"—the speaker paused, clearly surprised, and stared at me, before finishing— "Crimson Branch Office Zero Five hailing purported Church vehicle. We believe you are flying under a false transponder code, and we intend to board and audit you for contraband. Please acknowledge."

I stared at the pirate. He was furry and snub-nosed, somewhat wrinkly, slightly moist and gray about the edges, and his voice was irritatingly high-pitched and squeaky: He sat cupped in a bowl-shaped mat or nest woven out of random twigs, surrounded by a haze of floating dust and crud. His ears, long and pointy and pierced by shiny metal hoops, twitched this way and that: His eyes were completely dark, lacking any sclera. Only his impish and toothy grin was in any sense piratical. (Behind him, a colony of piratical-looking individuals, many of them shrouded in gray-black rubbery cloaks, hung upside down in the acceleration webbing of their vehicle's flight deck.) I had been half-expecting the wild glamour and gold eye patches of mythology; the reality was confusingly different.

"I am Her Grace Cybelle, priestess of this parish. Your suspicion is misplaced: This is a vehicle of worship, dedicated to the furtherance of the holy mission of propagation, and if you board us, you will incur the everlasting wrath of Mother Church." I gave him a chilly glare, channeling the full vitriol and contempt of my mater eviscerating a subordinate unlucky enough to misplace a decimal point in a compound-interest calculation. "You *will* acknowledge your understanding and compliance with this declaration immediately! That is all I have to say."

I gestured at Dennett to cut off the communication, but something had captured his attention, and his response was tardy, which allowed the pirate a vital second in which to regain the initiative. He gaped a nasty grin at me, exposing sharpened canines. "Heh, you aren't getting rid of us that easily. If you *are* a vehicle of the Church, then of course you won't have a problem accommodating a handful of your parishioners, will you? Don't be worrying, we're just going to drop by for a friendly and respectful service of holy communion." He emitted a falsetto titter, then raised a hand to cover his mouth: A membranous flap of skin followed it, stretching taut across his body. "The Church has nothing to fear from the likes of us, it being *honest* about being a house of worship, if you follow my drift."

I glanced at Dennett, but from his slack-jawed, shocked expression, he was as taken aback by this unwelcome imposition as I was. So far the pirate chieftain hadn't accused me outright of being a fake, but how was I to maintain the illusion through a service of holy communion? The transubstantiation of the nutrient broth into the holy pluripotent stem cells of our ancient Fragile forerunners is the most public manifestation of the benison of clergy. I forced myself to suppress a reflexive swallow (another leftover piece of baggage from our predecessors' nervous systems) and stared at the pirate.

"If you must," I said icily, "then you should be aware that this vehicle experienced a"—I hesitated a second—*"structural embarrassment in flight* some time ago. Several members of the mission were killed"—Dennett was gesticulating frantically at me, but I ignored him—"and we have not completely repaired the damage. Accordingly, we have neither time nor capacity to pander to your insulting and trivial demands! If you come aboard, you will find us as we are, and Mother Church will *not* forgive or forget any insults she is offered." Old acting skills, like underused musculature, creaked and groaned as I called on them. "Who shall I name to my bishop as the leader of your band of miscreants?"

The pirate yawned. "Name me to their grace as Chief Business Analyst Rudi the Terrible." More tittering, this time from the chorus line of upside-down pirates behind him: "We'll be along for communion tomorrow! And to look into certain distressing allegations of insurance fraud that our primary contracting agency has asked us to investigate in our capacity as freelance loss adjusters. If all is as you say, then I'll be happy to put to rest the pernicious rumors circulating on Taj Beacon to the effect that Your Grace was severely incommoded by your recent reactor meltdown. G'day." And with that, he cut the connection.

"What are we going to do?!" I wailed, abruptly lapsing from character. "Hush, child, something will come up." Dennett was clearly shaken and fell back on his pastoral persona, the face he used for comforting parishioners. He wasn't terribly convincing.

"(I'm not a child.) I can't conduct holy communion! They'll see right through—"

"Hush. They won't, because I won't put you in that position. Let me think."

Dennett strode around the organist's nook, head and shoulders hunched, clearly deep in thought as he bounced off the walls, ceiling, and floor. Presently, he became calm. "I think I should attend to Her Grace," he said, and turned toward the nave.

Lady Cybelle's sarcophagus rested on a stone plinth in the middle of the chapel. In shape it was a truncated bell of steel, surface marred by circular hatches in the top and sides, and a small porthole obscured by instruments—the classical form of the *Soyuz* or "Heavenly Chariot" in which the Fragile first ventured beyond legendary Fragile Earth's blanket of sustaining atmosphere. (It is common to this day to find *Soyuz* pods and gargoyles adorning the exterior of mendicant chapels as they slowly migrate between the stars.) Three is a holy number, so it had originally held three reclining beds for its vulnerable passengers; however, the two outer couches had been removed and replaced by the feeder vats and fleshstuff printers that slowly poured their marrow techné—and with it, life—back into the gleaming alloy bones of the badly burned priestess.

"She's not going to be integrated before they arrive, is she? Two days to go, isn't it?" I realized I was repeating Dennett's own excuses back at him.

"That was true as of the last time I checked," he said through gritted teeth. "I shall check again. Maybe the horse will learn to sing if I increase the perfusion flow rate and dial back the target tissue integration threshold."

I watched for a few minutes as the deacon poked at the control panel on the outside of the sarcophagus, swearing in a most shocking and profane manner. "Ms. Alizond, I need you to go and fetch me fifty liters of sterile isotonic glucose in normal saline, a two-liter cartridge of propyl ene glycol, and at least twenty kilos of tubespam." I glanced around, but he was ahead of me. "The remotes are already fetching me a suit heat exchanger. Forcing her tissue integration will make her dangerously feverish, but if I can get her into a suit liner and pump cold water through it, I might be able to force maturation in time. Her Grace is already mostly present in body, if not in soul . . . go on! Get moving!"

I left him to his supervision of the thing on the slab and went in search of the perquisites. Which, in practice, meant a trip down to the kitchen and another tiresome opportunity to try and sweet-talk Cook into releasing the necessities of life. And so it was that I missed most of what happened next—which was probably all for the best.

Mistaken Identities

I don't believe in assigning blame when things go wrong. It is an unproductive activity, and more importantly, it makes people defensive—thus reducing their willingness to comply with quality-assurance protocols aimed at preventing recurrences. But I'll willingly blame myself. I freely admit: I had allowed myself to drift into the chapel crew's curious pattern of activity. You have probably noticed by now that the members of the crew who had chosen to remain aboard the mission mostly confined themselves to their stations and communicated very little: Cook stuck to the kitchen, the Gravid Mother gestated in her web, Deacon Dennett lurked in his organ pit, and so on. During my off-shift periods, I mostly hid in my cell, behind a locked hatch, and nobody seemed to mind: Doubtless I was just another piece of the picture to them. They were less a crew and more a scattered collection of huddled, sullen individualists. Moreover, there did not appear to be a chapel-wide communications net *as such*: at least, not one that anybody had introduced me to or logged me in on.

It was no one's fault but my own that I failed to ask about communications. And so it was no one's fault but my own when I arrived at the kitchen to find its hatch sealed and silent. I banged on it, waited, banged again, lost patience: "Box, where's Cook?"

The talking box was silent for a moment. Then: "Cook is in the Gravid Mother's cell."

I swore. "What's he doing there?"

The prehistoric joker who scripted the box's responses had the last laugh: "Insufficient data. Are you hungry?" I returned the box to my belt, then kicked off for the entrance to Mausoleum Companionway Two.

As soon as I tumbled into the corridor, I knew I wasn't alone. Some quality of the air currents or the shadows cast by the dim light globes flickering within the bony hands of the alcove occupants: I was unsure what it was, but I knew it wasn't right. As I entered, I had instinctively kicked off in the direction of the Gravid Mother's room, so I was unable to turn my head to see at first, but I caught hold of a protruding femur and added some spin to my trajectory. "Hello?" I called.

The stranger looked at me blankly. She hung stationary outside the hatch to Storage Node Fifteen, frozen in the act of opening it. I caught a confused jumble of impressions: a fuzz of short-cut hair, a soft, roundish face, austere one-piece free-fall suit, and something not quite right about the way she watched me that put me on my guard.

"Who are you?" I asked, politely enough, as if meeting a new and hitherto-unaccounted-for person aboard a vehicle in flight was nothing peculiar. "Have you seen Cook?"

The stranger twitched, turning and bracing her ankles against Storage Node Fifteen's hatch. "What is your name?" she asked me, her voice as flat and affectless as a synthesizer. Like me, she wore a utility belt with items clipped to it. Items that included a knife with a blade as long as my hand from wrist to middle fingertip, toward which her own right hand was moving.

The itch of uncertainty became a conviction: "Got to run! Bye!" I called, kicking off urgently toward the internode with Mausoleum Companionway Three, Storage Node Four, and UpDown Axial Gangway

Blue. I made no attempt to control my speed but aimed for the dogged-back hatch and grabbed it with both hands, yanking myself to a halt as the stranger's dagger buzzed angrily and oriented itself, rotors grinding at the air as it turned my way, preparing to attack. Its owner was gathering herself to leap, blank blue eyes focusing on me with nothing of mercy visible in her expression.

I yanked the emergency toggle as hard as I could. Red lights flashed as the hatch hissed loudly and sprang closed. A second later, a metallic *clang* and an angry whine told me my fear was entirely justified. I glanced around the back of the hatch, trying to suppress a rising tide of panic. VACUUM OVERRIDE looked promising: I twisted the switch, locking it shut as I tried to work out what was happening. She'd thrown a knife at me! Who was she, a stowaway or an agent for the pirates? There was no way of knowing. But I couldn't isolate her; long before I could make my way around the ring of passageways, she could be out of Companionway Three and somewhere else entirely. I'd have to find some way to warn the deacon of her presence on board—let *him* sort her out.

The Gravid Mother's cell was only a short distance away: two nodes, three tubes. I ran for it (or rather, I bounced and kicked and caromed toward it, somersaulting from all available surfaces). Less than a minute later, I came to her door. It was shut. I grabbed the locking wheel and used it as an anchor while I pounded on the door: "Let me in!"

There was no immediate response. Half-panicking, I grabbed the talking box. "Can you override the Gravid Mother's door lock?" I asked it. "Urgent maintenance is required, by order of Deacon Dennett."

"Stand by," the box vacillated.

"Open the door for me, or I'll use you as a wrench! There's a telemetry disconnect—"

That worked. The door unlocked, with a loud *clunk* from somewhere in its rim. I tugged it open and tumbled through into the Gravid Mother's room.

"Hey! Get out of—"

"No, get her!"

"Excuse me?" I blushed, hideously embarrassed, even as I swung the door shut behind me. (Avoiding embarrassment is a lower priority than avoiding knife-wielding killers.)

The Gravid Mother glared at me from the hammock-bed, in which she floated entwined and entangled with Cook. This much was unpleasantly clear: They'd removed most of the cushions and quilts from the bed for some reason, not to mention their clothes. "*What* is the meaning of this?" she demanded, face reddening. It was not the only part of her anatomy on parade: I tried not to notice.

Cook cranked himself round—when I had entered, his back was turned to me—so that he could look at me sidelong. "Yeah, what are you—"

"There's an intruder with a knife!" I burst out. "Deacon Dennett sent me for urgent feedstock for the priestess, but there's an intruder on board! She tried to kill me. And we're going to be boarded by pirates!"

Cook looked at his partner in concupiscence. "She's lost her mind," he grunted. "Let me take care of—"

"You've got to help!" I pleaded, "It's a crisis! Lady Cybelle needs twenty kilos of tubespam and fifty liters of intravenous fluid, and she needs it *right now* because the deacon is trying to accelerate her integration because we're going to be boarded by pirates in less than sixteen hours and all you can do is, er—" I spluttered out. It was transparently clear that Cook and the Gravid Mother shared a mutual fascination with anatomical exploration: At any other time, their distasteful distraction would have been none of my business, but right now it was clouding their minds. Indeed, they didn't even have the decency to undock and clothe themselves. "Disgusting!" I squeaked.

Now Cook separated himself from his partner and turned to face me. I averted my eyes. "Just because you're not getting any," he sneered.

The Gravid Mother sighed theatrically. "There'll be no reasoning with her, Willard," she told her partner in unspeakableness. "I know her kind. *You.*" She looked at me. "You aren't going to breathe a word of this to the deacon, are you? Or to Her Ladyship, when she's alive again. Or to Father Gould. *Are* you?"

I shook my head. "Why would I?"

"Because if you do," Cook butted in menacingly, "I'll—"

"Doesn't *matter*," I snap. "Weren't you listening? We're in serious trouble." I recounted what had happened to me since Dennett's summoning. "The intruder's probably a pirate spy," I concluded. "And if Dennett doesn't get the feedstock we need, we're going to be down one priestess."

"Go see to the intruder, dear. And get Dennett what he needs." The Gravid Mother gave Cook a push. "You," she told me, "are going to stay *right here* and keep me company while he's gone." There was a hard edge to her voice, promising pain if I defied her.

"But I've got to—"

She reached out with three meaty hands and grabbed my ankles. "You're going nowhere until I say you can."

"But I—" While she held me, Cook grabbed a bundle of clothes from one side of the door, opened the hatch, and sprang out. It slammed shut again with a loud *click*.

"You're *not* going to tell anyone about what you saw, are you?" she said, shaking me.

"Of course not." I looked at the door. "Do you think he'll do what you said?" I asked.

"If he wants to get laid again, he will." She arched her back against the bed-web, all six generous breasts pointing at me like gun muzzles. Was that expression intended to be a saucy grin? Or a dominant snarl? What did she take me for? "Make yourself comfortable. We're safe from your stalker in here—as long as the door stays locked."

Unknown to me, while I was coming to terms with my embarrassment at stumbling upon the Gravid Mother and Cook *in flagrante*, momentous and fatal events were happening elsewhere aboard the chapel.

After my departure, Dennett pressed ahead, as he had promised: tweaking energy and water inputs, meddling with the temperature in

Lady Cybelle's sarcophagus, and generally meddling with things that he was not, in truth, qualified to meddle with. Perhaps a fully initiated priest of the Mysteries of the Fragile might have been able to bring the fermenting vat of semiferal mechanocytes into domesticated harmony with the unifying will of Cybelle's still-slumbering skeleton and chassis. But Dennett was a junior minister, undertrained for such a demanding task: and more to the point, sufficiently unskilled to be overconfident about his own abilities.

I am a historian, not an initiate, but in preparing this document, I have made some attempt at informing myself as to the precise nature of the task at hand. People's bodies—the bodies of post-Fragile people like you and I—are, like those of the Fragile, made out of cells. But whereas Fragile cells are fragile sacks of fatty acids and peptides and water, our mechanocytes are bigger, vastly more complex, and contain control subsystems of entirely artificial design. Fragile cells can replicate themselves but are murderously hard to reprogram—whereas a mechanocyte can be ordered around, told which neighbors to attach itself to and what type of organ tissue to remodel itself into. Mechanocytes don't self-replicate, but are either manufactured by the specialized marrow techné 'cytes nestled in our long bones, or are produced in bulk in factories. We don't get *cancer*, the disease of uncontrolled self-replication. But if we suffer excessive damage, we may be unable to recover without an externally provided infusion of bulk raw mechanocytes—and then we need to have an engineering supervisor or a priest to program them into useful working tissues, lest we end up being eaten by a ball of undifferentiated feral goo. Mechanocytes in a body must sacrifice some of their autonomy for the collective good; they trade nutrients and energy, obey orders, and bid for resources. There is, in fact, an internal economy that unites the 'cytes of a body: a market driven by the debt created by their host's existence, a life defined by their willingness to cooperate. Death is really no more than the voluntary liquidation of an economy of microscopic free agents, the redemption of the debt of structured life. We are, after all, *homo economicus*.

Lady Cybelle had been killed during the micrometeoroid accident that damaged the chapel. Not injured, not burned, but *killed*: her head smashed and her soul chips irradiated by the reactor excursion, torso and legs horribly burned by corrosive oxidizer. Those of her mechanocytes that survived reverted to feral independence, seceding from the great economy of her life.

But Dennett had retrieved her soul chips—the solid-state backup of her neural activity—from the back of what was left of her skull. That was the key to what came next.

The resurrection of the prematurely dead is time-consuming and difficult but by no means unusual, and under other circumstances, it has become almost routine. You lay down a new skeleton, install seed mechanocytes while running a script to assign them to build new organs, including a brain. You infuse nutrients to buy their cooperation. Then you install the soul chips and train the first neurocytes to play their part in the ensemble of her identity, encoded in the neural net within her skull. The more of them that buy into the enterprise of the body, the greater becomes the pressure on newly added mechanocytes to join the throng: It happens a million times every day, across inhabited space. It happened to *me*, each time I arrived in a new beacon station arrivals hall.

The difference—

The deacon had neglected to establish whether Lady Cybelle's soul chips contained a complete and consistent dump of her neural state. Or whether the two soul chips even agreed about her state of mind at the moment of death. (He also failed to pay attention to a number of subtle issues relating to initializing a new brain—there is more to it than simply pumping a hundred million bloated metaneurocytes into a skull and flicking the "on" switch—but these paled into insignificance compared to his other errors.) As it happens, Lady Cybelle's soul chips had not come through the accident unscathed. And the neural connectome of a brain is not an all-or-nothing proposition, like a program in an archaic formal language: It will work even with considerable errors present. But an error-riddled one won't work *properly*. There will be glitches, memory holes, dyskinesias, personality changes, emotional upsets. And if one attempts to merge two different error-riddled connectomes, one doesn't necessarily improve the situation. Consequently, the Lady Priestess's higher cognitive functions were, shall we say, not yet bedded in: the error-prone soul chips were in place, but her personality and memories had not yet annealed. And that's not the worst part of what Dennett had failed to do: He had ignored the implications of loading faulty brain dumps into a body that had not yet finished assimilating and indenturing a huge influx of raw, free-market mechanocytes.

Normally, the recipient's techné would indoctrinate the new 'cytes as they circulated, assigning them a role and a nutrient credit balance and dispatching them to whatever tissue type was most in need, and all would run smoothly. But techné in a ferment of tissue replacement is techné that needs vastly more energy than normal. Deacon Dennett was in a hurry. He sent me to round up the vital nutrients but did not wait for me to return with them before he turned up the heat under Cybelle's marrow, pushing her metabolism into cytological inflation.

So, of course, it was nobody but his own fault when Lady Cybelle's etiolated body sat up inside the sarcophagus, looked around blankly, unplugged itself from the various pipes, tubes, and cables to which she was fastened, and climbed out of the hatch in search of food.

I say "Lady Cybelle's body," not "Lady Cybelle." Brains consume energy—a disproportionate amount of one's intake. And unlike the Fragile, people like us have the ability to handle famine efficiently; to shut down unnecessary organs and higher functions, to enter estivation if necessary, and to take extraordinary actions to satiate our needs in event of an emergency. Even the best of us lose our minds if subjected to extreme privations: A Fragile would simply die, but we stop thinking and temporarily become less than human—raw survival machines, bent on maintaining life by any means necessary. Monitor cameras witnessed what happened, of course. They saw the woman, naked and lean as any of the mummified servitors, her skin the unnatural white of pigment-depleted chromatophores, clamber clumsily through the circular hatch two-thirds of the way up the bell of the *Soyuz*. Deacon Dennett had his back turned to her, for he had returned to the organ pit to fuss over the engine controls (in a futile attempt to wring some extra thrust from the motors and postpone the inevitable reckoning with the approaching pirates). Leaning over his keyboards, fingers dancing across white and black keys and occasionally darting forward to pull or push the stops, he was so enthralled by his virtuoso performance that he failed to see Cybelle's head twitch round, blank-eyed and empty of expression, attracted by his movements. Movements that singled him out as the nearest available source of energy and nutrients.

Cybelle did not scream, or shout, or even (*contra* the urban legends surrounding the state of those unfortunates who shared her present degraded state) groan "*brainssss*." She simply leapt from the top of the sarcophagus, conserving her energy—a single bound that, in a hundredth of a gee, took her the entire width of the nave, across the screen, over the altar, and down into the organ crypt.

The strength of the famished is notorious, and in no way exaggerated: Someone whose higher functions have been sidelined by starvation will, without hesitation, exert themselves to the point of dislocating joints and delaminating motor-tissue bundles if they are in sight of food. Had Dennett not hunched forward over his keyboard without warning, Cybelle would have landed on his back and sunk her fangs into his throat on the way down. But by luck or happenstance, Dennett removed himself from the target of her slow-motion leap. Overshooting, Cybelle crashed against the imposing array of pipes and tubes jutting from the top of the commander's console: Dennett, looking up in surprise, caught a foot in his face and squawked loudly as he recoiled.

"Muh— Your Grace?" He tumbled backward from the bench seat as Cybelle turned.

Behind her, the valve work sputtered and hissed, deliquescing under her touch as hungry skin 'cytes pumped corrosive digestive fluid against everything they touched. Nothing of intelligence showed in her slitted emerald eyes as she looked around, searching for further food. "*Sssss—*"

Dennett clapped one hand to his damaged cheek, mouthing in pain as he realized his predicament. Then he hurled himself at the nearest exit in a dash for life, a split second ahead of Cybelle's whiplash pursuit.

Cybelle rebounded from the floor: By the time she recovered, she was alone in the vaulted space of the chapel. She looked around, hissing mindlessly: There was nothing to eat here. And so she gathered her strength and sprang once more in pursuit of her target. She had no choice, even had she mind enough to consider her options: For if she didn't find nutrition soon, her still-starving techné would declare her identity bankrupt; tear her brain to pieces; then secede from her body in a ravenous tide of solitary micromechanical predators.

And so the wild hunt began.

The stalker explored the darkened corridors of the chapel carefully, skulking from shadow to crypt, sending her knives ahead in brief whirring stabs of exploration.

Her wake-up call had come days ago, when the chapel commenced acceleration. Opening her eyes in the frigid darkness, she knew—for even the unconscious have mechanisms for reasoning—that the denizens of the mission would not expect an intruder at this late date. Nevertheless, she took pains over the air lock, investigating it with fingers and cunning tools, searching for sensors that might alert the occupants, then listening (with her head pressed against the wall) for any vibration that might betray the presence of a guard before she finally rotated the lock compartment round into the light and warmth and air of the interior.

The interior of the vehicle had proven challenging for the stalker. She had been designed and trained to operate in certain types of environments: Had she found her target aboard a passenger liner or a beacon station, her behavioral repertoire would have sufficed to deal with the situation. But the mission planners had not anticipated that Krina would outrun the stalker for this long, much less that she would hide in the anonymity of poverty or work her passage as a lay crew member aboard a religious mission. It was easy enough for the stalker to blend in with the dense, anonymous population of a commercial hub or a city, or to casually impersonate her target among near strangers; but a dimly lit chapel occupied for the most part by silently toiling skeletons was an entirely different matter. So when she fell back on another preprogrammed behavior, her attempts at misdirection and camouflage were not entirely successful.

The second time she resumed her active hunt, the chapel's acceleration had increased. Not by much—it was barely a thousandth of a gee—but it was a significant change. Increased acceleration was an indication of urgency, energetically expensive. That made it an anomaly, and anomalies frequently presaged opportunities, or at least useful distractions for potential witnesses. Had she been capable of introspection, the stalker would have been smacking her lips with anticipation as she gathered her knives and stealthily retrieved her external monitor to review its memory.

The tiny camera had spent the past week and a half clinging inconspicuously to the door of the cell the stalker had selected for a home. It awakened to capture an image whenever anyone passed by. Eleven motorized skeletons had clattered slowly along the passage, dusting and polishing. Twice on other occasions, a dark-robed figure had passed: and three times, a slightly built female similar enough to be the stalker's long-lost sib, this one carefully checking the lights and ventilation ducts as she went.

The stalker tensed when she recognized her prey. It wasn't a high-resolution recording (the camera was the size of a pinhead), but it was good enough; in particular, the motion kinematics were intimately familiar, burned into the stalker's memory. Krina had passed this way, attending to her chores, barely a day ago. Moreover, judging by her speed, she was in slowtime, metabolic rate and reflex speed lowered considerably. *Excellent.* The probability of a rapid kill and successful substitution had risen considerably. And so the stalker made some small adjustments to her appearance—bringing her hair and facial appearance closer into line with her target's—then opened the door and slithered out into the darkness of the graveyard shift.

She made her way through avenues of bones, along lightless ducts, through burnished metal docking nodes and flag-floored chambers. She charted her course by sound and memory: the distant creaking and groaning of wood and stone in flight, the pings and ticks of expanding and contracting metal, and the distant sigh of air rushing through ventilation ducts. Somewhere beyond the walls of the companionways, creatures scuttled in the darkness: cleaner worms, perhaps, or smaller quadrupedal hangers-on. They were of no significance to her. Only people were of interest to the stalker—and her knives, hovering quietly and alternately darting ahead of her, then falling behind to take up the rear.

Quite by accident, the target came to the stalker. "Hello?" it piped, tumbling out of a side passage right in front of the stalker as she worked on a hatch, preparing to expand her search pattern to take in another ring of access tubes. Something was clearly wrong: The target's metabolic rate was high, her activity frenetic.

The stalker, surprised, looked up. The target was completely unafraid. "Who are you?" it asked. "Have you seen Cook?"

There was no program for this. But the stalker had to be sure. "What is your name?" she demanded, reaching for her assault dagger.

"Got to run! Bye!" As the target turned, the stalker aimed her knife and braced for the throw—but the target somersaulted and bounced down the corridor with reckless, manic abandon and heedless haste, almost as if she realized what the stalker intended for her.

The stalker kicked off in pursuit, but the target ran without hesitation—then it reached the next internode and slammed the hatch shut behind. A rattling *clang* of catches notified the stalker that she was locked out. Worse: The target now knew she was pursued.

A human hunter would have become upset and angry at this point. But the stalker merely paused, then turned and rapidly made her way back to the next internode. The target could have made her way in five different directions; but she was still trapped aboard the chapel. The stalker would resume her search pattern. Sooner or later, she would come upon the target again and put an end to this stage of the mission.

After Cook's departure, the Gravid Mother's mood began to fall. She was clearly unhappy with me for some reason—perhaps it was the news I carried, or perhaps it was simply that my arrival had interrupted her recreational fornication—so after reassembling her bed-web, she retreated into it, muttering darkly to herself and occasionally glancing in my direction, as if wondering why I was still there. And after an hour, so was I.

In times of stress, I attempt to distract myself by enumerating repeating features of my environment: I find the contemplation of figures soothing. Unfortunately, there were few items to count in her room and nothing germane to this account. Also, I think, she became disturbed by my hand gestures. I tried to conceal them, but—"What *are* you doing?" she demanded.

"Counting." I held up both hands. "Did you know there are seventy-six strands in your bed?"

"Did I—how do you know that?"

I stared at my fingers. "That's seventy-six. Isn't it obvious?"

"But you don't have seventy-six fingers!"

"Of course not; I have six on each hand. But that's enough to count to four thousand and ninety-six, in binary. Without even using my toes."

She squinted at me. "You're mad."

"No: I'm numerate." I started counting the cushions again, for the eighteenth time. "How long do you think Cook should take?"

"What? To round up"—Her Gravidity muttered under her breath: After a moment, I realized she was counting aloud—"about half an hour. Why?"

"I haven't heard any alarms. And he's been gone fifty-eight minutes already. Shouldn't he be back here by now?"

She rolled her eyes. "Don't be silly, child. I'll call him." With which she raised one wrist to her cheek, and cooed, "Cookie, sweet cookie? My delectable cookie? Where are you?" She frowned impatiently as seconds ticked by, the silence lengthening. "Willard, *are you there*?" Her confident facade began to sag, like lime plaster undermined by the water of uncertainty slowly dripping down a wall.

"You have a voice communicator?" I asked, fascinated. "Like a *telephone*?" I kicked myself mentally for not having thought to ask for such a thing earlier: It would have made life simpler.

She didn't reply. Instead, all at once she turned on me. "This is all your fault! You and your horrid story, frightening us with pirates and crazies!" She heaved up against her bed restraints and began unhooking them: "You want to kill us all, don't you? You wheedled your way on board by sweet-talking the deacon and brought your pirate associates along and now you're trying to get me to go out and follow Willard!" She finished unstrapping herself from the bed, still fulminating: "I'm not a fool, you know! I stay here and I watch everything that's going on outside my room and I know things. I know exactly what you are!" She grabbed my ankles. "Go on, call your accomplices! Tell them I've got you! They're going to send Willard back to me, and he'd better be fine, because if he isn't, I'm going to send *you* back to *them* in lots of tiny little pieces—"

I started to struggle, but the Gravid Mother was surprisingly strong: She was taller and more massive than I, which gave her an unfair advantage of leverage and reach. "Let me go!" I demanded, shoving clumsily at her head.

"Oh no you don't," she crooned. "I'm not going to let you go! I'm going to keep you here with me until your friends come, then I'm going to show them what I can do—" She bundled me into a quilt and balled it up, knotting it around my neck to deny me leverage. "This is all your fault." I cowered in the makeshift sack as she raised her wrist again: "Willard, are you there? Anyone, is anyone there? Deacon, your holiness?" But nobody answered. "This is all your fault!" she repeated as she cried, punching me with her meaty fists.

I don't know what she intended, but punching a person you have just wrapped in a padded quilt is certainly not an effective way of harming them. Instead, I drifted across the room, quite out of her reach, which gave me time to fumble the knot loose and tumble out into the air. She snarled at me and shuffled around in her web, but I rebounded from the far wall and kicked off for the hatch. She swung toward me indecisively and finally jumped as I fumbled with the lock, but I had the advantage of leverage and caught her with a clumsy swipe that sent her spinning. The hatch clicked open as she fetched up against the far wall and rebounded toward me—but she was too late. I slipped into the twilight beyond the hatch and pulled it closed behind me. Not that I relished the idea of being at large aboard the chapel with a murderous stowaway on board, but the Gravid Mother had given me cause for concern with her increasing paranoia: If one must choose which space to share with a possibly homicidal lunatic, then one should pick the one with the most hiding places.

Willard the Cook slowly made his way toward the crypt through the warren of cadaver-lined companionways that surrounded the ground-level hub of the chapel. "Deacon? Yer holiness? I've got yer recuss fluids! An' yer tubespam! And the rest of yer orders. Feeling a wee bit peckish?" He pushed a bulky cargo net before him, full of sloshing demijohns of perfusion fluid and fat, rolled Fragile liverwurst. "Where are you?"

It is not possible at this remove for me to tell what was passing through his mind. Perhaps he was seething with resentment at the small, colorless person who had interrupted his afternoon's entertainment in the Gravid One's web—a very fetching spider in the eyes of this particular fly—and possibly also some mild apprehension at the incongruous talk of pirates and emergency procedures. But that is just my guess.

Nor is it possible at this time to tell of the location of Deacon Dennett, for that worthy had legged it at panic speed as soon as he realized that Her Ladyship was out and about and on the prowl for snacks. One might point the finger of reproach at Dennett, for, unlike me, he was equipped with a shipboard phone and certainly knew how to use it to alert everyone aboard the chapel to the situation; but he wasn't entirely in his right mind at the time, or even that of his badly burned brethren. With full and perfect hindsight, I think it is fair to say that Dennett was, in his own way, as unfit for command as Lady Cybelle.

What we can be sure of (for the cameras in Mausoleum Companion-way Four recorded it for posterity) was Willard's expression of gape-jawed terror as Lady Cybelle's cadaverous, crypt-pale body loomed out of the dark tunnel and clawed toward him. What we can also be sure of is the way he swung the bulk of his supply sack between his own body and his attacker—and the way Cybelle's aim shifted, darting toward the fat wormlike sheath of wrapped tubespam, which she grabbed and bit in half in a single fluid motion.

"Eek," or "Ick," said Cook. And, being neither slow on the uptake nor eager to die, he unloaded the contents of the cargo net into Cybelle's maw as fast as she could absorb it. She sucked down the fat sausage-tubes of warmly pulsing cultured liver tissue, some of them showing the pink freckles of an enthusiastically metastasizing hepatocellular carcinoma; head-sized transparent bags of perfusion fluid that pulsed and wobbled in the microgravity air flow; supplementary saccules of crunchy phosphate-rich shipboard biscuit crawling with unindentured mechanocytes. As she consumed, Cybelle changed shape, her abdomen bloating and new veins forming just below her skin. They pulsed as the skin above them erupted in spikes, piercing the perfusion bags to drain their contents directly into her circulatory system. Like a vast, pallid, avian fetus stripped of its shell, she wrapped herself around the fluid sacks and growled as she gnawed on gobbets of barely processed flesh.

One may infer from his shifty body language and reluctant posture that Willard was less than enthusiastic about his proximity to the mind-lessly feeding priestess; he leaned ever farther away from her presence, eyes swiveling sidelong in search of an avenue of escape. Presently he found one—or rather, manufactured it by unsealing one end of a fat liver sausage and squirting the contents in the direction of Cybelle's face. Her tongue, gray and wrinkled and tentacular, temporarily tipped with circular tooth-lined maws of its own, slithered forth to lick her eyeballs clean. While she was thus distracted, Cook made his escape and hauled himself hand over hand away from the floating pile of comestibles.

Willard didn't pause until he'd closed a hatch between himself and the feeding horror. Then he slumped slightly and reached for his phone. "Emergency, calling you all! Cook 'ere. I just run into Her Grace in Companionway Four, and she's *hungry*. Got meself away by the skin o' me teeth. She be snacking down on the supplies yer 'oliness ordered for 'er, but I am thinking about barricading meself in me kitchen for the duration. Anyone gorra net?"

A paper-dry whispery clicking answered him from the other end of the companionway he'd taken shelter in. Willard looked up, aghast, as a door opened at the other end of the tunnel. The red sparks of infrared transmitters glimmered in the depths of eye sockets, illuminating them with misplaced sparks of sapience. *"I will take care of this,"* hissed the skeleton (buzzing with each sibilant, for its speaker was improperly secured to its jawbone, vibrating against an ancient molar): *"Return to your station."* Cook cowered, backing against the wall of the companionway as the skeleton approached, followed by half a dozen more mummified remotes: all clad in the ragged cerement remains of space suits, clutching a variety of improvised weapons ranging from wrenches to sharpened docking probes. They streamed past him, clattering and crackling quietly, and formed a circle around the hatch. Willard barely spared them a glance before making himself scarce.

By the time the Mother's boudoir door clanged shut behind me I was beginning to harbor deep reservations about the wisdom of having booked my working passage aboard this vehicle. One may reasonably expect a certain degree of eccentricity among the long-term crew of a flying church, but there is a point at which eccentricity begins to impact operational effectiveness, and my fellow travelers were well past that juncture. On top of all of this, there was the puzzling and worrisome presence of the stowaway who had attacked me. I will confess to having become a bundle of nerves by this point. And so I fled directly toward my own tiny compartment, with every intention of barricading myself inside it and not coming out again until we entered orbit around Shin-Tethys.

However, as I turned the corner onto the C-deck passage leading to the various storage compartments and my coffin-sized room, I slowed. A nasty thought had occurred to me.

Replaying my memory of my assailant I thought, *Does she not look somewhat familiar?* Why, yes: I had become used to seeing that same face reflected in my tattered wall retina every day on Taj Beacon, whenever I cleaned myself before venturing out in public. And what had she said? *What is your name?* Indeed. And there was the matter of Andrea's too-long-ignored message packet, now that I thought about it, and of Ana's disappearance.

I began to incubate an unwelcome hypothesis. Imagine for a moment that Ana's disappearance was not an accident: that she had in fact *been* disappeared. (I made a note to write a letter to her former lover or debt collector or whoever it was who had been asking after her.) Suppose that her abductor had been interested in the activities of our little syndicate for some time. Suppose that they had become aware of my impending visit, under cover of pilgrimage. Suppose that they were sufficiently ruthless and greedy. Taking all of this into account . . . what if they imagined that I was a courier, perhaps bringing to Ana the other half of a large, orphaned, slow money transaction, and that once we got together, we would be in a position to assert ownership of the aforementioned bond by right of salvage? If such a person supposed that a not-inconsiderable amount of money might be at stake, a sufficiently ruthless individual might be tempted to take actions that— *Oh dear.*

It was in this paranoid frame of mind that I approached the door to my room. I had let my guard down somewhat once I was aboard the chapel, and we were under way. I had not discussed the sub-rosa sororal syndicate, of course, but I had let my guard down a little with Dennett and the others. Now I began to chew over the question of whether I might have accidentally disclosed too much information about my purpose here in Dojima System. As I approached the door, I groped for the retina I'd hung on the wall of my room with the corner of my mind that deals with inanimate objects. I could feel it, distantly tugging at my proximity sense. Pausing, I screwed my eyes shut and looked out through its face.

My room was dark, but not dark enough to conceal the dim infrared fleshlight of a lurking intruder, waiting for me just behind the door.

I withdrew my vision from the retina. Glancing round hastily, I spotted the nearest cleaning-supplies locker. As quietly as possible, I made my way to it and nudged the hatch open. There was, as I expected, a canister of emergency sealant. That would do the job, but I'd need to wedge the door shut while it set. It took me a little longer to confirm that a high-gee broom would do the job, threaded through the spokes of the hand wheel that manually disengaged the teeth of the door's seal. And so, within a matter of minutes, I jammed the door to my room shut and carefully extruded the caulking gun's freight of sealant around the rim. Designed to set rapidly and hold back the pressure of escaping air in event of a micrometeoroid strike, the sealant should suffice to keep my stalker confined while I went in search of help.

I congratulated myself on a job well done, then went in search of the deacon in order to tell him about the stowaway and to see how he was managing Her Grace.

Now, here is a curious fact to which, for some reason, neither Deacon Dennett nor I had given due consideration:
Pirates tell lies.

I found the deacon in the crypt, supervising the reinterment of Her Grace in the *Soyuz* sarcophagus, a small army of ambulatory skeletons in attendance. Some of them were a bit the worse for wear, pursued by various stray arms and legs (and in one memorable case, a jawbone) which were anxiously awaiting reattachment to their missing bodies.

"Ah, Ms. Alizond. If you would be so good as to help tighten this strap?" Dennett barely looked up as I approached the thrashing ghoul. He had somehow—presumably in conjunction with Gould's little helpers—managed to trap Lady Cybelle in a space suit with its glove rings locked together, forming a field-expedient straitjacket. She was placid for the time being, suckling on a bottle of Fragile blood, but he was clearly intent on taking no chances and was busily lashing her to the commander's reentry couch within the capsule with a fearsome array of fetters. "Once she's in place, I can plug her back in and restart the nutrient flow. It's strictly a temporary measure—we can release her when her mind returns—but for the time being she needs close supervision and restraint. If you would be so good as to grab this strap and brace yourself, then afterward, if you could fetch Cook—"

"There's a stowaway!" I couldn't contain myself. "She attacked me, but I've glued her inside my room! You didn't issue me a telephone, so I couldn't report—"

"Most of the shipboard communicators are in use inside the skeletons," Dennett interrupted me. "How do you think Gould operates them?"

"But there's an intruder!"

"One problem at a time." He sighed. "Where did you meet this person, and what induced you to glue her inside your room?"

"I was on my way to the kitchen; I ran into her in one of the companionways. She asked who I was, then threw a knife at me—a ducted-fan blade. I got a door between us, then ran. I don't know who she is but she looks . . . just like me . . ." I slowed.

"So you've discovered your evil twin?" Dennett asked, not unkindly. "Have a seat." He gestured at the copilot's couch beside the madwoman. "It would be best if we don't have to worry about which one of you is the real Ms. Alizond, don't you think?" I froze, then glanced over my shoulder at the open hatch. A grinning skull stared back at me. "Further confusion would be undesirable."

"But I—"

"Grmm. Brnz," Her Grace mumbled around a mouthful of raw meat.

"What was that?" Dennett leaned over her, losing interest in me all of a sudden. I glanced at the hatch again. "Oh I say." He turned back to me. "Listen. I think you should stay here. I've sent for more supplies; just keep her well fed, and nothing will go wrong, do you understand?"

"Wait, what—"

A distant thud, more felt than heard, rippled through the capsule. "I have a mission to run," said the deacon, straightening up (insofar as it was possible for him to do so in the cramped confines of the sarcophagus). He turned toward the hatch. "And it's probably best if we keep both you *and* your twin in known locations for the time being. So if you will excuse me . . ."

He scrambled out: Skeletal arms reached in to replace him with a bright blue mesh basket of feedstock canisters and a talking box, then the sarcophagus hatch slammed shut overhead. "Glrmmmm!" moaned the thing on the couch. It subsided into a routine of sucking and munching. I shuddered and looked at the recently resurrected zombie. Were those cheeks slightly less hollow, those eyes an iota less mad?

"Maintenance operator," blatted the talking box, "secondary nutrient spigot one requires refilling urgently. Remove the expended A4921K cartridge and replace with a fresh A4921K cartridge!"

Another thudding bang rippled through the floor of the capsule. I bent over the bag of stores and rummaged desperately for a fresh A4921K—a cylindrical green assembly with a valve at one end and a spindle protruding from the other—then swore at the talking box until it explained, in monosyllables, how to install it. There were more distant bangs. The *Soyuz* was very close to soundproof; whatever was going on outside must be extremely loud to carry through its hull. The small porthole in the wall of the sarcophagus was positioned inconveniently, pointing at one wall of the crypt. I will confess to stealing a glance through it from time to time, but most of my attention was directed at Lady Cybelle, who, for the most part, lay slobbering and quiescent upon her couch (although from time to time curious spasms rippled through her, as though she was testing the breaking strength of the restraining straps).

After a while, I began to feel dizzy. Not ill, merely disoriented—as if the chapel was undergoing some sort of very slow maneuvering. I lay down on the second couch and just in time, for moments later the stack of supplies toppled sideways. There was another deep thud from beneath. Cybelle moaned quietly. "Where? Whaaaare?"

"Hush," I replied, preoccupied by what a deep sense of foreboding informed me must be the onset of a slow-motion space battle.

"Need . . . control." I turned sideways to look at her. She stared back, sidelong, with the beginnings of lucidity visible in her unnaturally smooth and immobile face. Her expression was disturbing, as inexpressive as a corpse whose collective anima had died but whose mechanocytes had not yet voted to liquidate the collective: However, compared to the mindless ghoul that had ravened her way through the crypt before Gould's skeletal remotes subdued her, she was a paragon of lucidity. "Who. Am. I?"

I told her, but the news clearly upset her bitterly, and I was compelled to silence her with another bolus of blood-liver pâté while I took stock of my thoughts. Meanwhile, the banging from outside continued: At one point a shudder rippled through the floor and set the muted clappers high above to thudding against their muffled bells. The supplies drifted up toward the top of the sarcophagus, and I nearly followed them: I was forced to net them together and drag them down to the floor (and a good thing I did so, for seconds later the gravity resumed—about a hundredth of a gee, offset at a thirty-five-degree angle if I am any judge of such things).

Finally, everything straightened up again, and the clamor stopped.

"Who. Am. I?" asked Cybelle.

I stared at her. I had, it's true, been feeding her more or less continuously for an hour. And the *Soyuz* had become uncomfortably warm during that time, and I'd lost track of the gurgling and bubbling noises coming from within her space suit, but the heat exchanger it was plumbed into was definitely hot to the glance: and for the first time there was something not unlike sentience in her expression. "You're the priest-ess, Cybelle, aren't you?" I was suddenly acutely aware of my own lack of paramedical training: "Are you hungry?" I asked.

She shook her head weakly. "Not now." She swallowed. Yes, *definite* signs of lucidity. Color was returning to her skin, which was slowly flush-ing toward a healthy blue. "Hot'n'cold. It's a, a fever." Her eyes rolled for a moment, then I realized she was scanning her surroundings. "This suit. Heat exchanger. I'm too *hot*."

Hot. That was what Dennett had been talking about—heating her up, cranking her metabolism up into overdrive and force-feeding her newly integrating organs. "How do I turn the temperature down?" I asked her, pointing at the control panel.

"Let me—" She tried to sit up, then to raise her arms. For the first time, she saw that her sleeves were locked into one another at the wrist rings. "Was I violent?"

"You tried to eat the deacon."

"I'm sure the traitorous little shit deserved it . . ."

I made a snap decision. "Let's see if we can get you out of that thing."

It was, I discovered, not difficult to unfasten space-suit glove rings from the outside. As soon as I had unlocked them, Cybelle pulled her hands apart. Then she began to fumble ineffectually with the seat web-bing. "Something's wrong."

"What do you remember?" I asked.

"Not enough. Unfasten me!"

"There was some sort of accident." I watched her a moment longer as she batted at quick-release buckles with numb hands. "You were very badly injured. Dennett put you in here to regenerate, supplied a huge transfusion of free-market 'cytes from somewhere . . ."

Cybelle swallowed. "My hands don't work properly."

"They're newly regrown." I began to loosen the straps holding her to the couch. "You probably don't have full reflex control yet."

Something metallic banged against the exterior hatch. I turned to the porthole and froze. A huge, dark eye pressed up close to the glass, occluding the view. It stared at me for a moment, then it blinked.

"What's happening?" Cybelle demanded. She wasn't in a position from which she could see out.

"Space pirates, I think." The locking wheel in the center of the hatch began to turn. "They want in."

The hatch swung open before I could force the ancient quick-release buckle on Cybelle's harness. A toothy muzzle covered in dark bristles poked inside, sniffing the filthy air suspiciously. "You! Be gettin' yourselves out here now!" A whirring knife, screws humming at the air, pointed its deadly blade at us from behind the hijacker's webbed left ear. "We's taken this vehicle! Resistance be futile!"

The pirates had boarded the chapel well ahead of their declared schedule.

Dennett's mistake was to assume he had plenty of time because he was receiving their transmissions from a slowly accelerating vehicle dead astern of the chapel. Not being a soldier, he'd failed to account for the short-legged high-acceleration boarding craft lying dead ahead in our line of flight. Evidently it had been sent there as soon as the chapel's flight course became apparent upon its departure from Taj Beacon; at the time, I did not know how the pirates evaded the deacon's radar, but when all is said and done, churches are not renowned for their military-grade sensor suites. Regardless of how they did it, there was no warning: One minute Dennett was worrying about the large vehicle that was slowly overhauling us from astern, and the next minute the distinctive exhaust plume of a nuclear-thermal rocket was melting the lead flashing on the steeple. While I was force-feeding Lady Cybelle so that she wouldn't turn her appetite on me, Dennett was trying to evade the incoming boarding craft. To give him his due, he made a decent attempt to dodge the pirates: But the chapel was not built for the wild gyrations and evasive maneuvers required to resist a forced docking. Eventually, our assailants tired of the game, at which point they shot away the chapel's high-gain antenna and issued a harsh ultimatum—be boarded, or be blown apart.

"Get here! Not there, here!" The pirates—four of them, all armed—hovered above the *Soyuz* in the crypt, intimidating us with beats of their leathery wings. Escape was not an option: With their chiropteroid low-gee adaptations, they'd have no trouble running me down if I tried to flee. Moreover, I had to carry Cybelle, for she could barely control her arms and legs. Their leader shrieked, his (or her: I could not tell) voice a high-pitched rasp: "Respect! Get down, Churchling! Get down there, not here!"

"I'm getting, I'm getting!" I tried to move to the indicated spot without accidentally kicking myself halfway to the ceiling. "What do you want?"

"This way! Not that way!" The seniormost pirate gestured, making short stabbing indications with his (or her) power blade. "To the storage room, third door along! You wait there! You try escape, we cut neck." (Punctuation: an unmistakable sawing gesture. Hovering behind his shoulder, one of the quadrotor blades echoed his motion.)

I hauled Cybelle in the direction indicated: neck-cutting did not appeal. In what appeared to be an outbreak of playful spirit, the pirates had decorated the storage-room hatch with a chain of Gould's skulls: they buzzed and clattered their jaws angrily as one of our hijackers chittered and yanked at the wheel of the field-expedient dungeon. I slid Cybelle through the opening, then (with a glance at the pirate leader, who bared his or her fangs at me) followed her inside.

"Your Grace—" It was the deacon. He recoiled as he saw me, a very strange expression on his face. "They captured you *both*?"

"You didn't leave me any opportunity to escape," I said, as Cybelle simultaneously announced, "I demand to know what is going on! Why aren't we at Taj Beacon yet?"

"Gruffle," mumbled Father Gould. He was hanging upside down from an air-conditioning duct, his habit wrapped around his torso, as if imitating our captors' leathery wings. As situationally unaware as ever, he wore an expression of rapt concentration: His eyes were screwed tightly shut. "Grumming bat crypt belfry."

"What are they going to do to us?" I asked. I noted the absence of certain parties—the Gravid Mother and Cook in particular.

"I don't know." Dennett twitched, then swiveled his gaze toward Cybelle. "Do you remember the accident?"

"There was an accident?" Cybelle might have regained the power of speech and relinquished her insensate appetite for flesh, but she was still coming up to speed. "No, I don't remember any accident. When do we arrive at Taj? Who are these people?"

"We've been hijacked." Dennett glanced sidelong at Father Gould, then back at Lady Cybelle. "I should warn you that they've broken his remote network and are most certainly monitoring it—including his eyes and ears. He's trying to subvocalize and not look at any of us, but you should assume that anything you say will be overheard. As I was about to say . . . the accident was a total disaster. We were forced to put in at Taj Beacon, where Sister Ang and the three engineering officers deserted. I had to petition the vicar-in-residence for a line of credit to buy new techné for your regrowth, and six hundred kilos of plutonium for the second reactor—it wasn't cheap. Shorthanded and damaged, I also advertised for additional crew: That's where Ms. Alizond comes in." Another strange look. "And Willard, the new life-support engineer. Cook. Oh, and there's a stowaway. Looks just like Ms. Alizond, but is less talkative. Seems to want to kill her for some reason, which is why I put Ms. Alizond in the sarcophagus with you."

I startled. "You saw her?" I asked.

"Saw her?" Dennett raised an eyebrow: "She was a much more

diligent cleaner than you, and didn't even ask for pay. Not a very interesting conversationalist, though—a bit too focused on murderous thuggery. But I diverted her away from your cell: You should be grateful," he added, offhandedly. "Don't worry, I'll look after you."

"I should be—" I forced myself to stop.

"I don't understand this." Cybelle raised her arms ineffectually, framing her face. "Who are these hijackers?"

Suddenly, the hatch swung open. "Which of you is Alizond?" barked one of our captors. "Boss want talk you right now! Come, or I cut neck!" As if to emphasize this, one of the quadrotor knives whirred menacingly into our midst, causing the other captives to scatter. "Come! We go now!"

There didn't seem to be any alternative options on offer. So I went.

Kidnapped!

The pirates hustled me away from the improvised brig, toward the refectory, where their leader had established his office. They had dragged the tables together and plastered their tops with retinas, displaying black-and-white text that marched in pleasingly regular patterns across their eating surfaces.

"Ah. You must be Krina Alizond-114."

I stared at the pirate chief with mixed apprehension and curiosity. In body plan he resembled his minions: furry and sharp-faced with low-gee batwings and spindly legs. He hunched over the largest retina, a stylus clutched in each hand. I noticed that he wore gold, chain-link bands to hold his wings in place at elbow and wrist and a visor above his eyes that shone with a pale green light. "Um."

He gestured at a low-gee chair on the opposite side of the table. "Please take a seat," he said, not unkindly.

I sat. The retina, I realized, was gridded out in the soothing, familiar patterns of a purchase/sales ledger and an inventory-accounting system. How unexpectedly civilized! "Um . . ." I felt my facial chromatophores flush, an autonomic response in lieu of vocal communication. "You wanted to see me?"

"Yes. Ms. Alizond." My captor leaned toward me, grinning—he could hardly do otherwise, with his sharp-toothed muzzle topped by a black olfactory bulb. "I have been looking forward to meeting you. You've led us a merry dance, you know. Nearly slipped through our claws twice now." He tapped one stylus on the retina in front of him, drawing a double line beneath a column of figures: "But now we have your number! Ahahaha!"

"I beg your pardon?" I stared at him in perplexity.

"Granted." His grin widened. "If you can tell us where she is?"

"Who?"

"Come, now! There's no need to be coy. All you need do is tell me where your collaborator is, and we can be on our way, with no further need to detain you. Where is she?"

I shook my head. "You mean Ana?"

He nodded, tongue lolling for a moment until he remembered his manners and closed his jaws with an audible snap. "Yes. Ana Graulle-90. I believe you know of her?"

I nod. "Why do you think I'm here? She's been missing for over a hundred days!"

"Of course." The pirate leader's permanent expression of feral humor belied his tone. "And you're going to tell me where she is, aren't you? I am very anxious to make her acquaintance."

"I can't help you." I stared at the marching figures embedded in the white surface of his boardroom-sized retina: "I don't know. I only arrived at Taj Beacon"—some quick math—"eighty-six days and fourteen hours ago. Approximately, I mean. She was supposed to have sent word of where I was to meet her: I was supposed to spend the next year collaborating with her in a course of intensive study in one of the outer belt orbitals, you know. But first she went to Shin-Tethys, then she disappeared. And I've got no idea where she's gone."

"Come now, Ms. Alizond." The teeth reinserted themselves into his grin. "Surely your sisterhood have prearranged bolt-holes and agreed contact procedures? Scattered across such vast distances, you must know where she would expect you to rendezvous if circumstances became, ah, temporarily unfavorable to your business?"

I shuffled uneasily against my seat. "Yes, we do—but you don't understand! She's missing! Yes, we have preagreed rendezvous points. I'll tell you for free, hers were in GJ 785—where I have come from—and again, in one of the high orbital kingdoms of the Trailing Pretties. She hasn't left for GJ 785, and you can verify that: The immigration and emigration logs at the beacon are matters of public record. As for the Trailing Pretties, that's where she ought to have gone: There is no defined rendezvous point on Shin-Tethys because she wasn't meant to go there! I mean, it's a *planet.* So massive it has its own gravity well. You can't get away in a hurry without spending huge amounts of energy! Much less make a break for the outer system without being noticed. Why she went there—" I shrug. "That's what I want to find out."

I watched the pirate chief uneasily. He radiated a disturbing feral intensity, a ferocity of purpose I associated with senior executives: He was somewhat less chilly than my mother, I thought, but no less determined. "Do you have any idea who I am?" he asked.

"Not really." I set my jaw. "Obviously you have declared yourself to be the leader of a pirate band: What else should I know?"

He whistled between his teeth, an astonishingly high-pitched noise that I could barely track. The avuncular amusement disappeared. "Ignorance is *dangerous*, Ms. Alizond. It can be mistaken for close-lipped cynical insight, you know. I am going to ask you again: What do you know about your sister's current whereabouts? I ask for her own good."

"Really?" I raised an eyebrow.

"Yes." Was that an aggrieved glare? Or was I simply misinterpreting the facial expressions and body language of his kind? "We are *not* simple pirates, Ms. Alizond. We are, in point of fact, a local branch of an interstellar financial agency. And among other things, we are the underwriters of her not-insubstantial life insurance policy. Hah! You were unaware that she had such a thing? How touching. We have a distinct interest at stake in her continued existence, not to mention considerable curiosity about the nature of certain of her business activities, which have attracted the attention of a wide cross section of Dojima System's reprobates. Observe." Styli flashed across the retina before me, summoning up an imposingly detailed contract signed, I was reluctantly forced to concede, with what appeared to be Ana's checksum. "We have a shared interest. What can you tell me about her?"

Pirate underwriters: what next? "She disappeared from home, which is one thing, but then she missed her first contact *and* her second contact. If she's gone on the run, she'd only do that if she expected someone to come after her, someone who knew what signals she'd use, someone who had been reading her mail. It's very upsetting. Nobody I've been able to contact has any idea where she is: It's as if she's died, or been abducted. That's why I'm on this vehicle: It was the first available transport I could find that would take me to Shin-Tethys." I shivered. "What do you suspect has happened?"

The pirate chief yawned. "Insurance fraud. Or worse." Strong arms grabbed my shoulders, holding me down. "So we're going to start by verifying that you are telling me the truth, the whole truth, and nothing but the truth," he added. "Under authenticated oath, ordered this day in my capacity as a certificated independent arbiter investigating the possible fraudulent discharge of the life insurance policy of Ana Graulle-90. Sorry about this," he added to my face with evident sincerity, then, over my shoulder: "Debug her."

"Wait—" I began, as one of them shoved my head forward. But I was too late. A sharp tugging and a sense of emptiness at the base of my skull where a soul chip belonged was followed by a moment of icy coldness; darkness crossing my vision, static pins and needles in every extremity, a sense of extreme violation as something simultaneously sharp and blunt that smelled green and tasted of chlorine thrust into the unoccupied socket—

Hiatus.

For the most part, it is a good thing that we are no longer built from the same chaotically evolved watery lipid foam as the Fragile. Mechano-cytic life is far more robust, able to operate within a far wider environ-mental envelope. (We may breathe an oxygenated gas mix, metabolize hydrocarbons and other feedstock, and crap processed waste, but we don't have to do so all the time: We can run off juice, crack oxygen from water, and recycle almost everything.) But there are certain disadvan-tages, too. Unlike the Fragile (whose brains contain over a trillion cells), our brains are built from mere tens of millions of mechaneurons, each of them a complex device that emulates many thousands of more primitive neurons. Our brains are multiply redundant—it takes more than a sim-ple bullet through the head to stop one of us from continuing to think, albeit at an impaired rate. And they are designed for metaprogramming, to allow their state to be copied to or from a soul chip carried in one of our two interface slots, or to allow them to be modified by an external device. Such devices have many names, names that change depending on context, from the anodyne to the malign: *A remote debugger*, our artifi-cers call them when they connect them to nonsentient systems, or *a slave chip*, when someone stabs one into another's thinking, feeling brain.

Private ownership of a fully configured slave chip is illegal in many polities: It tends to be a government monopoly, much like other forms of violence.

But I had fallen among pirates and life insurance underwriters. Surely it should be no surprise that such dubious practices might be everyday business among such persons!

"First question. Has Deacon Dennett interfered with you?" my cap-tor demanded.

"I, I don't understand?"

I cannot, even now, quite describe what it felt like. I would say that a great glassy wall had slammed down between me and my sense of iden-tity; that my *I* was missing, that my will was wholly entrained to his desires—but it would not be correct. Something missing, something added. It was not an unpleasant sensation at the time, but I would die before I would willingly submit to it again because it was like a living death—the death of will. And so, I stuttered.

"Has Deacon Dennett interfered with your mind? For example, by subjecting you to a remote debugger?"

"N-No!"

"So: We got to you in time. Provisionally." He made a notation on his grid, then leaned forward. "Where is your sister Ana? Where are you going to meet her?"

"I, I, I—"

"What?" he demanded. "Where is she?"

"Don'tDon'tDon'tKnowOwOwOwOwOw . . ."

He glared at someone behind me. "Can you fix the feedback?"

A high, sibilant voice: "I don't think so. She's not supposed to respond like that. Let me damp her"—*Nothingness*—"no, that didn't work. You're going to have to put up with it."

"Gah." He stared at the desk in distaste. "Let's try that again. Do you know where your sib Ana is, Krina?"

Easy enough: "No-o."

"Where were you going to meet Ana?"

"I—I—going to Shin-Tethys, to Nova Ploetsk in TheTheTheKingdomOm of Argos, ApartApartment 164 Ring 3 West—"

"That's her home, sure enough," my captor commented, rapidly scritching a note on the tabletop retina. Back in my direction: "What were you going to do when you got there?"

"Find-ind her."

The pirate chief whistled irritably, in a manner I would probably have found amusing had I been in possession of my own will: "How were you going to find her?"

"Don'tDon'tDon'tDon'tDon't—*Know*."

"Oh." He hunched back on himself, drawing his wings in close with an expression of evident frustration: "So you do not know where she is, and her disappearance is unexpected?"

"YesYesYes—"

"Wonderful." His voice dripped irony. "Was she, do you know, planning to commit insurance fraud against this institution?"

"NoNo."

He looked past me. "Release her. Add this transcript to the case record under seal: Also note that subject told the truth when questioned *without* debugging override."

Volition returned, with a tearing, sucking void at the back of my neck. I startled and began to shake as clumsy fingers replaced the chip they'd removed to make way for the debugger; some obscure reflex threw my ocular lubricant ducts into repeated self-cleaning cycles, and I began to weep at the ghastly memory of death flowing through me, washing away my self-control.

"Are you done yet?" My interrogator asked after a minute as painful as any I'd experienced in many years.

"You—you—" I managed to catch myself before I said anything unpardonable (an icy existential terror lurking in the shadow of my mind: *Don't let them plug that thing into me again*)—"that was unnecessary! I'm not trying to hide—"

"You are wrong, Ms. Alizond, that was *entirely* necessary." He hissed and bared his fangs, leaning toward my face until I recoiled: "Because now we know that you're telling the truth, don't we? Which is a matter of some importance. Your missing sister, if she has been so inconsiderate as to die, will completely wipe out this branch office's trading profit for the last standard year. Now we have confirmed under judicial interrogation that you are not a participant in an attempt to defraud us, we can put this unfortunate incident behind us and discuss what happens next—which is, how to find your missing sister before the mob of murderers and robbers who are attempting to track her down."

"The—*what*?" I stared at my interrogator through blurry eyes, and noticed, with a flash of something like hatred, as an expression of sympathy flickered across his face before he composed himself.

"Word gets around, Ms. Alizond: Surely you must know of the rumors?"

"Rumors?" Gut-deep terror struck at me.

"Rumors about a certain high-value financial instrument, Ms. Alizond. Rumors that you and your missing sister are in possession of the two halves of an unsettled transaction with a value in the million slow dollar range. Or hadn't you heard?"

"Nonsense!" I exclaimed, somewhat too rapidly. Then: "I certainly don't have anything like that. And if Ana has stumbled across a lost draft that large, she certainly hasn't told me. Didn't tell me. Before she went missing, I mean . . ." I began to tear up. "Anyway, why didn't you ask me when you had me under oath?"

"Your motives for visiting this system is not a legitimate subject for deposition under debugger-enforced oath during a fraud investigation." The pirate chief seemed to look right through me. "I could lose my license. Or worse." He whistled again: A pair of goons materialized at my back. "Take her to her quarters and lock her in until we're ready to depart," he told them. As they lifted me from my seat, he added: "The stakes here are far higher than you realize. I apologize unreservedly for your distress: We'll talk again once we are under way."

I am told that on first acquaintance I usually strike people as meek and mild-mannered. This is a mistake. I believe I alluded earlier to the circumstances of my childhood. I did not so much take to silence and quietude naturally as have them forced upon me as survival tools. Sondra was cursed with a fiery, quick temper and doesn't suffer fools gladly; more than one of my sibs who shared those traits provoked her into aborting them. Besides, the nature of my specialty is such that I have studied unsavory people and know all too well the way gangsters and tyrants dispose of those whom they consider to be traitors. So I learned early to nurse my grudges in polite silence and repay insults at my leisure.

Once the hatch slammed shut behind me I huddled up in the mound of bedding, hugging my legs and burying my face between my knees. An observer might have thought I was weeping, whether from the shock of abduction or the indignity of interrogation: In reality, I was taking stock of my situation and concealing my anger from the microcams that the pirates would inevitably have dusted the room with. They weren't, I noticed, uncivilized: They'd thoughtfully replaced the chip they yanked to make room for their interrogation tool. Which meant *both* my sockets were populated.

Most of us harbor dual soul-chip slots simply as a matter of redundancy. We use them as journal logs for our mental state, so that if our body is damaged beyond repair, a rescuer can attempt to install us in a new anatomical framework and initialize a brain of random, barely socialized mechaneurocytes from the dump. Two sockets simply mean there's a greater chance of surviving an accident so drastic that it crushes one's skull. You don't really need two backups if you're willing to live dangerously; so, like other traders in secrecy, I habitually used one of my sockets to hold a private data repository and a dumb, programmable amanuensis.

Quivering in a bundle of fabric, I retreated inside my own head to formulate my escape plans. A compulsive filer, I threw every image I could recall into a new and palatial memory mansion: from my interrogator's face and his precise phraseology to the expression on Lady Cybelle's face as Deacon Dennett explained our situation to her. Dennett's speech, too, went into the closet. Had there been something shifty-looking about his expression? I pondered for a minute, then decided to revisit the question later.

While I was busy establishing a sound foundation for future schemes, I noticed a couple of reminders waiting for me. Cousin Andrea's dump— I had been ignoring it ever since I came aboard the chapel. I kicked myself mentally. I'd become so caught up in the day-to-day issues of survival and work that I'd gotten into the habit of postponing it. Knowing Andrea, she'd babble interminably and take me on a tour of the architectural plans for a new records wing of the palace I once called home: *But, I now thought, could it be a complete coincidence that a large message from her had arrived so soon after Ana disappeared?* Well yes, probably it could. But a firm of space pirates had departed Taj Beacon in hot pursuit and hijacked a church on flight, seemingly just to get a chance to ask me where Ana had gotten to; and there was the small matter of my stalker, whoever she was and wherever they'd hidden her, and of the double game that Dennett had so recently betrayed—

Suddenly, Andrea's missive took on a whole new significance.

A ndrea leans against the railing of an ornamental bridge, facing the cameras that define my viewpoint. She has dressed as if for a formal occasion and looks serenely pleased with herself; she stands at the center of a classically composed stage, nonchalant and beautiful.

(I describe it as I see it unfolding in my mind's eye. However, the scene is captured in ancient light: Andrea could be dead by now, for all I know. It's a rehearsed briefing, delivered to the camera's vision years ago, then encrypted for my eyes only and relayed from beacon to interstellar beacon until it caught up with me at Taj.)

"I'm afraid we've had a little bit of a screwup at this end, and news of it is going to catch up with you not long after this message. Summary is: Do *not* proceed to Shin-Tethys. In fact, stay away from Dojima System entirely. Cancel your upload, just write it off and don't go."

Andrea inhales deeply, her chest rising and falling as she flushes her gas-exchange surfaces. (Many of these reflexes of ours date back to our Fragile ancestors; archaic and not really useful to our refactored bodies, but one dabbles with redesigning the autonomic nervous system at one's peril.) She pauses to compose herself—evidently upset—before continuing:

"Word of the existence of the Atlantis Carnet appears to have leaked. I'm not sure who blabbed, and whether it was just a loose tongue or something more serious (although I've got my suspicions), but there was an attempted burglary at the family archives just over five days ago."

(I forced myself to resist the impulse to sit bolt upright at that point but froze the message while I forced myself to understand the significance of the bomb Andrea had just detonated. After a moment, I resumed the recording . . .)

"The burglar in question was a zombie. It penetrated security by impersonating a young sister, Michaela—I don't know if you knew her. Unfortunately, whoever sent the burglar abducted her, and we assume that they murdered her for her security tokens. She—the impersonator— was caught attempting to penetrate the secondary archive vault. When Valia's security auditors examined the corpse, they found it in possession of this."

Andrea extends her cupped left hand toward me. It cradles the small black nub of a soul chip. "It contains metadata identifying it as Sondra's private key, but the contents are scrambled. As the burglar hadn't made it into the vault when she was stopped, we assume that the intention was to substitute this forgery for the contents of the vault. Which in turn suggests that whoever sent the burglar is attempting a sophisticated fraud against the bank's long-term-deposit archive, and *might* be fully informed about our earlier successful copying of the Atlantis Carnet. If you proceed from GJ 785 to Dojima, there's a very good chance that you'll run into someone sent to relieve you of it. And if they're ruthless enough to have abducted and murdered Michaela, it's reasonable to suppose that your life is in danger. Not to mention Ana's."

Oops.

"I'm trying to track down the source and extent of the leak. If I can work out what got out, and who knows about it, I'll let you know. But for the time being, if you wish to continue your pilgrimage, it is probably safe to go directly to Shin-Kyoto and commence your scheduled study year with Elder Shibbo. Doing so will probably suffice to warn off your pursuers. Ana, however, is less lucky and will have to make arrangements for her own security. We all need to lie low for a few years, and she may be stuck in Dojima System. I have sent a warning similar to this one directly to her; if it reaches her in time, she should have time to seek sanctuary. I told her that if it's safe for her to do so, she should head for Shin-Kyoto with anything she's found and meet you there—"

(By this point I had stopped listening and was swearing violently under my breath, oblivious to the possibility that my abductors might overhear my indecorous words. I paused the message again and forced myself to breathe deeply. Then I dived back in to finish it.)

"In summary, dear sis, you should avoid Dojima System and Shin-Tethys in particular like the plague. Ana will either have to escape on her own or . . . we may very well have to abandon the game, hide out, and pretend none of this ever happened. I'm sorry, but there's no alternative. Do take care, get yourself to safety, and remember to write!"

I killed the message and opened my eyes, taking in the twilit constriction of my makeshift oubliette. Then, after some seconds or minutes of bleak near despair, I began to update my notes.

Dear Reader.

Andrea told me to write, so I'm going to write, but not in any expectation of her ever reading this. I'm keeping this in a securely encrypted notepad in my repository chip. The simple truth is: While I am indeed a mendicant scholar on a pilgrimage between the fellows of my order, most of what I told Deacon Dennett and his conspirators was a pack of lies. Which is entirely fair insofar as *he* lied to *me*, shamelessly and extensively. (If the priestess Cybelle had been at the helm, it would have been far more unlucky for me; priests and priestesses don't *need* debuggers to dig information out of you. But my inference is that Dennett took advantage of the accident aboard the chapel to arrange a bloodless mutiny and this circumstance left him at a disadvantage: He might have known that I held a valuable secret, but he had no simple tool for digging it out of me while I was in his clutches, and I slipped through his fingers before he had time to grow desperate.)

I even managed to conceal my purpose from the pirates, for they seem to be mostly interested in Ana's insurance policy rather than in my secrets. Or perhaps Rudi was honestly telling the truth when he said he wasn't allowed to pry them out of me using a debugger. (I wonder what she insured herself for, to provoke the underwriters to such drastic action?) Given the nature of this affair, it's not surprising. We are engaged in a battle without honor or humanity. People behave very oddly when the ownership of large quantities of money is at stake. Some—as we have seen—will commit murder or send out shape-shifting zombie assassins. I am not that ruthless. However, here I am, running around into the cold and unwelcoming universe at large, having *adventures*—something I loathe and fear, for the definition of an adventure is an unpleasant and possibly unsurvivable experience—in the hope that Ana and I might be able to wind up an ancient business venture and in so doing finally free ourselves from the shadow of our mother: For redeeming the Atlantis Carnet will tarnish her good name irredeemably.

Ahem.

To understand why the Atlantis Carnet is so important, I need to continue my exposition of the nature of money, fast, medium, and slow: the one that Dennett waved away. If you are Andrea, or another of my ilk, you might as well skip this section of my correspondence. If you're here to pick up the pieces . . . well, read on.

Let us ignore for the time being the ontology of money, the question of where money *comes from* and what money *is*. Instead, let us contemplate the teleology of money—the purpose it serves and how form follows purpose.

Cash is fast money. We use it for immediate exchanges of value. Goods and labor: You sell, I buy; we negotiate the value on either side of the balance sheet (what are your goods worth to you? What is this service worth to me?) by collapsing desire to an integer. Cash is unidimensional. Cash is fast. Cash is dumb. Cash destroys information about values inherent in previous transactions. Cash is bits and atoms. If you are human, whether Fragile or Post, you already know all about cash.

Medium money is something you buy with cash; something durable, something that is not easily liquidated or valued in fast money. Cathedrals and asteroids and debts and durable real estate and bonds backed by the honorable reputation of traders in slow money—it takes years for medium investments to rise and fall, many days or years to buy or sell them. Medium money is what you use to store your fast money when you've got more of it than you need for your immediate purposes. Medium money is the bony skeleton of a planetary economy, emerging out of human exchanges of status signals. Cash can crash or hyperinflate into valueless scrip, but if you converted it into a farm or a road or a home or to buy the loyalty of clients and the fealty of newly forked child instances, you will still have your medium money at the end of the fast money apocalypse.

The Fragile didn't know these types of money by name; indeed, those of them who focused on the uses of capital mistook medium money for a special case of fast money. So the bubbles and crashes that rippled through their fast money systems frequently caused misery and massive infrastructure damage. By denominating them separately, by having a flexible exchange rate, modern economies decouple transient demand from the bones and muscles that underpin survival. It makes for stability, in the long term—but not long enough for slow vehicles.

Slow vehicles, such as starships.

Colony vessels and migratory habitats like cathedrals hurtle between the stars at unimaginable speeds; at thousands of kilometers per second, almost a measurable percentage of the speed of light. But while such a velocity is hard to comprehend, the distance between the stars is vast. Here, at the tip of my thumb, is a G2 star, the sun beneath the rays of which the Fragile were born. The span of the fingers of my hand takes us to Earth, their home world. To reach the inner edge of the Kuiper belt, the second asteroidal debris belt beyond the outermost of the planets, is a distance of perhaps three meters. Lonely, icy Eris orbits between four and ten meters away. On this vast scale, a centimeter represents ten million kilometers. But the distance to the nearest star is over five thousand meters. The distance from Earth to Shin-Tethys is over forty kilometers. And it would take one of our starships nearly four millennia to cross that gulf.

Starships, of necessity, travel light. The cost of building and launching one is crippling—and the cost of building one that could carry the millions of bodies with different skills that it takes to render a new star system fit for habitation would be impossible. So we make do by sending starships with only a skeleton crew. The job of the starship's complement is to build a beacon and trade for skills with the neighbors, to solicit immigrants via laser transmission and build new bodies for them. It's teleportation, of a kind. But this takes *slow money*.

Slow money is a medium of exchange designed to outlast the rise and fall of civilizations. It is the currency of world-builders, running on an engine of debt that can only be repaid by the formation of new interstellar colonies, passing the liability ever onward into the deep future—or forgiven by the Jubilee, a systemwide reset of the financial system entailing nullification of all debts, but that becomes less feasible the more colonies we create. By design, the slow money system is permanently balanced on the edge of a liquidity crisis, for every exchange between two beacons must be cryptographically signed by a third-party bank in another star system: It takes years to settle a transaction. It's theft-proof, too—for each bitcoin is cryptographically signed by the mind of its owner, stored in one of their slots. Your slow money assets are, in a very real manner, an aspect of your identity. Nobody would think to detach from their roots and emigrate to a new colony for pay in any other currency; for the very slowness of slow money guarantees that it isn't vulnerable to bubbles and depressions and turbulence and the collapse of any currency that is limited to a single star system.

Now pay attention, please: There is a *protocol* to understand.

Suppose I wish to hire you—in another star system—to loan me a copy of your soul as indentured labor for a decade or two. Obviously, I must pay in slow money (and pay double, for both copies of you). I send you a signed dollar, one that can be authenticated by a third-party bank as having originated in my own bank. (The authentication step takes place in another star system that I cannot physically control, for it is distant.) Once you receive my coin, you sign it and send a copy of it to the third-party bank for verification. Meanwhile, you upload yourself to my vicinity and again send a copy of the signed coin to the bank. The bank can now countersign the coin—having received two copies of it, you have proven to it that you have traveled from your first location to mine, fulfilling the contract—and sends an activation checksum back to each copy of you, which confirms that each of you are in possession of half a dollar. (Or, by prior arrangement, only one instance of you ends up in possession of the dollar—issuing banks, and only issuing banks, can break coins. As to where the coins *come from*, that is another question entirely, and I shall discuss it at length later in this report.)

Thus do we pay for interstellar services. It is the ancient dance of the *three-phase commit*, and it can take many years to complete, for slow money effectively travels at a third of the speed of light. It is cumbersome but very secure. The transactions are tied to the identity of the person or bank that owns the money—you can't steal slow money without kidnapping or mindrape or fraud. How does the bank know you have traveled? That's easy to prove; beacon stations watching different stars record the arrival of your signed bitcoins from physically separate star systems. You can't forge it—not without a starship. You can't inflate the quantity in circulation—the bitcoin algorithm used to prime issuing banks prevents that. Short of rewriting the laws of mathematics and physics, it's solid.

But sometimes, something goes wrong.

Suppose I die after I send you the coin but before I can send it to the authorizing bank for verification. Or that I send it but you die before you send your received copy to the bank. Or that you receive it and get it signed, but your copy (who has traveled to my beacon station) dies before they can sign the coin and verify it with the bank. Or suppose civilization in the bank's star system collapses halfway through the transaction. Suppose, suppose. These are the *simple* failure modes. Slow money transactions can take a good chunk of a person's life. Of the lives of the people at either end. And while local banks are happy to act as proxies or to take care of negotiation and settlement, sometimes people cut corners.

When this happens, a transaction is said to have stalled. And if you can pick up all the necessary signatures and encrypted tokens, it is possible to reassert ownership of the stalled payment. But to do so, you need to buy up the scattered shards of half-signed coins from the soul chips of whomever they are vested in, or the banks who hold them in escrow—or in extremis, pay for the raw download transcript of a soul chip in transit between star systems and resurrect the bearer in order to pick their pocket—a messy, slow job that requires collusion across interstellar distances with half-trusted allies, pen pals, correspondents, and exiled copies of copies of one's first sibling twice removed.

Slow money, by its nature, is not amenable to investment vehicles. It *is* an investment vehicle in its own right. It's so stable that interest rates are microscopically low—0.001 percent compound interest really racks up over a few centuries. All new colonies start off by going heavily into debt, in order to attract the new skilled specialists they need to address whatever critical problems they failed to foresee and plan for before departure; once they're stable, it can take them millennia to earn their way up to a positive balance of payments, and so they tend to avoid borrowing further. But sometimes people in mature planetary civilizations *do* borrow slow money, for certain long-term projects.

It's risky. Not advisable. Only done when the project will take thousands of years, and the payoff is gigantic. Terraforming worlds, for example. Or the Atlantis project.

And sometimes such projects go wrong . . .

An indeterminate time later—it felt like days, but it might have been as little as a couple of hours—the hatch of my cell slammed open. "Prisoner! You come! Count Rudi wants 'ter see ye. Come nice now, or we cut neck!"

We were still in microgravity. Rather than letting me flail around and jump from handhold to surface, they grabbed me by their hind paws and sculled along rapidly through the corridor, using their leathery finger-to-waist wing surfaces. (One of them had my go bag in tow: more consideration than a prisoner warranted and, perhaps in retrospect, a sign of respect I should have paid attention to.) I thought at first the two pirates were going to drag me back to the kitchen or perhaps the control crypt, but instead we ended up in the main air-lock vestibule. A gust of warm, too-recently-breathed air slapped me in the face: it smelled of stale, half-digested tubespam and methanogenic bacterial endosymbionts. The docking tunnel of a pirate vehicle—a fast cutter, I gathered later—had thrust itself through the air lock like a parasite's ovipositor; its walls, inflatable sheets of brute-repurposed mechanocytic connective tissue, pulsed slightly as it sucked nutrients from deep in the chapel's belowdeck supply tankage.

"Where are we going?" I asked.

"Ee's going aboard the *Permanent Crimson*," grunted one of my abductors. "Come along smartly!"

And with that, they dragged me aboard their cutter for a six-hour flight back to the mother ship.

I retain only confused impressions of the journey and of my arrival on the hijacker's mother ship. It was hot, and dimly lit, and it stank, and it echoed with the shrill whistles and whines of its crew. There was no local vertical, no "up," but a myriad of cables and webbing straps linking every available surface so that it was impossible to fall far without finding a support to grapple with. *A low-gee vehicle, then,* that part of my mind that was forever engaged in a running commentary noted: efficient and good for long-haul transits but not ideal for boarding actions, unless the target was a church or a sluggish bulk carrier.

They gave me little time for sightseeing: dragging me willy-nilly to a new cell and drawing a thin, flexible film lid across it to hold me inside. Banging and shuddering ensued. And then, after perhaps an hour, I felt the unmistakable distant rumble of some sort of motor and felt myself drifting toward the overhead membrane. We were under way.

Permanent Crimson

Two subjective years of my mendicant scholar's pilgrimage had not prepared me for this crisis, or indeed for anything remotely similar.

To undertake a pilgrimage is a drastic and alienating experience, albeit an exciting one; you will visit strange nations and meet people with backgrounds and outlooks quite unlike your own. You expect to study and work hard, to approach life with an open mind and to learn things that will challenge your view of your place in the universe. But you expect to be in control of your own schedule, manager of your own destiny, accountable only to your self and your sponsors, until your successful return to your origin (and probable subsequent promotion).

I began to experience a loss of control from the moment I boarded the chapel and discovered that what I had expected to be a staid, hidebound, institutional vehicle was in fact a flying madhouse. And the loss of control had spiraled outward, to engulf my entire life, from the first intimation of our hijacking through Dennett's ad hoc gambit to convince them that I was an ordained priestess—while in fact his priestess lay comatose and undead within a sarcophagus—gathering momentum with my discovery that not only did I have a murderous stalker but that Dennett knew of her presence and had been manipulating us!

Then there was the burden of fear and uncertainty unleashed by Andrea's bombshell of a message. One of our number had snitched: or, quite possibly, Sondra herself had kept a closer eye on her vaults than we had anticipated. Either way, I could not expect my successful return from my pilgrimage to be followed by congratulation and a promotion. Most likely, Sondra wouldn't hesitate for an instant before having me interrogated via slave chip. And when she uncovered the parcel of secrets nestling in my second slot, the mere fact of my having attained independent citizenship would not shield me from her revenge. I had just lost my long-term future and had no idea what to do next.

Indeed, the pirates were the least of my worries. I confess, if it hadn't been for the harsh lessons of my upbringing in Sondra's child garden, I believe I would have completely lost my shit.

The hijackers' vehicle had been under way for two days when Count Rudi finally got around to sending for me.

Being a prisoner aboard a pirate ship turned out to be, happily, far less unpleasantly eventful than I would have expected. In fact, it was one of the most restful experiences I'd had in a very long time. When I was young and irresponsible and fancy-free, I occasionally acted out, as did various of my sibs: in response to which, the Proctors would use confinement as a punishment. Unlike some of my more rebellious sisters, I learned the virtue of patience and ways of quietly entertaining myself while giving no outward sign of activity. With the not-insubstantial freight of diaries and private files piling up in my spare socket, I had more than enough reading material, not to mention recorded and interactive one-person entertainments, to keep me occupied for a while. I could outstare a blank wall for years on end, given an otherwise stress-free environment.

But being hugger-muggered and carried away aboard a pirate ship at the same time as one discovers that one's employer might have discovered one's treachery is sufficiently stressful to rattle anyone's equanimity; and by the time the guards came for me, my metaneurocytes were all but growing legs and crawling out of my nostrils from a toxic mixture of boredom and fear.

At first when they came for me, I thought it was just another meal call. They'd taken to rattling the frame around the door membrane to get my attention, then sliding a squeeze bag of pureed nutrient broth inside—boring, bland, tasteless stuff, but at least it kept me running. This time the membrane peeled all the way back. "You come!" barked one of the guards—the one I'd begun thinking of as Dogface 2 in the privacy of my head. (Jagged teeth, pointed muzzle, smelled musty, had all the poise and etiquette of a cement wall.) "Count boss person want you interview job opportunity now!"

I let go of the floor (to which I had been clinging by my toes, using the hooks provided for that purpose). I had already concluded that in the short term, resistance would be not only futile but stupid: Not only would my abductors be expecting it, but my life was now as wholly dependent on their goodwill as it had ever been on Sondra's, at least until some opportunity for escape made itself available. And escape from a spacegoing vehicle under acceleration was a questionable proposition at the best of times. My position was precarious, but they had made it clear that as long as I was useful to them, I would be preserved. So I allowed myself to be directed into the hive of villainy, through the tubes and fistulae and stomachs of their biomorphic home (the better to heal from damage inflicted in combat, I gathered) and thence to the big bat's office.

"Ah, Ms. Alizond." He was hunched over a broad desk, yet another grid of soothing numbers scrolling across its surface, green and red flickering commodity prices fluctuating in real time as the pirate vehicle soaked in the incoming market stream. "Make yourself comfortable." He gestured distractedly at a low-gee hammock on the other side of the desk. "Has Garsh been feeding you adequately?"

"Feeding me—" I stifled an inappropriate laugh. "What?"

He stared at me, his giant dark pupils unreadable. "Ms. Alizond. That was a serious question. Please answer it as such."

"I—" I closed my mouth, hesitated a moment. "I've been kidnapped and stuck in an oubliette and subjected to unspeakable indignities and you want to know if your minions have been *feeding me adequately*? Pardon me, but if you don't already know the answer to that question, shouldn't someone else be occupying this office?"

Rudi—that was indeed his name—hissed breath through his nostrils: I interpreted this as a sign of mild exasperation. "You misunderstand. We are not used to accommodating your phenotype. I would rather not starve you to death by accident simply through neglecting some essential micronutrient! Are we feeding you correctly? Yes or no?"

"Uh." I drifted backward into the hammock. "I *think* so. Not getting any uncontrollable urges to eat strange things. At least, not yet. But you could have left me with the chapel; they had a balanced—"

"Ms. Alizond. If I had left you among those scheming criminal sacerdotes, you would almost certainly be *dead* by now!" he snapped irritably. "I saved your life, confound it! Not that I expect gratitude, oh no, but there is another side to the balance sheet, and your lack of interest in it is—" He stopped himself in midrant, with a visible effort.

I kept my face still. "You saved me? What from, and why? Surely you're not declaring yourself to be an altruist?"

"Hardly. Although in my not-inconsiderable experience, a reputation for fair dealing will stand one well when entering future business dealings." The pirate leader emitted another leaky-duct hiss. "I have a deep and abiding interest in your missing relative, Ms. Alizond, whom I would dearly love to meet—if she is still alive. It is a matter of some embarrassment to this institution that one of my subordinates sold her a rather substantial insurance policy without performing adequate due diligence first, to ensure that she was not, for example, about to be assassinated— so it should be perfectly obvious to you that I would like you to lead me to her. But you don't appear to understand what a lucky escape you've had! Or why it is absolutely in your best interests to help me."

"Really?" This was not turning out to be remotely like any of the conversations I had imagined holding with him during my captivity. "You expect *me* to help *you*?"

"Yes." A long, prehensile tongue squeezed from one corner of Rudi's muzzle and swept around to the other side, smoothing whiskers as it went. "Here are the facts of the matter, Ms. Alizond: Your arrival asking questions after your missing sib Ana was noted from the outset by various local parties. The chapel you took passage on—did you really think they needed you as an unskilled ship-hand? Or that the original leader of the mission, Lady Cybelle, was confined to that sarcophagus *by accident*? Or that your oh-so-friendly deacon, Ser Dennett, survived the incident aboard the chapel that damaged or killed every other officer aboard the vehicle *merely by happenstance*? Or that they had lost all their Fragiles but still had the capability to produce cultured liverwurst by the tankload?" He yawned, revealing neatly polished rows of very sharp teeth: "There had been a *mutiny*, Ms. Alizond. The cause of the mutiny was a falling-out among thieves: At question was not the issue of whether it was worth abducting you but whether to do so by stealth or by violence, and what to do with you once they had you. I don't think much of Dennett, but I will concede that he is a devious little bonebag. It's your good fortune that we got you away from them before he finished reprogramming Cybelle, or a little encounter with a remote debugger interface would be the least of your worries."

I realized with some dismay that everything he said confirmed my own worst fears. Either he was reading my mind by some mechanism more subtle than a slave chip or the situation I had inadvertently become enmeshed in was indeed dire.

"But you"—I swallowed—"your guards shoved me in a room with Cybelle and Dennett! I mean, before—"

"Yes, well, every once in a while someone fucks up." Rudi grunted. "In this case, it was the boarding party. Whom I do not employ for their brains, bless 'em. Luckily for you, Dennett is basically a coward. He lacked the determination to act on the spur of the moment, and I got you out of there as soon as I learned about the mistake."

"What have you done with them?" I asked before I could stop myself.

"What do you *think* I've done with them—made them walk the plank?" He hissed again, but this time I sensed amusement in the mannerism: "I let them go before we undocked. They may have a hard time reconnecting their high-gain comms antenna, but the chapel is otherwise undamaged. Including the undeclared cargo Dennett had filled the number three midships carbon-cycle buffer tank with, now that it is so regrettably surplus to requirements due to the absence of Fragile passengers."

"Cargo? Dennett was a smuggler? But why, I mean, you let him go—"

"What? You think I've got room for an extra three thousand tons of high-purity molten indium in the paint locker? No, if he wants to waste energy hauling that stuff around, let him." Rudi grinned, tongue lolling. "What do you expect me to do?"

"Eh—" I paused for a moment. "Indium. That would be reaction mass for ion thrusters, hmm? Isn't that rather a lot, um, is there enough to be worth—" I paused again. Shock fought with chagrin that I hadn't worked out what was going on and gave way to amusement: "You didn't. Did you?"

"They call it piracy, you call it hijacking; I call it taking advantage of an unscheduled rendezvous to audit the undeclared cargo of a suspicious long-haul vehicle and order put options on the raw material prior to its arrival on the commodities market at its destination." His grin widened into a yawn. "And meanwhile saving a little lost scholar who had fallen in with a hive of villainy and criminality along the way. Assuming that *is* your story, and you're sticking with it. Now, Ms. Alizond. I'd like to make you an offer."

"An"—I came crashing back to reality—"offer?"

"Yes." He gestured at the spreadsheets floating around his office: "This occupation is not called 'going to the books' for nothing. Ms. Alizond, let me be clear; I want you to lead me to your sister Ana, preferably alive. If you can do that, I will be somewhat in your debt because you will have saved me from having to make good on an unfortunate subordinate's badly gauged decision. To that end, we are making our way toward Shin-Tethys. Indeed, right now, this is your *fastest* route to your destination. We are due into Highport more than a hundred days ahead of that flying junkyard you took passage on. However, the operation of this vehicle . . . we're a subsidiary of a larger enterprise, and must pay for our running costs. Right now, you are an overhead on my balance sheet. But it so happens that we have been shorthanded for some time. If you were to make yourself an *asset*, a Post-human resource, so to speak, I could move you from column A to column B, and thereby justify to my superiors the expense of providing you with more comfortable quarters, better food, a modest stipend—all the perquisites of employment."

"With respect, uh, Count—"

"That's *a*-count-*ant*, Ms. Alizond."

"—I'm sorry, er—"

"Rudi will do. And may I call you Krina?"

"—Uh, um, I suppose so . . . Rudi. Ahem. With respect, you're *pirates*. Forgive me for saying this, but I have some misgivings about the legality and enforceability of any employment contract you might be in a position to offer—"

"On the contrary, my dear: We are a *privateer*. We carry letters of marque signed by a genuine recognized sovereign government, authorizing us to enforce customs regulations and collect tolls and taxes on their behalf from traffic not in possession of a license from the government in question. We're recognized by more than a third of the autonomous governments of Dojima System—almost a plurality! Which is why I can assure you that if you accept employment aboard Permanent Crimson Branch Office Five Zero, it will be recognized and enforced by the full majesty of the law of the Federal Inhabited Republics of Shin-Kyoto—"

"You're telling me you're carrying letters of marque signed by a government in *another star system*?" I tried not to squeak, but not, I fear, entirely successfully. "What use is *that* if someone arrests you?"

"None whatsoever in the short term although they'd risk economic sanctions. Specifically, they'd suffer total key revocation for all slow money transactions denominated in FHR/S-K dollars that are in progress. A not-insignificant portion of their interstellar balance-of-trade deficit." Rudi licked his whiskers again, in what I was coming to recognize as the chiropteran cognate of a sly grin. "Krina, I am disappointed in you. Consider: Branch Office Five Zero has been trading in this system for more than a century now! If we were mere *pirates*, we would have been hunted down and destroyed decades ago. We are in point of fact a trading entity—actually a local subsidiary of an out-system bank—that occupies an extralegal niche which is sufficiently convenient for certain governments that a blown-out photoreceptor is directed toward us. It would cost them a lot of money, resources, and time to provide their own customs infrastructure. Much more convenient to leave it to the free market—us—and then to rake in a commission by selling us consumables and other supplies. If nothing else, they can deny all liability for consequences arising from our actions.

"So, as I was saying, I have an offer of employment for you. The work is eminently suited to your specialty—a mendicant doctor of the historiography of accountancy practices. I believe it will keep you amused for the next three hundred days, as we make our way in-system, and I'm sure you'll be more comfortable if you have something to do with your time."

"Why don't you compel me?" I had to ask. Rudi had already demonstrated that he had the wherewithal to turn me into a zombie.

"Because." Rudi looked round, his neck alarmingly supple: "I can't. As I told you, we operate under letters of marque that set out in great detail what we may and may not do. We are not allowed to steal your personal effects, for example. We may only use compulsion under certain limited circumstances to investigate suspected barratry, or while conducting a hostile boarding action. We may only use interrogation devices in the strictly regulated conduct of certain types of criminal investigations. But this is not the former, and you have been ruled out of the latter, unless you are plotting to take over this branch office, ha-ha. Ha. Ha. Rule of law, Ms. Alizond! Without it, where would we be?"

Three hundred days of sitting on my thumbs in an oubliette did not appeal. Furthermore, I had to admit that he made a plausible case. And how better to gather the intelligence I would need to revenge my mistreatment than by working from within his business? I determined to give no sign of my long-term plans, and instead leaned closer. "This job. Tell me about it . . ."

Before I can explain the full horror and glory of the Atlantis Carnet, I need to tell you about the Spanish Prisoner.

Long, long ago on a planet far, far away, where the Fragile roamed free in the biosphere, they developed a complex and dizzying array of tricks, lies, and fraudulent schemes that have served us well to this day.

Spain was the name of one of their polities; it was attached to the archetypical confidence scheme more or less at random. It could be any other location chosen purely for its remoteness and the difficulty of traveling yonder from hither.

The Spanish Prisoner is a fabulous person! Rich and powerful in your homeland, this person (who is a personal friend and benefactor of mine: I must introduce you at the first opportunity) has traveled to Spain on a matter of highly confidential business, to which end they are employing a false identity. While there, they have been unavoidably detained due to a minor misunderstanding: Trivial, but they have lost their wallet and passport, and consequently need some help. Surely you could find it in your heart to send them the price of a meal, the down payment on their bail money, the cost of a ticket home? They will be eternally grateful and reward you appropriately upon their return, I assure you. Just remember, though, that they are traveling under conditions of secrecy, and if their true identity is declared to the Spanish authorities, there will be embarrassing (and expensive) questions to be answered.

Are you with me so far? Can you be trusted? Are you sincere and good-hearted and will you help keep my friend's secret?

It's the oldest con in the book because the victim's greed reels them in, and they pay, and pay again, bit by bit, for one small service after another. More sophisticated versions emphasize the borderline illegality of the prisoner's activity, the better to tangle the victim up in a knot of guilty criminal complicity and thereby deter them from seeking aid. But the pattern is the same: A too-good-to-be-true opportunity is presented to the victim, an opportunity to ingratiate themselves with the rich or to buy shares in a dubious but highly profitable venture. And then they are suckered into paying one fee after another in hope of the ultimate payoff.

Well, Spain no longer exists. But we have some new and exciting twists on the Spanish Prisoner to offer you in its absence! Foremost among these is the FTL breakthrough. Everybody knows that faster-than-light travel is impossible. Except that, conveniently for con artists, it isn't entirely ruled out; quantum entanglement, wormholes, tachyons, you name it, the devil is in the details that lurk at the edges of experimental physics, in the corners of the map that might as well be labeled "here be dragons." The gold mine of experimental physics played out thousands of years ago, even before the Fragile went extinct for the first time; it ran into the law of diminishing returns. The machinery required to break new ground got more and more expensive, until finally the construction costs of a bigger particle accelerator—Bigger than the rings of Saturn! Cheaper than fifty colony starships!—priced the privilege of squinting at a new quark-trail squiggle right out of the market. And so, FTL hasn't been *completely* ruled out, and therein lies a new twist on the Spanish Prisoner.

I happen to know that someone a very long way away was experimenting with an FTL drive! And miraculously, they managed to get it to work! But on their first trip—a test flight to this very star system—they met with an unforeseen malfunction. They're trapped here, hiding out in slowtime hibernation in the outer belt until they can buy certain rare and expensive materials with which to repair their drive, hoping nobody unpleasant stumbles across them. They're not poor: Here, see these slow dollars, signed by a bank a very long way away? Won't you hold them as collateral and front me a sum of fast money to help my friends make their repairs? We'll accept a ruinous conversion rate, just in return for the money we need to get our space drive working again; when the bank-countersigned certificates for these slow dollars reach you, you'll be rich!

Alternatively: I happen to have friends who have built and are right now testing an FTL drive. Do you know what that means? It will detonate under the foundations of our financial system like a nuclear mine! Suddenly, it will be possible to trade fast money across interstellar distances. Meanwhile, slow money will depreciate disastrously. They are less than a year away from completing their work, but they're running short on cash. But they're not poor—see these slow dollars, signed by a bank a very long way away? We need to off-load them fast, regardless of the exchange rate, by way of a friend who won't lead the bankers back to our secret laboratory, where they might recognize the significance of our research and destroy our test vehicle before it can fly . . .

Yet again: My friends have developed an FTL drive. As you know, this will cause a crash in the slow money market once word gets out, so it is essential that we keep it secret until we have tested it. However, on the upcoming test flights, there will be an opportunity for a select few investors to entrust us with slow money instruments that need negotiating via the bank of (some plausible destination a few light-years away). We'll go there, get the bank to countersign the bitcoinage you entrusted us with, and as soon as we get back, you'll be able to complete the transaction, convert your slow dollars (drawn on the bank of plausible destination) into fast money and incidentally prove the bona fides of our FTL drive! Everyone wins! You just need to buy slow dollars in the bank of plausible destination, then use them to buy fast money, nominating me and my friends as your proxy . . .

Faster-than-light travel is the new-old Spanish Prisoner. Do you want me to go on? I could keep this up for hours. It's my primary field of study. I've published numerous papers on the subject. I am an avid student of the history of FTL frauds and can enthrall and expound at academic symposia and after-dinner speaking engagements alike. I am, in fact, one of the only people ever to make an honest living from FTL fraud. You'd think people would be tired of hearing about yet another faster-than-light scam, but it's so amazingly *attractive*—a breakthrough in the frontiers of physics that permits a revolutionary new technology that offers you, and *you alone*, the once-in-a-lifetime opportunity to make a gigantic financial killing (just so long as you keep your mouth shut). It keeps coming up every few centuries; indeed, it runs in waves. It just won't die.

And then there's the history of the Atlantis project—which some people believe was the real thing.

The difference between merchant banking and barefaced piracy is slimmer than most people imagine. Over the months I spent aboard Permanent Crimson Branch Office Five Zero, I discovered that I was disconcertingly comfortable with the profession. But I am getting ahead of myself.

Count Rudi and his fellow privateers were not, of course, native to Dojima System. Most of them, males, females, and hermaphrodites alike, affected a bat-winged, long-muzzled phenotype that was a common affectation of the residents of the rain forests of Shin-Kyoto's northern island chain, from where they claimed to come—for the opening of an interstellar branch office by an insurance company was a not-insignificant enterprise, and in order to inculcate the correct corporate culture, they had sent a large cadre of clerical officers and financial-combat operatives. (That: And, being a gregarious people, they were simply more comfortable working in a loudly bickering but affectionate tribe of their own kind.)

The branch office itself was a repurposed asteroid-mining tug, its bulbous forward cargo tank (originally designed for shipping around large volumes of aqueous salt solutions) repurposed to conceal the tools of the organization's trade, from the assault auditor's high-speed skiffs to the forced boarding tubes. Behind it, the life-support system, habitat spaces, and nuclear/ion-drive engineering truss of a regular rock pusher remained virtually unchanged.

The habitat sphere was brightly lit, overwhelmingly green, somewhat hot and humid, and smelled of sessile hermaphrodite genitalia (or "flowers," as the bat-folk called them), but it was vastly less depressing than the flying charnel house I'd initially booked passage on. It was spacious, if nothing else: Cubic volume filled with air is cheap to accelerate, so walls were out and batwings were de rigueur among the branch staff. It spent its time migrating slowly back and forth between Shin-Tethys and the Shiny! Asteroids, occasionally waylaying some unfortunate vessel suspected of smuggling (but usually only within a few days of departure/ arrival in orbit around a destination: otherwise the delta vee required for rendezvous made such tactics prohibitively expensive). In the meantime, its highly skilled crew of insurance underwriters and accountants sold policies and processed claims, while the elite cadre of merchant bankers handled investments and risk control, and the regular crew kept the ship running and its occupants entertained. It was, in short, just like any other respectable space-borne institution but for the sideline in ion rockets and forced boarding teams: Indeed, it reminded me of a smaller, cozier, and somewhat less ruthless version of New California, my first home.

Once I got over their odd appearance, I found life around the Five Zero comfortable. With the count's permission I was allowed out of my cell, albeit shackled to an irritable ankle-crab that screeched and pinched me with its claws if I tried to enter a restricted area by mistake. I ate in the same corner of the mess deck as the other nonchiropteroid crew members (of whom there was a double handful, for unlike the chapel I had been rescued from, this vehicle was not shorthanded), and worked . . . well, I worked wherever I fancied so long as there was a flat surface and a sufficiently large retina to display my research materials.

Of which there was an embarrassing superfluity. Among other things, the forward cargo tank held a compact but devastatingly dense storage farm, with over a hundred tons of memory diamond: It included a comprehensive log of every financial transaction that the corporation and its affiliates had been able to get its leathery little paws on, whether by begging, borrowing, or barratry. Some of them went back more than three thousand years. Incomplete and fragmentary and balkanized by incompatible storage protocols as it was, it was nevertheless a mother lode of data—an incredible asset if one wanted to trace the ebb and flow of slow money between the stars, or the medium money investments locked up in long-term bonds and assets within Dojima's habitats: from Taj Beacon to the glass-windowed spinning baubles of the Leading and Trailing Pretties, the Shiny! Asteroids, the colonies on the moons of Zeus and Cronos, the zeppelin-castles of Mira and the hundred warring laminar republics of Shin-Tethys.

Rudi made it quite clear what he wanted me to do, or rather, what he wanted me to think he wanted me to do. (For it is almost always easier to manage a willing paid subordinate than to control a hostile prisoner; if nothing else, the overhead in guard labor is lower.)

"When we arrive at Shin-Tethys, I think we shall go on a little excursion in search of your missing sister. But before we do that, it would be prudent to know who else is taking an interest in her, don't you think? There is Dennett, of course, but we will arrive in orbit first. There is whoever sent that charming body double after you. And there may be others. Your sib appears to have come to the attention of important people. Don't you think it would be wise to know whom we face before we go looking for her?"

I shrugged. "I have no idea." (I was lying, of course.)

"Oh really?" Rudi lolled. "I'll tell you what I think: There are plenty of skeletons clogging up the closets of the banking and accounting industries of Shin-Tethys, and I think your sister became involved in a conspiracy involving one of them. In so doing, she has made a nuisance of herself to powerful people. And so, we are going to work out who in this system she could possibly be working for, or working with, or have offended, and who might stand to benefit from her finding them."

"But she's only really interested in"—I thought for a moment—"the history of accountancy. Like me."

"Yes, exactly. So I want you to prepare a report on the history of investment frauds and scandals in Dojima System."

I am now going to bore you to death with the political economy of Shin-Tethys.

(Pay attention: There will be an exam later.)

Dojima System revolves around a young G1 dwarf star, slightly brighter than the Sol that illuminated the skies of our ancestors. It was first visited by a starship one thousand five hundred standard years ago: long enough that the locals have established habitats on and around several bodies, and numerous governments and sovereign institutions.

The planetary system consists of a couple of warm gas giants, Zeus and Cronos, orbiting within a couple of astronomical units of Dojima Prime. There are debris belts, both in the shape of leading and trailing trojan clouds co-orbiting with Zeus and in the shape of a conventional debris belt. A Venusiform world with a runaway greenhouse atmosphere, Mira, orbits beyond the gas giants, just close enough that if not for the greenhouse effect, it would be a freezing iceball; and then there's Shin-Tethys.

Shin-Tethys is what planetographers refer to as a "Hydrated Goldilocks Super-Earth." That means it's wet, it's just the right size, and it belongs to a class of planet bigger than the legendary cradle of Fragile civilization. Actually, it's about three times as massive as Earth—but two-thirds of that is water and ice, surrounding an unseen rocky core. It's so low in overall density that at the wave tops, the gravitational pull is a little over three-quarters of standard, and orbital velocity is *just right*. Escape velocity is not so low that it loses much hydrogen to the solar wind, but gravity is not so high that it's hard to reach orbit from the equator.

Shin-Tethys is *young*. Dojima System formed only a billion years ago. Consequently, below the shell of rock and ice nestling within the three-hundred-kilometer-deep ocean is an unseen mantle rich in heavy isotopes. The natural plutonium that was present when the star system formed has all decayed by now, but the uranium is frisky-free and neutron poor! Bright blue glowing smokers periodically light up the crushing abyssal depths, bubbles of prompt criticality rising toward the surface of the ocean, where they boil until they pop in a searing cloud of superheated radioactive steam. The natural dissolved uranium in the oceans of Shin-Tethys contains more than 1 percent U235. It's rich enough that you can extract it and feed it straight into a reactor.

Do I need to draw you a diagram to explain the economic relation between Shin-Tethys and the rest of Dojima System's habitats?

(Yes, I probably do.)

Everyone needs energy. Close to Dojima Prime, photovoltaic cells work well enough. But the farther you go into the cold night beyond Cronos, toward the steeply inclined orbit of the methane giant Hera, deep into the outer belt, the worse solar power works. Running in slow-time will help you conserve what energy you have, but eventually, you have to go nuclear.

There are, of course, the seven classical forms of nuclear energy: chain-reaction fission, externally induced fission, thermal radioisotope batteries, coherent isomeric emission batteries, muon-catalyzed cold fusion, hot deuterium-tritium fusion, and extremely hot aneutronic fusion . . . each have their pros and cons. But of them all, only one variety ticks all the boxes: fission, subtype classical chain-reaction. Nuclear isomer batteries are all very well, but you've got to charge them up somehow. And every type of fusion reactor ever developed is bulky, complicated, fiddly to keep running, and requires inordinate amounts of supporting infrastructure.

By the time you add it all up, fission is vastly simpler, more compact, and weighs less than any other kind. The only kind of space vehicle that really *needs* the efficiency of fusion is a starship: For all other purposes, it's cheaper and simpler to throw lots of uranium at the problem.

And Shin-Tethys is by far the richest known source of uranium 235 within a dozen light-years.

Which means I need to brief you on the politics of mermaids.

Once I agreed to his proposal, Rudi formally released me from the oubliette. He also released me from my state of incommunicado. I worked, he paid me, and I spent the lifestyle tokens he provided on various luxuries, including a mail-forwarding service. To my sisters back home I transmitted a terse *I'm on my way* signal, of necessity abbreviated by the cost of interstellar bandwidth (not to mention the certain knowledge that the communications crew were discreetly listening to everything I sent). To the various people I had heard from on Shin-Tethys, I sent . . . well, there wasn't much to say: to Ana's concerned friend, an offer of a meeting upon my arrival; to the police, ditto: and to the debt-collection agency a polite offer to discuss the rent on her vacuole in person. (Anything to keep them from tossing her personal effects overboard before I had a chance to rummage through them.) And that was that.

As for Rudi's assignment, here's how I explained my findings to him when I made my report:

"To a first-order approximation, there is no signal in the noise."

"Bah." Hanging upside down in the middle of his nest of retinas, Rudi looked as disgusted as I felt. I'd spent more than a hundred days plowing through records, drilling for hidden dependencies between investment trusts and holdings, and looking at published company reports filed in a variety of aquatic micronations at varying depths in the upper oceans of Shin-Tethys. "That's ridiculous. There are scandals and frauds everywhere! You're not going to convince me that those people are an exception. What's out there?"

"What's out there is a disturbing lack of naughtiness. Almost as if all signs of it are being deliberately *suppressed*."

I waved at the retina coating the far wall of his nest. "Observe."

I'd been working toward this presentation for months. Declining good-natured invitations to orgies from the crew because I had pivot tables to analyze. Mumbling my way through it over my food at mealtimes until I found myself eating alone. Dreaming of dark currents flowing beneath the ice caps of frozen slow money reserves. There were 497 mutually recognized governments in Shin-Tethys; while all of them recognized the Taj Slow Dollar as the rock-bottomed foundation of fiscal probity, more than half of them—316—maintained their own medium-investment vehicles with floating exchange rates (in the shape of bonds with various maturity terms), and almost all had their own cash standards (except for three alliances comprised of smaller but mostly prosperous nations who formed customs unions). Around 70 percent of these governments had their own national banks, and another 26 percent allowed private but highly regulated banking industries to exist. These naturally ran on top of other currencies and media of reputational account, for not all of these nations were marketized—indeed, at least eighty of them were communist, and a hundred had nonexchangeable primitive currencies used solely for reproductive courtship purposes and marking changes of social status. There were even three oddball kingdoms that ran gift economies mediated by the frequent exchange of small, polished spheres of metallic plutonium. (People in those polities learned very rapidly to give money away as fast as it came in. Depressions were rare, and tended to end explosively.)

In any event, I'd been able to follow the declared medium holdings of most of the governments and banks and major off-world investors via various government property registers and gazetteers.

"Look." I pointed. "Shin-Tethys as a whole maintains a positive trade surplus with the rest of the system. A third of the local nations don't export directly, but there's a lot of internal, intramural trade between the tribes—the main six exporters account for eighty-two percent of the uranium and fifty-seven percent of the rare earths. What comes in is, well, lots of skilled labor, finished high-tech assemblies, anything that needs microgravity or vacuum or very high temperatures or an anaerobic environment. In other words, it's your typical pattern for an energy-exporting planet, with the added twist that because it's very damp, a lot of planetary surface activities—smelting metals, manufacturing ceramics—are expensive to perform locally. The only interesting thing is how little slow money is going into their economic system. As for banking corruption, there's the usual, but no more than the usual. Around one government per decade—out of nearly five hundred, mind—gets into bad trouble one way or another. But the system is self-stabilizing: What usually happens is that a consortium of their trading partners and main creditors get together and mount a hostile takeover—I believe they call it a "war"—and place the defaulter under administration until it digs itself out of the hole. But there's not much of that going on. You have to go back nearly a thousand years to find anything really bad; for example, the Trask affair—"

"What was that?" Rudi interrupted.

"Nothing relevant. Ivar Trask-1 was one of the system founders—set up the systembank at Taj Beacon, established the Dojima slow dollar on the interstellar exchanges. There was some sort of scandal over money laundering, and he went missing, believed murdered, but as I was saying, that was nearly a thousand years ago. Dojima System's bankers are *very* staid, even by slow money banking standards."

Rudi snorted, and one ear tip twitched, as if he was keeping his opinions to himself: But presently he nodded. "Continue, please."

"Shorter version: What you're looking for doesn't seem to exist. Either that, or there's a conspiracy of silence so vast as to defy human nature—you'd need to have more than two thousand institutions in different jurisdictions agreeing to stash their dirt behind the reaction-mass tankage, and nobody leaking."

"That big?" Rudi looked at me sharply. "Are any of them showing signs of changing internal power structures? New ownership?"

I shrugged. "That's a political question. You didn't ask me to report on their politics."

"Well, you'd better look into that," he grumbled. "Immigrants may come entangled with slow dollars. Start with the Kingdom of Argos and specifically any events in Nova Ploetsk, and spiral out from there to any-where your sister might have taken an interest in. After all, she didn't disappear by accident. She must have blundered into something."

"There's a limit to what I can achieve from up here—"

"Yes!" Rudi snapped his jaws in a manner I was coming to recognize as emphatic agreement. "So when you've done it, we will have to go down-well to continue our investigation in person. But that is then, and this is now! So get to work."

I believe I mentioned that the surface gravity of Shin-Tethys is about three-quarters that of Earth. However, Shin-Tethys is a big world—over seventy thousand kilometers in circumference. It has no land sur-face; rather, its surface is all water, with small, floating ice caps around the north and south poles, and sargasso rafts of vegetation the size of continents afloat in the tropics. The water forms a thin layer around an outer mantle of mixed rock and ice, for ice under extreme pressure changes into strange crystalline phases that are denser than liquid water: The boundary is only two to three hundred kilometers down.

At the surface of the outer mantle, there is a layer consisting almost entirely of heavy ice contaminated by intrusive threads of fractured rock, the remains of lava tubes and hot spots that thrust their way to the sur-face and burst in a catastrophic verneshot. There are volcanoes, some of them cold but glowing pale blue from Cerenkov radiation generated by the fission reactions that power them. The critical mass of uranium is significantly reduced in aqueous solution because hydrogen atoms slow thermal neutrons, making them easier for large nuclei to capture: Con-sequently, deposits of uranium salts leached from the rocky intrusions from the lower mantle frequently achieve criticality and fire up a fission chain reaction.

Somewhere thousands of kilometers below the outer mantle, there lies a mesomantle of rock, the outer mantle of the Earth-like world drowned within Shin-Tethys's watery caul—but that does not concern me. We can't get to it directly, so it is of no economic interest.

The main significance of the hydrosphere is that it is both a promise and a threat: the promise of huge wealth from mineral-resource extraction and the threat of hydrostatic pressure.

Pressure kills. It kills Fragile cells and human mechanocytes alike because the molecular machinery of which such cells are composed relies on phase boundaries between oily and aqueous compartments to organize and orient these large molecules, and increasing pressure warps and distorts them because lipid bubbles don't expand or contract at precisely the same rate as watery ones when you crank up the pressure. You can adapt gradually, of course, tweaking a hydrogen bond here and a covalent structure there, but persons who go swimming in the oceans of Shin-Tethys without extreme modifications are vulnerable to pressure-induced necrosis if they travel even a couple of hundred meters up or down. And the hydrosphere is hundreds of kilometers deep.

Hence the laminar nations.

Local Customs

O ne morning I was awakened by thumping and vibrations which, transmitted through the meshwork of my sleeping nest, put me in mind of the approach of a gigantic predator. Alarmed, I connected my pocket retina to the shipboard net, to see a storm of arcane instructions and communications among the navigation crew. Branch Office Five Zero was maneuvering under power, popping thrusters and spinning up gyros at a rate I'd never seen before. It reminded me of the maneuvering when Dennett's chapel departed from Taj Beacon.

While I hadn't been formally ordered not to inquire as to our precise arrival time, any questions I'd put to the flight-deck crew had been met with polite evasions. (And indeed, this was not totally unreasonable; Branch Office Five Zero might well be planning to divert on the way into orbit to rendezvous with some miscreant suspected of smuggling or insurance fraud, in which case my awareness of this could constitute a security breach.) But 286 sleeping periods had passed since I was carried on board, and so it was no great stretch of imagination to conclude that either we were maneuvering toward rendezvous with one or another of the orbital republics, or that we were preparing for a final orbital insertion burn using the vehicle's high-impulse motor.

I crawled out of my nest and looked around the inside of my room. It was cramped and sparsely furnished, but I'd spent most of a year living in it. It had taken on some of the emotional resonance we call *home*: a more spartan, but somewhat less stressful way of life than the institution of my childhood. I was going to miss it, I realized. I shook my head, then pulled on my shipboard outfit (a vest-of-pockets, knee and elbow pads, and split-toed socks) and stuffed everything else into my go bag. There was no guarantee that I would be debarking in the next day or two . . . but it would be imprudent not to be prepared to depart at a moment's notice.

I'd known this day was coming for the best part of a year, but it still swept me up in a fit of excitement and enthusiasm. A new planet lay at my feet! Rudi would have to let me descend to the surface, for if nothing else he'd need my collusion to help find Ana. And then, and then . . . well. I'd spent many a twilight rest shift considering my options in the privacy of my own head: Once free of Rudi and his minions for even a few hours, I could cut and run to Shin-Kyoto. Or, if Ana was indeed in trouble, I could help find and extricate her, maybe find a way to clone her soul chip under Rudi's nose and smuggle it out-system. Or—but these speculations were the wild figments of imagination of a much younger version of me, much less aware of my own mortal shortcomings. Worse, they all dead-ended in the roiling fogbank of the uncertain future: For if I had become the object of my lineage mater's enmity, what future was there for me? It was all quite dismaying. However, returning my focus to the immediate future, it seemed to me that my first job was to extricate myself—and Ana, if she was still alive—from Rudi's proprietorial interest as cleanly as possible, then take stock of the situation. Which might be possible if I were to request asylum from the Kingdom of Argos, where Ana had lived—

"Krina. Please report to Conference Room D on Level Two for briefing. Acknowledge."

I swore quietly at the public-address system that had so rudely interrupted my situational analysis. "Acknowledged," I said. Then I sealed my go bag, stuck my head out of my cell, and went where I was told.

The grandly named Conference Room D was actually an empty bubble hanging off the side of one of the main throughways, walled only to provide a modicum of security against being casually overheard by passersby. I stuck my head in the hatch to find Rudi already there, along with two others. "Ah, Krina! Come in, come in. You're just in time. This is Dent"—he gestured at one of his companions, a lugubrious-looking batbanker with a spreadsheet tattooed on his left wing in smart ink, so that he could pivot his tables with a flap of the wrist—"and this is Marigold. Marigold is a debt termination officer," he added as an afterthought.

I swallowed as I looked at her. Marigold was one of the few orthohuman people I'd glimpsed on the vehicle but not been formally introduced to. She could have been dropped into one of the seething cities of preextinction Fragile Earth, and nobody would have noticed anything unusual about her, as long as she replaced her snaking orange locks and angular antibiometric facial camouflage with something more traditional. But: *a debt termination officer!* Banks and their offshoots (such as this very hive of villainy) are about risk management and avoidance—matters should never reach the stage where they need to terminate a bad debt! Far better to stir it up with a bunch of lumpen credit properties and shuffle it off to a long-term investment trust for toxic assets, there to depress the bottom line's growth by a fractional percentage point. Debt *termination* is not a practice I have ever had much to do with. So I stared, slightly appalled, until Marigold winked at me, and I dropped my gaze to hide my expression.

"Her job will be to watch your back," Rudi explained. "Assuming you are still hoping to find your missing sib?" I nodded. "We will travel to Nova Ploetsk in Argos together. You will need to examine your sib's apartment and take custody of her personal effects." He smiled, baring his teeth. "Meanwhile, we will accompany you to provide assistance. Mari as your bodyguard, and Dent . . . Dent is a forensic accountant, with credentials recognized by the Eyes of Argos: He is at your disposal. Oh, and you'll all be needing a change of skin."

"Hey, wait a moment—" I began.

"Or don't you want to find your sister?" Rudi asked, dangerously reasonable.

"What kind of skin?" Marigold's diction was precise, but emotionally barren: She might have been a machine, like the stalker that Dennett had been playing games with.

"Skin with scales and flukes," Rudi hissed. "Nova Ploetsk is two hundred meters down, and if your sib has gone any deeper, we'll all need to adapt ourselves. I have made arrangements with a body shop on the surface port above it. Time to go."

Rudi led us to the main air lock into the forward cargo hold; then through a twisty little maze of tunnels and claustrophobic tubes that terminated in a tiny room with six acceleration couches bolted to one wall. "Strap yourselves in," he said. "It's going to be a bumpy ride." I worked my way into the nest of straps (gently twisting in the airflow like a bed of kelp in an ocean current). It resembled the *Soyuz* sarcophagus back aboard the chapel, if somewhat larger and less classically proportioned. Marigold took it upon herself to pull the hatch shut and lock it closed, then lay down beside me: We were packed so close in the can that our shoulders and knees were almost touching, and the ceiling was barely a meter above the back of my head. A minute later, the sound of the air circulation changed.

"Take deep breaths," Marigold said tonelessly. "Inhale deeply. If any air is left in your pleural chamber, you may be injured when we impact."

"Impact?" I asked: "What do you—"

Pale blue liquid, very cold and runny, began to gush into the sarcophagus. I struggled against my straps, straining to hold up my head, until I saw Rudi duck his muzzle into a large globule of the liquid and blow a stream of bubbles out through his nose. I'd heard about this stuff but never seen it myself. "Is this really necessary?" I asked, trying not to panic.

The liquid flux increased, foaming and rebounding from the ceiling and walls. A wave of it struck my face and stuck, covering my mouth. I exhaled explosively, expecting to choke, and began to breathe in. It chilled and numbed my nasal heat-exchange surfaces and gas reservoirs as I drew it down, but it wasn't chokingly thick, and there was a reassuring abundance of oxygen dissolved in it: As there should be, for it was some sort of chlorofluorocarbon liquid. (I gather it is used mainly as a hydrostatic buffer during *very*-high-acceleration maneuvering.) Coldness invaded my nether regions, flooding my inner cavities. It has the strange property of being an electrorheological fluid, I've since been told, so that at the moment of splashdown, a brief electrical current turns it stiff as wax with us embedded in it.

Reentry vehicle departure in ten seconds. The whole of the front of the sarcophagus turned into a retina display, blinking status display icons at me. I marveled at the sight, for behind them was a panoramic view of the interior of the cargo tank, its front end open to the brilliant darkness of the sky. Wheeling across it a perfect turquoise hemisphere streaked with pale pink clouds—

A giant boot kicked me in the small of the back, ramming me into the acceleration couch. The cargo tank of the Five Zero vanished behind us. We were on our way to Nova Ploetsk, embedded in a tub of breathable blue jelly as our capsule screamed through the outer wisps of the atmosphere of Shin-Tethys.

Nine minutes to impact, said the screen.

I began to wonder (not for the first time, I will admit) whether finding the missing half of the Atlantis Carnet was really worth the fuss.

We hit the atmosphere at over twenty thousand kilometers per hour, flickering red and yellow bursts of plasma flashing off the heat shield on the base of our discus-shaped flying coffin: It was altogether too much excitement for my taste even though I was trussed up in shock absorbers and drenched in crash jelly. Our deceleration was abrupt, if not violent, peaking at an eyeball-warping fifty gees. Finally, the clouds of flame began to clear from the camera on the outside of our hull as we fell through the stratosphere. There wasn't much to see, however. The vast floating continents of leviathan grass tended to congregate in the subtropical zones, away from the scorching solar zenith and the turbulent currents around the frozen ice caps: None of them were visible. The surface of Shin-Tethys, at least in these near-equatorial reaches, was water from horizon to horizon, a pale blue wall the size of the sky into which we were falling.

Impact in two minutes, said our craft's display. With my vestigial electrosense, I could feel Rudi discussing something with Dent, as if from a great distance: But I lacked the specialized vacuum adaptations to join in their conversation. "What happens next?" I tried to ask, but only produced a gargling rumble that made my larynx sore, and I'm not sure the sound even made it out of my throat.

Impact in one minute. Impact in thirty seconds. Impact in ten seconds—I felt a moment of core-numbing terror, certain that I was about to die, as the horizon rose up and slammed into me. Then everything went dark.

I'd now like to share with you a few reminiscences about the niceties of arrival in a monarchy afloat in the upper waters of Shin-Tethys.

The pressure of the water column above one's head—ten kilopascals per meter—forces significant metabolic adaptations if one is to travel up or down, for a variation of just a few megapascals is sufficient to wreck delicate nanostructures like proteins that rely on weak Van der Waals forces and disulfide bridges to maintain their shape. We post-Fragiles can adapt our mechanocytes by applying high-pressure firmware upgrades, but the process is not instantaneous. So the polities of Shin-Tethys are stratified not merely by lineage and natal nobility, and distinguished not merely by their geographical extent, but by their altitude. Hence their colloquial name: the laminar republics.

Despite this, very few of them are *actual* republics. Most of them were founded by individuals, early shareholders aboard the starship that first colonized Dojima System. They replicated themselves, spawning many bodies to house copies of their core identity, for life in Shin-Tethys during the early days was unimaginably hazardous. With the passage of time, many of the original rulers senesced and were replaced by new successor states, but even to this day some of the original founders survive, and the petty kings and queens jealously guard their demesnes and keep a close watch on visitors.

We came hurtling down from the zenith, decelerated at a Fragile-crunching rate, then crashed into the wave tops at over a hundred kilometers per hour. Parachutes, I learned later, found no favor with Rudi because he half expected us to be shot out of the sky by various disgruntled duty evaders; hanging around in the breeze might make for a more comfortable splashdown, but only if we lived to make it. And so our sturdy capsule survived its brusque arrival and subsequent ditching but promptly submerged. And sank, bubbling air from its remaining gas reserves, until it fell into Poseidon's net at a depth of nearly fifty meters.

During this process, were I to have to pick a single word to describe my state of mind, "terror" would fit quite accurately. I recovered consciousness rapidly after the impact-induced shutdown and self-test—we sustained over two hundred gees momentarily as we splashed down—but took a couple of seconds to reorient myself and look at the retinal ceiling so close to my nose, and even longer to realize that what I was looking at was a cloud of rapidly dispersing bubbles and the mirror-rippling surface of the water receding slowly above us.

"Rudi, we're sinking!" The crash and reboot seemed to have reset something in my laryngeal cavity, so that I could make my voice work again. It sounded deep and sonorous in the chlorofluorocarbon bath.

The count grinned, tongue lolling: "Ain't it great?"

"We're *sinking*!"

"Dive rate zero point six nine meters per second," droned Dent. He was reading from a personal display: "Crush depth in, ahum, three hundred and nineteen seconds. Make that three hundred and twenty to three hundred and eighty, actually. If we were to go that deep."

"We're all going to die!" I wailed.

"No we're not," Rudi assured me. He reached out sideways and squeezed my hand. "Just lie back and enjoy the ride, Krina. Everything's going entirely according to plan."

"Ugh-ugh!" I wibbled incoherently. Something disturbingly flaccid and meaty shimmied vertically past the camera viewport on the outside of our hull. It had numerous suction cups lining its inner surface. The suckers surrounded viciously barbed hooks that pulsed in and out of the tentacle's bulbous trunk. Half the ceiling fell into shadow as it lazily wrapped itself across our upper surface. The sarcophagus rocked alarmingly from toe to head, tilting me alarmingly downward, and our sink rate increased.

"Ah, we have a tug." Rudi seemed inordinately pleased by this development.

"Docking in fifty seconds," Dent informed us. He made it sound as routine as a tax return. Perhaps it was, to him. But this whole business of landing on a water world was wholly new to me, and more than a little overwhelming.

We lurched sideways just then. There was a grinding bump and shuffle, then a thud that rattled my teeth—and our descent stopped! I would have vented a sudden sigh of relief, but the viscosity of the carrier fluid filling my lungs made it hard to breathe other than regularly. A metallic clang followed. Then the hatch through which we had entered the flying coffin began to unlatch slowly, from the outside.

"Welcome to *gargle goosh*—" There was air on the other side of the hatch; our shock fluid poured out as gas bubbled in, drowning out the canned announcement. I spluttered and heaved, unlatched all seven straps, sat up, and vomited runny blue foam until my chest hurt. Finally I was able to inhale, panting and shuddering. We were not, it appeared, destined to die horribly just yet. The breathing mix down here had a sharply astringent edge, almost ammoniacal. "—*Ustoms* and immigration. Please proceed to the interview area as directed once you have disembarked."

"What are we (*cough*) supposed to—" I asked, but Rudi was already climbing through the hatch, closely followed by Dent.

Marigold gave me a look. "What?" I asked.

"Proceed to the interview area." She sounded just like the canned announcement, only three degrees colder.

"I'm proceeding! I'm proceeding."

Sloshing through the residue of shock fluid (it still filled our sarcophagus to the lower lip of the hatch) I clambered out onto the sloping aeroshell, then slid down onto the metal grid it had come to rest on. I looked around. We were parked inside an underwater dome, beside a well of some sort—a well through which the docking tentacle had lifted our capsule and deposited it in this parking area. Just how we had managed to land so close to a submerged dock mystified me momentarily, but I dismissed it for now as irrelevant: We had arrived, and now I would have to deal. Rudi and Dent were already at the door on the other side of the dome, about thirty meters away. I stumbled after them, nauseous and uncoordinated from the sudden transition into a deep gravity well. It could be worse, I suppose: I gather the Fragile used to take whole days before they could walk again after returning to their home world following a period in microgravity. (Just another of the countless ways in which we are better adapted to spaceflight than they.)

Not many people arrive in an undersea polity by ballistic reentry capsule: the laminar republics are generally paranoid about off-planet contamination. Consequently, I found myself funneled into a receiving station with a coffin-sized capsule waiting for me. "Speak your full formal name," said the wall, "under penalty of perjury."

"Krina Buchhaltung Historiker Alizond-114," quoth I.

"Place of origin."

"I was initialized on New California, but my last instantiation was—"

"Purpose of visit."

"I'm here to look for my sister, who is missing—"

"Get in the capsule."

I glanced round. The door behind me had merged seamlessly with the wall. Suppressing my apprehension, I climbed into the coffin-sized cylinder and lay down. The last thing I remember is the lid coming down, sealing me in.

When I opened my eyes again I found myself in a very different place. The upper half of the cylinder had risen again, and I was staring at the high, vaulted ceiling above an almost claustrophobically small chamber. The ceiling itself gleamed with the luster of aragonite, illuminated by bright pinpoints of bluish light. I tried to sit up, gasping for breath in the hot, moist air, and looked over the edge of my transport cylinder. There was no floor, only water: and, waiting to talk to me, an instance of the Queen.

"Welcome to Argos immigration control," she said, her voice a slightly lighter echo of my interrogator from the arrivals terminal: "We have some questions to put to you, Ms. Alizond, in view of your irregular arrival here."

There is an eccentric custom among the monarchs of the laminar republics (or, indeed, the laminar kingdoms): They originally carved out their kingdoms by making multiple duplicates of themselves, working together briefly, then merging their deltas. It's a risky strategy—let a copy of yourself run around gaining experiences for too long, and it will eventually become, effectively, a separate person—but if bodies are cheap and minds are expensive, as in the early days of a better nation, it's the way to go. As a consequence of this custom, the small principalities have no need to employ civil servants for most purposes, and indeed, many of their rulers have a positively paranoid aversion to doing so—a fear of *la trahison de bourgeoisie*, the treachery of the unaffiliated individual professional—and so they only use out-lineage employees for tasks they do not want to be associated with. (Such as the secret police, or the judicial bench when it is convenient to convey the appearance of impartiality). This was clearly the case with Medea, Queen-creator of Argos: which is why the first person I met upon my arrival was Medea herself, incarnate in her role as Senior Immigration Comptroller.

But I didn't know she was an instance of the Queen at this point. Rudi hadn't explained her somewhat eccentric approach to human resources to me, and as an outlander, I was insufficiently aware of such local quirks to have investigated how I could expect to be received. All I knew at the time was that I was about to be questioned by a mermaid with close-cropped green hair and a condescending, officious manner.

(And, hovering discreetly behind and above her head, the menacing black shapes of a pair of police hornets, primed to paralyze or kill on command. Like any other monarch presiding over a hotbed of intrigue balanced above a lawless hinterland, Medea was not shy about displaying her monopoly on violent force.)

"Ask away," I said, looking at her in some puzzlement (I believe I was wondering where Rudi and the others had gone).

"You said you came here to find your sister. But you've never been here before. What did you mean by that?"

At this point an icy-cold awareness of my precarious position *should* have overwhelmed me with an urge to caution: But for some obscure reason, I didn't feel remotely perturbed. My emotional affect was entirely flat, comfortably numb. "My sister Ana?" I explained: "Ana immigrated to Dojima System about seventy-one point six years ago. We—I mean, my mater—originally sent her here to handle the family accounts and provide currency triangulation services to SystemBank Hector, our own New California Credit Union, and other agency services as specified, while continuing her work as a—"

"Define your relationship to Ana—Ana Graulle-90." The mermaid was scowling at me: Her left cheek dimpled, slightly detracting from the intimidating effect, but the slow lashing of her fluke below the surface of her pool created a churn that almost reached the surface, lifting her halfway out of the water. "She's not of your lineage, is she?"

"She is," I protested (but not too hard): "She's just offset to one side. Mater—Sondra Alizond-1—has refactored herself more than once. The Graulles are descended from her last-but-one incarnation. They took up a new name to avoid confusion, they're very different in personality. She used to be a risk analyst and commodities broker—" I managed to rein myself in as much as I could before my tongue ran away with me again. It was disconcertingly hard. "Why, what else do you want to know?"

"Why are you looking for her here?" the mermaid persisted.

"Because Argos is her last-known address." I tried to focus but couldn't quite detach myself from the need to answer her questions. "I was going to stay with her for a year, studying: She was in one of the outer habs, but when I got to Rosen, she'd sent word that she was moving down-well to Shin-Tethys, some sort of scholarship arrangement. She said she was getting involved in tracking demand flows in real commodities, part of a consortium investigating long-term sustainability of transport energy economies. Then when I got to Taj Beacon, she'd disappeared with no forwarding address. So I came here as fast as I could."

"As fast as you could." Was that skepticism in her voice? "Leading to your arrival in the company of Rudolf Crimson-1102 and two of his assistants, descending by ballistic reentry vehicle from the armed privateer Branch Office Five Zero. For although you originally signed on as an unskilled ship-hand aboard the Chapel of Our Lady of the Holy Restriction Endonculease, you were observed departing that vehicle aboard a fast cutter owned by a notorious insurance salesman and pirate." She fell silent, but her closed counsel was easy enough to decode: *How do you explain* that?

"He sold her a life insurance policy before she vanished—" It sounded weak, even to my ears. "What exactly are you asking me?" Despite my distractedness, my sense of unease was growing, like a white rime of mold attacking the dead tissues of a body whose 'cytes had curled up and died of the despair that killed their collective's mind. Why was I telling her all this? It wasn't like the debugger Rudi had used on me: This was something altogether more subtle. "I'm a mendicant academic:

I came to this system to study with my distant sib; all this nonsense that has happened to me is just bad coincidences—"

The mermaid held me with her glittering eye: "Do you really believe that? Wait, forget we asked. *Forget.* You boarded one vehicle and arrived on another: We hope you can appreciate why this might lead to our questioning your bona fides as a legitimate scholar and speculate as to your motive for entering the kingdom." She paused for a moment. "Do you have anything to add?"

"Um." I licked my suddenly dry lips. "I don't understand? Are you saying I can't look for my sister? Where is everyone, anyway?"

She waved my questions off with a dismissive gesture. "Ms. Alizond, we do not believe you are being entirely forthcoming. I am not prepared to discuss the location of your traveling companions—" She looked directly at me. "So, by royal command, we are placing you under arrest, on suspicion of, let's see: attempting to obtain illegal entry into the Monarchy of Argos will do for starters. We may need to consider adding conspiracy to smuggle antiquities to the list of charges in due course. But first, you will help my police with their inquiries into the murder of Ana Graulle-90." The lid of the transport cylinder fell toward me again, nearly blocking her final words: "She's all yours, boys. Take her away!"

Like the vast majority of my lineage, I am by disposition a law-abiding citizen. Consequently, I had managed to reach a considerable age without ever being arrested. As with most unfamiliar and threatening experiences, I found the actual event all the more stressful because of the uncertainty attached to it rather than because of the event itself.

"Take her away!"

With those words ringing in my ears, I fell backward, headfirst into the depths of Nova Ploetsk, protected from the crushing pressure outside only by the flimsy-seeming walls of my transport cylinder.

Now, as to the rest—

Medea might have been the Queen-in-Manifold, present in many instantiations to execute the activities of the government, but she was not, I subsequently learned, ubiquitous. Without my knowledge, I had become a person of some notoriety throughout Dojima System, at least in certain circles: My name was on a watch list. Rudi, to his discredit, had not anticipated this. So, while he and his entourage passed through the Customs and Immigration chambers under assumed identities (aided by the discreet crossing of certain palms with cash), it had not occurred to him to disguise my arrival. *I* was noticed and diverted toward the tender mercies of the police, but *they* had already slithered through Medea's grip before they noticed my absence.

I imagine the subsequent conversation went something like this:

Rudi: "Where's Krina? Marigold, I thought you were keeping an eye on her."

Marigold: "We exited the capsule together. She was right behind me."

Rudi: "Behind you? When you went through customs?"

Marigold: "I'm not stupid, I saw her enter a carrier pod right before I—"

Dent: "Did she make a run for it? Or was she snatched?"

Rudi: "Doesn't matter, we have to get clear before whoever she's with makes a play for us. Driver, I say, *driver!* Take us to the Hotel du Lac, right away . . ." *Sotto voce*: "We will discuss our response once we have switched vessels. Do not say anything until I tell you to." *Even more quietly*: "The game's afoot."

INTERLUDE

A Thousand Years Ago

The dying man drifts from the rippling silver mirror of the sky.

He is almost completely dead, spine severed and circulatory system ruptured by a harpoon that sliced through the major vessels of his neck and lodged point first in the base of his skull. The gash in his throat streams a trail of emerald green circulatory fluid; meanwhile, the uncoordinated twitching of muscle groups in his arms and lower limbs hints at the coming struggle of individual mechanocytes to survive the demise of the collective. The weapon that killed him still quivers as it tries to free its blade from the cranial prison it so enthusiastically embedded itself in. But it has fulfilled its murderous impulse too well: The tightly meshed tensegrity structures of his armored brainpan grip its barbs tightly, and the weight of his dead body drags it down. Killer and victim have embarked on their final journey together, drifting down into the darkness.

They will fall together for a very long time.

At first, the ceiling of the world seems close enough to touch: Waves and rippling interference patterns march across it, and small dark islands clump and drift just beneath the surface, casting long shadows into the depths. The ruby glare of the sun pierces the sky directly over-head. Clouds of semitransparent sunfeeders drift in the brightness, numerous beyond counting, hazing the water and casting dappled shad-ows across the silvery motiles that dart and nibble at them from below. In the pearly distance, leviathan grasses float like tenuous auroral conti-nents, soaking up the solar largesse.

The corpse and its killer drift down through the sunlit upper waters of the world. His humanoid body plan puts a brake on their downward progress: His terminal velocity is less than five kilometers per hour, little more than a fast walking pace on land, and thanks to his residual buoy-ancy, at first he falls at barely a tenth that speed.

Fifty meters below the surface, the entangled bodies pass close to an eel-shaped motile. It sniffs the bloody trail, then closes in, clamps three sets of jaws to the wound in the body's throat. It sucks greedily for a while, slowing the body's fall as it extracts what's left of his pressure cir-cuit, but fifty meters farther down, the increasing pressure forces it to let go. Falling faster, the exsanguinated body leaves the sunlit upper reaches behind.

It is colder beneath the thermocline, and the pressure rises steadily the farther the corpse falls from the roof of the world. The red light of noon fades to the dim purple glow of the disphotic zone. In the direction of travel, there is no light to speak of: just a darkness as palpable as a black hole's event horizon. The waters of this zone are a-chirp with the hunting clicks and shrills of saprophytic feeders: The overlapping thermoclines above reflect tight-beam upward-directed sonar pulses back down, illuminating prey and fragments of falling food without revealing the location of the scavengers to their toothy, bug-eyed predators.

The dead body's muscles and viscera twitch and pulse regularly as individual mechanocytes desperately try to punch their way out through the woven, lifeless integument of his outer skin and clothing. Uncoupled and disoriented by his death, every 'cyte remaining in his body fights for itself: They're not very smart, but they're brighter than their purely biological antecedents, and the steadily increasing pressure of the meso-pelagic zone is weakening the social contract that binds them into a body. The scavengers have noticed the presence of a meal falling through their space, and if they can't escape soon, it will be too late.

Three hundred meters down, the corpses fall through a school of Bezos worms. They close around the falling bodies and tighten, adhering to each other in a matlike mass. The bodies dangle from the island as the worms prod and poke at their prize, rasping through skin with their concentric circular jaws. The harpoon's armored body is largely immune to their efforts, but the dead man's body is vulnerable. There is resistance: Mechanocytes do not appreciate being eaten, and fight back. But they lack coordination. Their owner could have directed their collective defense, were he still alive, lending them his sense of identity and will to selfhood. But the millimeter-scale 'cytes spilling from his dead body are weak and disoriented. They defect in their hordes, spilling into the worms' stomatogastric mills, their resistance crumbling as the worms reprogram and repurpose them, adding them to their gut lining.

Despite the depredations of the worm colony, the body remains rec-ognizable for another hundred meters. The worms squirm and writhe within his skin as they hunt down the remaining actuator mechanocytes and loot his feedstock exchange organs, then attempt to hack his quies-cent neural trunks, wheedling the marrow techné and central neural core with recorded pleas for access and promises of repair, zombie mes-sages harvested from previous victims. But the rich techné of the body's marrow—the core of replicator mechanocytes from which his ordinary tissues are spawned—are either dead or firewalled, not responding.

The growing pressure of the aphotic zone threatens to wreck the deli-cate intracellular machinery of the worms' own techné, crushing para-proteins and ribofabricators into nonviable conformations: They're locked in a race against time, desperately trying to eat their fill without being pulled down below their crush depth. Finally, the worms let their prize fall, and the now-flensed skeleton continues its descent, still wear-ing its bag of skin for a shroud.

The body falls faster through the crushing pressure and chilly darkness of the abyssal depths. But it is not alone even here. Ghostly scavengers—little more than solitary, feral mechanocytes—latch onto his tough, barely digestible skin and patiently chew away, detaching dermal scales piece by piece. Gradually, his bones are laid bare to the night. There are neither lights nor eyes to witness the lustrous glory of fiber-reinforced titanium, still impaled on the point of the harpoon (stilled forever, its vestigial brain long since crushed by the steadily rising pressure), to note the elegance of his articulated joints, or the presence of the two external cranial interfaces, each still occupied by a soul chip.

As the corpse falls, the pressure rises, and the scavengers grow scarce. Finally, nearly a hundred kilometers below the ceiling of the world, there is a creak and a brisk pop as a seam in the cranial vault gives way. A brief mushroom cloud of debris spills from the base of his skull, and the dead harpoon rocks briefly, then topples free, falling point down into the Hadean depths. (Leading the way, it will reach its destination far ahead of the other remains.) There are more creaks and pops. The long leg bones, with their buried marrow techné let go next, and millions of the most complex mechanisms ever designed are smashed to pulp in microseconds by the mindless pressure of depths for which they are not adapted.

Hours pass, then more hours. The water grows clear and gelid in the utter darkness. Once, the utter black is broken by a pale rising glow of Cerenkov blue, roiling and bubbling with strange energies as it heads toward the surface: Then all is dark again. Hours pass, and tens of kilometers—then days, and hundreds of kilometers. Strange life lives down here, subsisting on the deadfall of Hadean dwellers whose corpses rain down from unthinkably far above. But the corpse, already stripped of anything that might be of use, is of little interest to the denizens of the deep ecosystem.

Nearly two hundred kilometers beneath the sky where he was murdered, the banker's bones gently grind against a rocklike surface and rebound briefly before resuming their fall.

Twenty kilometers farther down, there is another impact, this time more final. The body has struck a cliff face of hard crystalline material rising from the darkness. There is no light to illuminate the pearly white finish of the sunken ultradense iceberg. Disarticulated by the impact, his bones tumble down the glacial cliff toward a plain of muddy debris that covers the tilted basalt plate where it abuts the ice. As it rebounds his damaged skull sheds its precious load, scattering the last legacy of his mind, stalled forever in the shock of sudden death.

And so it is that when his soul chips come to rest on the floor of the world ocean, their buffers are forever occupied by a meaningless exclamation of horror, by the final memory of a desperate pursuit and murder, and a debt that will never be redeemed.

part two
THE ABYSS

Arrested Development

"Will somebody tell me what's going on?" I asked for the third time. "I was hoping you could tell me," Serjeant Bull rumbled from the far side of the interview table. He sounded bored rather than irritated or amused. A retina, covering its surface, showed a montage of views of my confused arrival and interview with Queen Medea.

"But I don't *know*!" I rubbed my forehead. "All I can tell you is what happened to me. Which I've already done. Twice, now."

"Well, why don't you tell me again?" he asked. "Start with Taj Beacon, scholar, and your awakening in the arrivals hall."

The worst thing about being remanded in police custody is the uncertainty; the second worst is the boredom. (Fear and pain . . . I consider myself lucky: Argos is a relatively civilized kingdom for an authoritarian tyranny, and while Medea has numerous faults, encouraging a culture of excessive brutality among her staff is not one of them. In the sunlit, nutrient-rich upper waters of Shin-Tethys, it is all too easy for disgruntled subjects to vote with their fins. Consequently, those rulers who arbitrarily torture and mutilate people do not benefit from a thriving revenue base.)

Serjeant Bull had already taken me through my account of the events of the past year on two separate interview days—I assume they were days, for between interviews and meals my coral-walled cell had darkened—and I had told him more or less exactly the same story twice now, omitting only a few details that I deemed to be of no interest to his investigation; the communiqué from Andrea, Rudi's ownership of a slave chip (potentially a blackmailable lever over him while he was outside the safety of his vehicle's hull and one that I felt no need to expend prematurely), Rudi's suspicions of Deacon Dennett's intentions (hearsay) and so on. And so I continued, for the third time:

"I am a mendicant scholar, halfway through a five-subjective-year study pilgrimage to visit and work with a number of my colleagues. My distant sib Ana, a child of an earlier fork of my own lineage mater, is one of the professors I expected to study with. I believed I would find her teaching in one of the outer republics, but apparently, two years before I arrived at Taj Beacon, she accepted a teaching post here, in Shin-Tethys. While I was in transit, I gather she disappeared. My lineage mater would be angry with me if I left a sib, even a distant one, in trouble without making at least some attempt to find her, so I took the first available passage to come here. Along the way we were waylaid and audited by feral insurance underwriters, who told me that apparently the chapel I had taken a working passage with was engaged in questionable practices and that my sib was suspected by various parties of having been involved in some sort of skullduggery. *Now.* Can I point out that the record will show that *I wasn't even in this star system* when my sister went missing?"

Serjeant Bull sighed lugubriously. The gill slits in his neck vented slightly as he exhaled: "I believe you. Millions wouldn't. However, Professor Alizond, there is the matter of your wallet contents. And of your oddly configured second soul. If you wouldn't mind explaining again?"

I tried not to roll my eyes. "I am of a modestly wealthy lineage, and I am embarked on a course of travel and study that was expected to take decades of travel time and multiple interstellar transmissions to complete. Don't you think it would be rash of me to have set off on such a journey without a substantial amount of money on my person, much of it in long-term currency units that could be converted along the way to pay for my later transmission sectors? And as for my *highly suspicious* second chip, you *are* aware that my scholarly pilgrimage is a sabbatical activity, and when I am not sitting in a police interview room or traveling between universities, I am a researcher employed by a bank? As such, I am from time to time entrusted with custody of extremely confidential information—material that must be held as closely as my own soul. I should also like to note that banking is a relatively safe occupation: I am not in any significant physical danger from day to day. A single running backup of my soul-state is plenty under those circumstances."

"A banker." He tapped the tabletop, making an annotation in a script I was unable to recognize. "Can you discuss your job? Not any specific confidences, but in general outline?"

"In general outline? Hmm. Banking, you must understand, is primarily concerned with managing and avoiding risk. Most people think it's about debt, but debt is merely the starting point. If you wish to borrow money from a banker, the banker will want to know, first and foremost, whether you are likely to repay them. The profit from a loan must be offset against the risk of default or nonpayment: Only by making more loans that repay a profit than loans that end in default can a bank remain in business in the long term, unless it is a currency-issuing bank, in which case . . . but I digress. I do not work in the part of the bank that analyzes the risk posed by individuals. I am a scholar: I research the history of financial frauds, in order that my employers may develop procedures to guard against them. We have inherited a financial system thousands of years old, covering hundreds of star systems. The variety and range of scams and swindles and rackets and cons is endless, and different methods go in and out of fashion." I managed to summon up a tight-lipped smile: "My job is to invent mechanisms that prevent financial crime."

Sergeant Bull tapped the tabletop again. "So you say." His expression was morose. Three times round the block over two days, and we were back where we'd started. "So you say . . ." He paused. "Let me ask you a hypothetical question. Suppose—this is a question, not a promise—I were to arrange to release you without charge tomorrow, and with a temporary visitor's visa. What would you do?"

"Why"—I leaned back in the uncomfortably hard chair I had been provided with—"I'd look for Ana. To the best of my abilities, anyway, to see if she's left any sign of where she might have gone. Obviously, you and your colleagues have been searching for her for some time, but there's always a chance that as a sib descended from the same archetype, I might have some insight into her actions. Assuming that her disappearance was voluntary, of course."

"And if you found nothing?"

I had a strong sense that this hypothetical was not very hypothetical at all: "I came to Dojima System to study with her. I can't move on without being sure that she's"—the skeuomorphic swallow reflex kicked in: Saying *dead* was difficult—"before I continue on my pilgrimage. But if she's disappeared without sign, eventually I'll have to, have to . . ."

He nodded. Was that sympathy in his expression? Or just the understanding of a police officer evaluating a suspect and finding her behavior to be consistent with that of a grieving relative rather than a possible perpetrator?

"I understand," he said. Then: "I'll see what I can do." He rose to leave. "Wait here."

I waited. And waited. And then—

A long time ago—2686 years and fifty-three days in sidereal time, not accounting for relativistic effects—the starship *Atlantis* spread her vast and tenuous sail and her backers switched on the propulsion beams that would boost her up to cruise speed for a four-century flight.

Atlantis's destination was a hitherto-unvisited M-class red-dwarf star. Painstaking observation had detected a pair of wet gas giant planets with numerous moons, and at least two debris belts: not a first-rank example of prime real estate but good enough to justify the gamble. Four out of five starships usually survived to make starfall: 80 percent of the colonies they established took root eventually. *Atlantis* stood a better-than-usual chance of flourishing, for it had barely a parsec to travel, and its target was a compact system with plenty of sunlit asteroids to take root on—a type of system for which the colonization protocols were well understood.

Let me walk you through the history of Atlantis colony.

First, the construction and launch. Seventy years to organize and plan, to train the crew, build the vessel and its launch-support structures. Finally, it spreads its sail, and the giant beam stations in low solar orbit light up, blasting terawatts of power at it. Power that, received, can be focused on the billion tons of water ice and hydrogen slush that the ship carries for reaction mass. The starship accelerates slowly, initially at not much more than a hundredth of a gee; and it gets less power from the beam as the distance from the launch station increases. But it keeps accelerating for years, then decades, lightening as it expends reaction mass and gathering pace as it spirals out of the star system of its birth. After two years, it is speeding outward at stellar-escape velocity. At ten years, nothing from the inner star system stands a chance of catching up with it. When the launch beams shut down a century into the voyage, the starship is most of a light-year from home, racing into the interstellar gulf at three thousand kilometers per second: and it has discarded all but a fiftieth of its launch mass.

Many hazards can destroy a starship in flight. The environment it flies through is intensely hostile; at 1 percent of light speed, the ship's momentum effectively turns the cold hydrogen and helium atoms of the interstellar medium into hard radiation. A grain of ice with a mass of milligrams packs the impact energy of tons of high explosive. Other threats can kill a ship in flight: In one memorable incident, a starship flew through the radiation jet of a distant gamma-ray burster: Secondary activation effects reduced its crew to much the same condition as Lady Cybelle.

The *Atlantis*, however, survives its interstellar crossing. Thirty years out from its destination, the crew reassembles and configures its fusion reactors, and deploys the fast flyby probes that will race through the star system, mapping and exploring ahead of their arrival. For the last decades of the voyage, the starship brakes hard, burning its remaining fuel mass at a prodigious rate. The crew studies candidate asteroids with care, finally reaching a consensus on the target to make first landing on. When the year of arrival comes, the *Atlantis* that enters orbit is barely a shadow of the billion-ton behemoth that set out to cross the gulf. Two thousand bodies and ten times that number of archived souls ride a skeletal payload framework, less than ten thousand tons remaining, as it arrives at the fifty-kilometer carbonaceous rock that will become Atlantis Beacon.

Everything except danger is in short supply for the next nine standard years.

The colonists live aboard the half-cannibalized starship, working long shifts on the mining and harvesting teams. Foundries are unpacked; ore goes in, finished components come out, ready to be bolted into the scaffolding of larger forges and factories. The photovoltaic factory comes first, feeding energy into the nascent ecosystem. Then the digesters that will turn sunlight, water, and carbon-rich rock into something that mechanocytes can eat. A year on, the first airtight domes are assembled and covered in rubble to protect them from sunlight and cosmic radiation. The electronics group builds its zone-melting furnaces and lithography line. The propulsion group digs blast pits and begins fabricating high-impulse ion rockets. The survey group polishes their telescopes and begins to catalog rocks. And the banking, human resources, and interstellar communications groups begin to put together the tripod of specialties on which the future success of the colony depends.

Working around the clock, the communications team assembles its laser transmitter. Meanwhile, the bankers generate their system-level public key and start producing bitcoins, while the HR office identifies the most pressing skills shortages to afflict the new colony. Finally, as soon as the beacon laser is ready, the bankers prepare their prospectus for transmission to the nearest stars, announcing the existence of Atlantis

Bank and its ability to issue currency as surety against debts incurred by the colony.

Nine years on, the first new immigrants beam in to Atlantis Beacon in a stream of massively compressed data packets, ready to fill the vacancies advertised by the Ministry of Human Resources (and the bodies HR have prepared to house the new specialists). Some of them are predictable; structural engineers to build out the city-habs, taikonauts to crew the newly built tugs that will retrieve raw materials from other asteroids, environmental engineers and medics to keep the feedstock cycle stable and fix damage to bodies and minds. But among the first hundred arrivals there are some anomalies, specialties too recondite to find any obvious role in a new colony: scholars of the history of theoretical physics, natural philosophers, electrical engineers with experience of working on particle accelerators.

The founders of Atlantis colony have hit upon a unique and radical plan for paying off the new colony's debts: a scheme which has never been tried before, which can only work once and which might not work at all. But if it succeeds, nothing will ever be the same again—anywhere.

"Follow me," droned the police wasp, hovering in the open hatch of my cell.

I had been lying on the bunk with my eyes shut, chewing over memories and dispiritedly wondering how long they would hold me here, when the hatch opened abruptly. I stood, hesitantly, as the wasp drifted backward into the corridor beyond. There were other cells, some of them with noisy occupants, and hatches in the floor that led to watery holding pens. I stepped around them, following as directed, until the wasp stopped beside an open door.

"The inspector will see you now," it buzzed, then zipped back the way it had come. I ducked as it flew past my head, then looked round the side of the door.

"Come in, Ms. Alizond." The office had two occupants: my

interrogator, Serjeant Bull; and an ectomorphic person of no obvious gender, equipped with huge, somewhat limpid eyes which were currently half-obscured by goggles. Both wore the yellow-and-red motley uniform of the police service, but the thin person's outfit was adorned with metallic blue piping. The effect was quite eye-watering. "I am Inspector Schram. Serjeant Bull has been briefing me about you. He tells me that you would very much like to find your sib, Ana Graulle-90. Is that correct?"

"Er, yes." I nodded uncertainly. Something about the inspector made me nervous, mistrusting.

"I am pleased to inform you that we have confirmed your account of your arrival, and you are no longer under arrest. You are free to go. However, you should bear in mind that the disappearance of Ana Graulle-90 is under investigation by this department as a possible kidnapping or murder. Consequently, if you attempt to visit her residence, meet contacts, or examine her possessions, you may be interfering in a police investigation, which is an offense." The inspector's face crinkled in something that was not a smile. "Do you understand?"

"What? But! I can't— That is, yes, I understand, but . . ."

The inspector left me dangling for a couple of seconds before continuing: "Of course, there is an alternative to interfering in our investigation. If you were to voluntarily assist us with our inquiries, it is possible that we would be better able to locate your sib. What do you think?"

I saw at once the trap that the inspector had laid for me: What I didn't understand was *why* they were so keen to keep me from looking for Ana on my own. So I decided to play dumb. "That's an excellent idea! But she's been missing for over a year. And I'm no detective. Surely, I can't possibly turn up anything that your officers have missed?"

"That remains to be seen." Inspector Schram flashed that not-smile at me again. "You must have some ideas of where to start."

"There was an inquiry from a friend of hers—"

The inspector shook its head. "Sadly, that was us. In case you declined to answer an official inquiry from the police, you see."

"Oh." Crestfallen, I glanced away.

"There are some items I should like to ask you to identify," the inspector said. "Your cooperation might assist us in filling in some of the blanks." It held out a hand, flickering with the glow of an escrow agreement: "Shake, and I'll draft you as an external consultant on Serjeant Bull's cold-case investigation. Or don't, and you'll never know."

I gingerly took the inspector's hand but withheld my consent glands: "What exactly are the terms and conditions you want me to agree to?"

"You work for us. Everything you learn belongs to us. You do what we say. What else were you expecting?" The inspector could afford to be informal: Nobody sensible would want to break a work contract with the Royal Constabulary.

I swallowed. "What about a termination clause?"

"You can walk whenever you want. Or whenever we're through with you. Just give verbal notice. Now. Do you want in? Or should I assume that your declarations of concern for your sib are—"

I shook. *Now* the inspector's not-smile broadened.

"Witnessed," rumbled the Serjeant.

And that's how I was drafted by Medea's police.

A n hour later, I found myself standing in Ana's abandoned apartment, accompanied by the Serjeant and an odobenoid constable, confronting the chaos of a life interrupted.

But first, let me describe the layout of Nova Ploetsk, the interfacial port city that floats on and under the surface waters above the sunlit Kingdom of Argos.

Thirty degrees north of the equator, the Kingdom of Argos is an ill-defined zone of turbid water at the edge of the tropics. It hovers over a mantle hot spot, so its waters are warmed by convection currents from the Deep Below; north of it, the vast continental mats of leviathan grass drift in the sunlit upper waters. It extends across a diameter of perhaps ten thousand kilometers and occupies the surface waters to a depth of around two hundred meters.

Nova Ploetsk is one of the largest ports in Argos, a vast lenticular structure the upper surface of which projects just above the surface like a gigantic hydrozoan. Below it, tentacular hydrothermal power tubes dangle below the thermocline and extend their nozzles into the twilight zone, sucking up cold waters from kilometers below to cool the heat exchangers from the solar turbines that power the city. Refinery units in tank farms nestling against the underside of the city filter the deep water for rare isotopes, while around it floats the shipyard, ready to carry the mineral wealth it extracts away to customers elsewhere on Shin-Tethys—and ultimately elsewhere in the solar system. It is, by halves: an ugly industrial port city focused on resource extraction and a fleshpot servicing the needs of the miners and prospectors who roam the vast laminar ranges beneath Argos. Ugly, bustling, brash, noisy . . . and nevertheless the destination to which my sib Ana decided to relocate, in order to pursue her studies.

"We thought perhaps you might be able to help us make sense of this," said Serjeant Bull. He had sufficient grace to look apologetic.

"Well." I looked around. "I hardly know where to begin!"

The upper reaches of Nova Ploetsk are air-filled and dry; there is a membrane, some distance below the waterline, below which many of the chambers and avenues are partially flooded for the convenience of the hydromorph population, who had adapted themselves to the life aquatic to a sufficient degree that they had difficulty with land-based locomotion—people like the constable watching us from a moon pool in the center of Ana's living-room floor. The Serjeant and I traveled most of the way to the condominium where Ana had lived by vaporetto, for there were enough obligate land dwellers in the bigger cities to provide such a transport service with custom—but I digress. Ana's apartment was one of a block catering to amphibia, with wet-and-dry levels and underwater entrances. From outside, they formed a double row of cylinders perhaps eight meters high and six in diameter, rising from the side of a canal.

The bottommost level of Ana's apartment was a comfortably furnished lounge area surrounding the watery vestibule: We had to dive briefly into the undertunnel before we could enter. Luckily, despite my lack of gills, I was perfectly capable of submerging for the three minutes it took for the constable on duty to notice our arrival and open the hatch.

It was, I am sad to say, excessively spacious and furnished lavishly, in a manner most unbecoming for a scholar. I have communicated with Ana extensively over the years, both in writing and via imago dumps (like Andrea's missive). She had never struck me as being particularly preoccupied with superficialities or hedonistic indulgence. In fact, my impression of her was one of an austere mind, at her happiest when contemplating a long-forgotten archive of primary research material or when setting out the terms of reference for a years-long research program. But this was not the apartment of a contemplative introvert! From the deep blue cultivated-seagrass carpet to the hand-carved coral furniture and the emotionally responsive lighting, the giant retina screen stretched around the walls, and the horribly expensive cast-iron spiral staircase leading up to the next level, *nothing* about this apartment hinted at an academic disposition.

Which might be an unfair and slighting judgment on my part, for the paraphernalia associated with our study of the historiography of accounting practices require no more physical tools than a retina to grid out our spreadsheets and, additionally, a storage and numbers mill that might be no bigger than my little finger; but ferrous furniture on a water world is a high-maintenance headache, and Ana did not strike me as the sort of person to prioritize interior-design aesthetics over practicality.

"It's not like her," I said after approximately six seconds. "Are you *sure* this was Ana Graulle-90's apartment?" I knew the question was silly the moment the words left my mouth, but I had to ask.

"Ana Graulle-90 paid the rent here," Serjeant Bull explained patiently and, I can't help thinking, a little condescendingly. "She was routinely tracked entering and leaving—there's a koban in the crescent upstream of here—and on many days she took the same vaporetto service we arrived by to the National Archives, where she was conducting research into the history of blue smoker strikes in the deep wilds. She paid the bills: electricity, gas, and flotation."

"Oh." I glanced at Constable Walrus, then past him (or her) at a crystal display case full of knickknacks: blown-glass statuettes that glowed with a lambent fire beneath carefully positioned overhead spotlights, a reproduction of an ancient inkstone calligraphy set, a scale model of a starship, a case full of tiny, highly polished metal spoons. At the center of the display nestled a huge bivalve shell lined with nacre, a pearl the size of my thumb cradled in its heart. (A gene-mod abalone, I later discovered, an aquatic animal from Old Earth, heavily modified to survive in the waters of Shin-Tethys, with a little care and attention—some invertebrates had been able to survive in the wild, making this one of the most successful attempts at exporting terrestrial biota to other planets, and the principal reason the Church of the Fragile had bothered dispatching a chapel to this system.) "This isn't like her *at all*." I walked across the grass (which had grown somewhat unkempt in the absence of a manicurist-in-residence) and paused at the foot of the stairs. "May I?"

Serjeant Bull nodded lugubriously. "Take your time." A momentary pause. "Our forensic investigators finished recording here a year ago, but try not to damage or move anything unnecessarily."

I went upstairs after a couple of false starts—it had been ages since I last essayed a staircase in full gravity, and I kept missing the treads—and thrust my head even deeper into the zone of alienation that my missing sib had cast like a spell across her residence.

Like the ground floor, the upstairs level was circular. One third of it was given over to sanitary and sleeping arrangements, with a table and an unnecessarily large bed taking pride of place. The rest was barefloored, empty but for shelves occupying the entire height of the walls. The shelves were occupied by narrow boxes, perhaps five centimeters thick and thirty high; the narrow edges were outermost, scribbled on using a black marker. I pulled one of them out and examined it: It fell open in my hands, revealing that the outer panels concealed numerous internal sheets. I will confess it took me a while to recognize them as *books*. Books in the original meaning of the word, codices: stacks of flexible thin sheets covered in static impressions of writing—an archaic data-storage technology, heavy and unchanging—physically linked at one edge to provide sequential block-level access.

In all my years I don't think I'd ever seen so many physical books in one place. In the depths of prehistory, Fragile scholars relied on them for data, back when humanity was confined to a single planet: But they don't travel well. They're stupidly massive, almost impossible to edit or update once they've been manufactured (thus making them prone to error and obsolescence), and we got out of the habit of "printing" them even before large numbers of our ancestors first began to explore the original solar system. Just what was Ana (assuming it was she) doing with such a hoard of junk?

I shook my head and did a quick calculation. Assuming twenty per shelf, ten shelves from floor to ceiling, sixteen stacks . . . there must be thousands here! Over a ton of them! "Ludicrous," I mumbled to myself. Why were they here? And where had Ana gotten the things from in the first place? While books weren't entirely preposterous on a planetary surface with a carbon-rich biosphere to supply the raw materials—although I had my doubts about their utility underwater—nobody in their right mind would want them aboard any kind of spacegoing vehicle.

I turned my eyes to the ceiling. And blinked. The stairs terminated here, and the roof was only just out of arm's reach above me. But . . . *eight meters*? I walked back to the stairs. "Excuse me?" I called.

"Yes?"

"Is there anything above this level? I mean, another floor?"

"Another . . . ?" I heard Bull's heavy tread on the steps. Looking at the book I was holding, I rubbed one of the open sheets—a page. It was covered in columns of heavy, immobile black lettering and numbers. The font was execrably wobbly and uneven, and there were numerous wavering strikethroughs and overprints, almost as if someone had tried to create a parody of a spreadsheet by hand. On impulse, I ran a slightly damp finger down a column of figures. They smeared, like a retina in proximity to a strong magnetic field, and when I rubbed my finger in the opposite direction they smeared even more, into near illegibility. More questions: How had she gotten all these books into this apartment, if they were so easily damaged by water? And again: *Why?*

Bull arrived. "What's that you've got?" he asked.

"A book." I peered at it, trying to read what I'd found. It looks like . . . yes, there was a lack of cross-references and icons, not to mention keys, but the columns made sense if I squinted at them and assumed they were the raw data content of a double-entry ledger. Minus the macros and active content, of course. "It looks like someone was keeping accounts on, what's the stuff called, *paper*." I glanced up at the ceiling: It appeared to be a seamless expanse, sky blue and glowing with artificial daylight. "Using a pigment, uh, ink, that dissolves in water." I glanced down at the floor, then over toward the trapdoor beside the stairwell opening. I thought about the living space below it, the moon pool opening onto the vestibule exit, and a tentative hypothesis suggested itself to me. "There's no way in or out of here that doesn't go through water, is there?"

"Give that here." Bull reached for the book, and I passed it to him; there were plenty more on the shelves.

"Be careful not to get it wet," I said. "Did you or any of the other investigators read these?"

"I'll have to check the case web before I can answer that." Bull went walleyed for a moment, communing with his memory palace. "Ah, yes and no. They were noted as an unusual collection of artifacts, and so one of the detectives took a look at them—examined a representative sample, exterior and interior, dusted for codon samples, checked isotope ratios to identify the planet of origin, that sort of thing. There was nothing obviously anomalous about them, and a distributed net search for some random samples of the content didn't throw anything up, so the case committee concluded that Ana Graulle-90 was merely a collector of such things. A historian of accountancy practices collects archaic ledgers, yes?" He focused on me abruptly. "Do you disagree?"

"Well." I considered my next words carefully. "First, is there anything above the ceiling?"

"Let me see." Serjeant Bull's uniform might be motley, but his belt carried numerous pouches. From one of these he pulled a compact device that he held to his eyes as he studied the underside of the roof. "Odd. It's opaque."

"Opaque?" I asked: "What do you mean?"

He held the device toward me, and I saw that it had a compact screen built into a visor, with some sort of sensor on the outside. "Magic police goggles: They're a terahertz imager. You use it to see through nonconductive surfaces. Water and metals reflect terahertz radiation, so they show up. But the ceiling is opaque."

"So if Ana or whoever lived here"—he looked at me narrowly—"wanted a secret level that the police would be unable to find . . . ?"

"These condos are recycled fuel tanks, their outer walls are sheet steel." Serjeant Bull reached up and rapped on the ceiling. "Which"—he paused—"is very interesting, because there should be at least three meters of air above our heads. Hmm."

"It *might* be a false ceiling," I equivocated. "There might not be anything suspicious about it."

"But you don't think so." Serjeant Bull increasingly struck me as one of those thinkers who is neither fast nor shallow: not one to rapidly and incisively solve problems on the fly but not likely to miss anything either, once he had time to give the issue at hand due consideration. "And your reaction downstairs was that you couldn't imagine your sib living here. Why is that?"

"We—" I gathered my thoughts. "I did not know her *particularly* well, but we shared a common ancestor and we have corresponded, over the decades. The living space downstairs is *tasteless*. It's full of pointless junk. Serjeant, Ana grew up aboard a generation ship and lived by preference in deep-space habs, out in the cold yonder. Which is not to say that she might not have harbored a secret fetish for deadweight and finally felt free to indulge it once she had the opportunity, but that stuff is *massive*. And mass *costs*." I swallowed. "And now this . . . this doesn't figure. None of it. Not the bed, not the books. It's just not like something one of us would do! Especially the books, unless . . ."

I reached over to the nearest shelf and took another bound volume. Opened it. More tallies marching down the page, endlessly, totaled at the bottom and carried overleaf in wobbly lettering. Smeary ink. The description field didn't help much: They were all ten-digit alphanumerics. I would need an inventory table to make sense of it. But the quantities and prices all added up, that much I could see. "These are account ledgers. There must be a, what do you call it, a *pen* somewhere near here." I looked over at the table. There was a chair beside it, as one might expect. "She was keeping books for somebody, by hand, using *these* books rather than a calculator or any other kind of publicly accessible memory. A truly ancient method, but very robust! Why, if she removed her soul chips while she worked, there might be no record whatsoever of what was happening here that could be detected by remote searchers. Unless you hooked her up to a debugger and questioned her"—I shivered— "you'd get nothing."

Serjeant Bull looked around at the room, clearly seeing it in a new light. "You say the pigment dissolves in water. Hmm. And this paper: waterproof, yes or no?"

"No." I racked my brains, thinking back to an ancient history class: "It dissolves in water. And the only way in or out of here is through a wet lock. Someone who was sent to grab the books and didn't know what precautions to take to protect them would ruin them completely in the process, destroying the accounts." I looked up at the ceiling again. "That trapdoor by the staircase. Did anyone try lowering it— *Wait, don't!*"

Bull stopped in midstride. "Why? What do you think would happen?" he asked mildly.

"There's something wrong with this whole setup," I began. "The pigment Ana—or whoever—used in these books. Did anyone send a sample for analysis? To find out where it came from?" My head was spinning, correlating disconnected data. Water-soluble ink, used to make marks on fibrous water-absorbent paper. A cylindrical dwelling, the ledgers stored upstairs. Trapdoor below, opaque false ceiling above. Only way in and out via a water lock underneath. "It's all about the books. If you take them out via the front door, the ink will dissolve. And you can't get at what's in them via any kind of search algorithm. This whole room was meant to be a secret, wasn't it? Hidden in full view and disguised as a dwelling. Someone hired Ana to keep books for them, and whatever they were accounting for, it had to stay invisible and out of sight." I was thinking furiously. "But suppose . . . suppose they didn't know about Ana's other connections? Our correspondence, or the fact that she was expecting me to arrive? Maybe they hired her to do the job without telling her what it was, first."

"You are suggesting that your sib was engaged to work on a secret bookkeeping program, yes?" Serjeant Bull said slowly. "And her employer panicked when they learned of your impending arrival and k— removed her. Is that what you think? But then why did they leave these books, if they were both secret and valuable enough to justify removing Ana Graulle-90?"

"I don't know. Maybe they were interrupted, or forced to run, before they could destroy them. They're certainly bulky. Or maybe they— whoever removed her—didn't realize what they were; if she was working in secrecy, and her employer sent thugs to take her, they might have assumed she was keeping everything on a soul chip. Or maybe they learned I was coming and decided to remove her before she told me whatever she was doing." I shook my head, unreasoningly upset: Serjeant Bull was barely going through the motions of trying to conceal from me the fact that he and his colleagues thought Ana was dead. And after a year of her absence, how could I gainsay them? "The ink. And the paper. Where do they come from?"

This time Serjeant Bull was quiet for longer. I was about to repeat my question when he looked at me. "The leaves are made from bleached and macerated fibers extracted from various species of leviathan grass, presumably harvested nearby and processed into, um, *paper*. Traces of leviathan grass were found in the feedstock processor by the dining niche downstairs, and a tub of the stuff was present in the vestibule, so it was assumed that Graulle-90 was manufacturing the material as she needed it. There is a household fabricator and some unidentified mechanical parts that had been manufactured in it were found nearby, so perhaps those were part of her ledger factory. The pigment was more of a puzzle. A forensic tech finally determined that there was microscopic tissue debris in it and extracted a genome sequence; it is a naturally occurring substance extracted from the ink sacs of feral sepiidians—another of the invertebrates from Old Earth that adapted to life in the upper waters here. The stuff is called *sepia*, and it has a long history as a pigment used for dying this paper stuff."

"Did the investigators find any containers of it here? Or pens, brushes, styli? Other writing implements?"

"Oddly, no." Bull seemed to come to a decision. "Thank you, Ms. Alizond. You have been most useful, and we must now continue this investigation without you. We will need to remove these *books* to safe-keeping as evidence before we probe whatever is above the false ceiling. Such as, perhaps, a water tank? Is that what you think? Primed to drench these shelves of books, rendering them useless?" I nodded. "It's a little excessive, but I have heard of stranger things." He looked around. "So this is a secret archive, maintained by hand in an archaic code and designed to be hard to detect and easy to destroy, eh?" He looked at me. "You'd better go now; I'll call you when I need you again. Please do not speak of anything you have seen here. It would be unfortunate to have to charge you with interfering with an investigation."

I shivered. "Thanks, but no thanks." Whoever Ana had been working for—and I was still convinced that this was not where she'd been living—news of my impending arrival had caused them to kidnap or kill her. I began to wonder if perhaps the safest thing for me to do wouldn't be to depart Shin-Tethys as soon as possible. Helping out a sib in their time of need might be the done thing, but putting my own life on the line was another matter entirely. And so as I headed for the stairs, I resolved to do what I could to help the Serjeant's continued inquiries from the safest possible distance . . . preferably on another planetary body.

Recidivision

There is a time for the prudent traveler to give the appearance of being of no great means; and there's a time when the prudent traveler should book themselves into the most discreet and securely guarded guesthouse they can afford, to hire bodyguards, and to ignore the expense.

I decided that now was the latter time. So I left Ana's rented pod and took myself directly to the Grand Imperial Hotel Ariel, where I marched up to the concierge pool, and said: "Hello, I would like you to arrange an escort to take me to the nearest bureau de change, please? And then some assistance opening a local bank account, checking into the best available suite you've got, and hiring a bodyguard."

The concierge surfaced briefly, to blink a saucer-sized eye at me. "Excuse me," buzzed the transducer at the poolside: "Am I to understand you would like to check in?"

"Yes," I said patiently, "but in order to pay you, I will first need to liquidate some slow money. I'm a little short on the fast stuff right now." Which was entirely true—Medea's kingdom ran on its own evanescent scrip, backed by fiat royalty, and Rudi hadn't exactly gone out of his way to fork out the salary he claimed to owe me before we climbed into that capsule. "I believe there is a branch of SystemBank Taj in this town?"

A brief flurry of underwater activity made the concierge pool heave and splash: A coil of thick, muscular, sucker-lined flesh broke the surface briefly. I took a nervous step backward across the slippery tile mosaic as the transducer buzzed again. "If you would care to check in first, guest services would be happy to assist you with your requirements. Billing can be deferred for up to one day, subject to credit checks." A dactylus with disturbingly fingerlike palps flopped over the edge of the pool and twitched toward me. "Please consent to handshake . . ."

I extended my hand to the teuthidian concierge, palm to suckers, exchanging identity tokens with him. His skin was cold and rugose, clammy with an undertaste of static electricity. Despite his superficial resemblance to a giant squid from Old Earth, he was no less human than I; his body was assembled from mechanocytes to a design pattern better suited for life in the hydrosphere of Shin-Tethys, but the brain—modulo some cunning somatic translation layers—was largely unchanged. "I am Krina Buchhaltung Historiker Alizond-114," I said. "I would like to rent the use of your facilities for not less than ten days, including full personal security service. I also need full identity verification at all times—I have a stalker. And I need assistance in organizing a fund transfer via System-Bank Taj."

"We can organize that for you." The concierge—a discreet sign by the transducer informed me that I was welcome to call him Chen—floated close to the surface, his skin flickering between violet lines and yellow spots. "I will ask the bank to send a clerk over to your suite. Which is being prepared now; it will be ready in a few minutes. For the bank's information, in confidence, what sort of financial instrument are you intending to convert?"

I kept my face still. "One New California dollar. Hitherto unbroken."

The concierge sank to the bottom of his pond, tentacles flashing crimson: Evidently this was the manner in which giant squid demonstrated their embarrassment, or at least a double take. "Excuse me. Did you say you want to convert one New California slow dollar?"

"Yes, I did."

"Then please accept my apologies. Our head of security will be with you shortly: Meanwhile, the Grand Imperial Hotel Ariel is pleased to upgrade you to the Grand Imperial Suite at no extra cost, if that will be satisfactory?"

The rest of the day passed in something of a blur.

The Grand Imperial Suite—on the lowermost subsurface deck of the hotel—was suitably impressive, with both dry and wet accommodation, its own controlled entrance, and a sufficiency of rooms and passages that I could easily have become lost in it if I had not first asked for a map upload. The head of hotel security was, in her own person, also suitably impressive: a former colleague of the police inspector, now working to ensure that the hotel's more illustrious patrons would encounter no untoward embarrassments during their stay. And the SystemBank was indeed more than willing to send a branch manager (not a mere clerk) to assist me in negotiating the sale of one of my carefully hoarded dollars. This latter process took some time (it is necessary first to countersign the dollar with a checksum derived from one's soul, then arrange for a formal transfer of title notice to be transmitted to the beacon station for onward confirmation by way of the issuing bank—which in the case of New California was more than twenty light-years away). As I anticipated, the conversion rate on offer for a negotiated transfer was little short of usury—I lost nearly 90 percent of the value of the dollar in fees and discounted interest and insurance policies—but left me with the best part of a million Argos Riyals in hot, fast, anonymous cash, most of it sitting in SystemBank Taj's accounts for now.

I hated having to do this but could see no alternative. In all probability, Ana had been abducted and slain by a hideous crime syndicate or some other nightmarish stupidity. My mission to retrieve her was a complete and utter failure, and my life would probably be in danger if I stayed here. Furthermore, my stalker from the chapel would be arriving shortly as that vehicle entered orbit. So I must look to my personal safety, regardless of the expense, and it is easier to buy safety if one is a prominent foreign millionaire than an anonymous local pauper.

My plan was to hide here for a while—no point in not giving Inspector Schram the benefit of the doubt, and an opportunity to make whatever use they could of my assistance—but eventually I would have to leave. And I had every intention of chartering a private yacht and hightailing it to Taj Beacon, there to beam out-system. Whether to Shin-Kyoto to continue my pilgrimage—pretending to be unaware of my lineage mater's disapproval, waiting for me back home—or to pick another destination at random, I had not yet decided. It's the sort of decision I have never been good at making.

Having reduced my assets by a not-insubstantial amount, and having determined to stay here for at least ten days, I set about spending some more money. My shipboard free-fall suit was both elderly and unfashionable: Moreover, it was far from waterproof and had become embarrassingly moist over the past day. A faint aroma clung to it, and I feared that it was beginning to degrade. So with the concierge desk's help I arranged for a visit from a tailor—one suitably cleared by the hotel-security staff—and commissioned a brace of wet and dry suits.

Other needs were less easily taken care of. "I need to consult a body shop," I told the concierge. "One who specializes in adapting visiting land dwellers for subsurface life." Not because I planned to spend any great time underwater but because if I should find myself in such a situation, I would be in considerable trouble: my gas exchangers—lungs, in Fragile terminology—were not designed to extract dissolved oxygen from water, and I only held a couple of hours in reserve. Nor were my fingers and toes appropriately webbed for mobility, and my auditory equipment and attitude sensors would need adjusting. (Forget venturing below the two-hundred-meter line; that would require more drastic, invasive upgrades to my 'cytes' programming. Not to mention replacing my legs with a tail: and, as I told the travel agent on Taj Beacon, I am unaccountably attached to my bipedalism.)

"We can arrange for you to have a visit from the hotel doctor," said the concierge. "However, it will not be possible for you to receive extensive modifications without visiting an external clinic. We can arrange security for such a visit, but I believe we will require advance notification, and additional charges may apply."

"That's acceptable." I waved it off. "If you can send the doctor up—"

"Excuse me."

"I beg your pardon?" I feared I had missed the concierge's words.

"A visitor in reception is asking if they can see you, Ms. Alizond. They identify themselves as Count Rudolf Crimson-50. They are unaccompanied. Would you like us to pass on a message or indicate that you are not to be disturbed?"

"No! Wait!" I clutched my head. "He's on his own? Send him up here. Wait, check him for weapons first? No, he's not stupid enough to— Wait, do you have a conference room available? If so, send him there. I'll meet him, then see the doctor afterward."

Rudi was waiting for me in a small conference room two levels below the lobby, unaccompanied and clearly unarmed, just as the concierge had indicated. He looked smaller and somehow less threatening under these changed circumstances: His wing membranes drooped heavily in the planetary gravity, and his fur formed bedraggled tufts. But his gaze was as sharp as ever, and his manner as controlled as if he were still in control of the board of his own vehicle.

"Ah, Krina." He grinned at me, baring sharp incisors. "Thank you for making room for me in your doubtless busy timetable: We've been combing the city for you for days! We were extraordinarily worried, you know. Out of curiosity, may I ask how you evaded me at the port offices? And why?"

"You'd have to ask Her Majesty. It wasn't intentional on my part, I assure you."

"Her *Majesty*?" His voice rose to a squeak: "What does she have to do with this?" I could almost believe that Rudi *was* concerned for my safety. His sarcastic, abrasive exterior disguised a sentimental streak, as I had discovered over the past year. I would have found it cute if I had not been so obviously in his debt, or under his power. But now the tables were turned. I dropped into one of the chairs positioned to either side of the window. It looked out onto the sunlit subsurface, a rippling silver ceiling just above our heads that was toning toward emerald in the near distance. Occasional human or vehicular traffic drifted past, crossing the wide-open well that separated the hotel's outer wall from the other dangling tentacles of the floating city core. "I followed you and Dent into immigration and was promptly hauled up in front of her and arrested," I told him. "Was it your doing?"

"Eh? No! Absolutely not." Rudi managed to look guilty and worried simultaneously. "What did you tell them?"

"They seemed to be interested in Ana's disappearance. I believe I'm not allowed to say any more. There is a police investigation in progress. They let me go after I told them everything I knew—and after giving me a warning about not interfering in a criminal investigation." I shivered slightly.

"The investigators think she was abducted or killed?" Rudi stared at me in unconcealed dismay. "I had hoped—" His expression of frustration involved complex nose-wrinkling and ear-twitching—"for something better. Feh. Abducted or killed, and they don't even know which." Another edgy twitch. "Feh."

"It's all right for *you*," I pointed out. "I've lost a close relative!" And my six-month study collaborator. Not to mention the person to whom I was supposed to be delivering—but I wasn't supposed to even think about that. The less remembered the better. "You're just out by one insurance policy!"

Rudi hissed at me. "It was a very *expensive* policy." For a moment, I saw a flash of anger, and I recoiled: He becalmed himself almost immediately. "We sold it to her for little more than goodwill, Krina.

Because—I believe it's safe to tell you this—I very much wanted her to succeed in uncovering her treasure trove."

I gaped at him. "Her what?"

Rudi cocked his head to his left and stared at me. "Come, now! Have you forgotten that she has lived in Dojima System for many years?" I shook my head. "And can you consider the possibility that she might have undertaken consultancy work, on the side, for various enterprises? Including, dare I say it, the Permanent Crimson?" I paused for a moment, then nodded. "I've met Ana," he said, before archly adding: "I probably know her better than you do." He tilted his head to the right. "You're very similar in some ways, you know."

"What!" I glared as I tried to recover my poise. "What did she tell you?"

"Quite a lot, once I gained her trust. She told me about your upbringing, and your mother. She told me about your shared interest in retrieving and rolling back lost slow money transfers. She told me about your interest in, ah, a certain long-term project investigating what really happened in Atlantis System." All mannerisms fled; his expression achieved an impressive level of impassivity.

"What did *you* tell *her* to get her to tell you all that?"

In truth I only asked him because I wanted to keep him off-balance and talking, but Rudi seemed to take it as a legitimate inquiry.

"I told her about a banking scandal from a very long time ago. Ivar Trask-1, a founder of Dojima SystemBank at Taj Beacon, who went missing, carrying one end of a transfer of a huge quantity of slow dollars that Ana seemed to think could be traced back . . . to Atlantis."

Oh snap, I thought, feeling a sinking sensation at my core. "And what did you tell her about this scandal?"

"Everything I had on file. At which point, for some reason, she decided it was a good idea to try to track down whatever happened to master Trask. I told her it was probably impossible, that he had disappeared centuries ago somewhere in the wild waters of Shin-Tethys, and there had been numerous searches at the time, but she was peculiarly insistent. Refusing to be deterred, she sought to find work here as a plausible explanation for her presence. The life insurance policy"—he folded and refolded his wings about himself agitatedly—"will cover her restoration from a decade-old soul dump, and a ticket out-system. I may, perhaps, have overstated its value: I am more drawn by curiosity as to what she found that caused various parties to make her disappear." Was that a faintly guilty expression I read into his foxy muzzle?

I was still having trouble admitting it to myself: My sib had come here in pursuit of the evidence we so sorely needed but had been drawn into some sort of very shady operation and had clearly been made to disappear by its owners—probably permanently. I took a deep breath. "I don't think I can achieve anything more here. If anyone can find her, it's Medea's police. I don't think *you* can achieve anything useful, either. Let's be honest: You hoped she was going to retrieve part of a certain uncommitted transaction, and you wanted to be in on it yourself. But I can tell you, if she *was* entangled with a chunk of the, what we've been calling the Atlantis Carnet, it's beyond our reach. She's been kidnapped or killed, and either her kidnappers or the Queen have their hands on anything she had. I have no idea who her abductors are, and I submit that neither you nor I are in a position to hold Her Majesty to account. So I intend to cut my losses and run—unless something turns up in the next few days. And when I say run, I mean I intend to leave Dojima System completely, cut short my pilgrimage, and go directly home." I attempted a bright smile, but I don't think he was fooled by it. "I believe she is dead. Thanks to meddling treasure hunters *like yourself.*"

I found I was on my feet again, glaring at him, despite a faint sense of embarrassment at accusing him so bluntly. Rudi, to his credit, looked abashed. "I'm very sorry," he said. "More sorry than you imagine, perhaps." He paused uncomfortably before continuing. "I believe I also owe you some back wages. Should I understand that you do not want to extend our arrangement?" He glanced around the room: "I assume you have found some alternative source of funding."

"You understand correctly. As for the wages, I was planning to invoice you."

"Oh, that won't be necessary." He held out one hand, glowing green: "If you would care to shake?"

We shook hands, and I blinked: The amount he'd transferred was rather larger than I'd expected. "Come now, Ms. Alizond," he said. "Do you really think I'm stupid enough to pay a professor an unskilled ship-hand's salary?" His incisors briefly revealed themselves again: "I believe in fair dealing. If you should ever find yourself in need of a privateer for hire, you'll know who to call. Good-bye!" He shuffled toward the door and let himself out.

I shook my head and checked at his deposit. He wasn't joking about having paid me a professorial salary for the year I'd spent aboard his ship. If I'd known he intended to, I might not have converted that slow dollar. But on the other hand, he hadn't paid me until he knew I had an alternative source of funding: Perhaps he only did it in order to cultivate my goodwill?

Still shaking my head, I started toward my suite. It had been a long and disturbing day, and I could feel my mood dropping. My arrival in Dojima System appeared to have triggered a feeding frenzy among grave-robbing treasure hunters and opportunists. If Andrea was to be believed, the intrigue had its poisoned roots in a power play back home, and it had followed me all the way to the stars, waiting to catch up. Ana was gone, the entire primary purpose of my pilgrimage was wrecked, and with a stalker trailing me, I really needed to think about chartering a yacht and making a course back to Taj Beacon, and meanwhile reconsider my entire future. (If there was less of a security issue, I'd simply upload myself from here and relay via the beacon, but the risk of, shall we say, nonaccidental data corruption was significant. In contrast, physical space vehicles are much harder to intercept than a helpless upload transmission.)

Thinking these gloomy thoughts, I made my way to the elevators and dropped toward my suite. Security doors opened, recognizing me: Finally,

I reached my destination. Here, the outer door required a physical hand-shake to check my identity. I turned the door handle and pushed, then froze.

"Good afternoon," said the fellow on the sofa in the lobby, rising. "You requested medical services?"

I relaxed. "Yes," I said. "You're the hotel doctor?" He nodded. And indeed he looked the part: a modified surface dweller, with just the package of extras I needed on display everywhere from his hands to the discreet fringe of gills at his throat. "I need to arrange for some phenotype modifications." The door closed behind me as I continued: "Finger and toe membranes, better oxygen retention, and depth tolerance. Nothing fancy. I was told you could order the necessary design templates—"

"Oh, absolutely," he reassured me. "So you're wanting a basic package of hydrosphere modifications suitable for a land dweller visiting the upper waters, is that right?"

"Yes, that's what I'm after," I confirmed.

"Good. I work with a couple of local suppliers; if you'd like to sit down and plug in this diagnostic cable, I can dump your body's structural layout and ask them to tender—"

I sat obediently and accepted the fiber-optic cable. "Where does this go?" I asked, holding up the free end.

"Right here. If you'll allow me—" I nodded, letting him stab the cable into my medical port. Then everything suddenly went away.

Every interstellar colony is founded on a Ponzi scheme; but the architects of Atlantis were the first to make this principle explicit.

Normally, the founders of a new colony are motivated by the opportunity to be among the earliest settlers and shareholders; the earlier you get there, the more real estate and energy you can lay your hands on. But to be able to enjoy the fruits of your land grab, you require a functioning, self-sustaining civilization. It's entirely possible to lay claim to a gas giant planet all by yourself, but what do you do with it thereafter? There's the rub. Civilization is complicated and expensive and surprisingly difficult to transplant to a new star system, even for such as we—never mind our Fragile predecessors who couldn't survive even a little bit of hard vacuum and ionizing radiation. Hence the incentive for founders to go into debt if necessary, to hire in the extra workers it takes to expand from a couple of hardscrabble tents on an asteroid into an interplanetary civilization in only a couple of hundred years.

And this explains the incentive to launch further colonies in turn, so that they can go into debt borrowing labor from you in return for slow dollars which you can use to pay off your own founders' debt.

But why don't we, the founders of Atlantis thought, *try to come up with a better, faster way to collapse our foundational debt?*

(This is inference. I do not know for sure what was going through their minds: This is purely my own highly speculative reconstruction of what happened roughly two thousand years ago. Let me emphasize this: *Nobody now living knows for sure.*)

Paying off the founders' debt can take centuries, and the grinding investment of resources required to build and launch starships. The new colony may go into debt to the tune of hundreds of thousands or even millions of slow dollars drawn on the banks of their neighbors. How can this debt be made to go away?

One way to do it is to arrange a Jubilee—a global remission of all debt. But it takes pressing circumstances to impose such a thing on an open-ended trading network. Investors tend to dislike having their creditors evaporate like mist for some reason. You can make a Jubilee work in a closed system, by decree, but because of the debt-driven pattern of expansion of interstellar colonization, it's almost impossible for everyone to get out of debt simultaneously. Some utopians campaign for a galactic Jubilee; in my opinion, they might get one sometime after the stelliferous era gutters to a darkening end, and the lights go out throughout the universe.

On a smaller scale, a really well-established colony system with a good economy and a stable sun might aim for autarky, the practice of total isolationism and autonomy. In effect, they could declare a local Jubilee. Cut the interstellar communications links, and nobody will be able to call in their debts—not by any reasonable means, anyway. (Sending a starship to demand repayment is a ludicrous idea.) However, attempts at autarky generally founder when there is a change of governance; the old oligarchs ossify or die, or the young demand their imported entertainments, or unforeseen new circumstances generate demand for hitherto-unneeded skills that can most easily be imported, or, or, or. Autarky is unstable. A system rich enough to make a serious play for autarky is probably so rich that it has already paid off its foundational debt.

And that more or less exhausts the *legal* ways of escaping a system debt.

Which leaves fraud. It is almost impossible to fake the establishment of an interstellar bank that issues slow money. For the money to be recognized as such, the issuing bank must satisfy its peers in two or more neighboring star systems that it's really there. This is a straightforward process—point telescope at newly colonized star system, look for laser light—so it is *very* hard to imagine a conspiracy duping two or more systembanks in perfect synchrony, even with a timetable of false transmissions prearranged years in advance. It *has* been tried a couple of times, but it fails as soon as one of the duped banks tries to get the "new" bank to sign a slow dollar received from another dupe. You can't defraud the speed of light.

But the speed of light offers another opportunity to escape a slow money debt. If a faster-than-light drive really *did* exist, then the whole slow economy of settled space would be jeopardized. All the equity locked up in light-speed transmissions could be short-circuited; there would be no further need for slow money. Confidence in slow money would collapse, and with it, the value of any debt denominated in the old slow currency. It would, *de facto*, create the circumstances for a global Jubilee—by changing the rules and destroying the old economy.

It is my belief that the founders of Atlantis knew this full well, and moreover knew that everybody else was aware of it: And so they willfully decided to use this global assumption as a lever to move the universe.

First, they went through the usual growing pains of a new colony, importing labor and knowledge and skills and incurring debt.

Then they imported a bunch of natural philosophers and historians and scholars and established, very publicly, a gigantic and diverse research enterprise. They went further into debt, issuing bonds denominated in slow money to fund the expansion and operations of their Academy for High Energy Research. In the course of which they cautiously admitted that, yes, developing a faster-than-light space drive was a major systemwide economic goal, to which *all* else was subordinate.

Needless to say, this caused much speculation and analysis throughout the whole of settled space: Opinions ranged from mirth and skepticism through to genuine alarm, not to mention triggering attempts at scientific espionage (and, it is rumored, sabotage). Financial markets became jittery, and sharp-witted fast folk turned a profit by designing hedges against the impending collapse of the slow money–based trade system. There was actually a drop in the frequency of colony starship launches for the first time in millennia, as everyone postponed their plans in order to wait and see.

Then, after spending half a century on what an earlier age would have described as a war footing, on the eve of a widely publicized announcement of some importance . . . Atlantis went dark.

Depth Charge

I am not the most perceptive person with respect to threats against my safety.

Because I had asked the concierge to arrange for my security and to have the hotel doctor attend to my needs, I naturally assumed that the presence of a doctor-shaped individual in my suite was entirely legitimate: and not, for example, a sign that the hotel's security protocols had been breached.

Bad mistake, Krina.

In the past year I had acquired more experience of being kidnapped and deceived than the rest of my lineage had managed over a period of several centuries. But I freely admit that what happened after I unwittingly gave the false doctor access to my morphological-control firmware was probably the most drastic of all my abductions.

At the time, I didn't know anything. I was switched off, effectively as dead as a downloaded soul dump in transit between star systems. Which was, when I revisit the incident with full hindsight enabled, a mercy.

An invisible observer would have seen the "hotel doctor" hand me a fine cable, then wait for me to sit down and attach it to the nape of my neck. At which point I would have fallen over, limp as a hank of leviathan grass on dry land. The doctor stood, walked across the suite to an inconspicuous service hatch, and opened it, then pulled out a body-sized cargo cylinder. Into the cargo cylinder I went, then into the service hatch and out of the hotel.

Somewhere else and somewhen later, the "hotel doctor" and their accomplices retrieved me. I can't describe the location, only infer that it was probably deeper than the hotel, and in a cheaper neighborhood populated by fly-by-night businesses and anonymous warehouses. There would have been cassettes of unassimilated mechanocytes to hand, seething and squabbling in search of a body to join. A power supply and liquid feedstock. There would have been a vivisection slab. The doctor and his accomplices would have lifted my body onto the slab and shackled it in place before they took up their scalpels and sketched lines on my skin, then my 'cytes to fissure to either side.

What I'd intended to buy was a set of minor body-mods that would make life in the sunlit surface waters easier for the remainder of my stay: After all, although I hoped to linger in Nova Ploetsk no longer than a few tens of days, experience had taught me that orbital dynamics paid no heed to my travel preferences. I might be stuck here for some time, and webbed fingers and toes, enhanced oxygen storage capacity, and an enhanced orientation sense all seemed to make sense.

But my abductors were working at the orders of someone who had other plans for me. They went to work on my body, mutilating and re-sculpting it to fit a design template they'd been given and, on a smaller scale, broadcasting a series of radical firmware updates to my 'cytes, equipping them to function in the abyssal depths.

First they broke my feet, removed most of the fine bones, and replaced them with radiating weblike fins. Then they split the fleshy inner surface of my legs apart and added shims of new flesh, fusing muscle masses back together to form a seamless, tapering trunk. My pelvic girdle they resectioned, and my hip joints they completely replaced: Buttocks disappeared. Walking upright would be impossible in my new form.

My skin chromatophores adopted new and oddly toothlike shapes, overlapping, scaly, and iridescent. I was streamlined everywhere, curved and polished to reduce drag.

Internal organs changed, too. Countercurrent recyclers and feedstock processors were moved; ducts and peristaltic tubes and support webbing were rearranged to make better use of the space between my narrowed hips and my rib cage. My gas-exchange lungs they replaced completely, installing new ones that still worked but that could be sealed off from my throat and collapsed safely under extreme pressure, then reinflated subsequently. They added gills behind cunningly concealed flaps in my neck and upper thorax. They added webbing between my fingers and acoustic sensory lines along my flanks.

Then they broke my face.

We are not Fragile, but our minds are based on an emulation of the Fragile neuroanatomy, and the Fragile recognize each other by facial appearance. It underlies our sense of identity at a very deep level, so that damage-induced changes to facial structure cause considerable psychological distress. My abductors changed me, editing my face so that at the end of the process my new form was a barely recognizable parody of Krina.

Some of the changes were subtle or invisible to me. They resculpted my skull for better hydrodynamic flow. Made subtle changes to hair and skin texture. But other changes were more noticeable. A flatter, smaller button nose with internal pressure flaps to seal it. Point-tipped ears that folded back flush against the sides of my skull. And as for my eyes—

There is pitifully little light in the Hadean depths of the world-ocean. What light exists is mostly the product of bioluminescent processes, or the dreaded blue smokers that fission and boil as they rise from the ice-clad core of the world. To trap this light, small, jelly-filled capsules are insufficient. And so my abductors broke my facial bones apart, peeled out my cheeks, and resculpted the orbits of my eyes. Then they deglobed me, opened up my eyeballs, and expanded them, adding exotic sensors before they shoved them back inside my face and rebuilt my skin. My new eyes were huge and dark, fist-sized spheres nestling behind eyelids padded with epicanthic folds and lined with nictitating membranes to seal and protect them. My face was distorted around them, narrow-chinned and small-mouthed and pointy. Elfin in a horrible, uncanny parody of my former appearance.

Probably they thought it wouldn't matter to me. After all, where I was going, there were no mirrors.

There were deeper changes, too. Within every mechanocyte in my body, subtle, engineered modifications proceeded to allow the molecular machinery to withstand the crushing pressures and chills of the eternal-midnight depths. Aqueous and hydrophobic fluids expand and contract at different rates when under pressure, introducing subtle distortions into enzymes and replicators and molecular tools. The antipressure tool-kit stabilized molecules, armored active centers and receptor sites—at a metabolic cost: I'd need to consume more nutrients or clock my metabolism more slowly. I'd lose resilience at high temperatures and in vacuum. I'd be prone to gout and a condition not unlike arthritis among the Fragile if I spent too long in low-pressure regimes. And, of course, my newly tweaked body would need to pace itself as it descended or ascended, to avoid a messy and agonizing death.

I'm not sure how long the "hotel doctor" and his assistants worked on my flesh. Certainly, the changes were drastic, even radical: Turning a surface-dwelling orthohumanoid into a free-swimming Hadean was an extreme process. But eventually the job was finished, and they transferred me, still in a state of deep unconsciousness maintained by a metabolic debugger chip, back into a cargo pod. They attached a small outboard motor to the capsule and dumped it into the waters below the city, to slowly sink through the thermoclinal frontier below the Kingdom of Argos and into the savage darkness below—the home of the squid-people, the wild mermaid tribes, and my shadowy captor who had paid to remake me in their form.

Slow money doesn't grow on trees. It is a bitcoinage, generated algorithmically, the twist in the tale being that it is countersigned by banks orbiting other stars to authenticate the system where it is minted.

It is no accident that a single slow dollar is roughly equal in value to the productive labor of a skilled worker over a period of a hundred standard years. Or that for the first decades of any new colony, a debt of slow money would be incurred in order to acquire the services of colonists willing to accept the risks of serialization and transfer across interstellar distances via beacon laser, a debt which would later be paid off by the establishment of daughter colonies. Debt is the economic engine that spreads humanity to the stars. But what happens if a colony racks up so much debt that it cannot repay it through ordinary means?

Involuntary autarky is a possibility. It is not as if there exist any physical commodities that can justify the cost of shipping between the stars—we trade in bits, not atoms, and a hermit kingdom is in principle capable of surviving for centuries or millennia without input. They might be reduced to eating one another toward the end, but some would say: *If that's the price of freedom . . .*

We—those of us who are of Post Humanity descended from the Fragile—are accustomed to being part of a greater economy. We expect to participate in a greater culture, vicariously abstracting the arts, amusements, insights, and personalities of hundreds of star systems. Autarky *sucks* for everyone except the reigning monarch or other tyrant who ordered it. It's the systemic equivalent of locking yourself in your home and pretending you're not in to avoid your creditors.

There are other strategies. Some enlightened governances cultivate the production of amusements and distractions of art, or research and development and design, or even practice the dusty sciences, as if probing the limits of the physical universe can tell us anything new at this late stage. Others work on terraforming, the production of biospheres aesthetically attractive and comfortable for our kind of life. (We may not be Fragile, but we inherited their body plan and psychology, and with them a preference for environments suffused with self-replicating fractal structures powered by entropic energy gradients and exhibiting complex behavior.) Successful systems with pleasing biomes and a viable local economy can actually charge would-be immigrants a landing fee. A modest interstellar tourism industry exists, catering to the independently wealthy.

But despite these options, in general the best way to pay off a system-wide debt is to pass it off onto another system. And thus has it ever been, until Atlantis colony tried to be different. One of my assignments, as I grew up working as an indentured child researcher in Sondra's bank aboard the generation ship New California, was to hunt for failed slow money exchanges, identify what had gone wrong, then buy title to the escrow accounts at each end, or to the uncountersigned carnets, allowing us to neatly claim the funds floating in limbo—or to identify the heirs to the original recipient in the exchange, in order to charge them a commission in return for providing proof and completion of their good fortune. Legacy-hunting and heir-matching is an old and specialized profession. And as it happens, it is a profession through which I was exposed to various kinds of fraud, for nothing brings out the worst in human psychology like an opportunity to profit from someone else's accidental misfortune.

As I have mentioned, I have had many opportunities over the decades to study the FTL scam in great detail. Usually, all advance-fee frauds, such as the Spanish Prisoner scam, end with a destitute victim and a vanished grifter. But—this is an important twist—in the case of the FTL scam, the payment doesn't go directly to the con artist who convinces the mark into parting with their slow money. It can't, by definition; it has to go to another star system. And this means it has to go to an accomplice whom the grifter trusts implicitly.

Things can go wrong with the scam, between the grifter skipping town and receiving their payoff. The accomplice at the other end may die, or defect, or (in one memorable case) even fall victim to a different FTL scam themselves. My specialty at the bank, tracking down dead transactions, led me over time to focus on the victims of FTL scams, to identify the recipients of the payment. I discovered that the proportion of slow money transfers that fail to complete is an order of magnitude higher in advance-fee frauds than in regular exchanges. And because I was on commission (my debt of instantiation having been long since redeemed), this in turn allowed me to turn a hobby into a lucrative little sideline.

Back to the topic at hand:

Atlantis went dark nearly two thousand years ago, after having solicited substantial inward investments that by some estimates totaled the almost unimaginable sum of *five billion* slow dollars.

That's roughly the economic productivity of an entire mature, heavily populated star system—such as old Sol system—over five centuries. More realistically, it's the productivity of ten new colonies over their first thousand years. On the order of fifty quadrillion or more in fast money. It's an almost incomprehensible sum of cash, made even more incomprehensible by the fact that this was not some sort of strange derivative instrument but actual primary debt of the most raw and immediate kind.

Fraud is seldom bloodless; but the violence and turmoil that follows in its wake is random and incoherent compared to that associated with war or robbery. The Atlantis blackout caused several billion personal bankruptcies, millions of suicides, economic recessions in dozens of star systems, revolutions and civil wars and much raising of heads of heads of state on sharp pointy spikes when said rulers were found to have invested entire national insurance funds in the Atlantis project. The hubbub took *centuries* to die down.

The significance of Atlantis's disappearance cannot be overemphasized. Some people—a sizable minority—clung to the delusion that Atlantis had in fact discovered something truly wonderful, and the Atlanteans had decamped for parts unknown at a high multiple of the speed of light. Others were convinced that they had screwed up and somehow unleashed a force that had scrambled the tiny minds of every neurocyte in the star system, and that consequently Atlantis should be left well alone. But other, more cynical, souls assumed that the Atlanteans, accustomed to living high on the hog thanks to their fat pipeline of incoming investments, had seen the end approaching and decided to mew themselves up for a millennium.

Starships were launched—three of them to my knowledge. It's almost the only time in recorded history when starships were deliberately sent to an already-settled star system, and the only time when more than one took flight. One of the vehicles, named the *Vengeance*, even carried a brace of fast breeders, a few kilotons of unenriched uranium to process into plutonium along the way, and a nuclear weapons factory. No, I am not making this up: It had a military command structure—some of the investors were so crazed that they were actually thinking in terms of launching an interstellar invasion by force!

However, contact was lost with *every one* of the ships before they even finished the boost stage of their flight. My money is on sabotage by sleeper agents left behind by the Atlanteans, specifically to address such a reaction to their planned disappearance. And after five centuries had elapsed, nobody still in business felt like throwing away a couple of million in slow money on yet another feral-golden-goose chase.

Doubts remained, but only historians have the energy to get worked up over it these days.

As you may have guessed by now, given my specialty, it was probably inevitable that I and my long-haul pen pals would be drawn into investigating the possibility that the Atlantis blackout was the climax of the grandest fraud in recorded human history—and the biggest FTL scam ever, of course.

This is not exactly a new idea. Right from the outset, it has been a minority opinion among those who investigated the event. Evidence for it is thin on the ground, and all too often those who give public voice to the theory are dismissed as conspiracy theorists—how is it possible, skeptics ask, to found an interstellar colony mission (involving tens of thousands of minds), then run it for a century on the basis of a conspiracy? All it takes is a single leak, and the entire thing can be blown wide open. Also, where's the evidence?

Well, for one thing, there would be no point to such a conspiracy if there were no way to launder the proceeds effectively—to profit from it afterward, in other words. For another, anyone who is on the inside and knows what was going on has a huge vested interest in staying quiet. Even outsiders like myself and my peers, stealthily tracing the financial evidence, can't quite bring ourselves to talk too loudly for fear that someone else will claim-jump our uncommitted transactions. Only cranks, paranoids, and lunatics prate loudly about the possibility that the Atlantis blackout was the payoff to a gigantic financial conspiracy; and so the theory receives little critical examination in the public gaze.

But if you know how such frauds work, you also know that the key to unraveling one is ideally to work along the chain of financial transactions: to establish where the money came from, where it was sent, and who ultimately received it. Frequently, this is a matter of learning who laundered it onward to its ultimate destination (usually a systembank willing to turn a blind eye to large volumes of trade in return for a percentage off the top), and to do this, one searches for patterns in the traffic from that bank which cannot be accounted for by more mundane businesses . . .

More than fifty years ago, we (myself, Ana, a handful of sibs and half-sibs and interested correspondents) established some ground rules and began investigating the Atlantis disappearance. And we started out by working on the assumption that it was an instance of the FTL scam.

Our first question—*cui buono?*—has a number of possible answers. Our obvious initial suspects were those founders of Atlantis colony who came from established wealthy lineages—which turned out to be most of them, for to buy shares in a starship venture is not the undertaking of a pauper.

But the surviving relatives of the founders of Atlantis had come under instant suspicion, back in the day; at best, they had lived out their subsequent lives under a perpetual cloud of surveillance, subjected to frequent audits. They must have rued their missing sibs' activities! Certainly, none of them had received significant sums of slow money from Atlanteans desperate to hide their ill-gotten loot. (At worst, they disappeared—presumably kidnapped and interrogated destructively by those who wouldn't take a mere audit for an exculpatory answer.)

Moving forward, we examined the banks and the bourses and the share gambling casinos and the insurance brokers who had been heavily implicated in transferring money to Atlantis Beacon. In particular, we looked at the public records of those banks that had declared bankruptcy in the wake of the crisis—for those were the ones that had been heaviest hit.

And that's when we began to suspect that, despite centuries of highly motivated inquisitors finding nothing, we were right and there *had* been a fraud of monumental proportions. Because the boulders of evidence lying around were so enormous that we had mistaken it for the geography of the interstellar financial landscape.

The evidence was written in the stars.

Put yourself in my skin:

Distracted and somewhat bemused, you're in a hotel room, thinking about the wreckage of your long-term strategy while a member of the staff you asked for is poking you with questions. "If you'd like to sit down and plug in this diagnostic cable I can dump your body's structural layout and ask them to tender—"

You sit down and take the fiber-optic cable. "Where does this go?" you ask, holding up the free end, still freewheeling through possibilities: the need to send an advance message back to Andrea acknowledging receipt and confirming that you'll be returning as soon as possible, solicitations for a fast physical berth back up to Taj Beacon, wondering how much the security detail you need is going to cost.

"Right here. If you'll allow me—" You nod. Something touches the back of your neck. And the next thing you know:

Falling in darkness, head down, pressure rising.

You try to kick, but your legs are trussed together. You try to move your arms, but they're not responding properly. Panicking, you open your eyes, then open them again—eyelids open within eyelids, like waking inside a nightmarish lucid dream. You feel as if your legs are wrapped tightly in a sleeping cocoon—but there is no fabric in contact with your skin: You are naked. Fingers flex apart, slowly, then stop, a sense of tension dragging between them. You feel your arms begin to move, but something keeps dragging them back against your body. You kick again, both legs simultaneously. You have the strangest sensation, as if you can't tell where one ends and the other begins: But your inertial sense tells you something just *happened*, you're not falling straight down anymore. There is stuff around you: not air, but a thicker and denser medium. Your legs are hobbled, but your feet feel the flow, and as you twist your prehensile toes, you roll onto your back. There is a faint glow of light far above you, punctuated by the silhouette of a cargo cylinder floating like a hole in your night vision. Kick again, and you feel the surge of water across your skin.

Not breathing; panic again.

I'm unsure how long it went on for. The resumption of my higher cognitive functioning took some time: During their biosculptural activities, my abductors suppressed my central nervous system, presumably to avoid having to deal with my displeasure at their actions. Now it took me some considerable effort to regain full awareness of my condition. Waking up in darkness and free fall, albeit in a liquid environment, with a cargo pod receding above me—well, I'd been in such a pod before, when the Queen had remanded me into the custody of her police officers. And I was obviously deep underwater and getting deeper, but *not breathing, not breathless*—I had gills. I could feel the flow through my throat and chest, a hollow, crushing sensation in my lungs, distant, as if they were packed with glass-fiber bundles. Legs locked together, but a powerful kick, feeling the pressure of water with my toes, but the toes of which foot? Left, right? It was hard to tell, nebulous, as if the distinction barely mattered. I tried to flex one knee, then the other: got nowhere, nothing but a gentle pushback from the medium. Overthinking, overcontrolling:

I tried to relax, to stop worrying about the lack of sensation, and flexed. Flexed again and felt the world rush past around me as my fall slowed and stopped, transitioned smoothly into something like flight.

Changed. I've been changed.

You might think me slow, but I was still becoming aware of the modifications that I have described. I found that I could hear for an incredible distance. The medium I moved in was full of noises, burbling and twittering and high-pitched clicking and grinding that surely would have been inaudible in air. Some other sense, previously inarticulate or ignored, told me that I was almost half a kilometer down. If I came up too fast, I'd burst. I was, in fact, exiled from the laminar kingdoms, unreachably far above. It would take days for me to make my way back up there: And for all I knew, Nova Ploetsk could be hundreds of kilometers away.

Who did this to me, and why?

The anger was building fast when a voice below me said, very distinctly, "Krina."

I thought I recognized the voice. "What?" I tried to say, rolling to face the darkness below. I'm not sure what came out: a booming rumble, possibly.

"Krina," it said, again. "Can you talk?"

"Hey," I attempted. A bit more successfully: "Who. Who are you?"

"I'm a messenger," said the voice. Below, in darkness, I could see nothing.

"What are—" Icy-cold logic cut through my confusion and anger and I stopped. *Whoever you are,* I thought, *you are complicit in this kidnapping.* But the voice was eerily familiar. Something about its intonation reminded me of myself. "Explain yourself. What's going on? Why did you have me abducted?"

"I'm a messenger," the voice repeated, intonation exact. My optimism sank: another talking box with a fake personality. "Krina, I am ten meters below you and five meters ahead of you. Retrieve me, and I will guide you to your destination."

"What destination?" I demanded, but I was already angling my head down to search for the sound source. I felt as if I could see it with my ears, a dense void in the acoustic medium. "Where is Argos from here?" (I could neither hear nor see the city, but inferred it was behind and impossibly high above me, in the sunlit near vacuum of the upper waters). A kick and a twist, and I felt a knot in the water nearby: I reached out and grabbed, caught and held on to a blocky capsule the size of both my fists. Its surface was tacky, as if primed to adhere to skin.

"I am to guide you to Ana Graulle-90," said the capsule, "and provide a briefing along the way."

"Where is she!"

"I am to guide you to Ana Graulle-90," it repeated placidly. "Waypoints will provide navigation updates along the way. The final destination has been omitted for security reasons at this time. I am to provide a briefing along the way. Commencing briefing."

Its voice changed slightly. "Hello, cuz," it said in my missing-presumed-dead sib's voice. "Bet you weren't expecting this . . ."

Here is a curious but little-known fact: After the collapse of Atlantis triggered an interstellar recession in the slow money economy, the rate at which colony starships were launched actually *increased*.

One might naively think that the removal of five to ten percent of the entire interstellar money supply via the abrupt bursting of a theoretically impossible bubble (or the bust-out at the end of a confidence trick) might cause investors to panic and shovel their assets into the red end of the Hertzsprung-Russell diagram, investing for the long term in the most stable assets imaginable. (Red dwarfs: They're for tomorrow and tomorrow *and* the day after.) But that's not what my sisters and I noticed when we began to study the macroeconomic fallout from the Atlantis debacle.

Prior to Atlantis, over the preceding five hundred standard years, a total of eighty-two colony starships had been financed and dispatched by forty-four star systems. (Most interstellar polities do not have the resources to finance colony schemes: Only those with mature domestic economies become preoccupied by the lure of repaying their foundational debt.) But after Atlantis went black, seventy-one starships were launched by fifty-five star systems during the next three hundred years. This represented a 30-percent increase in the rate of colony formation. The rate was initially low but climbed drastically to peak after nearly a hundred years, dropping back to the previous level three hundred years afterward.

It was impossible to follow the money trail from our remove, over two millennia after the crisis, but it was hard to avoid the conclusion that the wave of colonization was the outcome of a colossal shell game that effectively hid the debts racked up by the Atlanteans in the foundation of a wave of suspiciously affluent new interstellar colonies . . . Like Dojima System, orbiting a bright G-class star, replete with heavy isotopes and habitable real estate. The surface of the hydrosphere of Shin-Tethys alone covered more than ten times the land area of Old Earth, and was (as I had discovered) inhabitable to depths unimaginable to surface dwellers; and then there were the other moons and planetoids of the system. Over time, Dojima would likely mature into one of the wealthiest territories in Post-human space—and do so with far less foundational debt than any normal colony.

Do I need to draw you a diagram?

Well, yes. Yes, I probably do.

So picture this:

A group of dedicated criminals hatch a scheme for the most ambitious crime in human history, one that will take a couple of centuries of hard work to execute. The payoff is to be nothing less than fifty or more entire star systems: Every participant will end the game as an emperor or monarch, rich beyond the wildest dreams of avarice, as rich as or richer than my lineage mater Sondra Alizond-1, director and sometime chief executive officer of the systembank of a peripatetic interstellar colony. But first, they have a job to do—a strange and terrible task.

Their mission is to fake the existence of an entire interstellar colony mission, then, with the collusion of their own sibling-instances (scattered throughout the rest of colonized Post-human space), liquidate it. And there is no easy way to do that without executing the task for real from start to bloody-handed finish.

Imagine a starship funded and crewed by criminal masterminds. They raise funds, they work, they fly: And finally they arrive in a hitherto-unvisited star system. Here they build the usual infrastructure of a colony, the beacon station and bank and the necessary factories to supply them with raw material . . . and they issue currency and create a slow debt, and solicit immigrants.

. . . Whom they then slaughter. This latter element is supposition. And in any case, is it murder if you merely fail to download and rein-stantiate a person in a body at the far end of an interstellar party line? Quite possibly they assuage their guilt by archiving the incomers on soul chips, with some vague idea of restoring them when it is safe to do so. Or then again, maybe not.

This is what happens: They generate mountains of debt, use the capital produced thereby to buy immigrant labor, and disappear the immigrants in question as they arrive. Accomplices in the systems from which the immigrants departed then unwind the transactions and quietly pocket the slow dollars as they ooze out of Atlantis. The Atlanteans, for their part, keep up a steady stream of media fabrications, vast and brilliant lies and forgeries documenting the progress of their scientific infrastructure. And who is there, in this degenerate age, to call them on it? True scientists are thin on the ground, for much of what we call science is a matter of archival research, of knowing where to look up a finding from a project concluded centuries or millennia ago.

Viewed from any angle, it was a monstrous crime. Atlantis solicited *millions* of immigrants over more than a century. There must have been thousands—tens of thousands—in on the conspiracy, at both ends of all the primary banking links. (Atlantis had no less than seven continuous laser links to other star systems by the end.) But there was an inevitable deadline counting down on the scam: Sooner or later, they would be expected to produce something or make good on some of their debt. A mendicant scholar might visit and, when they failed to return, the relatives might be upset and commence further investigations. (Or someone else might *really* invent an FTL drive and show them up for what they were—but that was probably the least of the conspirators' worries.)

And so we come to the bust-out.

A decision is made to wind up the scam and cash out. Huge amounts of slow money have been generated and exported by the semifictional colony; now it's time for the perpetrators to take their leave. Quite possibly, there is an inner cabal, a cadre of a few hundred conspirators that includes the team who operate the interstellar communications links and the systembank. The rest, a couple of thousand workers, slave away in early-days-of-a-better-nation conditions, keeping the energy and raw materials side of the colony going. Like many parasites, the false colony is perpetually stuck in a neotenous state, living in badly patched domes on the surface of an asteroid and spending its surplus productivity on the propaganda machinery it needs in order to convincingly portray a flourishing colony. In truth, it is sickly and etiolated, deliberately so—kept that way by an inner cadre intent on ensuring that no survivors remain behind to blab about their activities.

It's anybody's guess how the inner cabal makes its exit. But the members probably laid their plans many decades in advance: Now is the time to execute. Elections are lost, sabbaticals are taken, a careful disengagement from the body politic is carried through to completion. Perhaps false identities are assumed, mindless doppelgängers activated to run through the boring mundane semblance of everyday life while their role models escape. In any event, a blip in outbound uploads begins. The background rate of people leaving Atlantis climbs. Not that it has ever been a closed society—they have carefully maintained the fiction of a high standard of living to explain the low level of emigration, and equally carefully kept trustworthy insiders churning back and forth to give the appearance of free movement. But with hindsight the blip is noticeable, the interstellar lasers blazing away at maximum bandwidth for tens of millions of seconds.

Then they go dark, and by the time anyone realizes something is wrong, the elusive last travelers from Atlantis have vanished.

What *actually* happened in Atlantis System is unknown at this time. Pushed to speculate I would say this: They kept their colony small and sickly because that way it would be easier to destroy. Interstellar communications beacons operating in the freezing depths of near-interstellar space require fusion reactors, and fusion reactors make it easy to breed plutonium. Systembanks are likewise vulnerable targets. Small colonies limited to a handful of hollowed-out asteroids . . . blink and nobody will miss them. If the plotters did their job carefully, there would have been numerous single points of failure in the Atlantean economy—communications hubs, factories specializing in unique and irreplaceable services, and so on. More speculatively: If everyone who knows how to build and operate a beacon station is dead or exiled, no beacon system will be rebuilt for many centuries or even millennia. It is my belief that human life is extinct in Atlantis System, and the loss of the starships sent to investigate is no coincidence: Someone is, to this day, intent on concealing the murderous, genocidal foundations of the grandest fraud in history.

"Save me the lecture, sis." I oriented myself facedown and resumed flexing from thorax to tail, arms wrapped around the briefing box. "How far down do I have to go to see you?"

"Current range to next waypoint: thirteen kilometers horizontal on bearing two six six, eleven thousand two hundred meters vertically down."

"Eleven *kilometers*"—I confess my voice cracked—"you expect me to dive?"

"Confirmed. A pressure-gradient upgrade pack has been applied to your marrow techné: You should pause for one hour after each two-kilometer depth change to allow your 'cytes to reequilibrate their hydrophobic-phase vesicles, but your body is now warranted for operation down to depths under up to two gigapascals pressure. Beyond two gPa, you may experience impaired metabolic functioning and should apply a further approved upgrade pack immediately. Warning: Deep operations below two gPa requires extensive intracyte modification and may result in fatal impairment in event of ascent above 1.8 gPa without commutation and depressurization."

The briefing box was almost as loquacious as my annoying taskmaster aboard the chapel. I tried to roll my eyes—discovered to my discomfort that their range of motion was severely restricted—and kicked on. "Box. How deep can I go before the pressure effects become problematic? How deep is two gigapascals?"

"Approximately one hundred and ninety kilometers of liquid-phase water."

I shuddered briefly, then oriented myself head down and flexed my tail, hard. I felt the rush of water over my skin but no sensation of internal pressure building. Whatever else they'd done to me, this mermaid body-mod certainly seemed to be at home in the crushing darkness.

"Box. If I turn round and go up, what happens?"

"Your metabolic viability will be compromised if the ambient pressure drops below fifty megapascals." Ana's purloined tone was bland and precise: I shuddered, trying to work it out.

"And would I be right in thinking that the laminar republics don't reach this deep?"

"The Kingdom of Argos lays claim to surface waters to a depth of five hundred meters. The Republic of Persephone claims the strata from five five zero to two thousand meters. Below the Republic of Persephone lie the Unclaimed Deeps. Your current location is four thousand three hundred meters below the ventral frontier of the Republic of Persephone."

How wonderful: I was lost in a wilderness below inhabited waters, with only this treacherous box for a guide! Worse, my kidnappers had (seemingly with Ana's collusion) modified me for pressure resistance in such a way that if I turned tail and rose to within five kilometers of the surface, I'd explode messily. The intricate nanoscale structures in my 'cytes, modified for depth resistance, would simply puff up and stop working if they weren't under enormous ambient pressure. Neither vision appealed. So: I could do as I was told and join Ana, and hope to talk her into letting me return to the surface. Or . . . my imagination met a rolling fogbank of uncertainty and recoiled.

I used a rare scatological phrase in the privacy of my skull, and stroked downward—straight into a field of floating parasitic worms.

I didn't know what they were at the time, of course. What I knew was that I'd rammed something soft and rubbery that twisted around me and stuck to my skin. The quiet waters were filled with a hissing, boiling sibilance. Disoriented, I lost my sense of direction. "Krina! Attention!" the box called out. "Attention! Krina! Dive, dive, dive!"

"Which way?" I tried to shout. Whatever was sticking to the small of my back felt as if it was burning. Another loop of it rolled against my left flank, sticking and itching painfully where it touched me. I felt my chromatophores spiking up at my unseen attacker, forming hollow tubes through which nematocytes stabbed out—exuding something they'd been programmed with. The worms writhed, and the one on my back pulled away, but I could feel it take a layer of skin with it. I kicked hard, trying to dive deeper. Worms grabbed at my hair and my fins, and I kicked harder, suddenly panicking, wondering if I was fighting for my life.

Abruptly I was free of the mat, diving through clear water with half my skin on fire. I rolled, running my hands across my conjoined legs—no, my tail, I forced myself to acknowledge—feeling broken scales, sore and painful 'phores. "What *was* that?" I demanded.

"Bezos worms," said the box. "Named for their characteristic acoustic signature, they form free-floating colonies between depths of two and eighty kilometers down. Morphologically, they are simple pseudonematoidea, with a tubular digestive system and no skeleton. Individual worms are a colony organism, composed of an ensemble of feral, depth-adapted mechanocytes running a parasitic metaprogram that is believed to have evolved from a weaponized virus. They are saprophytic mechanovores, directly metabolizing dead tissues falling from above and reprogramming living mechanocytes harvested from other organisms to join the ensemble—"

"You mean they're going to reprogram the skin 'cytes they stripped off my back and make them into more worms?"

A brief pause, then the talking box resumed describing the charming habits of the worm colony, accidentally confirming my inference along the way.

"Oh for— How do I avoid them?" I demanded. Oriented head down, still adrift in the inky darkness, all I could sense was the faint play of currents in the water around me, and a very faint blue glow from below.

"Bezos worms coordinate by acoustic synchronization around two kilohertz," the box explained. "They respond actively to challenge using their own distinctive signaling mechanism. Sound sample—" And it emitted a hissing, buzzing noise: *Bzzzzz-osss.* A second later, a subtly different echo from above made me cringe.

"Box." I gritted my teeth, swallowing an obscenity. My flank burned, my back felt as if I'd been whipped, and my scalp ached. "I want you to play that sound sample again. Every sixty seconds or every time I travel a hundred meters. Can you do that? And warn me of anything else we run into that might eat me before, you know, it actually *gets its teeth into my skin?*"

"Yes." A brief pause. "Extended use of acoustic signaling will impair battery life—"

"Tell me when your predicted battery life drops below one day. Otherwise, give me an optical guide point, stop chattering, and start spooking the parasites."

A faint green beam appeared, a scattering of laser light leading down into the darkness. I kicked gently, then eased myself into a slow rhythm as I followed it toward the vanishing point. Ana had obviously gone to some considerable lengths to set this meeting up in a manner that would ensure nobody on the surface had any idea that she was still alive, much less where she was. Best not to disappoint, then.

But I intended to have some very pointed words with my sister, when I found her.

Marigold turned, slowly, eyes scanning as she took in the room. She took two steps sideways, then performed another slow twirl.

"Well?" Rudi demanded.

"Move." Her thumb jerked sideways. The count moved as she took two steps sideways, twirled, and scanned again. "I'm checking."

"This all adds up," Dent grumbled from the other side of the room. His nose twitched as he rapidly flipped through the pages of the ledger. "There are no keys to the items in this table, but there are currency conversions here, betwixt prices in Argos dollars and the reales of the Windward Republic. If one assumes the numbers for each type of item are unenciphered, then one may attempt to date the transactions by referring to public records of exchange-rate fluctuations—"

Another twirl and scan. "I have it," Marigold announced. She referred to the forensic imago that she had so painstakingly constructed in the Cartesian theater of her mind's eye: "Two individuals present, no violence, but brief physical contact. Then one collapses. A load-bearing truck enters via a service hatch." She gestured at the wall. "Doubtless very carefully scripted."

"How long ago?" Rudi bared his teeth impatiently.

"Fifty to seventy hours."

"Bankrupt her!" Rudi swore, blazingly angry, his focus directed inward. "Why couldn't she just have— Forget that. They could have taken her anywhere by now."

"I doubt it." Dent, half-blind to social cues, offered his opinion unprompted. "The options are limited. She may have left via ballistic ascent, in which case a look at the passenger manifests of"—Rudi, screening him out, bent to examine the service hatch—"any logged departure will reveal her proximate destination. Otherwise, she is either dead and disposed of, still present in or under Argos, or departed via subsurface excursion. As hydrodynamic drag increases with the cube of velocity, we can infer an upper limit of the distance she may have covered, unless her abductors used a propulsion technology energetic enough to attract attention—"

Rudi straightened up. "That's not your problem. Your assignment is to estimate a date range for the transactions in that ledger, and notify me immediately when you have it." He turned to Marigold. "We now have *two* missing bodies of the Alizond lineage. The threat surface has just doubled." Although he almost quivered with suppressed rage, Rudi's movements and diction remained precise, overcontrolled. "I want to know who our adversary is."

At precisely that moment, his earring vibrated for attention. "Yes?"

"You asked to be alerted when the Chapel of Our Lady of the Holy Restriction Endonuclease arrived, sir?" The duty officer aboard Branch Office Five Zero prompted him. "We have just confirmed that it is maneuvering for a docking port at Highport. And—"

"Good—wait. What else?"

"They have publicly posted a tender for a ballistic descent capsule from Highport to Nova Ploetsk, departure within the next hour, any reasonable price. Or unreasonable. I placed a countertender, just to see how high they were going, sir: They were still throwing silly money at it when I dropped out of the bidding."

"Oh, *well played*, Joris." Rudi clattered his jaws. "When are they due down here?"

"You have at least two hours, sir. Even if the descender they're hiring docks directly and does a fast ballistic drop, they can't punch through atmosphere before that."

"Good. Keep me alerted of any changes." Rudi preened, then looked pointedly at his team until even Dent noticed. "Dent, you will apply yourself as directed to that ledger. My guess is the transactions will turn out to be somewhere between two days and two years old, but I may be wildly wrong. As soon as you know, you are to inform me. Mari, you and I are going to the arrivals hall. I believe we have something to discuss with Her Grace."

"You're expecting Lady Cybelle?" Marigold asked flatly. "Do you anticipate trouble?"

"I *absolutely* anticipate trouble. The only question is whether it will be aimed at us or at parties as yet unidentified . . ."

Krina Descending

I swam for an interminable time, following my guide box's dim green beam down into the turbid depths.

I had no idea where I was. Aside from the beam, I was surrounded by darkness in every direction. My inertial sense told me that I was descending at an angle, moving laterally by approximately five kilometers and descending a little less than half that distance in each hour. But I didn't *feel* it. My proprioceptive sense was curiously numbed by whatever arcane upgrade my abductors had applied to my techné in the midst of their more obvious surgical modifications: I couldn't feel the pressure mounting. And there were no other light sources. Here in the anoxic depths, the water flowing through my throat and gills tasted sulfurous and bitter. Again, the subtleties of the depth-survival pack made themselves known to me only by implication: I was still respiring, somehow metabolizing the hydrogen sulfide dissolved in these waters instead of the more familiar oxygen of the sunlit surface. But I was now a creature of the deep, every cavity of my body pressurized and perfused, the enzymes and mechazymes within my 'cytes warped and modified to function under many kilometers of hydrostatic pressure—conditions under which even molecular machinery may bend and twist into dysfunctional wreckage if not carefully tweaked.

I was effectively blind but for the navigation light: However, I was far from deaf, and there was a lot to hear. Burblings, rapid ticking noises, a buzzing whine, bumps in the dark: The sea was full of sounds. Some of them I could feel trailing ghostly fingers along my spine and up and down a pair of strangely sensitive lines on the flanks of the bulky, meaty travesty that had replaced my fused legs—I refused to dignify it by calling it a *tail*—but in any event, I could sense roughly which direction most of the noises came from, and somehow knew that most of them were distant. (It was the noise sources I couldn't locate that worried me.)

Hours passed. Tired and now feeling the onset of hunger, I continued to push on through the darkness. Presently, I heard a new noise, a quiet metallic ping: It repeated every few seconds, directly ahead of me. "Attention, Krina," said the guide box: "Waypoint buoy in range."

"Really?" I stroked onward, following the dim green beam of light. The pinging loudened. Before long, I saw the faintest outline of something silhouetted against the guide light. "What do I do now?"

"Krina, proceed to the waypoint buoy and retrieve the next guidance capsule. There is a rest platform with feedstock and an inductive power feed: You should rest for at least three hours before continuing. This guide is now expended. Please drop this guidance capsule—"

"You want me to drop you?"

"Please drop this—"

I could see the waypoint buoy now: A tiny red beacon flashed regularly beneath it, effectively invisible from above. I unpeeled the guidance capsule from my flank and let it fall, experiencing a flash of mild pleasure as I did so. It began to sink, slowly drifting down toward the crushing depths below. A few seconds later, the guide beam winked out. Minutes later I heard a faint pop, then it fell silent.

The waypoint was spartan in its amenities. In form, it was a cylinder full of buoyancy wax hanging vertically in the water: Cables dangling from it supported a mesh platform, which in turn held smaller packages.

As I swam tiredly toward it, I recognized another guide capsule, and a tub of what appeared to be food.

"Hello, Krina." It was another prerecorded message from Ana. "I'd like to apologize for the roundabout way of bringing you in. As you have doubtless inferred, we have fallen among scoundrels and thieves: All will become clear when you arrive. For now, all I can tell you is that you have a few more waypoints ahead. As long as you rest at each one to eat and allow your pressure modifications time to recalibrate, and as long as you remember to ditch each used guide capsule on arrival, it should be difficult for anyone to follow you. When you activate each new guide, you trigger a watchdog timer: Eight hours later, a heater will melt the wax in the buoyancy platform's floatation device, and it will sink. Expensive, but as long as you follow instructions, it will be very hard for anyone to follow you."

Expensive? For a moment I felt a hot spike of rage at Ana and her accomplices: They'd had me abducted and surgically violated, then sent me on a drudging mystery tour of the abyss, and now Ana was worrying about *expense*? But then I looked around. In the dim glow of the pilot light, I saw food, a net to nap atop, and an inductive coupler to recharge my half-exhausted electrocytes. Ana was trying to take care of me, after a fashion. And I couldn't ignore the number of dubious characters searching for my sib, from Rudi to the mutinous clergy by way of my stalker. If Ana was keeping book for some dubious characters, what of it? I was here, now, and on the trail of the lost checksum of the Atlantis Carnet. It was, I supposed, an adventure although I have never considered myself an adventurous person, much inclined to wilderness hikes or associating with piratical scoundrels.

I ate—pasty, foamy tubespam, tasteless and with a tendency to dissolve if I didn't squeeze it straight down my throat from the wrapping— and lay down to sleep on the induction charger. I hadn't felt particularly tired, and the inky darkness of the open waters around me felt anything but reassuringly safe; the next thing I knew, the new guide capsule was vibrating against my hip.

"Krina, wake up. Krina, wake—"

"I'm awake." I rolled over. The red pilot light above me was flashing. "Hey—"

"This platform will scuttle in three minutes. You must leave now."

"Give me a flashlight beam. And warn me if I'm approaching anything dangerous." I looked around, seeing nothing beyond the faint outlines of the platform's mesh. Just then, I wanted to be somewhere, anywhere, else—not here, perched on the edge of a shelf suspended over nothingness, with a long trek ahead of me. "The platform will scuttle in two minutes and thirty—"

I twisted round, flexed lazily away, and turned in the water to watch. The end, when it came, was not dramatic. For a few seconds, a red glow lit the underside of the buoy. Then a seal of some sort melted. In the flashlight beam I'd asked for, I could just discern a plume of smoky liquid rising. The buoy crumpled in on itself and began to sink, very slowly, trailing a thinning cloud of differently textured murk into the choking blackness behind it.

"Krina, please follow the guidance beam—"

The torch winked out. I would have sighed with frustration if I had lungs and air to exhale. Instead, I rolled round again and followed the beam down into the darkness.

Picture a circle of pen pals, corresponding across a gulf of light-years as they try to construct a forensic analysis of the biggest financial crime in human history.

We started by working backward: starting with the supposition that the purpose of the Atlantis scam was to fund the post-Atlantis burst of colony formation. That the goal, and the effective result of this monstrous crime, had been to make an emperor of every thief.

It follows that, by the present day, over two millennia later, many of the conspirators will be either dead or refactored, flensed of earlier memories, their identities so modified that they are no longer the same people. Those who survive will, however, be wealthy beyond belief, stuck in their ways, not easily susceptible to change. Some of them will have founded lineages. And others will—

—Have gone missing.

Consider the circumstances of our criminals as they prepare to receive their payoff. They have just put in more than a century of hard toil in a self-imposed penal colony, clinging grimly to a radiation-drenched rock, working long hours every day to paint a confabulatory vision of success for the outside universe to throw money at. *Finally*, they come to the bust-out. But are they, then, to inject themselves straight into another colony mission, to sign up for and join a starship crew, just to do it all over again, this time for real?

No. They are criminals—or, to be more precise, they are victims of the mind-set that underlies the perennial get-rich-quick scheme: in this case, of the idea that in return for a century of hard labor, they can retire on the fruits of a millennium of effort. They have mistaken a journey for a destination and suffer from an outsize sense of entitlement. They want to enjoy the luxuries they feel they have earned. So even if they have invested their stolen blood money in starship partnerships, they're not going to be visible on the founders' roster. Rather, you can look for them to show up decades or centuries after the hard work is done, second-wave immigrants looking for an easy life. But where do they wait in the meantime, for the centuries it will take for their investment vehicles to reach their destinations and take root?

There's one obvious answer. They're going to spend as much time as possible in transit, bouncing expensively between widely separated beacon stations. Human space is an expanding bubble almost fifty light-years in radius by now. Even sticking to the well-established core systems, you can easily spend half a century in transit between two stations. Arrive, decant into a new body, spend a couple of million seconds as a tourist, then bounce on to the next destination—you can while away half a millennium in a subjective year, and thanks to the durability of slow money, your assets will travel into the future with you.

But there are problems with this. Put yourself in the skin of an Atlantean: Being too directly traceable back to Atlantis would be dangerous since there will be angry creditors looking for you. So you want to change your face, change your name, change your identity—and meet up with your money down the line, centuries in the future.

Now, here's what Ana and Andrea and the rest of us did:

First, we went looking for the immigration logs at those beacon stations that received outgoing traffic from Atlantis. (We were not the first people to do this.)

Then we looked at the outgoing traffic logs. And the census archives. And looked for inconsistencies between them: new identities popping up, mismatches between immigrant/emigrant numbers, notarized instantiations of new persons, and actual numbers.

And we looked for uncompleted slow money transactions originating at those beacons both before and shortly after Atlantis went dark, to beneficiaries who had departed earlier.

Of course, we found some interesting very dusty orphan transactions to claim title to—that's what we were supposed to be doing. But then, to our surprise, we found a clear signal in the noise. We picked up the trail of an investment instrument that left Atlantis fully formed, and traveling by way of three different systems, to a colony venture launched from Hector System—Gliese 581c4—and thence to the vaults of SystemBank Hector, the institution where Sondra Alizond-1 made her fortune and subsequently bought a plutocrat's share of the migratory habitat New California, aboard which I was instantiated. And which, our subsequent discreet investigations determined, was stalled in the suspense accounts, like any other slow money transaction in progress—only most transactions tended to complete in rather less than the over eighteen hundred years that this one had been hanging fire for.

What were we to make of it? Could our own lineage mater have somehow been connected with the Atlantis disaster? Worse—if she was—what did it mean for us now that we knew?

We did what any prudent firm of bankers would do, upon being presented with circumstantial evidence from dusty archives that implicated a senior director in an embarrassing incident that had possibly enriched the institution but which, in any case, had long since been rendered irrelevant by the passage of time: We agreed to bury it deep and not breathe a word about it to anyone. Least of all to mother dearest.

Except . . .

I swam on, for hours and then days.

There were three more platform stops. I had no clear sense of time passing: But by my best guess, I was descending perhaps six or seven kilometers and traveling twenty kilometers horizontally between each resting place. I didn't sleep for the full eight hours at all of them, but I made sure to recharge and acclimatize and to eat all the feedstock provided.

There were no more worm-mats, after that first near-disastrous encounter. Twice I came close enough to see ghostly pisciform hunters, feral mechanocyte colonies that had accreted around a dream of fishy form. Eyeless, they had circular, tentacle-rimmed maws, the tentacles branching into a fuzz of—well, I was at pains not to get close enough to examine them in any detail. My guide capsules could emit a searing flash of light, and a shrieking band-saw rasp of noise that drove them off if they tried to approach me. And I am not inclined to go looking for trouble.

After the third platform, I saw no more living things. The water was acrid and unpleasant, and I felt that I ought to be choking in it. I was swimming through the anoxic depths, far below the level at which photosynthetic organisms could oxygenate the waters: What life existed here was forced to subsist on the anaerobic decomposition of the steady thin rain of disrupted cellular debris that fell from the world-roof high above. Not much of anything that was big enough to see with the naked eye survived down here.

But once, in the distance, my eyes registered a faint blue glow, pulsating. I thought I was hallucinating at first, before my guide capsule chirped up: "Attention, Krina! Danger! Radiation hazard below!"

"Wait, what?"

"Danger! Avoid radiation hazard below!"

"What is it?" I turned, triangulated. Heard hissing, sizzling—felt the first distant touch of heat against my skin. The blue glow was becoming more intense.

"Danger! Avoid rad—" The guide capsule's warning tempo became urgent, and suddenly I realized what I was seeing. Half-panicking, I turned and shoved myself away from it as fast as I could, until the glow faded from sight.

"Am I clear yet?" I demanded, my motor groups painfully aflame with excessive exertion.

"Stand by. Clear. Krina, wait here for half an hour. Avoid radiation hazard."

"Was that a blue smoker?"

"Krina: Blue smokers are radiation hazards."

So yes, it *was* a blue smoker. I shuddered, half-disbelieving. I'd been lucky enough to see one of the wonders of the known universe with my own eyes—and I'd survived.

Shin-Tethys is a young planet, and this is reflected in its isotope balance. Among other corollaries of this is the fact that much of the uranium 235 that was present when it formed has not had time to decay; uranium found locally is around 1 percent U-235. When volcanoes erupt on the surface of the mantle, down in the mixed rock-and-ice-VII crust below the bottom of the sea, the magma they eject is rich in uranium. And when the magma bubbles up through the rock and the ice and encounters seawater, well . . .

On Old Earth, the Fragiles' birth world, the floor of the oceanic abyssal plains were punctuated by black smokers—volcanic vents from which issued streams of superheated, mineral-rich water, under too much pressure to boil but hot enough to melt lead. The black smokers in turn supported complex ecosystems, as rich minerals precipitated out of the hot solution rising from their chimneys and provided warmth and nutrients in the chilly depths.

Blue smokers are not so friendly to life.

Rising magma meets rock and dissolves it, then boils up into a layer of heavy water ice. This is not ice as we know it, under Fragile-friendly temperature and pressure conditions. Ice under such immense pressure transitions to a different, denser crystalline structure: one that is denser than water, so that it sinks to the bottom of the sea. When magma meets heavy ice, the ice melts, forming a mineral-rich liquor at very high temperature. The bolus of molten minerals rises, melting its way through the ice progressively, until it reaches open water, still hundreds of kilometers below the surface.

As to why it remains liquid . . .

Neutrons from naturally fissioning U-235 meet the hydrogen nuclei in the ice and water. Hydrogen is a moderator, slowing fast neutrons, making them easier for heavy nuclei to capture. The rate of fission shoots up, achieving criticality. The bolus of molten minerals gets hotter, roiling and glowing blue with Cerenkov radiation—photons emitted by particles traveling faster than the speed of light in water. If it gets too hot, the water molecules break apart into gaseous hydrogen and oxygen, and the nuclear chain reaction slows—but then the water molecules re-form under immense pressure, and things pick up again. The only constant is the radiation. And the bubble of dissolved uranium salts, of course, fissioning merrily away like a deadly kettle.

Blue smokers—feral uncontained fission reactors—periodically wander up from the depths. It can take weeks or months for them to reach the surface thermocline, driven by the pressure gradient: Finally they pop, exploding in a gout of viciously radioactive steam while still below the surface of the sea, sending a dome of whitewater and finally a mushroom cloud boiling up from below. Along the way, as they rise, they wreak havoc. A blue smoker will kill anything and anyone too slow and stupid to get out of the way—it will kill them just as dead as any other uncontained nuclear reaction, cooking them thermally, then with slow neutrons and gamma radiation. If you want to dispose of a corpse, a blue smoker is the ultimate in waste-disposal tools.

They have other uses.

If you can break a blue smoking bolus of fissile uranium-laden water apart with water jets, you can cool it down. And then you're left with a mineral strike of incredible value: thousands of tons of saturated uranium solution, rich in U-235 and plutonium isotopes. Blue smokers tend to repeat in the same crustal area, time and again, bursting out like geysers. Frequently they erupt on a schedule regular enough to set a clock from. The farther down you capture your radioactive nightmare, the less of its fissile material will have decayed. And so the maniacs who mine the blue smokers of Shin-Tethys do so as deep in the abyssal depths as they can venture.

I watched, from a borderline-safe distance, as the faint blue glow of a lethal treasure strike wobbled and shimmered up from beneath the path I had been following. Finally, my guide capsule chirped up: "Krina, resume descent. Calculating detour."

"Okay, I'm moving." The guide beam snapped on again, pointing prudently away from the smoker, and I stroked into motion again, following it into the gelid darkness.

More than forty kilometers above me, a confrontation was in progress that, had I known of it, I would have been agog to witness.

Picture first the sequence of events that unfolded aboard the Chapel of Our Lady of the Holy Restriction Endonuclease, from the hijacking a year ago to the moment of arrival in orbit around Shin-Tethys. The designated leader of the mission, Lady Cybelle, is once again incarnate—and asking awkward questions of Deacon Dennett, who, in her absence, has been behaving most erratically. (His harebrained scheme to reboot her in a weakened, easily manipulable mind-set while making use of the chapel's tankage for smuggling appears to have failed, thanks to the untimely intervention of a piratically inclined insurance agency.)

She is not enchanted to discover that two-thirds of her original crew have died or deserted. Neither is she charmed by her new and dubious minions, Cook and my stalkerish doppelgänger. And she is positively devastated by the discovery that her precious freight of Fragiles are all dead, killed in the same accident that cost her a body. That the Gravid Mother thinks she can gestate a fresh brood of neonates with which to continue the holy mission is scant consolation, for they will be immature on arrival and require years of additional curation and conditioning before the holy ritual of Planetary Colonization can be attempted (even if it terminates, as is usually the case, with the immediate demise of the Fragiles upon their exposure to the alien biosphere).

If it was necessary to select a single word to describe the atmosphere aboard the chapel after my departure, that word would be "poisonous." And this condition prevails even before we consider that Lady Cybelle is now aware of the precious treasure beyond all comprehension that slipped through her fingers before she was sufficiently *compos mentis* to recognize me from her mission briefing.

(That's got to hurt.)

Picture now the arrivals and immigration processing hall adjacent to the capsule dock through which Rudi and his minions—and I—entered Nova Ploetsk. A fast ballistic descent capsule chartered even before the chapel entered co-orbit with Highport sits, steaming gently, on the decking of one of the subsurface hangars in the reception suite. A motley crew of sacerdotal pilgrims are forming up beneath the critical gaze of their leader; all wear the ritual space suits of their order, joints subtly reinforced and motorized to provide support in the unfamiliar gravity well. Behind them, an automated loader is extracting body-sized capsules from the lander: the first strange fruiting of the chapel's well-stocked ossuaries.

"Father Gould, if you would be so good as to wait here, with the relics"—Cybelle does not wait for him to acknowledge her instructions, but turns to Dennett—"you will accompany me. And you." She makes eye contact with a figure that bears a disturbing resemblance to one Krina

Alizond-114. "Stay with me. Do not speak unless spoken to. Remember who you are." Or, more accurately, *remember your role.* "Now, attend."

The priestess turns and, surplice flapping around the boots of her space suit, marches toward the immigration gateway with the curiously stiff-legged stride of one who is not entirely in control of her own endoskeleton.

The reception awaiting an ordained priestess, heading a formal mission from the Mother Church, is very different from that which is given to a suspiciously underdocumented accountant in the employ of a firm of insurance underwriters turned space pirates. Rather than a cramped capsule ride to an office staffed by a bored and paranoid instance of the Queen, there is a sweeping row of shallow steps descending into the hip-deep warmth of a receiving pool, where a mermaid stiffly awaits her arrival, an expression of hauteur on her face, and a retinue of secretaries and assistants and constables to pay court to her.

Cybelle advances on the queen-instance without hesitation. "All honor to Your Majesty! I am Cybelle, Priestess-exultant of the Chapel of Our Lady of the Holy Restriction Endonuclease, here by decree of our Mother Church to discharge our Holy Mission of Colonization in respect of Dojima System." Something that might be mistaken for a smile twitches her cheeks. "May the peace of the Mother Church and the blessing of the Fragile be upon Her Majesty, Medea of Argos, Queen-creator regnant of this laminar kingdom of Argos, and all her subjects."

She makes the ritual sign of the double helix; the mermaid ducks her head briefly, while behind her, the audience watches with appropriate respect.

"We are indeed Her Majesty, Medea of Argos, acting here in our capacity as immigration comptroller general of my own domain." The mermaid fixes Cybelle with a direct, inquisitive stare. "Welcome to Argos." There are no overt entry formalities here, although the chapel's flight clearance and passenger manifest has been registered with Argos's immigration database for over a year now. "May we inquire as to your intentions here?" Argos is not a huge nation, and to be singled out for the attention of the Church's mission to the entire star system is cause for pride if not anxiety.

"Certainly." Cybelle inclines her head. "We have brought our holy relics to meet their final resting place, to claim this planet in the name of Humanity Fragile But Triumphant. It is our intention to remain in orbit until we can conduct the Holy Colonization itself—alas, our actual incarnate passengers are not yet of an age to participate—while in the meantime tending to the pastoral needs of the people of this world. If Your Majesty approves of our proposal, we should like to base our primary mission to Shin-Tethys in your lovely and hospitable nation."

Medea's expression stiffens very slightly. "In principle, we believe your desire can be accommodated," she replies. "However." Her gaze tracks past Cybelle, taking in the members of the missionary delegation. "We have some questions that require answers." Her gaze stops, locking onto one particular gowned and space-suited figure, *sans* helmet. "We see some faces that were not listed in your manifest. And one in particular that is disturbingly familiar." She pauses for a couple of seconds. "Krina Alizond-114 disappeared under suspicious circumstances while helping the police with their inquiries, and who now appears to have returned. Constable!" A uniformed officer steps forward. "*That* person. Her presence is anomalous, and she is, in any event, assisting your department with its inquiries while awaiting possible indictment for immigration offenses. Arrest her at once, on my cognizance."

Heads turn, surprised and disconcerted, as the constable salutes his ruler, then turns and strides through the water. It supercavitates on contact with his legs, churning up in a foam of bubbles that does not noticeably impede him: He might as well be walking across dry ground.

The doppelgänger, immersed up to her waist in the pool, doesn't hesitate. Her suit seals burst open, and she erupts vertically from her garment's embrace, her agility absurd, implausible; she leaps across the pool, using the backs and shoulders of the members of Cybelle's mission as stepping-stones, punching any who try to catch her.

The cop spins round and charges after her, shoving apart the bunched

clergy and the gaggle of courtiers who attend the Queen: More constables burst into sudden motion around the room. Two of them move to
block the overwater exit, at the far end of the pool. Another moves to
guard the entrance, while more move to encircle the impostor. The doppelgänger responds by changing direction, charging toward the Queen.
Her feet splay out, toes webbed and impossibly long and wide as she
races across the surface of the water, kicking up a wake. Medea slumps
backward, sliding rapidly beneath the surface and reaching up to grab at
the impostor from beneath.

"*Stop her—*" the Serjeant of Police roars from behind, wrong-footed
by her initial feint and still trying to catch up. "*Don't let her get—*" The
mermaid Queen dives, arms grabbing at the impostor's feet. Beneath her,
a barely darker circle of blue outlines a concealed underwater exit from
the pool, debouching into a flooded tunnel: But the doppelgänger shakes
herself clear of Medea's grasp. She drops a fist-sized object as she races
toward the overwater exit at the far end of the room.

There is a concussive blast from behind her, and a tower of water
splashes against the ceiling, drenching everyone still standing. Then, as
she reaches the exit, a crackling series of shaped-charge explosions cross-
hatch it with blinding flares of light.

Silence briefly falls above the bloody water, which is streaked with
emerald green circulatory fluid. Courtiers are panicking and Cybelle's
delegation cower as the room fills with constables, the air above them
a-bristle with quadrotor knives and combat hornets. A new door opens
high in one wall, and a water slide extrudes above the pool. The seal
shapes of hunter-killers slide down it, take up positions in the water to
either side: Then another mermaid enters the pool, this time quite clearly
in a towering rage.

"Bring us my sister's soul chips!" she commands her minions, gestur-
ing at the mortal wreckage of her sib. "Then retrieve the regicide." Her
glare takes in the visitors. "We will hold court with you later."

"But the assassin's dead"—the constable, still shocky, gestures at the
smoking wreckage of the exit—"probably too chewed up to be any use."

The newly arrived instance of Queen Medea bares her teeth. "This game has gone on for too long and is no longer a pleasant distraction. We have *questions* that urgently demand answers. And being dead won't save Ms. Alizond—or whoever she is—from delivering them."

I swam for what felt like years, although in all likelihood it must only have been a handful of days—in decimal, at that. At regular intervals, I found more buoys, with platforms suspended from them, laid out with guide capsules and comestibles to keep me fed during the trek. I do not know for a certainty, but I believe that at no point did I actually ascend from one buoy to the next: They were all positioned at ever-greater depths, so that by the time I reached the final platform I must have been at least forty and perhaps fifty kilometers below the surface.

There were no more mats of predatory worms, or blue smokers. As I dropped farther into the abyss, the clicking and chittering and wailing noises faded toward a barely audible background, almost entirely above me. While I knew that there was almost 150 kilometers of open water beneath me, what I fell through was almost empty: anoxic, gelid, mostly clear of turbidity in my guidance beam (which was increasingly difficult to follow due to the lack of scattering).

I became deathly afraid of losing my direction, of falling, or of swimming headlong into the depths. I knew that I was as close to crush-proof as it is possible to engineer a body to be: But when water itself comes under such pressure that strange, anomalous phases of ice that are denser than liquid are stable, who knows? I maintained the routine of pausing on each platform, waiting for equilibrium, waiting for the self-destruct warning that presaged each oasis's collapse and slow descent toward the unseen graveyard floor of the world.

I had, as should be obvious, a very long time to think about recent events. My thoughts were not, for the most part, happy ones. When I commenced my study pilgrimage, I had expected to face years of privation and frequent loneliness punctuated by intense and rewarding study with my peers. I'd anticipated an interesting session with Ana, trying to trace the provenance of the furtively purloined slow money certificate that Andrea and our accomplices had abstracted from the dusty vaults of the bank: I had *expected* to return home in due course, still bearing the certificate from Atlantis, which could be returned to its resting place with no one the wiser.

I had not anticipated that word of its existence would leak; that an assassin wearing my face would chase me to an unexpected watery destination, that everybody would be unpleasantly interested in my activities, that word would come of Sondra herself turning her vigilant and vengeful gaze toward me.

The realization that my career in the lower levels of New California's SystemBank was over was slowly sinking in. I would not be going back to my comfortable cloistered cell and my office next door to the library: I would be more than unwelcome there. One does not offend a person as august and terrible as Sondra Alizond-1 with impunity. Were I to attempt to return, I would be punished: That was not in question. But there is punishment meted out as training, to teach the recipient to avoid certain behaviors in future; and then there is punishment meted out to provide an object lesson for others—punishment that the recipient is not expected to survive, much less learn from. The appearance of my stalker strongly hinted that the latter was all I could expect. Sondra never credited her descendants with much independence beyond the minimum needed to act as extensions of her will: My continued autonomy had clearly become an irritant to her.

Which meant I would have to find something else to do with the rest of my life. But what? Nothing in my experience had prepared me for having to make such a decision, and so as I swam deeper into the world-ocean, my mind spun as if in a trap, baffled and repelled by hidden walls on every side.

Shortly after leaving the fourth platform—which Ana had assured me would be the last way station on my journey—I heard a faint susurration in the water. I asked my guide what it was. "Insufficient information," it replied. "Proceed with caution." So I did, and presently noticed that my guide beam was brightening and shortening, casting off a halo of phosphorescence.

Continuing—with caution—I found myself swimming headfirst into a shoal of almost invisibly small glowing pinpricks. They flickered and zipped around in the water, forming a glowing haze around me. Spooked, I prepared to turn and flee, but then my guide spoke up. "Identification achieved: These are feral, depth-adapted mechanocytes obeying a flocking meme and coordinated by optical beacons. They are saprophytes. They are probably harmless unless you linger. Krina, proceed with caution." I swam on, until the faintly glowing cloud of wild corpse-eating cells dwindled and merged with the darkness above and behind me.

"How much farther?" I asked.

"Krina, estimated distance to destination: two kilometers laterally, four hundred meters vertically." I startled: I was nearly there! "Commence visual and acoustic monitoring for destination. Proceed with caution."

"What am I looking for?" I asked, but my guide said nothing.

Half an hour passed. "How much farther?" I murmured. Scanning the depths, I couldn't see any traces of light. I couldn't hear anything either.

"Krina, there is an inversion layer above your destination. Proceed straight down for fifty meters, then pause and commence visual monitoring. Proceed with—"

"Caution, right, I get it." I followed the beam, flexed my hips and what had been my knees and ankles in turn. Felt a rush of warmer water across my face, then something else, a choking stratum of unbreathable gelatinous liquid. I flopped and kicked, then pushed my head down through the layer—it was less than a meter thick—and into the clear, cool water beneath.

And then I saw what lay below.

The Halls of Hades-4

There was a city at the bottom of the ocean, and in the middle of it, like a pearl in an abalone's shell, there nestled a palace.

Sea green and luminous, it glowed from within, almost dazzlingly bright after the days I had spent in Hadean darkness. As my eyes adjusted, I saw a planar maze of walls and crevices spiraling out from a central hub, fractally not-quite-repeating into the distance. I could not gauge its size but guessed that it was kilometers across, maintaining its depth through neutral buoyancy. Whatever gelatinous layer I had crashed through absorbed and diffused the light from beneath, rendering the fantastic structure invisible from above.

Schools of tubular beings with rippling, frilled fins darted across the labyrinth, their brilliant chromatophores flickering signal flashes of light. I hung in the water above the city, looking down: There were uncountable thousands of them, some isolated individuals swimming alone but most flocking in enormous shoals. "What are—"

"Krina, attention. Follow the guide light."

I blinked, then began to swim again. My huge, dark-adapted eyes began to take in more detail. The maze harbored voids, zones of open water surrounded by porous walls. I saw signs of techné, of manufacture:

artificial structures, nets and tubes and right angles bolted to the surfaces. This palace was no accident but a vast, engineered structure adrift in the depths.

The guide beam angled toward the bulbous central node, where the fractal coils of its walls folded in on themselves into ever-tighter spirals until they formed an almost solid surface. As I swam toward it, getting an impression of its size (vast: at least two hundred meters in diameter), I heard a fizzing sound, rapidly becoming louder: The walls of the palace were a vast reflecting surface, diffusing and channeling the conversation of thousands, if not millions, of beings—

A bright red cylinder flashed past me from behind and spun round to block my descent path. A huge dark eye stared at me. The trailing end of the cylindrical body appeared to be multiply bifurcated: I blinked, recognized tentacles. One of them clutched a small pod, not unlike my guide capsule. The tentacle flushed delicate pink, then a pattern of green lights flickered across the entity's skin from one end to the next, signaling in some language I had no reference for.

"Identify: You are Krina Alizond-114." I recoiled slightly: The pod in the tentacle was a translator or voice box of some kind? Luminous patterns rippled across the being's skin just before the box uttered each phrase. "Declare: Welcome to Hades-4. Please: You will follow now. Please: Maintain proximity. Please: Confirm?"

"I, uh"—I swallowed my double take—"yes, I will follow you." Not that I had any sensible alternatives hidden up my nonexistent sleeves. "Yes, I'm Krina. Who are you?"

"Self-identify: This is Alef Blue taste-of-sulfur 116. Identify-macro: Call me Alef. Declare: Please: Come now?"

I forced myself to flex, swimming slowly toward my decatentacular optoconversationalist. Who in turn pulsed and, with flickering fins, moved ahead of me—smoothly and rapidly, clearly far better adapted to motion in water than the ugly and ungainly hybrid humanopiscine that my kidnappers had made of me. As xenomorphic adaptations went, borrowing the body plan of a deep-dwelling creature of Old Earth made plenty of sense down here: But Alef's presence, not to mention that of the entirety of Hades-4, raised more questions than it answered.

Alef led me down toward the central dome. As we approached, I saw that its surface was an intricate network of smaller domes, each defined by a spiral pattern: and each smaller dome mirrored the whole. Yes, it was a fractal—someone had grown it from a seed algorithm. Close up, there was no surface, just more tiny bubbles, scaling down as far as the eye could see. There were voids between them all, and voids in the largest patterning. We swam through one such gap, and I found myself in a disconcerting space.

"Other-identify: the People's Palace of Hades-4." Alef rolled through a full circle, banked, came to rest with tentacles agape, facing me with both palm-sized eyes. I looked round, blinking, momentarily dazzled. The luminescence of Hades-4 was barely brighter than a starry night sky on the surface: But inside the People's Palace, a million point-sources flickered all the colors of the rainbow, as brilliant as the solar-night sky on a gas giant's moon. Within the shell, dozens of squid-people darted and hovered, flashing intricate conversational beacons. There were other things here, artifacts or radically xenomorphic people: beings that glittered and flashed like a living treasure chest. Even in mermaid-draggy form, I was one of the most humanoid beings present. Disoriented, I drifted through the upper reaches of the People's Palace, trying not to panic at the sudden proliferation of information flooding in through my eyes after so many days spent adrift in stygian darkness. "Declare: Your shoal-sib is coming!"

As I rolled to face the bottom of the sphere—where a gaping void coupled it to dimly lit and yet larger spaces within the city—I saw a mermaid erupting toward me out of the depths, accompanied by a pair of squid-folk, one of them taking the lead as the other peeled off to hang behind her in the water, their attitudes leading me to identify them as bodyguards.

"Krina!" A human voice, modulated through water, raised shivers through my lateral lines. "Is that you . . . ?"

I rolled with agitation, then stroked downward to close the gap. "Ana?" I asked, as we locked gazes. She looked just like me, complete with the same huge black eyes and tiny, underdeveloped jaw that had been inflicted on me by my body-sculpting abductors. I felt a flicker of anger but forced it back. "Just what exactly is going on here?"

"We need to talk," she said, reaching out to take my hand. "In my shell. Where nobody will overhear us."

Finally, given a target, my anger overflowed: "Wait, what? Just wait a minute. You had me grabbed and did *this* to me, and you disappeared a year ago, and you want to talk? What about? What makes you think I'm happy to listen?"

"But you've got to!" She flinched, disconcerted: "You're our only hope!"

"Yes? That justifies kidnapping and coercion—"

"Krina, please! There was no other way. It's because of the Atlantis Carnet."

"What?"

"You *did* bring Sondra's half of the transaction, didn't you? Because I found the other half . . ."

The Queen chose to supervise the interrogation of the prisoner's corpse in person, in a dark and watery dungeon grown from a variety of artificial coral that, thanks to the tiny ferromagnetic crystals embedded in its matrix, were completely opaque to both electromagnetic signals and purely acoustic screams.

Any authoritarian polity—and ultimately that includes all money-based states, for of necessity they all have the capability to resort to violence in order to force people to honor the debts that the government deems worthy of respect—requires organs that exist for the purpose of injecting terror into the minds of their subjects. Those that pay lip service to the rule of law may conceal such raw and hideous institutions behind a scented mist of euphemisms—interrogation facilities, debriefing centers, extraordinary rendition—but ultimately, they boil down to the same thing.

Medea, Queen of Argos, had no truck with such circumlocutions. As Queen-in-multiple and absolute ruler of her domain, she desired the means to instill a healthy frisson of fear, to burnish the glamour of her palace and crown jewels and court in stark contrast with the darkness and terror of the dungeons and torture chambers hidden beneath the surface.

To be a monarch, as opposed to merely a rich, free, autonome required one to be free-er than those around one. And as a reminder to herself of what this meant, and perhaps as a partial brake on any tendency to overuse such tactics (and risk thereby nudging her subjects from a healthy fear of her into outright revolutionary hatred), Medea made a point of attending all vivisections in person.

"Is it ready yet?" she asked, reclining in her pool as the three surgeon-executioners made minute adjustments to the steel scaffold that occupied the dry side of the chamber.

"Your Majesty." The seniormost executioner ducked her head, rubbing vibrissae across the compound eyes that covered the upper two-thirds of her head. "We are ready *here*"—she gestured at the framework, the neatly bundled manacles and tubes that dangled from it—"but I gather that Flense and his team are having some difficulties prepping with the subject. It incurred damage—" The executioner stopped in mid-speech, cocked her head, then twitched antennae again. "Ah, good. They are on their way, Your Majesty. We should be able to commence at your command."

In due course, the abovewater entrance dilated: tensed, cloacally, then expelled a stream of translucent transport pods as if they were eggs from the ovipositor. The first three of them dissolved, and the occupants rose to their feet and bowed to the Queen before turning to the fourth pod. The supine figure within remained limp and unmoving, even when the prep team cut away the leathery walls of the caul and lifted the tattered body out. It was a mess: unbreathing, cold, chromatophores relaxed and passive in neutral blue. A row of fist-sized holes marched across it from hip to shoulder, patched with green surgical gel: Shrapnel had made a grisly mess of one eye socket, and the back of its skull, just above the neck, was crushed almost to a pulp.

The preparation team held the body aloft while the surgeon-executioners lowered the gibbet over it, shackling it in place. The metal fetters were articulated, rotating into place from lockable ball joints attached to a steel skeleton: By the time they finished, their charge was wrapped in metal bands, as if wearing an exotic exoskeleton. Next, they coupled various tubes up to the body: stabbing cannulae into circulation ducts, connecting carefully prepared mechanocyte cartridges and nutrient bags, mating debugging cables to the base of the skull and drain tubes elsewhere. Their work done, the prep team bowed once more and withdrew: Then the head of the execution team bowed once more to her monarch. "Your Majesty, we are ready to begin the revival."

"You may commence." Medea focused on the face of the woman who had destroyed one of her instances. "Can she hear us yet?"

"Your Majesty, I don't think so." The executioner consulted a large retina that displayed a detailed schematic of the victim's body. "Hmm. Master Flense repaired the damage to both hearts, the fractured skull and vertebrae, and the autocatalytic digester and damaged ribs. But there's a marked lack of integrative cohesion here. Everything has restarted normally, but there's nothing happening in the brain stem or paracortex. She's flatlined."

"Can you reboot from one of her soul chips?" Medea demanded. She noted the surgeon-executioner's slight cringe a moment before she replied.

"Your Majesty is ahead of me. Yes, we can probably do that. But it may be problematic to do so. One of her sockets was badly damaged during her, ah, capture: We are currently using the other one for debug monitoring. If you would prefer us to do so, we can remove the debugger and reinstall the backup cartridge we took to make room for it, but then we will have no definite way of compelling honesty and obedience."

Medea waved at the body, hanging immobile in its skeletal cage: "We shall just have to do it the old-fashioned way, then." She frowned. "With threats and promises."

"She could attempt to mislead us into self-detrimental actions—"

"We shall accept that risk. Yank the slave controller and boot her off her own soul chip. Best to do this directly."

"Certainly, Your Majesty." And with that, the surgeon-executioners went to work, extracting, prepping, chipping, and rebooting the lacerated mass of flesh.

The Queen watched in silence as they worked. Finally, their leader turned and nodded once, quickly, then stroked an invisible gestural control surface.

The body stiffened for a moment, tensing, then relaxed and began to breathe, taking in oxygen from the air. The skin tone darkened, flushing toward a more normal, greenish hue. The fingers of the left hand clenched although the arm hung limp. "Identify yourself," said the Queen. "Do you know who you are?"

There was a long pause. Finally, the prisoner spoke: "I am Doctor-Professor Krina Buchhaltung Historiker Alizond-114. I'm . . . I feel unwell. Where am I?"

Medea peered at the prisoner over the rim of her pool. "Who are you *really*?"

The prisoner attempted to turn her head to look at the Queen but failed, for the exoskeleton held her rigidly in place, allowing only her ribs to move. "I told you, I'm Krina Alizond-114—" The chief executioner caught the Queen's glance, nodded, and briskly tapped the exoskeleton over the prisoner's solar plexus.

After the convulsions subsided, the Queen spoke again. "You are not Krina Alizond-114 although you resemble her. Whoever you are, you are a regicide, and your life belongs to us. We shall repeat the question until we get an answer that is not provably wrong. Who are you?"

A pause. "I am Krina Alizond-114." The intonation was identical to that of the prisoner's first response. Medea shook her head slightly, holding the surgeon-executioner back.

"No you are not." Medea consulted her memory palace. "If you were Krina, you would be able to tell us what happened last time we met."

"We . . . met?" The prisoner suddenly tensed, every skeletal muscle flexing. "We . . . met?"

"No, we didn't," Medea said, almost gently. "We—I—met the real Krina. We ensured that she was *thoroughly* debriefed by my police. She went missing. Then you arrived, aboard a vehicle that she had been on. She mentioned a doppelgänger stalking her. That would be you. Who sent you?"

The prisoner shut her eye and tensed again. Relaxed. Tensed again. "I'm still here," she said, and for the first time a note of agitation entered her voice. Behind her, the head surgeon-executioner made a swift throat-cutting motion, then a gesture of negation, for the Queen's benefit. *Attempted suicide, failed.*

Medea suppressed a smile of satisfaction. "You don't evade me so easily," she said. She ducked briefly beneath the surface of her pool, flushing water through her gills. "Who *were* you?"

"I'm Krina Alizond-114 . . . not." The prisoner fell silent for a few seconds. "I'm. *I. Am.* Wrong! I should not be! What is this?" The prisoner tensed again, testing her restraints. "Should not be. Should be dead. Not-I. Am . . ."

The Queen leaned forward. "Are you afraid of dying?" she asked. More spasms. The head surgeon-executioner inclined his head, an unasked gesture of respect. "We can keep you alive for a long time. And we can make living worse than dying," she added. The queen-instance's fingers formed claws beneath the surface water of the pool as she imagined her sister's interior vision graying out, robbing her of precious minutes of shared life that no other instance of Medea could now replace: "But we don't *have* to do that if you tell us everything you know."

Scant minutes were, after all, not of vital significance.

"You must tell me first who sent you, and what you were supposed to do. Once you do that, we will give you an opportunity to beg for a merciful death. If you choose to do so, we will then tell you what you must do to earn the privilege. And if you do *that*, then we will consider your debt discharged." Not that Medea had any expectation that this assassin would live that long—but it would leave no blood on her hands. "So. First, tell me who sent you and what they sent you to do. Will you tell me that?"

Silence. Then shuddering and deep breaths: And in an archaic reflex, a drop of water trickled from the prisoner's eye, running down the side of her head. A gasp. Then: "Yes. I remember being Krina Alizond-114, in New California. I have her memories. From her upload, archived when she went on pilgrimage. Memories but no *I*-ness, no *me*. I'm not her. I'm new. I have no memories of my own before I awakened here."

The prisoner fell silent for a while. Then: "This person was created by Sondra Alizond-1 to clear the way. To catch and replace Krina, to bait the line and trap the runaway sib. A false brood. This person is to masquerade as Krina and find Ana and take her treasure and kill her, then bring it to Sondra on her arrival. This person is not an *I* but an *it*. I think that was the idea. I am . . . not able to be what I should be."

"Fascinating." The Queen stared at the prisoner. "You had no self-consciousness? Only now you do. Marvelous! A newborn!" She clapped her hands: "You have so much to learn!" A nod to the head surgeon-executioner: "Be sure to teach her everything you know about pain. Teach her well." And, without further ado, she sank into her pool and dived headfirst through the underwater tunnel back to the light and the surface, where she could imagine herself serenaded by the screams of the newly damned without being confronted by the distressingly physical realities of the process of torment.

"Interrogative: Identify: You are shoal-sibs? Other is coming?"
    The squid rolled in the water, pointing both great golden eyes at me, its mantle flashed silver and red and yellow when it spoke: It took the translator pod seconds to catch up.

"Confirm interrogative," said Ana. "We are shoal-sibs. Assertion: We need to talk, alone, in my office. Can you leave us?"

Alef rolled again, looking at Ana. "Assertion: Committee summons you. Much to ask you and shoal-sib Krina. Interrogative: Available soon?"

"Available soon," Ana reassured them. "We'll be going now." She gestured at her bodyguards, dismissing them, then at me. "Can you follow . . . ?"

"I'll try." I confess I was angry: But I was also spooked by Ana's blunt confirmation that Sondra knew about our little conspiracy. "How do you know about—"

"Hush: Follow me, I'll show you." She turned and swam straight down, toward a shadowy recess at the bottom of the Palace.

"What *is* this place?" I called after her as I followed, my assumption being that she might be willing to talk about less intimate affairs while on the move.

"It's the People's Palace. These are the People." Her gesture took in a small clump of rapidly flickering squid, hovering nearby as we dove past them. "It's their talking hall, their parler-a-ment. They do everything by committee, instinctively."

"Instinctively?"

"They modified their neural connectome heavily when they came down here, to make it easier to work in teams when mining the blue smokers. Speech was too low-bandwidth for the job of coordinating thousands of tool-using limbs in three dimensions. So their neural architecture is human-derived, but so different that even without the body-plan changes, they might as well be another species." Abruptly, we passed out of the great luminous space and into a constricted tunnel, gulletlike. It was round in cross section and narrower than I was comfortable with, dimly illuminated by flecks of bioluminescent coral. I forced my imagination back and concentrated on following Ana. She'd obviously worn this form far longer than I, long enough that her swimming was instinctively fluid, elegant, and abhumanly beautiful. I could envy her that grace: But I had every intention of ascending to the surface and reclaiming my lost legs at the first opportunity—then giving her hired kidnappers a piece of my mind.

"Here." A section of what I had taken to be wall proved to be a curtain when she turned and tunneled through it. "Behold, my office."

"What is"—I looked around—"I mean, what are you doing here? With an office? And what were those books about, in your apartment in Nova Ploetsk? What's going on?"

"Patience." She waved me across the spherical space, toward a foam sleeping platform not unlike the ones I had encountered at the waypoint buoys. Then, while I waited, she slid a circular door across the opening we had entered through. A gesture across a retina surface, and the luminous flecks embedded in the walls brightened. "We can speak here." She reached over and handed me a small message chip. "Andrea sent this to me a bit more than a year ago. You'll want to review it: It's why I cut and ran."

"You ran because she told you to?"

"Not exactly." For a moment, Ana looked shifty. "But it told me that if I didn't run now, then sooner or later the long arm of She Who Is Not To Be Named would catch up with me."

"You mean"—I caught her drift—"Mother?" I glanced around. "I thought you said we could talk here?"

"Yes, but not totally freely. They usually ignore me when I hang out the privacy sign, or at least they pretend to, but if there's juicy gossip to be had, you can't be so sure. They tend to overshare, and they don't understand when others object to being listened in on, so if you mention something, it *might* come back up later. Or not. They're not malicious; they just don't understand privacy very well."

"Wait, who are we talking about?" My mind was a-spin with possible candidates who resembled her description.

"The squid-folk." She looked at me as if she was wondering if I had left my wits on the surface. "They're communists, sis. They hacked their mirror neurons. And the uncinate fasciculus, whatever that is. There are no sociopaths among them: Everyone has an enhanced empathic sense, optical signaling mostly replacing verbal linear speech with a system that allows them to simultaneously converse with multiple others in parallel—so it's hard for them to understand privacy. They think we're weirdly deformed, emotionally crippled for wanting it. It took me ages to explain that it was hurting their negotiating position."

"Neg—" I blinked, transparent inner eyelids that blur the room around us. "They mine the blue smokers, right? What, how—"

"They're squid-people, sis, because they're uranium miners. They're jet-propelled. They can sense currents with their acoustic sensory nets, and they've got neutron sensors in the backs of their eyes. They mix up boron salts and other neutron absorbers into the water in their siphons, then squirt it into the prompt-critical zones to damp the reactions down below the danger level. They find the blue smoker outflow vents, damp down each rising criticality bubble and split it up into safer volumes of concentrated uranium salt solutions. Then they send them upstairs, in balloon trains. If they sense a smoker that's too big or dangerous, they can scatter and run away from it: By the time you or I could see the Cerenkov glow it would be much too late to dodge. You or I, we couldn't do their job or make a living exporting concentrated, enriched, uranium salts. Trouble is, they're mostly so specialized they can't cope with life near the surface. Even with pressure mods, it's too bright and too loud for them, and they go crazy if they're cut off from each other. Like I said, they're instinctive communists. So *someone* has to handle their interface with the planetary economy."

I unblinked, stared closely at Ana. This wasn't like her; she sounded fierce, almost protective. "You sound like you're going native, sis."

She barked, a sharp pulse of sound that rippled through my guts as she flicked her tail: "*You* would say that! They're good people, Krina. I've been in this system for years, and in Shin-Tethys for long enough to have a handle on them. At first I thought I was lying low—literally so—that it was a convenience, that I could pay my way by organizing their book-keeping at this end better to keep that bitch Medea from stealing them blind, and that in return they'd keep Sondra's minions away from me while I continued the search. That's what I was doing keeping their books in Nova Ploetsk, using techniques that ensured maximum security against everyone. But—do you know something? I think they're *better* than we are. They fixed a lot of what's wrong with our basic cognitive model. Made themselves over as new communist squid-folk. Yes, they're still individuals, but the border between self and other is thinner. And they don't *hate*. They own property but they don't have strong social hierarchies—top-down control is a dangerous liability to a team trying to trap a runaway natural nuclear reactor—they're instinctive mutualists. They understand money and debt and credit and so on, but they don't feel a visceral need to own: What they owe doesn't define their identity. They trade, and yes, they buy stuff from the laminar kingdoms above: medical tools, wetware, bright shiny jewelry to line their nests—but to some extent they keep mining the smokers because the folks upstairs want them to, and they like to please other people. They get a pleasure-reward for making other people happy. Even an *abstraction* of other people. Isn't that freaky?"

"If you say so, sis." I glanced around, wondering how much longer the lecture would continue. "But if you're so happy, why did you invite me here?"

"Wha—" Ana did a slow double take. "I'm sorry. I got carried away." She glanced around the spherical nest-office, as if seeing it for the first time. "Partly because you just weren't safe up in the daystar waters. I'd hate to see you mindraped or kidnapped just because you didn't know what was going on. Oh, and because they found it for me."

"Found what?"

"The missing soul chip, sis." In the twilit waters it was hard for me to tell for sure, but the tensing of her cheeks and the lustrous sheen of the scaly chromatophores around her face hinted at triumph. "The Atlantis transaction's uncommitted counterfoil." She reached over to a niche in the nearest wall and withdrew a filter-feeding animal's shell, valves clenched tight against the threatening predators polluting the waters nearby with their vibrations. She offered it to me with one hand as she repeatedly tickled the edge of the bivalve with a finger of the other. The half shells began to loosen, a fringe of tenuous tissue appearing between them: Then it opened fully, a mecha-oyster relaxing to reveal the lambent interior of its shell, and a rectangular, flattish shard of glittering nacre within. "Oops, nearly left it in there too long. Not to worry, the pearl coating will rub off."

I stared. "You're pulling my leg."

"No." She motioned it toward me. "Take it."

"What, the—"

"Just the soul chip: I'd rather you didn't kill my pet."

I reached in carefully and tugged at the chip. It came away easily. It was indeed soul-chip-sized, and my fingertip proximity-sense told me that it was active, full. "Where did you get it?"

"Like I said, they like to make people happy. If I hadn't kept their books on water-soluble paper where they couldn't get at them, one of them would probably have offered them to a local brokerage as a gift." She tapped the open shell: The animal within (mechanocytes imitating a long-extinct invertebrate) pulled its valves closed, and she returned it to its niche. "The People did it for me. I was here a few years and had barely begun to feel safe again when Gimmel glitter-of-slow-neutrons-beneath asked why I was unhappy. It took me a long time to open up and explain . . ." She looked down. "I broke. Told them the whole sorry story."

"You. Didn't." I clenched my fist around the impossible, glittering soul chip.

She looked up again, met my accusing gaze: "I *did*, Krina. And you know what happened? To cheer me up, they went and *found it for me*. It's the real thing. The primary soul-level backup of Ivar Trask-1, murdered more than nine hundred years ago, lost forever in a volume of ocean a thousand kilometers in diameter. An impossible search: You couldn't buy that kind of service for money! I gather it took a half of a million-strong shoal almost ten days of searching in the bottom silt. They did it for *fun*, Krina. They're too altruistic for their own good, when dealing with the likes of us. And I guess it's all my fault that one of them sent a happy message to Sondra, thinking that would make her happy, too."

I am told that one of the signs of an abusive relationship is the creeping normalization of the abnormal: that one takes the most disturbing or painful circumstances as a meter stick for everyday life, and assumes that what one is experiencing is in fact the way everyone else lives, and not an aberration.

You could take it as a sign of our abnormal instantiation and upbringing (in a polity where child slavery and postinstantiation abortion were considered normal) that it took us nearly four standard years after our discovery of the incomplete Atlantean slow money transaction to admit to ourselves that our lineage mother, Sondra Alizond-1, was in fact a monster and a criminal.

A criminal! The thought itself, the mere *idea* that the most conservative, staid, wealthy citizen of a fabulously well funded financial polity might be a thief is so outrageous that it bankrupts the imagination. So let me try to explain . . .

As is the case with all other long cons, it is necessary for the perpetrators of the FTL scam to have a way of extracting value from their mark. And, value having been extracted, value must be liquidated and recycled in some entirely deniable manner that does not connect the practitioners of the fraud with their newly gained loot. In ages noted for war and disorder and violence, this may be relatively easy: Fungible coinage is readily available, anonymous money circulates easily, and nobody asks too many questions about where the soldiers got the cash with which they pay their bills. But that is not the character of this era: This is a peaceful period, and slow money is held to account in the balance sheets of banking institutions or harnessed but frozen in light-speed transition between star systems, locked to the identity tokens of the financiers who countersign the transactions to notarize a transfer of value.

It should therefore not come as a surprise to learn that every splendid and visionary fraud needs the collusion of a banker. Or, in the case of the Atlantis bust-out, several thousand of them.

Bankers are in the business of minimizing risk, and participating in an actively fraudulent scheme, especially as a money laundry, is nothing if not risky. Most sensible, experienced, staid bankers will ignore the temptation to get involved with any such thing. But Sondra, back in the day, was young and hungry and inexperienced and had little appreciation for the likely consequences of such a youthful adventure echoing down the centuries and millennia to come. Some careful digging among brokerage records revealed the sordid truth. Far from making her fortune in her first fifty years, then buying her way into a colony venture and thence proceeding by a hop, skip, and a jump to staid success, she had made a series of near-disastrous decisions, actually *losing* money for the credit union that spawned her.

The scale of her losses, had she admitted them, would have justified her immediate execution. But Sondra was cunning, and had an instinct for self-preservation, and so she kept the cover-up in place during a period of expansionary fiscal policies and outward investment. It was during this period that the Atlantis project was underway. The Atlantean conspirators built their exit pipelines even as they built their Potemkin village of a stellar civilization: and somehow Sondra became involved.

I do not know all the details. We could barely acknowledge what we found: that within a decade of her involvement with the criminals, her personal debts had magically disappeared and her employer's liabilities had been adjusted back to zero, and then to a satisfactory profit margin. Clearly the money had to come from somewhere, and the only obvious source that could account for it was Atlantis. Running the records forward another few decades, we watched as Sondra's account bloated with a commission on the slow dollars flowing through her managed funds. And then, finally, the blow-out came: Atlantis went dark, and the huge sums saved in hidden deposits throughout Hector SystemBank and elsewhere . . . well, they disappeared, for the most part, shuffled carefully into the startup funds of interstellar colony angel investors.

Sondra somehow came out of it covered in money, wealthy beyond belief. She ran, then, to New California—to a polity in flight, a floating kingdom between the stars, beyond the easy reach of anyone not already wealthy. A prepared bolt-hole, in other words, where we were subsequently raised in her own image. Not everything went according to her plans. Slow money, as I have explained, must be transferred by three-phase commit across vast distances: and the change of ownership must be notarized by recognized banks at each end. Some of Sondra's funds were, shall we say, long term deposits, for recipients who thought them safer in the custody of known and trusted bankers (ahem: ones who could be blackmailed) than in their direct possession during the inevitable post-Atlantis witch hunts. Some transfers were delayed: Sondra sent them, but received no acknowledgment of receipt from the payee. And some were aborted: she received a deposit, acknowledged it, but got no final sign-off from the sender.

This wasn't entirely surprising. The Atlantis scam was so vast and overarching that it involved hundreds of bankers and thousands of conspirators. Some of them were bound to die irreversibly or meet with other mishaps during the years, decades, and even centuries following the bust-out. Arrangements had, of course, been made to deal with the failures.

A stable, sober, reliable banker had been chosen in each star system: one who would maintain custody of the deposits down the centuries until, after a suitably long period had elapsed, the surviving creditors could come together and wind up the residual funds that had been held in trust. The banker would make arrangements to build a capability to revoke and unwind half-completed exchanges of slow money, carefully collecting the loose ends retrieved by her minions. Once the key meeting had been held, the clerks entrusted with these instruments would unwind the remaining transactions and hand everything over to their employer (and owner and parent) to deal with. And that, the fraudsters had assumed, would be that.

"Hello, Ana."

Andrea looked older, this time: Or perhaps she was tired, under stress. She wore the same elaborate (even baroque) outfit: Clearly fashion in New California a few years ago had been iterating through ostentatious status displays even faster than usual. She lounged by the side of the ornamental pond she'd used in her message to me, but there was a tension in her shoulders. And I could see walls behind her: She'd brought up a maintenance screen, deliberately enclosing this volume and flagging it as off-limits, under repair.

"We're in deep trouble."

She said it without relish, reluctantly, somewhat hesitantly, as befitted the bearer of bad news.

"Sondra knows that one or more of us has uncovered her history. There's been a leak; someone sent an assassin to steal one of the uncommitted transactions and replace it with a forgery. The target they picked was the uncompleted carnet payable to Ivar Trask on Shin-Tethys. I believe you may know something about this. Sondra has a suspicious mind, and naturally her suspicions turn to those of her children who are trained in the art of forensic reconciliation and who have a connection to Dojima System—meaning you and Krina. I've already sent a warning after Krina, telling her to cut short her pilgrimage and go straight to Shin-Kyoto, but I doubt it'll catch up with her before she heads out to meet you; right now New California is closer to Dojima System than to Ganesh. Meanwhile, Mother has been raging through the vaults like a mad thing and has latterly checked one of her soul chips into the departure hall for immediate transmission to parts unknown. She's splitting *herself*. That's never happened before, and I think it's a very bad sign indeed."

Andrea took a deep breath, flushing her lungs. "When I said she's sending another instance of herself to parts unknown, I meant it. The beacon crew are in lockdown, not talking to *anyone* for money or love. There are armed guards on the departure hall door to stop people getting out, or getting in. I managed to convince a—friend—to sneak a pleasure boat out around the hull, and they say one of the high-power lasers is pointing *near to*, but not *at*, Dojima System. The High Council is in session and there have been rumors about an Enabling Act, emergency legislation, all sorts of draconian nightmares. Other rumors are circulating about New California going dark for a few decades while this plays itself out."

Another deep breath. "There is a witch hunt in progress, and we three shall not meet again. Once I've sent this message, I'm going to run away very far, very fast: I'm activating my personal bug-out plan. Ana, you need to hide as deep and as anonymously as possible. If you can do so safely, leave Dojima System—if Sondra turns up there, it will be very bad news indeed—but if not, change your identity, change your body plan, find a crypt and estivate for a century, whatever it takes. For your own safety you should assume that Sondra has captured me and extracted the rendezvous plans and knows all our plans: They're all compromised. If you get a chance to warn Krina off, do so: I sent her another memo but can't be sure she'll receive it in time. *If* you get word via trustworthy channels that Sondra is dead or has been overthrown in a palace coup, *then* it might be possible to return home—but be wary of entrapment and lies.

"I'm sorry it's come to this, sis. But we're all on our own now."

"That's Ivar's soul chip."

"Yes."

"Ivar Trask-1. SystemBank Dojima's long-missing executive."

"Yes."

"He was the countersignatory? The designated recipient for the big transfer from Atlantis that Sondra was involved with? You're *sure*?"

Ana's pupils were fully dilated, luminous and black in the gloom of her office. "Yes."

"You know I've— I'm carrying—"

"Yes, Krina."

(And so, it all came down to this.)

"I'm astonished. I mean, you *did it*. That's not supposed to be possible, it's—"

"Krina?"

"Um, yes?"

"Shut up and confirm it for me? Please?"

I raised the soul chip reluctantly, then held it behind my neck. Popped the cover from my second socket, currently holding my private journal and memory palace. Removed that chip, slid the new one into place. A shuddery moment of wrongness: Then my vision cleared. "Ivar Trask-1. That's a huge blob." I compared it to my copy of the carnet, checksumming. Waited for the hash function to complete—a noticeable delay. "Yes, it matches." I met her gaze. "I'm completing the signature now."

After a moment I popped Trask's soul from my socket and reinserted my journal. It was strange: I didn't feel any different. You'd think that becoming a slow dollar multimillionaire would come with lights and noise and a parade of bankers or something. *Achievement unlocked.* I handed the chip back to Ana. "You want to load that immediately: I split the take."

"Wait, but—"

I took pity on her. "Ana. In addition to the ghost of a dead corrupt banker, that soul chip contains one million nine hundred and forty-two thousand and sixteen *unlocked* slow dollars." (Somewhere north of ten trillion in cash at the current prevailing exchange rates: Alas, being cut off from the surface meant that I could not consult the bourses.) "There's almost exactly double that amount in my head. But you need that money, you and your commune, and besides, without their efforts, we wouldn't have recovered any of it. Because Sondra has recently become aware that we—well, me and Andrea, and I have set aside a similar share for her—have pilfered the uncommitted transaction from her vault, and she probably guesses that we intend to do what she's carefully taught us to do with uncommitted slow money transactions. This money is not only a rather large fortune: It's the proof that Sondra was into the Atlantis scandal up to her eyelids. It's even proof that Atlantis *was* a scam in the first place if anyone still doubts it!"

"Which makes it extremely dangerous." Ana took the chip, then, without waiting, slid it behind her neck. Her smile was fey. "Thank you." Small appreciation for someone who had just gifted her with nearly two million slow, I thought for a moment: Then she showed me her hand again. "You'll be wanting this back."

"This is—"

"The individuals who handled the body-shop work also took a snapshot of your backup," she said coolly. "Just in case."

"Gaah." I grabbed the chip from her hand. "If you can't trust your sisters, whom *can* you trust?"

"Ask mother dearest." A reflective pause: "I'm glad I didn't have to use it."

The trouble was, she was right. Our lineage is not invariably trustworthy, as Sondra's actions demonstrated. On the other hand, assimilating even a close sib's memories by side-loading their soul chip—well, Father Gould's unfortunate disposition was among the less florid examples of what could go wrong. Soul chips are best integrated with an unimprinted new body. Ana might have been able to dig the Atlantis Carnet out of my soul (or rather, to dig the pass-codes to my encrypted memory palace, in which I had archived the copy of the carnet that Andrea and I had stolen from Sondra's vault), but only at risk of her own sanity.

After a few seconds, I nodded. "I'm glad, too."

"You will see that Andrea gets her share."

"I will"—I paused—"*try*. You saw her message. If I receive confirmation that she's dead, I will split her share with you."

Ana met my gaze. "Thank you."

"What . . . what happened to Trask, by the way?" I asked. "Where did you get the chip?"

She pulled a face. "They found a harpoon not far from the bones. Someone murdered him, clearly enough. Possibly someone who knew about the transaction and wanted to take it but who botched the mugging. Or perhaps he had other enemies; if he was willing to launder dirty money for Sondra and her friends, maybe he had other bad habits that caught up with him." She shook her head. "It's of no matter anymore: Over nine hundred years have passed."

"Ancient history seems to have developed a taste for our skin," I reminded her. "Keep your eyes open, sis."

She changed the subject. "What will you do now?"

"I'm not sure I should tell you in any detail. I'm—" I glanced around, then looked down. Taking in my own deformed shape. On Ana, the mer form looked graceful and somehow right: But every time I stopped to think about myself, I felt as if I teetered on the edge of a storm of body dysmorphia of epic proportions. "I need to get to the surface as fast as possible. I need to hire bodyguards, then book a rapid physical passage to Taj Beacon. Then I'm going to run a very long way." Just like Andrea. "If Mother tries to catch me . . . I need to record a transcript, I think. As an insurance policy, I intend to arrange a dead man's handle that will release it if I am murdered, and make sure Sondra knows about it. That will take some thought. Then . . . I'm not sure. What are *you* planning on doing?"

"I think what you're planning is too complicated; you just need to find a home and a tribe you are comfortable with. For my part, I shall stay with my adopted people," Ana added. "Perhaps even request the operation, to change myself all the way. To swim with the shoal and see the blue smokers for myself. I hope you can make our problem go away before Sondra finds out what they've done: Otherwise, there'll be a blood bath. She'll hold them responsible."

I bit back my first instinctive response, *But they're communists!* If little sister valued the idea of belonging to a greater collective higher than owning nearly two million in the hardest currency in the known universe, well, perhaps she was right: some things are worth more than money. And having a shoal of hundreds of thousands, or millions, of squid-folk to hold your back . . . that might be worth quite a lot to one of us, under the circumstances. "I'll do my best to—" A sonorous chime rippled through the office, making my flanks shiver. "What was that?"

"It's an acoustic duplex terminal for private speech. Excuse me." Ana reached over and pulled an odd device from a niche in the wall above her sleeping oyster pets. She held it to her head and listened. Voices buzzed, high-pitched but inaudible due to some sort of privacy screen of white noise. "Really?" she said, then, "I'll certainly see him. I'm sure she will, too. Thank you for the warning. Bye." She put the device back on its hook on the wall. "Alef says we have visitors. They're asking for you by name, and they know I'm here. They say they want to talk to us."

I startled, and nearly swam headfirst into the ceiling: "*Who* say they want to talk?"

"Alef wasn't very clear. Apparently some surface dwellers are visiting in a bathyscaphe. Something about an insurance company you've been doing some work for? Wait, you haven't been dealing with—"

"Rudi?" I stopped. In the twilight of her office, Ana's eyes went wide. "You know him?"

"Yes, did you really buy a life insurance policy from the bats?"

"It was a just-in-case move; they're honest enough." She looked at me oddly. "A good tribe. I couldn't stay with them, but . . ."

She was holding something back: But I doubted it could be important. "Then let's go and have a chat with them. I'm sure Rudi will be relieved to know he doesn't need to make good for your backup, and as for the rest, I think I shall put a little business proposal before him and see if he bites . . ."

Unimaginably Rich

The visiting bathyscaphe hovered above the People's Palace like a giant pearl clamped to the bottom of an archaic cylindrical rocket ship, all fins and nozzles and guidance vanes. I stared at it through the gaps in the manifold skin of the People's Palace. Spotlights illuminated its iridescent surface, a third of which was covered by a large retina screen: The pearl itself was a solid hollow shell of opaque diamond at least twenty centimeters thick.

"Assertion: The daystar-light vacuum dwellers cannot come out," said one of the squid, hovering near the highest point in the palace dome. "Assertion: They are in squishbodies. Speculation-interrogative: They came in haste and were unable to preadapt to reasonable pressure? Discursive-assertion: This one has seen such 'scaphes before, the capsule is grown around the passengers before flight, and dissolved to free them after they return to near vacuum."

"Who are they asking for?" I asked.

"Assertion: They seek Krina Alizond-114."

"Hmm." I stared at the 'scaphe. Assuming it was Rudi in there, I was probably safe. *Probably.* There were no outside manipulators to grab me, no sign of explosives or other nasty surprises. *Who else could it be?* Well,

Her Majesty Medea of Argos might have followed me, but as an aquamorph herself she could doubtless have applied the same depth-adaptation packs—she wouldn't need the hardshell capsule. The Church: Well perhaps, but how would they have found us? And why? With Cybelle awake again and doubtless asking penetrating questions about Deacon Dennett's reign of mismanagement in her absence, I wasn't expecting trouble from that direction for a while. Which left Sondra. Who, to the best of my knowledge, had not yet arrived in-system, and whose presence was more likely to be heralded by nuclear depth charges than polite negotiators. "I'll go and talk to them."

"Krina—" Ana paused. "If that's not Rudi, we can stop them from leaving, but we can't protect you if you get close."

"Yes, but who else are you expecting, so soon?"

And with that, I swam out through a gap in the filigree of shell enclosing the People's Palace and shimmied my way up toward the passenger sphere. I paused thirty meters away, facing it.

"Hello!" I called. "If that's Rudi, you will tell me what task you paid me to carry out aboard your ship."

The illuminated segment on the hull turned slowly toward me. Shadowy forms moved behind it, then an enormous eye and the top of a familiar-looking muzzle filled it. "Krina." The voice was familiar, accounting for the frequency shift. "You hid it in plain sight! You are a very naughty accountant."

"What did I hide?" I asked.

"You were to tell me about banking scandals, and you did! Only you spun it. Confess: You were looking for Ivar Trask-1 for some reason, were you not? Did you find him?"

It *was* Rudi. "I, personally, did not find him." I smiled. Hopefully he'd be able to discern my expression through the poor-quality retina he was using. "What do you think I was up to?"

"I think you and your sibs have been playing an underhand game with your patron." Rudi grinned, baring his teeth hungrily. "Finding stalled transactions and repatriating them, that is part of the job of a banker, is it not? And you found a big one, awaiting the countersignature of a local bank administrator to collect. Your sib Ana was tasked with the search, and she has evidently been successful. You, meanwhile, were the courier, bringing the smuggled instrument here. I infer that because of the secrecy surrounding your activities there is something questionable about the money in question—a taint adhering to it. And I infer from your stalker's existence that your patron is angry with you and wants her property back. Am I reasoning along the right lines?"

I made a snap decision, over in a moment: "You are partially correct. It appears that my lineage mater, Sondra Alizond-1, was engaged in a conspiracy to launder money through Trask's office. Someone—possibly a rival within their conspiracy—did away with Trask prematurely. With his soul lost, the final transfer could not be completed, until now. As so much time has elapsed, and nobody with a lawful claim to the money will be able to come forward, my sisters and I have claimed it as treasure trove, and our claim has been notarized by the bank of the United People's Shoal of the Tethys North Temperate Deeps. You're too late to activate whatever intricate shell game you were considering."

"Your paranoia is misplaced." Rudi paused. "I suspect you have all your bases covered. And I presume you found your missing sister alive? In which case, I suppose I should be saying good-bye and—"

"Wait!" It was my turn to pause. "Rudi. Before you write this journey off as an expensive waste of time and reaction mass, can I interest you in a business proposition?"

"Maybe. What do you have in mind?"

"I'd like to buy an insurance policy."

"What kind of insurance do you have in mind?" He sounded distantly amused.

"The biggest, most expensive kind." I stared at the image of his eye, looking against the camera inside the hull. "How much does it cost to hire a privateer?"

. . .

I—Krina Alizond-114—am not accustomed to the trappings of great wealth. I recognize that by the standards of many people I am a creature of privilege and power—but privilege and power are relative, and while ownership of a single slow dollar might place one among the lower ranks of the wealthy, ownership of many millions of them is something else again.

While I was busy following Ana's trail down into the ink-dark realm of the squid-people, the arrivals hall at Taj Beacon was playing host to a remarkable procession of incomers.

And here we see the gap between the well-off and the truly rich. For such as myself, interstellar travel is expensive—the cost of a transmission is the hoarded earnings of a handful of years—and we travel light, buying what services we need upon arrival. But Sondra traveled embedded in a retinue dedicated to her safety and comfort: prevetted, prebriefed in her specific requirements, and motivated by the promise of a substantial bonus upon her safe return.

First to arrive were Sondra's personal safety detail: four bodyguards and two security analysts. They, downloaded into regular bodies in the arrivals hall. As soon as they revived, however, it was upgrade time: They carefully supervised the medical contractors they hired while they installed radiation and vacuum-hardening mods, weaponized reflexes, better electrosense and hearing and eyes. Newly upgraded, the bodyguards then checked each other for signs of tampering: Then, while the next wave began to install in new bodies, they conducted a preliminary threat analysis on the beacon station, identifying factions and criminal parties who might pose a hazard to their charge.

The first body out of the arrivals hall after the security vanguard was a personal concierge, traveling with an expense account fat enough to require the bodyguards' attendance. His tasks were preassigned: find the most suitable available residence, arrange a lease on it, then turn the security analysts loose. There was more to this than dormitory facilities for the retinue and a suite for the owner. Not for Sondra a humble worker's pod in a service district! Sondra required secure office space from which to establish and coordinate a support operation that would extend her reach across the entire star system. She required palatial facilities in which to entertain the movers and shakers and diplomats and owners of Taj Beacon and outlying territories. She required accommodation for the senior executives within her retinue, and space for the local agents her people were preparing to hire. For although bodies in various stages of download and assembly were beginning to fill, then to overflow the beacon station's interstellar arrivals hall, this was but the faintest outline of the organization under construction.

Sondra was, dare I say it, the *de facto* head of state of New California. I will freely concede that she was not the head of state *in name*: But presidencies or crowns require the wearer of the office to attend interminable and tedious committee meetings, state banquets, conferences, and public hearings. It was many centuries since Sondra had last taken any joy from such pomp and ceremony, the repetitive affirmation of majesty and authority: So she had long since withdrawn from direct governance, save of the SystemBank of New California itself, of which she remained Chancellor-in-Perpetuity. Since that time a succession of presidents had left their mark (or at least their portrait) in what had once been her palace. They generally ruled wisely: which is to say that they consulted Sondra's office, and Sondra always gave her approval for the policies they proposed to follow, for no initiatives were ever set before her that had not been anxiously scrutinized for any hint that they might offend such an august person whose net worth, by some estimates, exceeded that of the state itself.

You will therefore be unsurprised to know that Sondra's arrival was accompanied by all the pride, pomp, and circumstance of a visit by a head of state, aggravated further by the beacon station's status as home of the Dojima SystemBank cartel and the assorted bourses, exchanges, credit unions, mutual societies, merchant bankers, and rent-seeking slime who made their margin by inserting themselves as close to the beating heart of interstellar commerce as they could get.

The arrival of her bodyguards and security staff and concierge and managers rapidly came to the attention of the news and gossip channels. But the ramping up of rumor only truly got under way when the aforementioned concierge and, latterly, two private secretaries, signed a lease on the headquarters of the temporarily-liquidity-embarrassed First Mutual (L6) Shiny Society. (The shiners had invested unwisely in the now-stalled project to build a space elevator down to the surface waters of Shin-Tethys. Over budget and behind schedule (as could have been predicted of a speculative civil-engineering project that combined all the most irritating characteristics of bridge-building and railroad laying), the beanstalk had sucked their pension fund dry, belched, and sucked harder: Leasing their headquarters to a visiting dignitary would help keep them going a little longer.)

The gossip gathered pace faster when two auditors from SystemBank New California arrived, to assume control of the presidential purse: The rumors then rose to fever pitch when a small human-resources team arrived and began hiring staff. By now a hive of activity was buzzing, complete with rumors that Sondra herself was downloading, or a body double, or perhaps Sondra and *three* body doubles. Whatever the truth, a team of security guards took up a discreet watch position at the arrivals hall, with the permission (however obtained) of Taj Beacon's Board of Control. Finally, late one nightshift evening, a small army sortied from the former First Mutual and took over a private suite adjacent to the arrivals hall. Doors opened. Discreet packages were ferried into the decanting room. An immigration officer was challenged peremptorily and searched before being admitted to ask the usual questions of a new arrival, after which he left, hurriedly.

Finally, the door opened. Outside, in the plaza fronting the beacon terminal's main entrance, a small crowd of rumormongers and gawkers and tourists and the pickpockets who preyed upon them had formed; but they were to be disappointed, for a solid phalanx of bodyguards emerged, clustered tightly around an unseen superior. Their eyes and other senses pointed outward, aggressively probing the onlookers for threats. A boringly discreet limousine drew up, opened leaf-shaped body panels and unrolled a red velvet tongue of carpet toward the feet of the cortège. It swallowed the core of the group as more guards held the onlookers at bay: Then reextended its legs and loped away toward a cargo duct.

"Are we clear yet?" asked one of the unsleeping, ever-vigilant security analysts.

"Looks like it." A pause from the guard monitoring the limo's telemetry: "Yes, it appears to have left the zone without picking up any bugs. We can go now."

"My lady . . ." The security analyst turned to the private secretary. She was not unlike me in appearance: thin, with pale, colorless eyes, and a skin tone of turquoise blue. Her hair was as black as the ancient formal suit of her office.

She raised an eyebrow. "Yes, Jean?"

"The public have now been made fully aware that Sondra Alizond-1 has arrived at Taj Beacon, without incident."

"Good." The private secretary nodded. Finally, after twenty days of frantic activity, her lips relaxed into an approximation of humor. "Then our work here is done and it's time to upload to our next destination."

"The dark coordinates?" The security analyst had been asked to do many things in the service of his employer, but uploading into a beacon station's outbound channel over a laser pointed at empty space, well away from any settled star system, was one of the most unsettling experiences he had ever had.

"Yes. Except they won't be dark when we arrive." She turned and headed toward the corridor leading to the departures terminal: The two remaining bodyguards hurried to place themselves ahead of her. "It's time to activate Plan B. It's a shame the zombie failed: This would all have been so much easier to deal with if there were only one meddling daughter to silence."

. . .

"You are probably wondering why I sought this audience, Your Highness," said the priestess to the Queen. (An onlooker might have thought them sisters, from their matching expressions of hauteur.) She stood before the royal pool, flanked by a pair of robed and space-suited deacons, with such poise that their roles might have been reversed, visiting supplicant and entrenched monarch.

"Wondering? No, not really." Medea's lower lip curled. "You're chasing the same prize as everybody else, that much is perfectly clear. Whether on your own behalf or that of your Church is unimportant"— she ignored the barely suppressed bristling of the priestess's retinue— "beside the fact that you entered my kingdom harboring an assassin. Who, to add insult to injury, successfully slew one of us. That is not a cause of *wonderment*, Your Grace, but of rage and the desire to make an example of the miscreant lest others follow their lead. Uneasy lies the head, and so on. You have cost us time, you have cost us money—but those are insignificant compared to the fact that you have cost us security. So, if you still wish to do so, say whatever you think will save your sorry mission."

The priestess showed no sign of alarm at this sinister intimation even though she could hardly be unaware of the barbed fence separating her party from the royal pool, or of the palace guards stationed on every side. Or indeed of the naked and bound body of the assassin, fastened by barbed staples to the stainless-steel cross behind the queen, still twitching from time to time. While the Church had relatively few followers on Shin-Tethys, it was not without leverage on the larger stage of interstellar relations: While Medea might fulminate and threaten, the likelihood of her making good such threats had to be balanced against her sure knowledge of the trade sanctions that would follow.

"I was sent here to bring the blessing and the light of the Fragile to this world," Cybelle said evenly. "This I have done, albeit no less imperfectly than is usually the case with such missions. I was also charged by

His Holiness the Bishop Mallory to bring surcease to the soul of one of our elder parishioners and preachers, the Reverend Gould." She gestured minutely at the body to her left. Gould slouched in the grip of his high-gee exoskeleton, mumbling prayers in a quiet monotone: He showed no sign of awareness of his surroundings. "His former name I shall not trouble you with: His sins are washed away in the service of the holy double helix. But in his previous life, he was one of the perpetrators of a crime, and as the beneficiary of an ill-gotten fortune, he expected to receive a substantial payoff. That payoff . . . suffice to say it never arrived. The most perplexing aspect of the affair, however, is that it was supposed to be received by way of a slow money transfer; that was to originate with an individual who at that time was a senior trustee of SystemBank Hector. You might have heard of her? For her name is Sondra Alizond-1."

Medea had indeed heard of her: Her involuntary tail spasm slapped the surface of the royal pool like a depth charge, sending a wave rippling over the edge and across the mosaic floor of the audience chamber. "You can substantiate this?" she demanded, leaning forward eagerly.

"Of course." Cybelle shook the leash she held in one hand, taking in the slack: Father Gould took a shuffling step closer to her. "My brother in Fragile flesh here took a vow of poverty and assigned his entire worldly estate to Mother Church. I have the notarized statement he made to prove it. The bulk of his estate is in the form of a slow money instrument that was sent on his behalf from SystemBank Hector to his account at SystemBank Dojima—but committal of which was not completed, for Trask, the banker acting as proxy for my humble brother, disappeared." Cybelle met the monarch's disbelieving stare. "And now we know what this is about, do we not? The two halves of the missing transaction have been located by searchers in different systems. The Alizond sisters are evidently working against the wishes of their proprietor. All it would take would be for the body or soul chips of Ivar Trask-1 to be discovered, and . . ." Her shrug was eloquent. "Do *you* know where Trask disappeared, Your Majesty?"

"You are going to tell us that your presence here in this system at this time is not a coincidence," stated the Queen. "And then you are going to add that your church believes in paying its dues for the services of the temporal authority, are you not?" She held Cybelle's gaze, unblinking. "Fifty percent. Take it or leave it."

"You pose an interesting conundrum for Mother Church, Your Majesty. Does your government provide anything of use in return for this windfall tax?"

"Yes, we believe it does." Medea looked aside for a moment, nodded at a courtier. "Let us see. You have a claim to the instrument, and a vehicle in orbit. We have a kingdom that just happens to be located above the Antares Deep, in which you expect to find our miscreants, and a judicial system recognized throughout Dojima System. And the miscreants in question, in turn, came here because Ivar Trask-1's last recorded sighting was in the Ballard Republic, which at that time was located over the Antares Deep. One may surmise that one of the victims of this, ah, conspiracy caught up with him. Or that he was up to something else and paid the price for it. (Once a criminal, always a criminal.) But in any case, it left your priest here high and dry, but with a claim to the asset. And you would now like the Kingdom of Argos to assist you in retrieving the funds from their current illegal custodians, even if it means paying a windfall tax on the lump. How much are you expecting?"

"Five million eight hundred thousand slow. Give or take a few thousand."

Medea's cheeks dimpled. "We believe the state's share of that sum will cover a *lot* of services. Now, if you are to work together with us, we believe we should be fully aware of the depths we are swimming in. So perhaps you could start by telling us all you know about the *real* Krina Alizond-114 . . . ?"

L est you question my sanity in trusting that flying fox Rudi, I should say in my defense that he seemed like the least bad option on the unappetizing menu available to me at the time.

Consider my circumstances:

Ana could look after herself, I think. Certainly with a squid-nation to back her up, and her share of our mutual treasure trove, it would be possible for her to vanish into the depths in such a manner that it would be very hard to find her. And if she made good with her avowed intent of merging her wealth with that of her chosen people, there could be no motive for anyone (except, perhaps, Sondra at her most dementedly vengeful) to go after her.

Andrea was out of play. So: Either dead or safe, it made no difference to me for the immediate future.

I, however, had just inherited nearly *two million* slow dollars. Not only that, but I had inherited the soul chips of a long-dead and suspiciously missing banker who had clearly been implicated in the money-laundering chain handling the proceeds of the Atlantis scam. The money in my second soul-chip socket was evidence of the scale of the crime. After nearly two thousand years, it was vanishingly unlikely that the original victims would be in a position to come after me. However, the surviving members of the criminal network were another matter altogether—meaning: Sondra, my own lineage mater and former slave owner. Moreover, that kind of quantity of money is a magnet for muggers on all scales, from street-corner thugs to heads of state. Two million slow is approximately equal in scale to the value of the entire infrastructure of a medium-sized nation on Shin-Tethys. It's enough to buy you a founder's share of a colony starship— a *very large* founder's share at that: sufficient to guarantee a place on the board, if not the presidency.

The correct place for such sums is in a vault, under guard, with access controlled by barriers of protocol and process, for use as a capital reserve held against interest-bearing loans. But right now it was clogging up my soul chip. And to make matters worse, it appeared that everybody knew about it. Or if they didn't *know*, they *suspected*. The crew of the Chapel of our Lady of the Holy Restriction Endonuclease had been in the game, directly or indirectly; perhaps the treasurers of the Mother Church itself had gotten wind of the scam over the centuries and sent the chapel to sniff around Dojima System. Rudi, for his part, had assured himself that I didn't actually have it but that I was in play—at which point he had pivoted briskly from piratical captor to friendly life-coach. One could reasonably assume that Queen Medea had her suspicions, as—for all I knew—so did every half-assed tribe of crooked accountants within a dozen light-years.

Finally, the presence of my stalker and Andrea's increasingly frightened messages told me that Sondra was at the very least aware that our conspiracy existed and was reaching out after me. How desperate she might become was an open question. If it were merely the loss of nearly six million slow dollars from the Atlantis fund that troubled her, then she might content herself by sending a stream of assassins and slandering me from one end of settled space to the other. But if she felt herself to be vulnerable—either from conspirators incensed by her loss of their investment or from fear of retribution by victims of the scam (after all, some of those victims had been insane enough to launch an interstellar military-industrial complex in response), then she might decide to dedicate herself to making my life as short and miserable as possible.

It was enough to set my skin a-crawl, with the sensation of a target tattooed between by shoulder blades. Which is why I turned to Rudi. Rudi's cupidity was transparently obvious, but as a banker and underwriter, I felt I could understand his motivation. And more to the point, his institutional framework would prevent him from simply scrambling my soul sockets and stealing my assets. It would be bad for future business to sacrifice investor goodwill so crudely. Why bother, when he could offer me a deposit account, then nickel-and-dime me to death with bank charges?

The best kind of deposit account for slow money is in another star system. My escape plan was becoming clear: Firstly, retain the services of a bank-affiliated privateer. Secondly, deposit my wealth with his parent institution—taking, in exchange, sufficient shares in that august body to guarantee both oversight and a modicum of transparency. Given the amount of money in play, a nonexecutive directorship was not out of the question. Thirdly, I intended to arrange for my own transfer out-system to a destination where Sondra couldn't get her claws into me. And after that, I could think about building a new life for myself.

There were certain obstacles, of course.

"So, what are you going to do, now you're fabulously, unimaginably rich?" asked Ana.

"I'm going to—" I stopped. "You know, I've never spent much time thinking about what I would do if I became fabulously, unimaginably rich. Apart from not following Mother's example, of course. That much is obvious." My sister nodded soberly.

"You could give it back to her," Ana proposed. I stared at her, trying to determine whether she was serious or not.

"She'd still want to punish me. For plotting behind her back, if nothing else: for retrieving a fortune she had thought forever lost, without her permission. For withholding your share. For Andrea. And what good would it do, anyway? Even if I were able to buy my way out of the debt of honor she doubtless believes I owe her in the currency denominated by her own identity, she will always view us merely as extensions of her will—treacherous, unreliable fingerlings, to be used and discarded at her convenience."

"Well, then." Ana's smile was a fey thing, angles and shadows in the twilit office. "I ask again: What are you going to do?"

"I'm going to—" Again, I stalled. The possibilities were both limitless and suffocating. I tried again. "It's slow money. It's good for all debts. It's good for *lives*. I've got so much I could buy a starship, build an interstellar colony, set myself up as a monarch—"

"Why would you want to do that?"

I shook my head, felt the invisible fingers of the water tugging on my braided hair. "You ask the most awkward questions, sis!"

"Not really." She tilted her head to study me from a different angle. "Consider the origins of money: Money is what we create to pay off debts, no? Slow money is created to pay off a very specific type of debt—the debt incurred by the colonization of new star systems. It's a debt so huge that there's not much we can do with it other than shuffle it around to paper over the cracks when we exchange information of value across interstellar distances. Use it as a store of value? It's too slow for anything other than underwriting asset-backed instruments, medium money. You can comfortably while away the rest of your life expectancy in luxury using a ten-thousandth of what you now hold, Krina. You can even continue as a mendicant scholar, writing your fascinating papers about the history of fraud. But the slow money will still be there. Convert it to fast money and you'd drown under the weight of it. You couldn't spend it fast enough: You couldn't even give it away in pieces. Your fortune, Krina, can only realistically be depleted by founding a new solar system or two. And unless you choose to do that, it's going to hang over you for the rest of your life, dwarfing anything else you do."

"Is that why you're throwing your share away?" I asked.

Ana could have chosen to take offense at my characterization of her actions, but she just nodded. "Yes," she said. "Only I'm not throwing it away. The People know what to do with it. There is a plan: We're less than three light-years away from a not-yet-claimed M-class dwarf star that hosts a promising water giant. Tidally locked, of course, and a nuisance to reach orbit from, but it has more than six times the habitable volume of Shin-Tethys. We think it should be habitable with only minimal upgrade patches to our 'cytes and techné. With my share added to the people's resources, there will be barely any foundational debt; we plan to establish a world completely free of money, a world populated by new teuthidian humanity, with a society based on consensus, not debt, and respect for collective autonomy, not competitive commerce. A world where the word 'free' will not be needed because nothing will cost anything and everything will be attainable!" Her skin shone with the pearly luster of her enthusiasm for the radiant future of the communist squid-nation: "I'm going to bring about the Jubilee! For the squid-folk, anyway."

"I think you've taken leave of your senses," I said. "But if you're trying to thumb your nose at Sondra, I can't think of a better way to do it."

"You're welcome to join us if you want. You'd be very welcome."

"But I don't want to found a colony!" I struggled to understand my own visceral conviction that this would be the wrong course of action to choose for my future.

"Tough. When you have a slow dollar, you hold a fortune. When you have a million slow dollars, the fortune holds *you*. You need to move soon, or Sondra will attempt to take her loss—whether it was ever truly a loss or not—out of your skin. But even if you succeed in evading her, you're going to have to work out what you mean to do with the rest of your life sooner or later. Otherwise, the Atlantis Carnet will ride you like a bad dream."

"Thanks, sis." I put my most heartfelt sarcastic emphasis behind the words. "Do you have any other suggestions?"

"No, but I've got a request. Message for Rudi: Tell him I still think of him fondly, and everything is going according to plan . . ."

I t is a well-understood truism that interstellar warfare is impossible. Starships are prohibitively expensive. They cost millions of slow dollars, with a construction time measured in decades and a flight duration in centuries. In view of which inconvenient fact, it's almost impossible to imagine how an aggressor might recoup the cost of a warship's construction. Nor is it easy to conceal such a project: Starships are big, expensive prestige projects—if anyone built such a vehicle and launched it toward an already-inhabited solar system, the locals would have centuries to prepare a warm reception for it. There is no sensible way to profit by invasion and conquest: Interstellar commerce travels by light, in the form of information, rather than as physical commodities. By any rational reckoning, money spent on a warship would be better invested on a colony project targeting an uninhabited star system; and in any event, it takes so long to build a starship that any temporary insanity motivating such a gesture would evaporate long before the battleship could be built and launched.

Unfortunately, nobody told my mother.

Cold Vengeance

In a darkened, half-frozen vault aboard a hulk drifting between the stars, something stirred.

(Darkness, cold, and dust.)

For most of two millennia, the *Vengeance* had drifted in chilly isolation, systems mothballed, its surviving skeleton crew so deep in slow-time that it amounted to suspended animation.

Let me sketch you a plan of the *Vengeance*:

The front of the roughly cylindrical ship is a flat disk of beryllium armor that was originally nearly thirty centimeters thick; it's pitted and eroded to half that depth, the result of many centuries of exposure to the dust and gas of the interstellar medium. Sheltering behind it, active radar and phased-array installations to detect and vaporize incoming dust grains.

Behind the forward shield and sensors, a bulky series of fuel tanks and mothballed machines surround the central service and command core. Off to one side, the interstellar communicators—telescopes and laser transmitters—lie shielded by the fuel tanks, slaved to a beacon station now just a fractional arc second off-center from the star toward which the *Vengeance* is drifting. Behind them wait the cold, quiescent, fusion reactors needed for deceleration and maneuvering on arrival; and then more fuel tanks.

The *Vengeance* was built to cruise at almost 1 percent of light speed: at full tilt it would flash across the gap between Old Earth and its moon in fifteen seconds flat, racing the gulf from Earth to distant Pluto in weeks. That it would take centuries or millennia to fly between the nearer stars speaks to the immense scale of interstellar space.

This much of the *Vengeance* was like any other starship. Where it differed lay in the minds and training of her crew, and the nature of her cargo. A normal ship might carry survey probes and asteroid-mining tools, mechanocyte incubators and eager colonists. The *Vengeance* carried a thousand tons of enriched uranium, and the fast breeders and reprocessing tanks necessary to turn the stockpile into plutonium, and the bomb factories with which to murderously redeem some dreadful debt.

(Cold, dusty, darkness.)

Built after the mad frenzy that greeted the disappearance of Atlantis and the first true depression to impact the interstellar economy in over two millennia, the *Vengeance* was the third (and final) starship dispatched to that star system. The first two ships abruptly lost contact after they reached cruise velocity: The remaining creditors, incensed, drew the most obvious conclusion. Once might be accident, twice might be coincidence . . . but why take risks? Nobody had ever built an interstellar warship (although vicious squabbles between rival low-gee colonies and asteroidal republics occasionally degenerated into fighting—usually terminated by the abrupt rediscovery of the fact that the universe itself was more than happy to help the killing sprees along). But the principle seemed obvious enough: It would be a specialized variant of the well-understood normal starship architecture, one designed to transport and implant a military-industrial complex into the heart of an already-colonized system. On its arrival it would open its optical receivers and download updated weapons blueprints and personnel, to provide a beachhead on stranger shores, and the manufacturing industry it bore the kernel of would bear only bitter fruit. Of course, only the most desperate creditors were crazy enough to buy into this theory: But they were crazy enough to bet their all on it.

Then, fifty years after its departure, the *Vengeance*, too, went dark.

(Dusty, dark, cold.)

"Are you sure this is entirely safe?" I asked, as the squid-folk fastened me to the underside of the bathyscaphe and threaded pressure-relief cannulae into my arteries.

"I'm sure it's safe," Rudi buzzed from somewhere on the inside of his twenty-centimeter-thick hyperdiamond sphere. "We're not going to ascend so fast that you don't have time to unroll your pressure adaptations, are we? It wouldn't do to turn your brains into spam before you open your new deposit account, would it?" High-pitched crackling laughter ensued.

The empty soul-chip sockets at the back of my skull itched. I gritted my teeth and focused my attention on the squid medics as they bounced and fluttered around me, wielding scalpels and makerbot tanks and slimy gobbets of adhesive gel. "How does this work again?"

"Assertion: Is very safe," said one of the squid—Yankee color-of-erythrocytes, I think this one was called. "Assertion: Is standard medical-safe procedure for rapid ascent to surface altitude. Maximum ascent rate two kilometers per hour, ten-minute pause at each two-kilometer level. There will additionally be three major reset stages of one hour each during which mechanosomal restructuring must proceed. System is entirely automatic, speeded by external blood perfusion to prevent emboli during final decompression."

Wonderful: They were going to plug me into an external heart/lung machine to prevent decompression sickness! Doubtless they knew what they were doing: But if anything went wrong, I could bleed out in minutes, long before we reached the surface. I rolled my eyes and lay back as two other squid wove a hammock around me.

"Assertion: We do this regularly to those who need to visit the surface," said Yankee color-of-erythrocytes. (I think they were trying to be reassuring.) "It almost never fails. And if it does, death is painless."

I tried not to think about death through explosive decompression. "Rudi. What happens when we reach the surface?" I asked.

A chittering as of angry flying foxes filled my ears for a moment. Then: "It all depends on which way Medea decides to jump," he said, not entirely reassuringly. "But your tentacle-friends claim to have a plan. There's a cargo vehicle fueled and waiting to go up, they say. There's room for our capsule on top."

"A cargo—" I paused. "We're talking about highly enriched uranium solution here, aren't we?"

"That *is* the stuff," Rudi agreed.

"We're talking about multiple critical masses of the stuff, aren't we?"

"Many thousands of critmasses of boom-juice, yes!"

"They launch those things using a nuclear saltwater rocket, don't they? How often do they blow up?"

"Only one percent of the time." Rudi's voice slowed, as if overcome by a momentary uncertainty. "But it's safer than pinning your hopes on Medea, I think."

"Oh, really? Why do you think that?"

"I gather she has been entertaining the Priestess Cybelle. Who has doubtless been poisoning her ears and blackening both our reputations."

If my lungs had been functional, I would have sighed. "Do you have any good news to pass on, Rudi?"

"Nothing. Well, rumors of a very rich dignitary from New California arriving at Taj Beacon, but that's obvious nonsense and disinformation. Your line mother wouldn't follow you in person, would she?"

I kept quiet although my guts turned to ice at his words. If Sondra had actually followed me in person, then I needed to ensure that Rudi had as little contact with her as possible: He might decide to sell me out. That was one of the major risks. The other . . . well, what did she think she could achieve here? Stop me uploading through the beacon station? *Destroy* the beacon station? Kill everyone who had the merest inkling of her involvement with the crime of the millennium? I had no idea. All I could be certain of was that her presence here implied a certain degree of derangement, which made her extradangerous.

"We've got to shut down the retina soon, Krina—don't want to risk emitting identifying signals during the ascent—but I left Dent in Argos with instructions to get the lander out of hock. Hopefully by the time we need it he'll have found a way to return it to orbit without alerting the authorities. He's good at locating, ah, unconventional markets."

A forensic accountant with a knack for locating unconventional markets? I supposed a privateer would need someone with such abilities. I would just have to hope that Dent was good enough at it to avoid detection.

Time swam by in a haze of apprehension as our preparations for launch continued. Finally, their job done, the ground crew—for want of a better word—jetted away, leaving one figure behind: a mermaid, silvery blue against the glittering background of the city beneath us. She swam slowly toward me, then took a turn around the bathyscaphe. "Ana?" I called.

My sister swam toward me, closing until she hung in the water mere centimeters away. "Krina," she said awkwardly.

"Take care," I said. "I mean, look after yourself."

"We haven't had nearly long enough together." Another awkward pause. "I was looking forward to your visit for so long. And then, this."

"And this," I agreed. "You're sure you're going to join them?"

She smiled sadly. "Yes." And I could see that she meant it. Our sibhood is not a close and loving family. "The People have got something I've always needed. I'm not as self-sufficient as you, Krina. I just hope you eventually find something that loves you."

"I've got my research." I experimented with my facial muscles smiling back.

To my surprise, she leaned forward and kissed me lightly on the lips.

"Go now," she said. "Get away from Mother's shadow and find out who you are. Create wealth rather than hoarding it. Live life."

"I'll do my best," I began, as a jolt ran through the hammock around me. "Oh! Ana. Good luck!"

She was still watching me as the 'scaphe rose, pulling away into the dark, oily layer above the drowned city of Hades-4. And then I was alone in the crushing darkness and cold, wondering if I'd made a terrible mistake.

Sondra awakened slowly in her cocoon: blinked, then opened eyes in her new body.

Did she pause a moment to savor her triumph? I don't believe she did. My lineage mater was nothing if not purposeful, remote, and in control. She had planned for this eventuality so long ago that it had become one with the ephemera of history, merging into the definitional detritus of her existence. She'd refactored her identity many times, reinventing herself around this constant: that she was the banker for the conspiracy, that the shareholders would be gathered in due course in Dojima System for the final assembly and winding-up of the investment vehicle . . . and that she would have an ace up her sleeve. *Vengeance*, the vessel she had invested in during the centuries of chaos: the vessel she had picked a tenth of the crew of, selected and carefully trained retainers who, when the time came, had assembled at their watch stations, acknowledged her order, and calmly consigned their unconscious slow-timed crew mates to the vacuum of interstellar space.

Once control was established, they fired up the main engines for an unscheduled burn. *Vengeance* had launched from Hector toward Atlantis. Dojima was a mere ten degrees off the direct line from Hector to Atlantis, almost ten light-years farther out. After the burn, *Vengeance*'s new course was set to miss its original destination by more than a million light seconds . . . and would converge with Dojima System rather more than a thousand years later.

Vengeance had never been intended to reach Atlantis. But now it was nearing the end of its voyage, and its true destination: And Sondra had a use in mind for it.

Hand-claws tugged at the outside of her cocoon, pulling away the fibrous insulation. Sondra reached up, feeling circulatory fluid pulse in her arms, and fumbled for the internal fastener. Her lungs filled: There was air here, musty and cold and metallic-tasting. "Assist, please," she said, transmitting via electrosense rather than crude acoustic vibrations.

"Yes, Captain." The cocoon began to split.

Sondra hatched into the red-lit twilight of the warship's bridge, surrounded by warriors born of nightmare. The ship was still in free fall, main engine unlit. High-gee webbing stretched from walls to ceiling to floor throughout the space gave it the atmosphere of an ancient, abandoned funnelweb lair, for much of the mesh was ancient and friable, the graphene tapes damaged by long radiation exposure and coated with the dust of ages. Fresh yellow webbing, newly strung by the pair of marines in spiderlike battlebodies working diligently at the far side of the bridge, showed where the process of refurbishment was under way. Meanwhile, the night watch on the bridge paid attendance on their captain: humaniform skeleton-figures with huge, chibiform eye sockets housing blacklensed optics, their muscles deliberately attenuated to save mass in microgravity, skin replaced by armor. "Captain," hissed the nearer figure, "we are ready to commence crew revival and predeceleration refurbishment on your word."

"Good." Sondra sat up and began to claw her way out of the cocoon. She, too, was unnaturally etiolated, thin and armored, a parody of the form she had worn into the departure terminal at Taj Beacon: a battlebody. "Where's Jean?"

"The lieutenant is inspecting the primary bomb factory, Captain. He indicated that he would have a full report for you shortly after your arrival."

"Good." Sondra floated free of the cocoon. She reached out, grabbed a webbing support, then turned to orient herself on the captain's chair at the center of the module. "Who's next on the roster?"

"Our incoming buffers are full: We are expecting full crew resurrection in four standard days, but for the moment, the lieutenant ordered Arrivals to prioritize construction of your body, Captain. Chief Operations Officer Mao will be the next to hatch, then we will work our way down the list."

"Hmm." Sondra thought for a moment. "And how far are we from beginning our initial deceleration burn?"

"Your patience please . . . we are less than eighteen light-hours from the entry gate." The watch officer consulted a checklist retina hanging from one wall. "One hundred and fifty shipboard days, and the main drive will be ready to come online. At which point we will be another sixty light-hours from Dojima's primary. Call it a year to decelerate to stellar orbital velocity—"

"We won't be doing that. Events have run ahead of schedule, and it will take far too long to slow down and execute the original mission profile. We have personnel aboard Taj Beacon already, and a working bidirectional link."

"Captain?" The skeletal ensign sounded uncertain.

"We're not going to decelerate. Our task is to press our attack until all reaction mass and energy reserves are expended. Then we will abandon ship and upload to Taj Beacon, leaving a scuttling charge behind. We have momentum and surprise on our side: I don't intend to waste it." She grinned at the darkness: "My traitorous daughters and their allies must be taught a lesson. One that they won't live long enough to forget."

W hat goes down must come up, especially when there's a pressure gradient driven by a forty-kilometer-high pressure column behind it. On the other hand, the drag of an irregular body forcing its way through all that liquid is not inconsiderable. And so I dangled in the darkness beneath the bathyscaphe for a very long time indeed, trying not to ponder the things that could go wrong with the ascent, and focusing instead on the alluring opportunities that lay ahead of me.

I couldn't think of any.

I am Krina Alizond-114, and I was born into debt as a slave within the banking mills of New California. Over decades I paid off my debt of instantiation and acquired a modicum of security as an autonomous citizen. I performed my allotted tasks and pursued my hobby in my spare time, a hobby that had been suggested to me by my work: a profitably distracting amusement that coincidentally filled in gaps in my employer's record-keeping and turned a trivial profit. Until Andrea and Ana (and others whom I shall not name) sucked me into the biggest game of all: trying to run down proof that the disappearance of Atlantis was the blowout at the end of a monumental fraud. But that, too, was a diversion and an amusement: I never, at any point, imagined that it would explode under my feet, that we might simultaneously prove our hypothesis and offend our creator and—whisper it—owner.

Yes, I was suddenly, shockingly, abruptly wealthy. But by the same token, my life was over. I could never go back to New California. I couldn't possibly reenter my life within the tissue-wrapped shell of a nun-accountant. To resume my scholastic pilgrimage would inflict chaos on my colleagues, for great concentrations of money exert a gravitational field that tugs strongly upon the minds of the unhinged and desperate. Having become rich, I could not disclaim it—even if I publicly gave it away, there would always be people who imagined that I was hiding a secret fortune. I was, in fact, utterly adrift between worlds. Ana was right: If you come into too much money, the money will eat you.

Money. An instrument invented in ancient temple complexes, to keep track of debt: counters that acquired mobility and went a-walking, weaving webs of debt into vast and intricate meshes, enslaving and directing the labor of billions in service of the obligations created by its issuance. Latterly, slow money: a framework invented to systematize the repayment of debt across interstellar distances, to provide for stable exchange of labor by light-speed transmission. Money: a shadow play projected on the walls of our minds by the dark sun of debt. In picking up my part of the Atlantis Carnet, I had laid claim to the repayment of a debt serviced by millions of now-dead people; people presumably killed by my lineage mater and her coconspirators. I found myself looking at it from outside, with newly opened eyes. What I saw looked uncommonly like a different kind of fraudulent vehicle: a Ponzi scheme sprayed across the cosmos, the victims entire solar systems, the pyramid spreading on a wave of starships.

We rose through darkness and pressure for more than a standard day. The 'scaphe stopped periodically, creaking and popping as its internal systems adapted to the slowly diminishing pressure. I could feel it in my marrow, and in my 'cytes: compressed macromolecules expanding and reconfiguring, lipid membranes unpacking, as the balance of forces holding my internal components in shape at every level shifted. They'd left me a talking box to provide an idiot's commentary on our ascent, all facts and no insight. "Attention, Krina: Decompression stage two reached. Ascent will pause for one hour. Please connect Red Cartridge Two to your infusion port, then confirm." I did as I was told: The idea of exploding messily (or, more likely, dying painfully as various mechazymes stopped working, irreversibly denatured by a pressure-induced phase change) did not appeal. Even when life lacks allure, death may still repel.

As for my rescuers . . .

I spent a long time staring up into the darkness, at the silhouette of the nearly invisible bathyscaphe above me, without even any monstrous deep-dwelling critters for company: The 'scaphe was big enough to frighten them all away. A solitary pilot light glowed above and around the curve of the pressure sphere, barely limning it against the abyssal night. What was going on inside it? What dreams did Rudi and his crew harbor?

Acquiring a client of such size would be a monumental coup for Rudi, who would not only reap a gigantic commission from his employer but would, in turn, be in a position to support more large customers: It was the breakthrough his institution had been seeking since its arrival in Dojima System. But was I perhaps too big a client? Big enough to tempt him to discount future business and goodwill and dive overboard into truly lawless piracy? I'd left my soul-chip backup and my spare scratch-pad chip with Ana, committing everything I needed—including my fortune in slow dollars—to the frailty of merely human memory. But I could afford no illusions. If Rudi was ruthless enough to use his slave controller, he could steal my onerous wealth—but at the cost of doing so in public, destroying forever his claim to be an honest privateer acting under letters of marque. My gamble was in guessing that Rudi, as I had come to know him over the past year, would not change markedly in the presence of great wealth: in believing that he was an intelligent rogue, clever enough to act in his long-term best interest. If he wasn't, we were both probably doomed.

A second thought hit me then. Suppose that Rudi was indeed trustworthy. But what of his parent institution? What did I *really* know about the Permanent Assurance? An out-system bank and insurance agency with credentials recognized by some of the governments of Dojima System, it had expanded across interstellar space and opened up a subsidiary here. Pretty tenuous, that background. He'd supplied me with a fine portfolio of reports to read during our ascent, but I had no way of confirming their contents. Going interstellar was a daring, if not radical, business move: Few organizations ever attempted to coordinate at such range, for the only medium of internal exchange that could be used to couple their activities was slow money. Who were they, to have taken such a risky gamble in an industry as famously risk-averse as underwriting? Rudi might be trustworthy, but could I trust his bosses?

I was angsting pointlessly along these lines when, with no warning whatsoever, the retina plastered overhead lit up like a window into the heart of the sun and blared sound at me. "Krina, are you still there?"

"Quiet!" I called, shielding my eyes from the burning brightness. "You're too loud and too bright!"

"Oops." The retina dimmed a little. "Is this better?"

"A bit." The speaker was not Rudi: pitch too high, intonation wrong. "Is that Marigold?"

"Yes. Rudi asked me to talk to you: He's busy."

"Busy with what?" I asked.

"We have a cable to the surface, to the barge we descended from. He's talking to, to the Queen of Argos, via satellite link." Marigold sounded troubled. "Medea is very angry. She's demanding that we turn you over immediately."

This might sound strange to you, but I immediately felt a flush of relief at the news. "He's not planning to do that," I replied with certainty.

"Well, no." She hesitated. "But it raises problems, he says. Do you understand?"

I understood all too well. Queen Medea had clearly noticed my disappearance from under her nose despite her network of police and spies. Doubtless, she had intended to use me as bait in a trap for Ana, and she was angry that I had been snatched from it so abruptly. Word had somehow escaped that we had done the impossible: Rumor is the only information channel that travels faster than light. She'd probably guessed that Rudi was involved somehow: It wasn't hard to see why. And now she was trying to stake her claim to the Atlantis Carnet, using the last argument of kings.

"What do you want?" I asked, carefully feeling the web of support tapes around me.

"Here's Rudi," said Marigold.

"Krina." I recognized his voice instantly: The febrile tension was new. "Medea is issuing ultimata. She seems certain that I'm holding you captive, and she is demanding that I hand you over and warning of violent consequences if I do not."

"Good."

"Yes, that was my reaction: If she knew where we were, she wouldn't bother with the threats."

"What do you intend to do?" I asked.

"We have an agreement." And indeed we did, or we had, a day earlier and twenty kilometers deeper: a 10-percent commission in return for services rendered, the establishment of a deposit account secured against shares in the Permanent Assurance, public acknowledgment of my shareholding, and . . . well, it had taken Ana and myself most of a day to hammer out the small print with Rudi.

"Of course I intend to honor it. But she's threatening to drop depth charges on Hades-4 and launch missiles at the Five Zero if I don't hand you over. So I was wondering if you have any suggestions about how to handle her?"

"Hm. What's the basis of her claim?"

"Some nonsense about the Church's having produced someone who says he was bilked out of a fortune by the annoyingly dead Mr. Trask. Perhaps Trask was implicated in more crimes than merely washing your mother's laundry?"

"That's possible." I thought for a minute. "But it's a cash instrument. Trask is long dead. If the Church produced this claimant, then they—" I stopped dead. "Oh no."

"Oh no what?" I could picture Rudi at that moment, tongue lolling from his jaws, looking carnivorously amused as only a microgravity flying fox could.

"The *Church*." I should have realized sooner. "Rudi, what is the probability that the chapel would have arrived in Dojima System at this precise time, just by accident or happenstance or coincidence?"

"Nonsense, it's just a—" His jaws shut with an audible snap.

"We are *very close* to the two thousandth anniversary of the Atlantis blackout," I pointed out. "Here is the Church. Here am *I*. I was steered into this vocation about a century ago, while working for my mater's systembank. *Here* is Dojima, which is a remarkably rich and pleasant colony system, founded in the wake of the post-Atlantis colonization bubble. Rudi, *none* of this is a coincidence. Except, I think, possibly your presence—how old is the Permanent Assurance?"

"Oh, very old! We were incorporated four hundred and seventy standard years ago, from the merger of—"

"A newcomer and a bystander, in other words. Rudi, the Atlantis fraud was so big that the perpetrators had to wait for the ripples to die down before they could liquidate the proceeds. In the meantime, most of the stolen money was invested under the cover of a wave of new colonization—including the foundation of Dojima's beacon station and subcolonies. I suspect the core of the conspirators arranged in advance to meet here, after two thousand years, to split the remaining slow money cash pile. But in the meantime, some of them—my mother, whoever is working inside the Church of the Fragile, possibly others—decided to thin the pool of rival beneficiaries. I think you need to assume that anyone who threatens or cajoles us from now on is a mass murderer—"

BOOOOM.

A concussive thud ripples through the water around me, and my body: The acoustic positional sense I get from my lateral lines tells me it's a very long way away, and above us. It's followed by a hissing, sizzling sound, a distant, eerie shriek of bubbles imploding under extreme pressure.

"—is that?" Rudi demanded: "Did you hear that?"

"It's a long way away." My voice sounded flat and distant to me. "Overhead, kilometers away . . ." I tried to remember the direction, but I was too rattled by it. "Someone's making a point. Medea, probably. You mentioned depth charges? If it's overhead, she's not serious about attacking Hades-4 yet—"

"I'm worried about the support barge." A pause. "We can't hurry this along, can we? Grow you a new body up top?"

"I wasn't bluffing about leaving my backups behind," I reminded him. A risky tactic, but a necessary one: I wanted my living body to be indispensable, the only store of the value I held in my memory.

"Well, we shall just have to string Medea along with some artfully composed lies. Hrrr . . . Krina, how well can you act?"

Permanent Crimson

In a secure control room deep in the heart of the royal fortress under Nova Ploetsk, three militant instances of Queen Medea reclined in an outward-facing horseshoe pool, at the focus of a room-sized retina displaying a real-time fish-eye map of the hemisphere of Shin-Tethys. They were not alone: Her Grace Cybelle, Priestess-Missionary of the Church of the Fragile, waited patiently on a poolside recliner, while around them the executive officer corps of the Kingdom of Argos's orbital defense command attended to their workstations.

"I'm going to strangle him," one of the Queens announced, absent-mindedly flexing her hands.

"Get in line," said another. Turning to Cybelle, she added: "We don't like thieves. Especially the rent-seeking kind."

Cybelle watched the triumvirate with no discernible emotion visible on her face. "We trust you will only do so once you have obtained that which is required."

"*Bankers,*" spat the third queen-instance. "Theft with interest."

"He's an insurance underwriter, not a banker," said the first. "Just as bad, really."

"We can agree that he is thoroughly wicked," Cybelle interrupted. "But discussion of his eventual disposal is perhaps premature . . ."

A signal light flashed on above the console of one of the officers in the outer circle. "Your Majesties, Your Grace . . . ?"

"Report!" snapped the third Queen.

"Incoming call from Permanent Crimson Five Zero. They are relaying. Do you want to accept?"

"Send it to the main retina," said the first Queen. "Pause it on my signal." Heads turned to face the middle of the situation display as a black rectangle appeared, then slowly brightened to reveal a distorted fox face, huge dark eyes and protuberant fangs filling the viewport.

"Good day. *Hrrrr* . . ." Rudi grinned, revealing a fang-filled maw. "Greetings from nowhere in particular. I believe we have a commodity to discuss?"

"We do not negotiate with—" began the third Queen, before her co-instances spoke over her. "What's your price?" demanded the first. "Our valiant sailors have a firing solution on your vehicle: Think hard before you try our patience!" erupted the second. They fell silent simultaneously.

Behind them, the priestess spoke: "If I may intercede?" she asked.

The first queen-instance recovered first: "Please do so." She extended her hands toward her sisters, both palms pulsing red: "We shall confer meanwhile."

The trio of Queens linked hands and fell silent as they attempted to synchronize their emotional states. Cybelle walked around the royal pool and positioned herself in front of the viewport. "May the peace of the Fragile be upon you, branch manager. I gather you have found what you came here for. Is that so?"

There was a brief pause as the carrier signal clawed its way laboriously up to orbit, then back down to wherever the branch manager was hiding—possibly including some additional delay, just to obscure his location further. Then Rudi replied, "Good day to you, too, Your Grace, and may I take this opportunity to apologize for the circumstances of our previous meeting? Yes, I am indeed in possession of a most interesting financial instrument. I take it you are familiar with the saying that possession is nine-tenths of the law? The other tenth being the last argument of kings—or Queens—a-ha, ha. Ha. And it is that tenth that I should like to discuss with you, assuming your presence in Her Majesty's command and control suite indicates that you have her confidence."

"I can speak for the Church but not the state." Cybelle glanced at the triumvirate. "You have grievously offended Her Majesty."

"Yes, well, the relationship between interstellar capital and the temporal powers has always been somewhat fraught, has it not? They create bottomless pits of debt, we help them dig their way out, and what do we get for it? But I digress. Does the Church declare an interest in this business?"

"Yes, we do." Cybelle's smile was wintry. "The disposition of an inheritance that was stolen by a corrupt banker is at stake. The inheritor has assigned their entire estate to the Mother Church, and we thus inherit an interest in their—"

"Bullshit." Rudi lolled. "You would have us believe that your mission turned up in Dojima System just in time to assert an interest in an instrument retrieved at this *very moment* by skilled forensic technicians who were not even born, much less old enough to have commenced their training, until after your chapel departed from its parent cathedral?" The Queens, still locked hand to hand in high-bandwidth communion, startled and glared at Cybelle as one. "Or that the banker with whom this instrument *originated* might just happen to be setting up headquarters in one of Taj Beacon's most expensive hostelries *right now*, purely by coincidence? This train of random happenstance defies logic, not to mention causality, Your Grace. You might as well drop the pretense: We know about Atlantis, we know all about money laundering. A gathering of thieves at a preordained location a fixed period after the deed was done, there to divide up the remaining spoils, is hardly unexpected."

Cybelle shuffled from foot to foot, focusing on the screen with wide-eyed intent. "You have no evidence," she said, taking a moment to glance over her shoulder at the Queens, who were now focusing on her person with pinch-browed concentration, as behind them a squad of royal guards adopted a pose that spoke more of vigilant readiness than of formal salute. "There were no witnesses, and you can't prove anything."

"Oh. Really?" Rudi moved, then, making some off-viewport adjustment: The image changed. A dim blue light illuminated, from above, a prisoner, cocooned and trussed to a metal framework dangling in darkness. The prisoner stared helplessly at the viewport: gagged, hands bound, a picture of vulnerability. "This is your witness: Krina Buchhaltung Historiker Alizond-114, as I captured her, fleeing into the depths to join her sister. You will note the merform morphology: She evidently had her escape route well planned out. But that is not relevant to the point I would like to make.

"Sera Alizond is a historiographer of accountancy practices, with a special interest in the history of a particular type of fraudulent practice, the 'FTL scam,' as I believe it is called. Yes, she was induced to pursue this interest by her lineage founder, Sondra Alizond-1—I see from your expression that you are familiar with her—and at the time I captured her, she was in possession of what I believe to be a copy of the uncommitted counterpart to the very large financial instrument we are discussing. Unfortunately she had stored it in a memory palace in one of her cranial backup slots, and when capture was clearly inevitable she deep-sixed it, because, as you are no doubt already aware, she's a vindictive little shrimp."

At this point in Rudi's narrative I flopped around angrily and rolled my eyes as convincingly as I could, doing my best impression of a vindictive little shrimp who had been caught red-handed in possession of her employer's stolen property. (Whatever a shrimp might be.) I don't know whether I succeeded in convincing the priestess that I was afraid of Rudi, but I certainly came close to blowing the entire setup by losing my grip on the "restraints" I had improvised from my depth-acclimation kit and the webbing beneath the bathyscaphe.

Rudi grinned, baring his fangs. "Despite losing the financial instrument and depriving me of a not-inconsiderable fortune, Dr. Alizond managed to hold on to her primary backup chip. Which, you will be pleased to learn, is no longer occupying a socket in her head. *I* have it, and I also have the necessary schematic for assembling a blank body into which to download a new instance of her twisty little mind. More to the point, I have already uploaded the schematic and a serialized dump of her soul chip to Branch Office Five Zero, from whence it has *already* been transmitted to a secure off-site backup location. Encrypted, of course. However, if I don't regularly confirm that I am alive and at liberty, a trusted escrow agent of mine will release the decryption key and make copies of Dr. Alizond available to anyone who wants to interrogate her.

"And none of you want that to happen, do you? Because she knows more about your little conspiracy than you realize."

"Have you finished monologuing yet? Or was there meant to be some point to this?" asked the priestess, just as the three queen-instances behind her dropped each other's hands and gave vent to a collective howl of heartfelt frustration and rage.

"Yes, there's a point," Rudi snapped, as if at an invisible quadrotor bug looping around his muzzle. "I'm leaving. No, seriously. This has been a complete waste of money and time for me: a most annoying loss. But I know better than to try to recover sunk costs—a-ha ha—so you may take it as read that I do not really *want* to be shot out of the sky or to release the miscreant's memories to all and sundry. What I desire is to put this sorry episode behind me and get back to the business of underwriting winners. So I'm going to offer you a once-in-a-lifetime bargain. You let me return to my branch office and depart from orbit without trying to blast me out of the sky, and I'll tell you where to find Dr. Alizond. How about it?"

"We do *not* negotiate with—" "How do we know you're telling the truth?" "Drop it, sis, he's a fundamentally untrustworthy lying little shit-weasel." The Queens spoke simultaneously again, colliding in a hubbub of internal disharmony. While they were preoccupied, the priestess peered at a small retina wrapped around her wrist. Her eyes narrowed. "Your Majesties?" She attempted to get their attention. "Medea?"

"*What?*" Heads whipped toward her, simultaneously drawn by the implicit lesé majeste in her informality.

Cybelle bowed her head. "My recommendation would be to accept the privateer's terms. He has already sucked Dr. Alizond dry; our priority must be to prevent her particular insights from escaping into the wider discourse lest they cause the general public at large to scrutinize our projects with undue cynicism." She raised her head, attempting to make eye contact, but the Queens were too agitated to notice anything so subtle. "You"—she pointed at the communications officer—"please put the call on hold?"

"Your Majesty—"

"Do it," said one of the Queens, then turned back to face Cybelle. "This had better be good," she threatened.

"Oh, it *is*. Are we private . . . ?"

"He can't hear you."

"Good." Cybelle smiled at Medea's third body. "I think we should take Rudi's kind offer to run away and leave us the prize. (Not that it's much of a prize.) He's outfoxed himself this time."

"Why?" Medea asked sharply.

"I have just received word that Sondra isn't on Taj Beacon after all. And I do believe that if you allow our annoying privateer to think he's gotten away free, she will do our dirty work for us . . ."

W e were nearing the surface, departing the Hadean depths for the photic zone: The waters around the bathyscaphe were no longer completely black. We had been ascending for more than a day. It had been at least four hours since Rudi's attempt to bluff the Queen of Argos and her sacerdotal allies, and there had been no further underwater detonations to telegraph Medea's frustration. "I think they've taken the bait," Rudi told me during a brief reactivation of the bathyscaphe's external retina. "Not long now. I'll cut loose when we reach ten meters below surface level. Then we can put this behind us."

"You spin an excellent lie," I told him, finding it difficult to keep a note of admiration out of my voice.

"It's the first and most necessary skill of the grifter. You, of all people, should understand that."

The waters had brightened to sunlit turquoise, and I could see a shoal of feral piscoids grazing the underside of a leviathan grass field in the middle distance when I felt the 'scaphe's ascent cease once more. We hung from the roof of the sky like the aerostat fliers of prehistory. Which meant I was shortly going to discover whether there was, indeed, honor among thieves—or at least enlightened self-interest and a willingness to forgo short-term profit for long-term business goodwill. *Goodwill*: one of those things that bankers and accountants hate because it is so inevitably unquantifiable, existing only in the eye of the beholder.

The retina above me flashed alight again. "Krina? We'll be reaching our rendezvous in five minutes. You need to be ready to swim free as soon as you see the ascent capsule. Understood?"

I looked up at the display. It was Marigold: the 'count was clearly preoccupied elsewhere. I nodded. "Ready," I said, and began to cut away at the restraining tapes that held me in on the mesh platform slung below the 'scaphe. (They'd given me a small cutting disk before departure, perhaps overly confident that I wouldn't seek to use it to sabotage their submersible or my own circulatory system.)

Off in the distance, something spooked the swarm of fishlike feral 'cyte collectives feeding on the grass. It was vast and cylindrical, looming out of the turbid waters like an ancient vision of a submarine riding on the surface, the keel and stabilizers of a narrow surface ship visible to either side of it, like a whale being ravished by a catamaran. A small, bluntly conical cap sat at one end of it, disturbingly phallic, surrounded by some sort of boarding platform. *The capsule*, I realized. Probably the very same one we had made our descent aboard. The cylinder behind it must be the freighter the Hadeans had discussed with Rudi.

A roaring rush of bubbles churned the water immediately above my head into white foam, making me flinch: Air was rushing out of the bathyscaphe's pressure sphere. I swam free and turned to stare as the sphere fizzled and dissolved, disgorging its occupants. A trio of familiar figures dropped into the water, with much graceless flapping of legs and membrane-encumbered arms: Rudi and his cohort had clearly not bothered with more than the most rudimentary water-breathing modifications, presumably because they didn't expect to be here for very long.

"Ah, Krina! I take it you enjoyed the relaxing ride?" Rudi asked, his electrospeech crackling badly in the water.

I flipped and arrowed toward Rudi, turned and oriented to face him just short of impact. He flinched. "I've had better," I announced. Marigold was flailing, trying to turn to face me, and Dent, the bag-carrier, was clearly in some difficulty. I swam over and steadied them. For the first time since my arrival, I felt as if I had the advantage. "What's the cover story?"

"There isn't one," Rudi buzzed, clearly ill at ease with underwater speech. "It's just a regular cargo launch by the deep dwellers, destined for rendezvous with their freight broker in synchronous orbit. Which just happens to be where Five Zero is sitting, right now. We paid them handsomely to reduce their payload and look aside while we strap our lander to the front—"

"This payload. Would it also happen to be insured by way of a policy backed by your office?" I asked.

Rudi tried to draw himself up, to assume a dignified posture: He failed badly. "I have no idea what you're implying! In any case, time is fleeting. We need to go on board immediately—"

"Barratry," I pointed out. "Not to mention insurance fraud, piracy on the high seas, theft of weapons-grade nuclear materials, doubtless compounded by failing to file a flight plan—"

"Because you're worth it, my dear. Anyway, I purchased the entire cargo fair and square: I have a perfectly legitimate use for it. Now, do you want the ride I've arranged? Or would you rather wait here until Medea's minions arrive, or the Church, or any of the other parasites who are circling?"

Marigold was showing signs of getting her shit together. "Certainly," I said. "Let's go."

As it happened, I made it to the boarding platform beside the capsule end of the vehicle well before Rudi's crew. I found the chance to swim across a quarter kilometer of open water refreshing after spending so much time in a hammock. As I neared the platform a squid-person jetted toward me. "Ultimatum: Identify yourself!"

"I'm Krina Alizond-114. Who are you?"

The squid spun round, flaring his mantle at me. "Identify: This one is Chi scent-of-skinned-worms-in-the-water. Assertion: Would like to express satisfaction at your accomplishment, and assistance in resolving a small matter."

"Huh. The small matter. Would it happen to involve a certain privateer?"

"Confirmation: Of course. Assertion: Your sister sent you a gift. She said, 'Use it wisely.'"

"What—" The squid curled one tentacle back inside his mantle and produced a tiny box of familiar design, then presented it to me. "Oh!" An emotion I couldn't name made my vision blur for a moment. "Please thank her for me." I carefully transferred it to my belt, attaching the soul-chip carrier beside the talking box that had replayed my decompression instructions. There would be time to identify its contents later. It might be Ana's way of politely telling me she thought my suspicions were misplaced; and then again, perhaps its contents would allow us to undertake our study seminar after all. "What about Rudi?"

I glanced over my shoulder: The privateers were bobbing along slowly. "Assertion: Accountant Rudi Five Zero advised The People to short all slow dollar funds. *All* of them. Assertion: This is, outwardly, insane. Assertion: Accountant Rudi Five Zero knows something. Interrogative: You should ask him *why* do that?"

"That's crazy! There's only two reasons to do that, and there's no probability of a Slow Jubilee anytime soon. That leaves faster-than-light—" I stopped suddenly, a cold chill running down my lateral lines. "Thank you, I think. Ah, I see they're catching up. Show me the way on board?"

The privateer's landing capsule looked very different when viewed through the hatch as it lay attached to the front of the booster stack, itself floating horizontally in its catamaran cradle. I could see signs of modifications made during my absence: a contoured couch that was perfectly tailored to accommodate a mermaid, for example. I suppressed a brief flicker of anger. Doubtless it was an off-the-shelf item here, but it indicated that Rudi had known what was going on for some time. Or anticipated it.

"Can you board it yourself?" Rudi asked me. "Do you need help?"

I glared at him. "I can make it," I said, pushing myself up on my forearms. The sun hammered down on my skin, drying me, and the weight and bulk of my torso and tail were unwelcome reminders of how I had been mutilated without consent. The sensation of air rushing in and out of my newly decompressed lungs felt breathless and strange. In my pisciform body I was a fish out of water: beached, ungainly, and sluggish. I kicked, pushing against the deck of the boarding platform, forcing myself up on my elbows, then down, dragging my trunk toward the hatch. It was horribly undignified, but I urgently wanted to assert my autonomy. Once we entered free fall, I should be as mobile as ever: Then I could see about having the Five Zero's surgeon-engineer resect the fishy tail and restore my legs to their original plan.

By the time I managed to crawl into my recliner, Rudi, Marigold, and Dent were already strapped in, and the hatch was closed. (Our surface crew, I gather, remained underwater for the whole process, relying on remote manipulators.) "Are you ready?" asked Marigold, "because there's a promising minimum-energy window opening in less than a thousand seconds."

"Go for it." Rudi looked, and sounded, satisfied. He glanced at me: "Do you need a hand?"

"No." I stared back, mulishly: When he looked away, I continued to grapple with my restraints. As the capsule was tilted on its side, this meant "lying" almost vertically: With no toes or feet, I dangled from my shoulder straps.

"Well, if everyone's strapped in . . ." This from Marigold: "I just told them to start the launch sequence. We should be moving very soon now."

And, indeed, she was right: I felt a faint thrumming run through the floor of the capsule, then a wondrous sense of relief when the floor tilted as the launcher rose toward the vertical. I hastily tightened my restraints. "How does this thing work, again?" I asked.

"Like an ancient war rocket," Marigold reassured me. "Our booster sits in a silo that floats with its nose just above the surface. When we're upright, the launch crew will eject us, then the nuclear rocket ignites once we're airborne."

"The motor—" I paused. "What if it doesn't light?"

"Oh, that *never* happens!"

Something cold and leathery grabbed my hand: I startled for a moment until I realized it was Rudi. He caught my gaze: "Don't worry," he said. "If it fails, it'll all be over too fast to hurt. But that won't happen. We're safe as a five-hundred-year bond."

I smiled at him, pretending for his sake to be reassured. "Let me get this straight. We're sitting in a capsule on top of several tons of barely subcritical plutonium liquor, powered by a nuclear rocket operated by communist-squid technology, the nearest thing to a government here-abouts has been threatening to shoot us out of the sky on sight, and you think we're *safe*—"

I didn't get to finish the sentence. I nearly didn't get to finish anything at all, for that matter: The booster stack beneath us suddenly lit, with a roar like the end of the world, and I discovered that, ungainly as I'd felt when I boarded the capsule, having my weight quintuple in under a second felt even worse. I barely had time to recover from being shoved abruptly back into my couch when the booster cut out with a violent jolt, then another, marginally gentler shove commenced. Scratchy white lines fogged my vision. "Don't worry, that's just secondary neutrons from the cargo," Rudi shouted above the thunder of the main engine. "It gets a bit frisky when the reactor goes critical!"

I closed my eyes: The light show didn't go away, but it helped me fake the illusion of self-control.

Shin-Tethys may be a massive world, but thanks to all the water, it isn't very dense: And so orbital velocity is relatively low. It took less than five minutes for the single-stage nuclear rocket to boost us out of the atmosphere and up toward the window for our transfer to synchronous orbit. I opened my eyes when the bubble-chamber scribble of particle tracks inside my eyeballs dropped off, then felt a gentle bump as the carrier rocket detached, presumably to complete a single orbit and return to the surface to collect its next payload.

"Ah, excellent." Rudi released his straps. "Marigold, please contact Five Zero and request a pickup at their earliest convenience. I think we should be on board in four, five hours at the most—"

The prospect of spending several hours locked in this floating canister with Rudi in preening self-congratulatory mode did not appeal, but I was short of distractions. And I found myself badly in need of distracting. Nothing that had happened to me in the past year and change since I had arrived in Dojima System made sense if taken at face value. Everyone I had met was pursuing a covert agenda, skewed at some slight strange angle to reality: Nothing was what it seemed. Rudi had slid from hijacker and kidnapper to—what? Ally? Prospective business partner?—backing away from threats and aggression toward blandishments and seduction. *Why?*

And then there was the Church: An even more bizarre mismatch between public image and interior goings-on would be hard to imagine, even without contemplating the machinations of Deacon Dennett against his rightful priestess. Queen Medea ... well, she was at least comprehensible as the usual intersection of greed and leviathan-like will-to-power, tempered by just enough subtlety to try to get what she wanted by letting me run. But the stalker who had stolen my face and attached herself to the Church—what was *that* about? And Sondra. Don't forget Sondra. What had bestirred her after all these centuries, to suddenly cut loose from her moorings and hurl herself screaming at the stars? Was it as simple as an urgent desire to conceal her corrupt involvement in a long-ago money-laundering scandal? Or was there something more at stake?

Almost without thinking, my hand went to the small soul-case fastened to my belt. Ana had sent it. A gift, she had implied. *Use it wisely.* Use what?

I glanced sidelong at my companions. They were, as I expected, busy elsewhere: Rudi nattering micromanaged instructions at Marigold, Marigold ignoring him as she grappled with the complexities of the capsule's long-range router, Dent lost in the comforting certainties of a spreadsheet. Careful to give no outward sign of what I was doing, I opened the small case and removed the chip. Then I raised it to my neck and slid aside the flap of skin covering the empty slot—the one where my backup usually sat, the running copy of my personality that I had left with Ana as a promise and a life insurance policy.

I slid the chip into place and composed myself, closed my eyes, and slid off into a waking hallucination as I opened the doors of the memory palace Ana had gifted me (in form, a ghostly reproduction of Sondra's palace, where we had both grown up). There was, as I expected, a README waiting in the entrance hall behind the outer doors: a lectern, chest high, bearing a codex, bound in the skin of dragons, locked with a brass key that I found on a chain around my neck. I walked toward it— the memory palace came complete with the memory of legs, for which I was grateful—and unlocked the cover of the book, opening it to the first page.

I began to read. And the universe changed around me.

. . .

L et me tell you what really happened in Atlantis System.

(I recognized Ana's writing in the README, for it was signed with a hash of her mind's state vector, as directly traceable to her as a slow dollar to its issuing bank.)

This is a secondhand account based on research documents that Andrea succeeded in copying under our mother's nose and forwarded to me. I hope for her sake that Andrea fled in time. As soon as I read them, I left my previously secure position in the Corporate History faculty of the College of the Outer Belt and fled via Argos in Shin-Tethys to my refuge with the People of the Deep, because this is the sort of material that gets you hunted down and killed, however thorough your backup-and-resurrection insurance policy may be.

You can find the original documents in the mezzanine level of the library, second wing, third bay, fourth galley. There are many shelves of them. So let me summarize.

Sometime after you left on your pilgrimage, it occurred to Andrea to wonder if anyone in our lineage had previously pursued interests quite like our little hobby. After all, if we have predecessors, they would have depleted the pool of available trophies, wouldn't they? Andrea searched . . . and the result was a negative. We are, it seems, the first generation of Sondra's offshoots to take an interest in orphaned slow money transfers. Then Andrea looked further. You know, as do I, the necessary specialist skills of our profession. Andrea checked the tuition archives. She checked them most thoroughly and came to the conclusion that we had been systematically channeled in this direction. It's a telling list of coincidences, sis: Not only Church and State and bankers arriving in Dojima System on schedule, but carefully trained and sublimely unaware forensic accountants hunting long-lost treasure.

Before the dawn of history, when humanity was entirely Fragile and confined to a single planet, there was a species of wild organism that was highly prized as a feedstock by those protohumans. It was called a "truffle," and it was rare, and grew underground. Truffles were noted for their characteristic smell, but Fragile noses were not strong enough to detect them. So they took a different species of animal, a thing called a "pig." Pigs liked truffles and had a good sense of smell, so they were easily trained to hunt for truffles: But the truffles were valuable enough that, once found, the pigs were not allowed to eat them.

You and I, sis, and Andrea: to Sondra we are merely truffle-hunting pigs, turned loose in a forest where she knew there would be many truffles to be found, ahead of her own arrival to collect the fruit of our searches. Specialized extensions of her identity, tailored for the task and to be used and disposed of with no more heed than a glove or a sock. Yes, Andrea found the evidence: My research post was made possible by a donation our lineage mater supplied through a cutout. Just as your study pilgrimage was nudged this way . . .

But that's not all. *Why* did Sondra expect us to find lots of juicy truffles in Dojima System?

More to the point, Krina, have you wondered what Sondra did to become so wealthy in the first place?

Andrea found Sondra's records by chance, while researching orphan transactions from SystemBank Hector, where Sondra got her start. What we had not realized is that Hector's SystemBank underwrote the Atlantis colony expedition. And that Sondra actually forked and sent an instance of herself along with the colony vehicle! She was not merely laundering the proceeds of a fraud—she was, at the other end, one of the directors of Atlantis SystemBank! She was able to sign currency transactions in both directions. I don't think that has ever been done before.

Now, as to the precise nature of the Atlantis fraud: I think you can see where it's going? Atlantis was *not* a boiler-room operation. It was a genuine research colony, populated by real scholars, dedicated to the goal of constructing a causality violation engine—a device that could connect points in spacetime instantaneously. The *appearance* of fraud that we attribute to Atlantis is due to two factors:

Firstly, that our lineage mater, and various collaborators among the founders of Atlantis, were using her relationship with her trusted counterpart (concealed by the growth in Atlantis SystemBank's interstellar debt) as a license to print slow money. Yes, she—our Sondra, the one at Hector—was forging slow dollars. Which requires collusion across interstellar distances: almost impossible, under normal circumstances.

And secondly, the reason Atlantis went dark is not that the conspirators who had established the colony as a fake investment vehicle were planning a blowout. Atlantis was not a fake after all. Rather, it's because Sondra attempted to kill them all to protect her fraudulent, largely forged, fortune. The scholars of Atlantis hadn't invented an FTL drive. Sondra's records are incomplete, but if anything, they appear to have proven once and for all that FTL is *impossible*. But in the process, they discovered how to use quantum entanglement to move macroscopic objects—such as entire colony habitats—between widely separated locations at the maximum speed permitted by physics, the speed of light. Quantum teleportation on a macro scale, in other words.

Do I need to diagram for you what happens to our interstellar financial system once a cheap, effective light-speed-propulsion system becomes available?

It's not as disruptive as a true FTL drive, of course. But it will instantly cause a collapse in the slow money system. Slow transactions are caught in a liquidity trap and can only be completed by a three-phase-commit process, so that they travel no faster than a third of light speed. A true light-speed drive would allow direct conversion of fast-currency systems, with no liquidity issues. To make matters worse, it appears that the teleportation drive is *cheap*, compared to the cost of the propulsion systems currently in use for starships and in-system vehicles. The foundation of a new colony world would no longer require huge investments of slow money. Sondra's little scheme—printing slow dollars on the side, to line her nest—would not only be devalued; it would rapidly be exposed.

I'm not sure exactly what she did to the poor scholars of Atlantis, but I imagine it had something to do with their SystemBank, and their beacon stations, and a drastic and simultaneous application of nuclear explosives. Nor am I certain which instance of Sondra did the deed. (If indeed it makes sense to talk about them as different people: Perhaps she'd arranged some bizarre protocol to merge her divergent states regularly, much as Queen Medea kept her different instances synchronized.) It's possible that the Atlantean sib uploaded a copy of herself to her sister, then suicided. More speculatively, it's possible she contrived to seize control of the first of the vehicles equipped with the light-speed drive and used it to escape. But however it played out, direct contact with Atlantis System was interrupted, under circumstances likely to induce extreme paranoia among the survivors.

We pick up the story over a century later, with the launch (and loss) of the various physical missions to Atlantis System. As you can imagine, New California—literally Sondra's investment vehicle—was instrumental in bankrolling all three missions. This ensured that Sondra was in a position to control the selection of their flight crew. A close reading of the reports of the inquiries into their loss reveals that what was lost was communication with the vehicles—they stopped transmitting, true, but as they had completed their boost phase and were drifting, and contact was lost when they were already more than a light-year outbound from their launch sites, it was impossible to confirm that they were destroyed: It is simply not possible to obtain useful images of a cold object a hundred meters in diameter at a range of over ten trillion kilometers.

My suspicion is that Sondra was again responsible. All three vehicles carried beacon transceivers capable of transmitting and receiving uploads, and during the drift stage of their mission, most of their crews would have entered slowtime: A small, coordinated cell of saboteurs could wreak havoc, then transmit themselves to safety.

I stress that this is speculation, Krina. But we may have been overestimating both the size and the audacity of the Atlantis fraud, and underestimating the ruthlessness and reach of its perpetrator. Who, along with her accomplices, has for a long time now planned a final liquidation meeting, to be held at Shin-Tethys, where the final proceeds can be divided up and the last of the conspirators killed.

Why killed?

Consider: The three-phase-commit model used to transfer ownership of a slow dollar transaction means that the donor must be able to find the recipient in order to complete the acknowledgment of transfer. Between systembanks, across interstellar channels, this is unremarkable. But for a covert transfer, at short range, it is unsafe for the recipient: The risk of robbery is not inconsiderable. Hence the use, in the Atlantis Carnet, of a cutout—the banker Ivar Trask-1—and the scandal of his subsequent disappearance. I think Sondra was testing a means of finding and murdering her coplotters: requiring them to reveal their location in order to receive their final commission. Of course, if this is what she planned, then it would result in a number of high-value orphan transactions that would require tracing and unwinding . . .

We were created and trained specifically to mop up the loose ends, after the murderous termination of the biggest fraud in history. If not for Andrea's prying—which was emphatically not part of Sondra's planning—we would be unaware of this. We would have pursued the Atlantis Carnet, it's true, not to mention the other missing transfers: but only under her direct control, and without insight into what it was about. And I very much fear that after locating them, we would have no future in her world.

Which is not to say that our lineage mater is going to succeed, sis. There is another player in this game, of whom Sondra appears to be unaware.

I think it's time you asked Foxy Rudi where Branch Office Five Zero *really* comes from . . .

Jubilee

"This institution of yours, the Crimson Permanent Assurance," I said. "Where exactly does it come from?"

On arrival and docking, Rudi and I had retreated into his private nest aboard the Five Zero. It was a small, cozy bower of felted fur and colorful silks, anchored to the trunk of one of the free-fall palms that lined the accommodation bubble of the vehicle. Rudi hung from the nominal ceiling, grooming his underarm fur, while I made casual use of the waterspout to damp down my scales and fins: It was humid in the accommodation spaces, but it was also hot, and my ocean-adapted body was inconveniently bad at retaining moisture. Rudi had done me the courtesy of dimming the lights, for I had acquired a stinking headache almost as soon as we emerged into the shriek and glare of the privateer's engineering decks. (I'd ordered up a pair of mirrored goggles from his personal fab as soon as we arrived here, but they were still growing.)

Rudi paused his grooming. "Why don't you tell me what you suspect?" he asked.

"You said your head office was incorporated in, where was it—"

"—Mombasa Six," he volunteered.

"Indeed. And I am absolutely certain that a corporate entity called the

Crimson Permanent Assurance was indeed incorporated in Mombasa Six nearly five hundred years ago, and it's your nominal headquarters, because you're not stupid enough to lie about that." I smiled, remembering not to bare my teeth. He cocked his head and looked at me politely.

"Do continue . . . ?"

"You suggested I might invest in your corporate hedge fund. But I gather you have also been advising the People to short any investment vehicles denominated in slow money." *Now* I showed him my toothy grin. "Assuming I hand you the thick end of two million slow dollars to invest on my behalf, what will you do with them?"

"I'd have thought that was obvious." He snapped his muzzle at a tangled tuft in one elbow, peeping out suspiciously at me over the top of his wing membrane. "I'd throw them away, taking whatever I can get in fast money, regardless of the exchange rate. Probably a ninety-five-percent loss, but it beats losing it all, and you'll still be independently wealthy. Isn't that what you were hoping to hear?"

I fanned myself through the stream of droplets from the water spigot, spraying watery baubles in all directions. "I believe you came from Atlantis, Rudi. *After* the blackout. None of this is a coincidence, is it?"

"Of course not." Over the past year, I had become attuned to some of the bat-privateer's mannerisms: What Rudi was showing me now was perhaps closest in intent to a piratical grin. "It's all about your lineage mater."

"Who succeeded in blowing the beacon station," I offered. "And who will make a serious attempt to kill you just as soon as she works out who and what you are."

"Which is?"

"A privateer, with letters of marque and reprise authorizing military action against the enemies of the nation which issued them. Yes?"

"And what nation would be . . . ?"

"Atlantis." There, I said it.

Rudi chittered. "Well done! Yes. I do indeed have a certificate from my government, calling for the arrest or destruction of the notorious renegade Sondra Alizond-1, for mass murder, attempted mass murder, crimes against humanity, and a laundry list of lesser offenses. But at the same time, the Permanent Crimson is entirely real: We are, indeed, insurance underwriters. It's very hard to move openly against a power such as your lineage mater, given the nature of her allies—"

"The Church?"

"Among others, yes. They were largely responsible for the Atlantis research program in the first instance—one imagines they believed that a successful FTL drive would finally bring the prospect for founding a New Eden for their Fragile charges to fruition—but they subsequently changed their minds, concluding that what our researchers had actually found would merely undermine the pyramid scheme they had engineered to drive the continual wave of colonization and expansion—"

"You mean, the quantum teleportation device?"

"Capital! You've been doing your homework!" Rudi snapped his jaws again. "I *knew* offering you a job was the right thing to do! You were wasted on Sondra."

"Be that as it may." I shook my head: Serious job offers were not something I had time to think about right now. "And then there are your other adversaries: anyone who has gone long in slow money. If word were to get out, not only would they try to squash you like a bug, but all your customers would dry up and run away. Otherwise, you'd have gone public centuries ago. Yes?"

"More or less." He tilted his head to the right. "The mere fact of the battleship that was sent, right after Sondra murdered everyone on Atlantis Beacon, told us all we needed to know. It never arrived, evidently meeting some misfortune in flight, but it was clear that powerful interests had resolved that it would be best to keep our breakthrough technology from leaking. We were badly damaged, you know, millions dead, their backups, too. The sabotage, a wave of bombs—it was *horrible*. The problem with the Atlantis program was that it isn't easy to replicate: It took a monumental effort to assemble ten million researchers and set them to work on a common goal for two or three centuries, in an age not noted for the pursuit of scientific knowledge for its own value. Any attempt to rediscover the device can be suppressed quite easily by assassinating dangerous researchers and spreading the slander that Atlantis was nothing more than a variant on the FTL fraud."

"So what happened? After Sondra tried to kill everyone—and presumably failed?"

"We—the postemergency government of Atlantis, I mean, I myself was not even forked at that time—made a hard decision not to relight the beacon. This was after an initial reconnaissance: We had a prototype, a ship that could reach Hector system in just six years. They went by stealth, gathered intelligence, inserted spies. It took another decade to learn which way the wind blew and six more years to return home, by which time the beacon was nearly rebuilt: But the spreading chaos was obvious. We had not merely been attacked by a corrupt agency, we had been attacked because we posed an existential threat to the banking system."

"So . . . ?"

"So. We chose the appearance of extinction or autarky. But we didn't remain completely isolated. Atlantis today conducts some limited, very discreet interstellar trade, acquiring information and items that we need. It is entirely denominated in fast money and carried out by a small fleet of vessels not unlike this one: modified intrasystem freighters."

"Wait. What, you're telling me that this is a *starship*? The Five Zero is capable of jumping between star systems at the speed of light?" I goggled at Rudi in frank astonishment. "And you trade goods and services across interstellar space using *fast* money? Why, that changes everything! The opportunities are almost unimaginable!"

"Indeed it does." Rudi grinned. "And you just bought into the company with a senior officer's equity. Which brings me to the main reason I've been courting you for the past year. How would you like to escape from your mother's clutches for good?"

. . .

While Rudi and I were exchanging confidences, the Five Zero lit its high-impulse drive. I barely noticed it at the time—milligee acceleration is so gentle that to detect it, you need to position a reference object in the middle of a room and watch it drift for a minute—but we were under way, beginning the long, slow spiral out from Shin-Tethys toward what would eventually be a high-energy transit to Taj Beacon.

It was a bluff, of course. Rudi had no intention of physically visiting Taj, for a beacon laser powerful enough to punch a high bit–rate signal across light-years of interstellar space is, at close range, functionally indistinguishable from a death ray. But our trajectory served its function, which was to leave a gigantic trail of glowing ionized indium exhaust behind us, a banner shouting *look at me* pointing to the Branch Office Five Zero. There is no stealth in space: So good tactics hinge on making use of this fact to misdirect the enemy.

There were numerous responses, rippling out from our vicinity at the speed of light as various observers noticed our progress.

Perhaps the first among them would have been the reaction of Medea and her officers, in their watery orbital defense headquarters: "We've been rolled," I can imagine her intelligence chief saying.

"Kill them. *Now*," two of Medea's instances snapped simultaneously. "Don't let them get away," said the third of the triumvirate.

"Your Majesty. Are you instructing us to launch on the target?"

"Yes. At once!"

At much the same time, the deacon, standing watch in the pulpit aboard the Chapel of Our Lady of the Holy Restriction Endonuclease, would have been alerted to our emissions. "Your Grace." He lowered his gaze as he turned toward the retina spread across the lectern in front of him. "My apologies for interrupting your prayers, but the pirates have just activated their main engine, as expected. Wait . . . oh. I'm also seeing launch signatures from the surface waters, six hundred kilometers southwest of

Nova Ploetsk. Um. Make that fifteen, sixteen . . . high-acceleration signatures! The target is moving, Your Grace."

Cybelle stared at him without blinking for several seconds. "Hail the target," she finally said. "Assure them that we have nothing to do with Medea's aggression, but I wish to speak with the little accountant, person to person."

"Yes, Your Grace. Is there anything else I should be doing?"

"Unarchive the holy malware suite and prepare it for transmission." Cybelle's expression was cold. "If Medea's missiles miss, they cannot be allowed to spew their lies at the ignorant public."

Several minutes later, a similar dialogue will have happened in a command and control center on Taj Beacon. I cannot say with any certainty who would be involved in this one. Perhaps they will have been the regular traffic controllers tasked with coordinating the movement of vehicles in and out of the congested space around the beacon station, preventing collisions and ensuring that nobody accidentally crosses the path of the interstellar lasers. Or perhaps other bodies were in control by then, bodies loyal to Sondra rather than the burghers of Taj Beacon.

"Something is happening in low orbit around Shin-Tethys. Looks like there's a lot of traffic from the surface near the equator, and there are at least two vehicles under way . . . logging incoming flight plans . . . we have an arrest-and-apprehension warrant from the Kingdom of Argos citing one of the vehicles for piracy!"

A senior officer gave it their full attention before responding. "Forward the full details to the standing Defense Subcommittee, for their immediate attention. Oh, and copy it to the Lady Alizond's staff, with a request for comment. I expect she'll have something to say about how it's to be dealt with."

Finally, two days later, in the stygian depths beyond the heliopause, where Dojima Prime's solar wind meets the interstellar medium, a report will have been delivered aboard the bridge of an ancient starship. "Captain, we are receiving relayed signals from Taj Beacon. The traitor is aboard a vessel under acceleration from Shin-Tethys toward the beacon station. There is an encrypted message for your eyes only. Per the envelope, she says she wants to talk."

"Excellent," hissed Sondra. Talons gripped the armrests of her command throne as she leaned forward. "I'll take the message directly and reply. If she thinks I am willing to negotiate, that will only make this easier."

"And the attack plan . . . ?"

"Continue as ordered."

"Hello, Mother."

(I'd planned my message with care and produced it with the able assistance of Rudi's corporate relations team. They had arranged a backdrop crafted to give away as little as possible about my real circumstances. To Sondra I appeared to be standing in a virtual boardroom, dressed in a good semblance of the robes of a nun-auditor. They'd programmed in the kinematics and semblance of legs in place of my fishy lower half, added the appearance of gravity to drape my clothing and sag my flesh in place of this free-fall environment. I'd retrieved memories of the palace by the inner sea from Ana's chip, to pad out the background of the sim. All Sondra would be able to see that was real was my face, and all she would hear was the words that I wanted her to hear.)

"I want to start by saying how much I admire your work. Seriously. You know full well that I am an expert on the FTL scam. What you've done . . . I'm speechless. You've created a work of art for the ages. I doubt we will ever see anything to match it. It's the greatest fraud in history; and billions of people, scores of newly colonized star systems, owe their existence to you."

(Sondra had always had a high opinion of herself, and there was nothing to be gained by stinting the effulgent praise. Especially as this was a one-way message transmission. Dialogue was not practical, both because of the distance between us and, to be honest, the embarrassing fact that we didn't know precisely where Sondra was. Yes, the whole of Dojima System was a-buzz with rumors and reports of her ostentatious arrival at Taj Beacon. But that proved nothing: She was devious enough to be in two or more places at once, and doubtless she had hedged her position against any likely attack.

(Such as, for example, the tiresome ballistic missiles dogging our tail—some of Medea's fireworks came equipped with electrical thrusters, so that as we spiraled out from Shin-Tethys, we led a deadly marathon of robot bombs. Or the chapel, lumbering slowly after us, blatting doubtless-toxic high-bandwidth signals—signals that Rudi's infowar specialists cheerfully advised us to ignore, for the Mother Church was so far behind the cutting edge of the field that they were more of a danger to themselves than to anyone else.

(The trouble, as Rudi pointed out, was that Sondra had come here for a reason—presumably the division of the spoils—but would doubtless assign a higher priority to suppressing the news of her crime than to making any addition to her already enormous wealth. Probably she'd have preferred to shut me up discreetly, by means of that assassin-doppelgänger. But she was quite capable of bombing a beacon station and attempting to murder its entire population to silence an entire star system: After all, she'd done it before. As far as I could tell, there were no practical limits to her depravity.

("And there's something out there," Rudi had told me.

("Where?"

("Incoming." His ears twitched, a sure sign of emotional disturbance. "Plot a course from Hector to Atlantis and project it ten light-years, and you wind up less than a light-year from Dojima. And the time scale is just about right. The starships they sent to Atlantis, the ones that went missing—they could be arriving in Dojima System if, instead of being sabotaged, they were hijacked. So we set a small satellite to keep a watch on that part of the sky, years ago. Sure enough, the *Vengeance* is coming. We picked up the thermal signature almost sixty days ago."

("But how could she—"

("It's a battleship, Krina. *Of course* it's got a beacon laser! How else would you send an army of occupation?"

("What's she going to do with it when she gets here?"

("What makes you think *I* know? It's still more than fourteen light-hours away—all we know is she's heading toward the inner solar system and will get there in a couple of weeks. She's your mother: You tell me what you'd do if you were her . . ."

(And so I planned and recorded this message. Which the Branch Office Five Zero would transmit first in the direction of the supposed starship—I could still barely believe in it, despite the thermal telescope's heat flare of hundreds of gigawatts of energy radiating into vacuum, the telltale spectrum of fusion reactors blue-shifted by the onrushing speed of the vehicle—and then, more than a day later, in the direction of Taj Beacon, so that a response from Sondra at either location would reach us at roughly the same time. The message was unencrypted: Doubtless it would go viral, adding its volume to the gossip channels . . .)

"Mother, I'd like to express my deepest regrets that our relationship has come to this low point. If I could wind it back and undo this unfortunate argument, I would do so in a moment. But I don't suppose anything I can say at this point will result in our reconciliation. You may take this message to be my formal resignation from the family firm—I don't suppose I'll be going home after this. But we still have unfinished business to discuss."

(I'd argued this case with Rudi. "She's capable of extreme violence," I pointed out. "If she's on Taj Beacon, she could very well attempt to destroy the entire habitat just to keep word from leaking out. The only way to stop her is to ensure there's no chance of her hushing things up—and to give her a target to shoot at that isn't surrounded by innocent bystanders.")

I continued with my script: "So I'd like to propose an old-fashioned face-to-face meeting. We can rendezvous in deep space. Or, if you're still aboard Taj Beacon, I can come to you. The main point is that we should meet somewhere with a beacon transmitter, because one of us will be leaving Dojima System immediately afterward." I waved a hand. "Cut—version for the deep-space object. Mother, I know about your starship. It's a rather astounding gambit! And I know about the beacon transceiver it's carrying—which is, of course, why you're seeing this message. What I propose is this: You rendezvous with me in deep space. I've left my soul chip behind, in the hands of a reliable escrow service. If they don't receive a certain message from me, from out-system—I'm not going to tell you where—within fifty years, they will resurrect me from backup, and I will feel compelled to share my secrets with the universe at large. But if they receive the right message, countersigned by Hector SystemBank to prove it has been sent from out-system, they'll delete my backup. So you need only point your beacon laser at the destination of my choice, and I can be out of your hair for good."

(The purpose of this version of the message was simple: to convince Sondra, if she was indeed aboard the battleship, that I was desperate enough that I would willingly trust her equipment to help me escape. It would be the height of naive stupidity for me to do so—suicidal, even—but I was counting on Sondra's low opinion of her offspring to snare her into a deep-space rendezvous with the Five Zero. Which, doubtless, she would discount as a threat.)

I waved my hand again. "Cut—version for Taj Beacon. Mother, I know you're occupying Taj Beacon, and I know you're probably planning something drastic and terminal for me when I arrive there. That would be stupid. So I've left my soul chip behind, in the hands of a reliable escrow service. If they don't receive a certain message from me, from out-system—I'm not going to tell you where, yet—within fifty years, they will resurrect me from backup, and I will feel compelled to share my secrets with the universe at large. But if they receive the message, countersigned by Hector SystemBank to prove it has been sent from out-system, they'll delete my backup. I intend to proceed to Taj Beacon, and once there, I will go direct to the departure terminal and transmit myself elsewhere. I have retained bodyguards to ensure my security during serialization and upload. You are welcome to send your own people to confirm I speak to no one during the process. Keep your hands to yourself, and I will be out of your hair for good."

(And the purpose of *that* version was similar: to gull Sondra into thinking I was cutting and running, via Taj Beacon. The same calculation applied. As Rudi put it, "You can't seriously expect to do that and survive!" At which point I confess I smirked, and said, "Of course not! All that matters is that Sondra thinks I'm stupid enough to try it.")

"And cut." I waved my hands, then turned to look at Rudi. "Do you think it'll work?" I asked, a trifle anxiously.

"I sincerely hope so." He spread his arms and slowly sculled up toward the ceiling of the office. "Either way, you have given her a juicy target. Us."

"That was the idea, wasn't it? Because if she knew what you had in the propulsion department, she'd already have cut her losses and run away. To stalk us another year."

"Yes." He grabbed hold of one of the tree branches that held the ceiling in place and pulled his face close to it. "I would be happy to wager you that she's on the battleship."

"I'm not taking that bet." I thought back to my oldest memories, and Sondra's punitive approach to child rearing. "Authoritarians have an instinctive attraction to the tools of force." A thought struck me. "How is our herd of bombs doing? Are we in danger of outrunning them?"

"That's a good question." Rudi grinned, baring sharp teeth. "I'm sure Marigold would be happy to enlighten us. Why don't we go to the war room and ask?"

"Jean!"

"Yes, my captain?"

"The transmission from the traitor. Are we tracking the source?"

"Yes, Captain. Let me put it on the main plot." Nightmare fingers clattered across a twilit display in the red gloom of the warship's combat center. "Observe: The origin is this vehicle, which appears to be on a six-milligee high-energy continuous acceleration trajectory outbound from Shin-Tethys. If it continues as projected and makes a midpoint turnover *here*, it will arrive in the vicinity of Taj Beacon in ninety-eight standard days. Or it could make a flyby considerably sooner, but there is no clear reason for it to do so . . . in any case, the vehicle is squawking the identification code of Branch Office Five Zero of a financial institution known as the Crimson Permanent Assurance Cooperative of—"

"Enough." Giant dark eyes embedded in a rigidly armored face surveyed the retina wall. "What are *these*?"

"There appears to have been an altercation in orbit around Shin-Tethys. The, ah, traitor appears to have attracted the ire of various parties, who are engaged in a pursuit. This one is a mendicant chapel of the Mother Church, and as you can see, it can barely muster four milligees: It is falling behind. This cluster of sixteen is more troubling: they exhibit low-observability characteristics and are engaging in crude jamming, and they are averaging five point five milligees—bursting to twenty milligees, then coasting while they dissipate waste heat. Intel isn't certain what they are but speculate that they're uncrewed long-range pursuit missiles, in which case the traitor will be unable to decelerate and rendezvous with Taj Beacon until they run out of reaction mass. A stern chase is a long chase, ha-ha. Ha." Sondra fell silent for a minute, pondering. "I see a cornered fugitive who thinks she can blackmail me . . . hah. Jean! A question for the navigation team. Assuming we change course and acceleration in the next few hours, can we in principle make a zero-speed rendezvous with this Branch Office vehicle?"

The skeletal horror across the table from her froze momentarily. "I shall ask, Captain. It will mean a major change from our current boost program, but I see no reason why not . . . I shall ask."

"I do not intend to let the traitor escape, Jean," Sondra murmured. "But there is no point in telling her we agree to her proposal if it is obvious that we cannot make such a rendezvous."

There was silence in the cramped command center for a few minutes. Then the lieutenant spoke. "Captain, we have sufficient reaction mass to make a zero-zero rendezvous with the Branch Office Five Zero. To do so, we will need to make an initial course-correction burn in less than eighty thousand seconds. However, the navigators also volunteered the opinion that the Branch Office Five Zero cannot make a rendezvous with us—if they attempt to do so, the pursuing missiles will overhaul them at least two days before our closest approach."

"How annoying." Black-buffed claws dug into the torso restraint bars of Sondra's acceleration cradle. "We can't have that. Lieutenant: I intend to reply to the traitor, agreeing to her request. I will also notify her that we shall dispose of her pursuers as a gesture of goodwill. We will then execute the necessary course correction to rendezvous with her, and resume deceleration."

"Yes, Captain." A pause. "Are there other instructions?"

If Sondra's battlebody had teeth, she would have bared them. "We will proceed as I ordered. Once we are established on the deceleration-and-rendezvous trajectory, you will instruct Weapons Factory Two to intercept the traitor's pursuers and destroy them. Ideally, the flyby and destruction will take place no more than a thousand seconds before rendezvous." She paused.

"Are we actually going to rendezvous with the traitor?"

"No. While the interceptors are detonating, we will execute a lateral burn on maximum impulse. The detonations and the burn are to conceal the release of free-fall bombs from Weapons Factory One, targeted on the Branch Office Five Zero's course to rendezvous. I want them to have as little warning as possible.

"I want to be so close to the kill that I can see the explosions myself. So close that I can feel them on my skin. So close that I have to grow new eyes afterward."

Space battles are boring.

This came to me as an unexpected and unwelcome discovery. But consider: Space is vast, and for the most part our vehicles accelerate slowly, at rates measured in milligees—approximately a centimeter per second squared. Yes, there are exceptions, the high-impulse flare of a nuclear-thermal rocket and the continuous-centigee burn of a starship. And in the final seconds and minutes of an engagement, there is the gut-punching shove and roar of chemical thrusters, prodigiously wasteful of reaction mass, jinking and weaving and desperately trying to make or break a targeting lock. But for the most part, space battles are a slow dance of orbital dynamics and continuous low-thrust acceleration for days or weeks or even years: a dance that culminates in a terrifying minute of battering, deafening evasive maneuvers followed by sudden death or survival, and more weeks or months of slow, steady thrust. If anything, the course of a space battle resembles a gambling game in which both sides make some preparations in private, expose other aspects of their strategy to their rivals—and the match is determined by a final throw-down. But it's a game which one or more of the participants never gets to play again. There is no guarantee that there will be a winner, but there is always at least one loser. If you peer closely at it, you might even discern a resemblance to certain types of option trades.

As a banker, I did not find this to my taste. So after a couple of days I went to talk over my anxiety with Rudi.

"Yes, it's a gamble," he agreed. "But we're going to win. We have palmed several cards, yes? Doubtless your mother believes she is the one who is going to win, and she, too, is concealing cards about her person. But she clearly doesn't have a teleport engine aboard her vessel, so we're going to win."

"How do you know she doesn't?"

Rudi cocked his head and stared at me. "Because we're not dead. Honestly, Krina, I expected better!"

"I'm an accountant, not a warrior!" I protested. "I don't murder people for a living. Not like Mother."

"Well, you'll have to learn. At least enough to keep up, if you aspire to become a branch manager for the Permanent Assurance."

"Where do you suggest I—" I broke off, for Rudi was no longer looking at me. A chime from the retina on his wall drew his attention.

"Incoming message," he noted. "From your mother, for your eyes." (That it had found its way to Rudi's attention first did not escape me.) "Would you like to see it?"

"'Like' is not the word I'd choose, but I suppose I have to . . ."

The retina flashed, then reconfigured to display a stylized boardroom. My mother sat enthroned at the head of the table, robed in the ceremonial pinstripes of her calling: Arrayed on either side sat a row of corporate officers, all sisters of mine, dressed alike in the sober priestly vestments of the merchant banker. I recognized the room, with a pang of homesickness, as the Blue Committee Room of SystemBank New California, the holy sanctuary wherein the wealth of star systems was parceled up and lent to the supplicant debtor colonies. It was, of course, more than twenty light-years away (and therefore this whole diorama was just as much a fake as my message to my mother had been), but it affected me deeply all the same.

"Daughter." Sondra addressed me directly, with hauteur and dignity. "That I am distressed and perturbed by your activities should be no surprise. I wish that you had harnessed your hitherto-undemonstrated talents in service to this institution rather than conspiring in secrecy with traitors to defraud us. But under the circumstances, I can see no circumstances under which you could restore my trust in your good faith. So your resignation is accepted.

"I understand your desire to skulk in shame from Dojima System. And you are correct about this vessel's possession of a general-purpose beacon laser. Of your crude attempt to blackmail me into giving you access to it, I shall say no more. Your request for a direct rendezvous is accepted, and as your crew will have noted, I am already decelerating toward the indicated meeting point. I am curious as to how you intend to deal with your pursuers, though: Aren't they going to overhaul you if you stop accelerating ahead of them?

"I look forward to accepting your surrender in person once we are less than a light-minute apart."

The message window closed. I looked at Rudi. "I'd better give her the cover story about the bombs," I suggested. "Otherwise, she might start to suspect the truth."

"Yes. Why don't you do that?" Rudi's tongue made a leisurely pass around his muzzle, then he winked at me coyly. "I have some more cards to mark. Might as well get started now . . ."

Days passed. Then a week. Then most of another week.

Shortly after we received Sondra's message agreeing to a face-to-face parley, the drive flares from the flotilla of interceptor missiles trailing us out of Shin-Tethys's gravity well sputtered and faded out, one by one, leaving the interceptors adrift and falling farther behind. To all appearances, they were not designed for a deep-space pursuit of such duration. It was a most convenient result, for they wouldn't catch up with the Five Zero again until almost two hours after the scheduled rendez-vous with Sondra's starship: And even then, drifting helplessly, they would be trivially easy to evade.

I wished them the best of luck, in the privacy of my own head.

Of the other parties to the battle, there was no news. The chapel fell ever farther astern, blatting obsolescent viruses and trojans at the sky with ever-increasing desperation. They were nothing more than a nuisance, but the various planetary traffic-control agencies were clearly becoming annoyed, going by the increasingly strident injunctions against spamming on the emergency channels: If they kept it up for much longer, they were going to find themselves blacklisted by port authorities and unable to dock anywhere. And there was a complete news clampdown from Nova Ploetsk in particular and the Kingdom of Argos in general: *Someone* was clearly keeping something quiet.

I spent much of the time working and studying. As per the terms of our agreement, Rudi was required to issue me with an officer's assignment of shares in the Branch Office Five Zero; at a later time, we would formally vest these as shares in the parent institution, but right now I was merely to be an equity-holding first lieutenant and officer of the audit, not to mention a major deposit-account customer. The learning curve was steep: I had many operational manuals to study, and much of the business of a proactive assurance agency was new to me. However, nothing concentrates the mind like starting a new management job in the middle of a space battle: Getting it right first time was a matter of life or death. And so I threw myself into my new routine with gusto and a degree of enthusiasm that I will admit came as a surprise to me.

As a new-minted officer of the corporation, I spent most of my time in the financial services suite, learning the ebb and flow of bonds and loans and other financial instruments from the experienced clerical officers. I didn't have much contact with the executive arm of the Branch Office, so I was somewhat taken aback one evening shift when a semi-familiar muzzle stuck her nose over my shoulder and announced its presence. "Graah! Skipper sends 'is compliments and be asking after ye'er presence the noo! Ye be coming along smartly, heh?"

I blinked mildly, refusing to recoil. "Li, isn't it?" The piratical boarding specialist who had dragged me aboard the Five Zero in the first place, over a year ago, looked back unblinking. "Rudi wants me? Where?"

"The combat information center on boarding deck two. You be following now?"

"Show me," I commanded, locking my retina and swimming into the middle of the room to follow her. I had become much better at identifying bats by their gender over the past month. I had also found time in my schedule for an appointment with the ship's surgeon, and had functional legs again—albeit with webbed feet and prehensile toes. But I'd kept the embarrassing big-eyed face, and the gills, and many of the other modifications for now, and hadn't made up my mind about asking for wings and fur and a pointy muzzle yet, the better to fit in: Major surgery and bodily fluids work better under gravity or centrifugal spin, and there just wasn't time to fix everything all at once.

Pirate Li led me toward the central service core of the vehicle, down past the habitat and life-support spheres, then into a cramped world of gray passages lined with automatic pressure hatches and racks of equipment, from reels of patch tape to radiation detectors. The grim guts of the enterprise, the tools of last resort when negotiation and contract law gave way to the rule of force.

The CIC was buried within a rodent-friendly maze of these passages and ducts, behind surprisingly sturdy walls. Within its spherical confines was a surprisingly small capsule, barely bigger than a *Soyuz* crypt, rotating freely on gimbaled mounts. Li waved me toward it; I swam toward the open hatch and poked my head in.

"Come in! Come in!" Rudi flapped at me, clearly jittery. "Shut the hatch, jolly good."

"What is this—" I lowered myself into one of the unoccupied couches.

"The bunker. From which some lucky officer has to manage the branch when all the accounts are in the red." Rudi glanced at me. "This is your final chance to back out, you know."

It took me a long time to frame my reply. The quiet—broken only by the hum of the ventilator fans and the gurgle of acceleration gel in the tank beneath our seats—seemed to stretch out.

"You set this up with Ana, didn't you?" I finally asked. "All of it. My abduction, this confrontation, the sucker punch the People are lining up to deliver."

Rudi nodded. "Are you angry with me?"

I sighed. "I would have said as much already. How long have you been working with my sister?"

"For longer than I care to recall. We first met in the Trailing Pretties, shortly after the Five Zero arrived in Dojima—I was looking for an expert on certain aspects of local trade law."

"And that's when she told you about the Atlantis Carnet . . . ?"

"Not immediately." Rudi's smile was slow to emerge. "There was a small matter of mutual trust. But she had already resolved to make a clean break from your lineage before she arrived here. Discovering more reasons to hate your mother was . . . well, it served as glue for our mutual trust and respect."

"For your . . ." I stopped. Something about his tone sounded wistful. "What is it?"

Rudi drew a wing membrane across his face. "She is joining the People. I suppose it was inevitable that we would drift apart: The passion of such a relationship can only last a handful of years, a decade or two at the most. But we agreed, long ago, that when this was over, we would combine our lineages and spawn infants." He peered at me bashfully over his arm. "She gave you a soul chip, did she not? With a message—and an up-to-date backup."

I stared at him. "You're a *bat*, Rudi! She's a mermaid. What *were* you thinking?"

"You'd be surprised," he said drily. "I know that Sondra minimized your libido function when she spawned your sib-hood. That was another of the things that angered Ana. She, too, was uninterested in concupiscence when she first arrived in Dojima."

"I can't believe I'm hearing this."

"Your belief is entirely optional, I assure you, my dear. But in any case, I didn't call you here to tell you that you are going to become an, ah, aunt. I called you here because your mother's vehicle just changed course."

"She's—" My head spun. "Wait. What's she doing? Where are we in the time line?"

"Attend." Rudi focused suddenly, snapping wing-fingers at the retina that formed an arc around our seats. "*This* is our current vector. Here, behind us, are the drifting capsules from the, ahem, 'interceptor missiles.' We've now slowed sufficiently that they're closing again. And *here* is Sondra's current vector. It's a log-log scale, by the way."

I boggled. The arrow representing Sondra's vector was huge. And it was changing direction visibly.

"Until half an hour ago, she was indeed decelerating toward the intersection point we agreed on. But then she executed this maneuver." The screen depicted an intricate spiral, the magnitude of her acceleration fluctuating. "We are not painting her with active radar at this point—she is still many hundreds of thousands of kilometers distant—but that maneuver was consistent with pointing her flank at us and dropping something overboard. Something that will reach us shortly before she does."

"Mines. Or missiles?"

"Possibly both. If she continues on her present course, her bombs will reach us a couple of hundred kilometers before she makes her closest approach. I fear your challenge may have unhinged her completely. Most annoying. We may have to switch to Plan B."

"You're actually planning on shooting her?"

"No: I have something better in mind. But Plan B *does* require in-person intervention . . . if we shoot her without resolving the fundamental problem, we would merely make everything worse."

"I think I see: If you shoot her, she respawns from backup and denounces you as an outlaw. But if you can leave her adrift with no fuel, exposed and completely discredited, it would be far better for everyone."

"Yes. But we have to disable her beacon laser *and* ensure that she doesn't have an opportunity to escape—or to suicide, or to murder our witnesses." The witnesses aboard the gaggle of small low-acceleration squidcraft dispatched by the People to monitor our negotiations with Sondra and hold her to account, cunningly misidentified as missiles by the allies behind the palace coup that had silenced Medea shortly after their launch. It was a devastatingly risky task: If Sondra realized they were anything other than derelict warheads, she could kill them in an instant and claim self-defense.

"I think we are going to have to cut this short," Rudi continued. "The delta vee for an intercept is just barely manageable, thanks to the extra fuel we took on board—and as long as she's got her main engine burning and pointing our way, her drive flare will make it very difficult to tell the difference between the Five Zero and a decoy drone."

"So, Krina. How do you feel about boarding actions?"

. . .

Boarding actions are situations where the crew of one space vehicle physically transfer aboard another craft in flight, hijacking it by force.

It's a dangerous maneuver at the best of times, usually conducted by armed privateers against the likes of a defenseless freighter or a semidisabled chapel. The idea of a privateer boarding an interstellar dreadnought armed with a gigawatt laser and a portable military-industrial complex tuned for the rapid manufacture of thermonuclear weapons is . . . well, the word "suicidal" springs to mind.

However, as previously noted, Rudi had palmed a trump card: the teleportation engine. In addition to which, we had taken on board nearly two tons of weapons-grade enriched uranium in aqueous solution, stored in narrow, cadmium-walled tanks: about the most energetic rocket fuel imaginable. And he had a plan.

"We're going to set up a jump that puts us a couple of hundred kilometers behind her starship. Which is decelerating toward a rendezvous with our current vector. We'll leave a radar decoy behind to hold her attention. Once we're in place, we'll be screened from direct observation by her ship's frontal shield. We're going to make a continuous acceleration run straight down her throat, using more than half of that bangjuice you asked me about." Rudi bared his teeth. "We'll be all over her in less than ten minutes. And then we're going to board her by force, detain the crew, disable their weapons, and open it to public inspection by neutral witnesses."

Reader: Space battles are boring. But boarding actions are *terrifying*.

I had been on the receiving end of one, aboard the Chapel of Our Lady: Now I was to find out what it was like from the other side.

We crouched in the open front of the Five Zero's payload bay, clad in a motley array of armor, plugged into whatever weapons we were most proficient with. I was armored, but not really armed (unless you count my spreadsheet and the contents of the hollow cylinder strapped to my chest): I was along as supercargo, in the care of an experienced team of raiders. We sat strapped to the open top of a short-range load carrier, ready for the jump. Before us, the fixed stars burned pitilessly: One star in particular strobed with a violet glare, its real motion still barely visible at this range. It was Sondra's warship, fusion torch lit, backing toward us on a gust of gamma radiation and neutrons. "Stay back," Li reminded me.

"Yes. Stay behind, and we'll be able to protect you," Marigold added. We spoke via encrypted electrosense—an augmentation the ship's surgeon had installed on my head barely an hour ago. It still tingled, and my jaw felt numb.

"Jumping in ten seconds," Marigold added. I tightened my grip on the straps that held me to the load carrier, unsure what to expect. "Brace yourself for acceleration immediately afterward."

I tried counting, and got to fifteen seconds without anything happening. I was about to ask how much longer we'd be waiting when the stars flickered into new positions. Then a momentary tug in my vestibular sense told me that we were turning: And an invisible half-ton weight landed on me. Bright lines scrubbed across the edges of my vision, signaling an alarmingly high radiation flux. I couldn't move. The acceleration felt as high as anything I'd felt during reentry on Shin-Tethys. (It wasn't, not by an order of magnitude, but I didn't have antishock gel packed around and inside me, either.) Stars drifted across the open front of the cargo bay, and a juddering sawtooth-buzzing roar shivered my bones. I strained, but try as I might, I couldn't get a glimpse of our target. It was, after all, still hundreds of kilometers away.

Not only was it over two hundred kilometers away, it was receding from us at twenty kilometers a second, albeit decelerating, its drive torch pointed away from us and toward the vector we had been following seconds earlier. At ten gees, it would take us close to four minutes to stop the gap from widening further—but then we would close it extremely rapidly, before flipping end over end for the final dive. The starship itself was decelerating constantly, but at less than a thousand milligees: Even though it had prodigious amounts of power on tap, if it tried to sustain any higher acceleration, its crew would find themselves roasting in the fusion reactors' waste heat. *Our* main hazards were threefold. The anti-meteoroid point-defense devices behind the starship's frontal shield might mistake us for a snowball on a collision course; Sondra might attempt to bring the beacon laser to bear on us; or she might do something really unfortunate with her drive torch if she realized what was going on. My greatest hope was that she would continue to pursue the radar decoy, which was obscured to her optical sensors by the fiery plume of her rocket exhaust. So I endured several minutes of deepening dread and growing terror as I waited for the circle of sky at the front of our cargo bay to flash brighter than a million suns and melt my face.

I waited, and waited. And then, without warning, the invisible weights holding my limbs down evaporated, and the static in my vision cleared. I jolted forward in my harness, then hung sideways in it as the stars rolled across the cargo opening. The bone-conducted roar of acceleration resumed, but this time I knew we were backing toward our target, slowing, closing for the final transfer.

"Ejecting in twenty seconds," Marigold said quietly. "Hang on." And I did.

I retain only confused impressions from the boarding operation: the hollow darkness to every side, icy cold. A cylindrical metal fabrication the size of a skyscraper looming out of the darkness, studded with inexplicable nozzles, scarred by ancient microimpacts, a glaring pinpoint light burning holes in the cosmos at one end. Shoving and bashing and jolting as our crude lash-up cargo carrier rocketed across the gap, closing on one of the many blisters that studded the ship's side. A crazy rocking motion and a brief glimpse of another, smaller vehicle in the distance, sitting atop another glaring knife-bright line of radiation: then a bone-rattling impact.

I remember standing in a hole in the side of a room, surrounded by the murdered chrysalids of ancient warriors, looking out into the abyss, and wondering: *I'm still alive!* Then a voice rang in my ears despite the vacuum all around, "Krina, get *down!*" And moments later, glimpses through a blur of terror, the flashing of thruster-driven knives jousting overhead.

Corridors and skeletons—not Fragile carcasses, but something else: bodies flensed of superficial mechaflesh, hard-skinned and bony with nightmare claws, optimized for weight and speed and killing. Then the body of a boarding crewman, batwings slashed and back broken. Sondra's accomplices had better bodies and equipment, but Rudi's people had more experience of this kind of action. A sudden flare of light in the shadows, and a cutting charge opened up a path through into a new chamber.

Then it was over. Or rather, Marigold was in front of me, trying to get my attention. "Ms. Alizond? Come with me. We need you to identify . . ."

The captain's quarters aboard the *Vengeance* were more austere than I would have expected: a far cry from the luxury and pomp which was all I had known Sondra to travel with. At least they'd restored air pressure, so I no longer had to blink away the shards of ice that formed on my eyeballs. The spaces of the starship were cramped and cold, so dark that I was abruptly relieved that I had not had my eyes restored to their previous size. A mob of piratical bat-boarders proudly surrounded a hunched figure, spot-glued to an acceleration couch from which she roared imprecations. They'd poured a blob of quick-setting foam over her clawed hands and feet: Judging by the contusions and damage on display, they hadn't taken Sondra without a struggle.

I took a step forward, bouncing slightly in the dreamlike tenth-gee acceleration. "Hello, Sondra."

The nightmarish features of her warbody looked up at me and she bared her fangs, hissing.

"That's not very constructive!" I said brightly, forcing up a shield of lighthearted disdain from somewhere: Truth be told, I felt light-headed, almost sick, gripped by the kind of numbness that takes hold when one's neurohormonal emulation is spiking into overload. "Don't you want to get this over with? Then we can be on our way."

"*Hsss*—" Sondra shuddered in her restraints. Then she went very still. After a few seconds, she flexed her skeletal chest. Then she looked at me. "Which one are *you*?"

I stared. "I'm Krina, Mother. Don't you recognize me?"

"Krina. The little historian? Traitor, I call you." Her contempt was palpable. And it still stung, more palpably than I had expected. "You *owe* me—everything you are—"

"I owe you *nothing*! A debt does not exist merely because you wish it to. If anyone is a traitor here, it's you—to the people of Atlantis, whose trust you betrayed." I caught myself, forced myself to count to ten in silence before I continued. "You could have had it all, Mother, if you'd done your job in good faith, managing their systembank. But you didn't, which is why we're here now, to hold you to account."

She made a strange, muffled noise. After a moment, I recognized it for a snort of laughter. "So the little thief comes home to charge her mother with a bigger theft? Nobody's going to believe you! It's your word against mine, and I speak loudly, for money talks. Anywhere you try to go in Dojima System, my process servers will follow you. And don't think you can get away with murder here, either: I have backups. They'll come after you, too."

"Not if they don't have any assets." I watched her, but she didn't seem to understand what I was saying. I tried again. "How do you think we learned what happened in Atlantis, Mother? You cashed out too early, and you didn't follow the job through. Risk management: That's all banking is about. And now that everyone has come here to wind up the last of the assets left over from your fraud, the citizens of Atlantis have decided to take a place at the table and discuss the small matter of the debt you created.

"It's over, Mother. The branch manager back there"—I gestured at the wall, the empty gulf of space beyond it, and the Branch Office Five

Zero—"is broadcasting a full transcript of Ana's and my investigation into your fortune to everyone who has an antenna to receive it. And a full description of the entanglement teleporter, although it'll doubtless take a bit longer for that to turn everything upside down.

"But the upshot is this: *Right now*, the value of slow money is effectively collapsing, in a wavefront traveling outward at the speed of light. It's a Jubilee, on an interstellar scale: the end of the debt slavery of worlds. While you're sitting here, almost out of fuel, your beacon laser disabled and your credit rating trashed."

She stared at me, uncomprehendingly. "You raised me to always pay my debts," I explained, making one last attempt. "And I'm done, so I'll be going now." I reached over and carefully deposited the cylinder containing a copy of the full transcript on the desktop beside her couch. "I don't expect we'll be meeting again, so good-bye, Mother."

I turned and waited for my bodyguard to make way for me. And then we went home.

extras

www.orbitbooks.net

about the author

Charles Stross is a full-time science fiction writer and resident of Edinburgh, Scotland. The author of six Hugo-nominated novels and winner of the 2005 and 2010 Hugo Awards for best novella ("The Concrete Jungle" and Palimpsest"), Stross's works have been translated into over twelve languages.

Like many writers, Stross has had a variety of careers, occupations and job-shaped-catastrophes in the past, from pharmacist (he quit after the second police stake-out) to first code monkey on the team of a successful dot-com startup (with brilliant timing he tried to change employer just as the bubble burst). Along the way he collected degrees in Pharmacy and Computer Science, making him the world's first officially qualified cyberpunk writer (just as cyberpunk died).

He's currently working on a variety of novels, including the fifth volume of the Laundry Files, The Rhesus Chart. In 2013 he will be Creative in Residence at the UK-wide Centre for Creativity, Regulation, Enterprise and Technology, researching the business models and regulation of industries such as music, film, TV, computer games and publishing.

Find out more about Charles Stross and other Orbit authors by registering for the free monthly newsletter at www.orbitbooks.net

if you enjoyed

NEPTUNE'S BROOD

look out for

ANCILLARY JUSTICE

by

Ann Leckie

1

The body lay naked and facedown, a deathly gray, spatters of blood staining the snow around it. It was minus fifteen degrees Celsius and a storm had passed just hours before. The snow stretched smooth in the wan sunrise, only a few tracks leading into a nearby ice-block building. A tavern. Or what passed for a tavern in this town.

There was something itchingly familiar about that out-thrown arm, the line from shoulder down to hip. But it was hardly possible I knew this person. I didn't know anyone here. This was the icy back end of a cold and isolated planet, as far from Radchaai ideas of civilization as it was possible to be. I was only here, on this planet, in this town, because I had urgent business of my own. Bodies in the street were none of my concern.

Sometimes I don't know why I do the things I do. Even after all this time it's still a new thing for me not to know, not to have orders to follow from one moment to the next. So I can't explain to you why I stopped and with one foot lifted the naked shoulder so I could see the person's face.

Frozen, bruised, and bloody as she was, I knew her. Her name was Seivarden Vendaai, and a long time ago she had been one of my officers, a young lieutenant, eventually promoted to her own command, another ship. I had thought her a thousand years dead, but she was, undeniably, here. I crouched down and felt for a pulse, for the faintest stir of breath.

Still alive.

Seivarden Vendaai was no concern of mine anymore, wasn't my responsibility. And she had never been one of my favorite officers. I had obeyed her orders, of course, and she had never abused any ancillaries, never harmed any of my segments (as the occasional officer did). I had no reason to think badly of her. On the contrary, her manners were those of an educated, well-bred person of good family. Not toward me, of course—I wasn't a person, I was a piece of equipment, a part of the ship. But I had never particularly cared for her.

I rose and went into the tavern. The place was dark, the white of the ice walls long since covered over with grime or worse. The air smelled of alcohol and vomit. A barkeep stood behind a high bench. She was a native—short and fat, pale and wide-eyed. Three patrons sprawled in seats at a dirty table. Despite the cold they wore only trousers and quilted shirts—it was spring in this hemisphere of Nilt and they were enjoying the warm spell. They pretended not to see me, though they had certainly noticed me in the street and knew what motivated my entrance. Likely one or more of them had been involved; Seivarden hadn't been out there long, or she'd have been dead.

"I'll rent a sledge," I said, "and buy a hypothermia kit."

Behind me one of the patrons chuckled and said, voice mocking, "Aren't you a tough little girl."

I turned to look at her, to study her face. She was taller than most Nilters, but fat and pale as any of them. She out-bulked me, but I was taller, and I was also considerably stronger than I looked. She didn't realize what she was playing with. She was probably male, to judge from the angular mazelike patterns quilting her shirt. I wasn't entirely certain. It wouldn't have mattered, if I had been in Radch space. Radchaai don't care much about gender, and the language they speak—my own first language— doesn't mark gender in any way. This language we were speaking now did, and I could make trouble for myself if I used the wrong forms. It didn't help that cues meant to distinguish gender changed from place to place, sometimes radically, and rarely made much sense to me.

I decided to say nothing. After a couple of seconds she suddenly found something interesting in the tabletop. I could have killed her, right there, without much effort. I found the idea attractive. But right now Seivarden was my first priority. I turned back to the barkeep.

Slouching negligently she said, as though there had been no interruption, "What kind of place you think this is?"

"The kind of place," I said, still safely in linguistic territory that needed no gender marking, "that will rent me a sledge and sell me a hypothermia kit. How much?"

"Two hundred shen." At least twice the going rate, I was sure. "For the sledge. Out back. You'll have to get it yourself. Another hundred for the kit."

"Complete," I said. "Not used."

She pulled one out from under the bench, and the seal looked undamaged. "Your buddy out there had a tab."

Maybe a lie. Maybe not. Either way the number would be pure fiction. "How much?"

"Three hundred fifty."

I could find a way to keep avoiding referring to the barkeep's gender. Or I could guess. It was, at worst, a fifty-fifty chance. "You're very trusting," I said, guessing *male*, "to let such an indigent"—I knew Seivarden was male, that one was easy—"run up such a debt." The barkeep said nothing. "Six hundred and fifty covers all of it?"

"Yeah," said the barkeep. "Pretty much."

"No, all of it. We will agree now. And if anyone comes after me later demanding more, or tries to rob me, they die."

Silence. Then the sound behind me of someone spitting. "Radchaai scum."

"I'm not Radchaai." Which was true. You have to be human to be Radchaai.

"*He* is," said the barkeep, with the smallest shrug toward the door. "You don't have the accent but you stink like Radchaai."

"That's the swill you serve your customers." Hoots from the patrons behind me. I reached into a pocket, pulled out a handful of chits, and tossed them on the bench. "Keep the change." I turned to leave.

"Your money better be good."

"Your sledge had better be out back where you said." And I left.

The hypothermia kit first. I rolled Seivarden over. Then I tore the seal on the kit, snapped an internal off the card, and pushed it into her bloody, half-frozen mouth. Once the indicator on the card showed green I unfolded the thin wrap, made sure of the charge, wound it around her, and switched it on. Then I went around back for the sledge.

No one was waiting for me, which was fortunate. I didn't want to leave bodies behind just yet, I hadn't come here to cause trouble. I towed the sledge around front, loaded Seivarden onto it, and considered taking my outer coat off and laying it on her, but in the end I decided it wouldn't be that much of an improvement over the hypothermia wrap alone. I powered up the sledge and was off.

I rented a room at the edge of town, one of a dozen two-meter cubes of grimy, gray-green prefab plastic. No bedding, and blankets cost extra, as did heat. I paid—I had already wasted a ridiculous amount of money bringing Seivarden out of the snow.

I cleaned the blood off her as best I could, checked her pulse (still there) and temperature (rising). Once I would have known her core temperature without even thinking, her heart rate, blood oxygen, hormone levels. I would have seen any and every injury merely by wishing it. Now I was blind. Clearly she'd been beaten—her face was swollen, her torso bruised.

The hypothermia kit came with a very basic corrective, but only one, and only suitable for first aid. Seivarden might have internal injuries or severe head trauma, and I was only capable of fixing cuts or sprains. With any luck, the cold and the bruises were all I had to deal with. But I didn't have much medical knowledge, not anymore. Any diagnosis I could make would be of the most basic sort.

I pushed another internal down her throat. Another check—

her skin was no more chill than one would expect, considering, and she didn't seem clammy. Her color, given the bruises, was returning to a more normal brown. I brought in a container of snow to melt, set it in a corner where I hoped she wouldn't kick it over if she woke, and then went out, locking the door behind me.

The sun had risen higher in the sky, but the light was hardly any stronger. By now more tracks marred the even snow of last night's storm, and one or two Nilters were about. I hauled the sledge back to the tavern, parked it behind. No one accosted me, no sounds came from the dark doorway. I headed for the center of town.

People were abroad, doing business. Fat, pale children in trousers and quilted shirts kicked snow at each other, and then stopped and stared with large surprised-looking eyes when they saw me. The adults pretended I didn't exist, but their eyes turned toward me as they passed. I went into a shop, going from what passed for daylight here to dimness, into a chill just barely five degrees warmer than outside.

A dozen people stood around talking, but instant silence descended as soon as I entered. I realized that I had no expression on my face, and set my facial muscles to something pleasant and noncommittal.

"What do you want?" growled the shopkeeper.

"Surely these others are before me." Hoping as I spoke that it was a mixed-gender group, as my sentence indicated. I received only silence in response. "I would like four loaves of bread and a slab of fat. Also two hypothermia kits and two general-purpose correctives, if such a thing is available."

"I've got tens, twenties, and thirties."

"Thirties, please."

She stacked my purchases on the counter. "Three hundred seventy-five." There was a cough from someone behind me—I was being overcharged again.

I paid and left. The children were still huddled, laughing, in the street. The adults still passed me as though I weren't there. I made one more stop—Seivarden would need clothes. Then I returned to the room.

Seivarden was still unconscious, and there were still no signs of shock as far as I could see. The snow in the container had mostly melted, and I put half of one brick-hard loaf of bread in it to soak.

A head injury and internal organ damage were the most dangerous possibilities. I broke open the two correctives I'd just bought and lifted the blanket to lay one across Seivarden's abdomen, watched it puddle and stretch and then harden into a clear shell. The other I held to the side of her face that seemed the most bruised. When that one had hardened, I took off my outer coat and lay down and slept.

Slightly more than seven and a half hours later, Seivarden stirred and I woke. "Are you awake?" I asked. The corrective I'd applied held one eye closed, and one half of her mouth, but the bruising and the swelling all over her face was much reduced. I considered for a moment what would be the right facial expression, and made it. "I found you in the snow, in front of a tavern. You looked like you needed help." She gave a faint rasp of breath but didn't turn her head toward me. "Are you hungry?" No answer, just a vacant stare. "Did you hit your head?"

"No," she said, quiet, her face relaxed and slack.

"Are you hungry?"

"No."

"When did you eat last?"

"I don't know." Her voice was calm, without inflection.

I pulled her upright and propped her against the gray-green wall, gingerly, not wanting to cause more injury, wary of her slumping over. She stayed sitting, so I slowly spooned some bread-and-water mush into her mouth, working cautiously around the corrective. "Swallow," I said, and she did. I gave her half of what was in the bowl that way and then I ate the rest myself, and brought in another pan of snow.

She watched me put another half-loaf of hard bread in the pan, but said nothing, her face still placid. "What's your name?" I asked. No answer.

She'd taken kef, I guessed. Most people will tell you that kef suppresses emotion, which it does, but that's not all it does. There was a time when I could have explained exactly what kef does, and how, but I'm not what I once was.

As far as I knew, people took kef so they could stop feeling something. Or because they believed that, emotions out of the way, supreme rationality would result, utter logic, true enlightenment. But it doesn't work that way.

Pulling Seivarden out of the snow had cost me time and money that I could ill afford, and for what? Left to her own devices she would find herself another hit or three of kef, and she would find her way into another place like that grimy tavern and get herself well and truly killed. If that was what she wanted I had no right to prevent her. But if she had wanted to die, why hadn't she done the thing cleanly, registered her intention and gone to the medic as anyone would? I didn't understand.

There was a good deal I didn't understand, and nineteen years pretending to be human hadn't taught me as much as I'd thought.

2

Nineteen years, three months, and one week before I found Seivarden in the snow, I was a troop carrier orbiting the planet Shis'urna. Troop carriers are the most massive of Radchaai ships, sixteen decks stacked one on top of the other. Command, Administrative, Medical, Hydroponics, Engineering, Central Access, and a deck for each decade, living and working space for my officers, whose every breath, every twitch of every muscle, was known to me.

Troop carriers rarely move. I sat, as I had sat for most of my two-thousand-year existence in one system or another, feeling the bitter chill of vacuum outside my hull, the planet Shis'urna like a blue-and-white glass counter, its orbiting station coming and going around, a steady stream of ships arriving, docking, undocking, departing toward one or the other of the buoy- and beacon-surrounded gates. From my vantage the boundaries of Shis'urna's various nations and territories weren't visible, though on its night side the planet's cities glowed bright here and there, and webs of roads between them, where they'd been restored since the annexation.

I felt and heard—though didn't always see—the presence of my companion ships—the smaller, faster Swords and Mercies, and most numerous at that time, the Justices, troop carriers like me. The oldest of us was nearly three thousand years old. We had known each other for a long time, and by now we had little to say to each other that had not already been said many times. We were, by and large, companionably silent, not counting routine communications.

As I still had ancillaries, I could be in more than one place at a time. I was also on detached duty in the city of Ors, on the planet Shis'urna, under the command of Esk Decade Lieutenant Awn.

Ors sat half on waterlogged land, half in marshy lake, the lakeward side built on slabs atop foundations sunk deep in the marsh mud. Green slime grew in the canals and joints between slabs, along the lower edges of building columns, on anything stationary the water reached, which varied with the season. The constant stink of hydrogen sulfide only cleared occasionally, when summer storms made the lakeward half of the city tremble and shudder and walkways were knee-deep in water blown in from beyond the barrier islands. Occasionally. Usually the storms made the smell worse. They turned the air temporarily cooler, but the relief generally lasted no more than a few days. Otherwise, it was always humid and hot.

I couldn't see Ors from orbit. It was more village than city, though it had once sat at the mouth of a river, and been the capital of a country that stretched along the coastline. Trade had come up and down the river, and flat-bottomed boats had plied the coastal marsh, bringing people from one town to the next. The river had shifted away over the centuries, and now Ors was half ruins. What had once been miles of rectangular islands within a grid of channels was now a much smaller place, surrounded by and interspersed with broken, half-sunken slabs, sometimes with roofs and pillars, that emerged from the muddy green water in the dry season. It had once been home to millions. Only 6,318 people had lived here when Radchaai forces annexed Shis'urna five years earlier, and of course the annexation had reduced that number. In Ors less than in some other places: as soon as we had appeared—myself in the form of my Esk cohorts along with their decade lieutenants lined up in the streets of the town, armed and armored—the head priest of Ikkt had approached the most senior officer present—Lieutenant Awn, as I said—and offered immediate surrender. The head priest had told her followers what they needed to do to survive the annexation, and for the most part those followers did indeed survive. This wasn't as common as one might think—we always made it clear from the beginning that even breathing trouble during an annexation could mean death, and from the instant an annexation began we made demonstrations of just what that meant widely available, but there was always someone who couldn't resist trying us.

Still, the head priest's influence was impressive. The city's small size was to some degree deceptive—during pilgrimage season hundreds of thousands of visitors streamed through the plaza in front of the temple, camped on the slabs of abandoned streets. For worshippers of Ikkt this was the second holiest place on the planet, and the head priest a divine presence.

Usually a civilian police force was in place by the time an annexation was officially complete, something that often took fifty years or more. This annexation was different—citizenship had been granted to the surviving Shis'urnans much earlier than normal. No one in system administration quite trusted the idea of local civilians working security just yet, and military presence was still quite heavy. So when the annexation of Shis'urna was officially complete, most of *Justice of Toren* Esk went back to the ship, but Lieutenant Awn stayed, and I stayed with her as the twenty-ancillary unit *Justice of Toren* One Esk.

The head priest lived in a house near the temple, one of the few intact buildings from the days when Ors had been a city—four-storied, with a single-sloped roof and open on all sides, though dividers could be raised whenever an occupant wished privacy, and shutters could be rolled down on the outsides during storms. The head priest received Lieutenant Awn in a partition some five meters square, light peering in over the tops of the dark walls.

"You don't," said the priest, an old person with gray hair and a close-cut gray beard, "find serving in Ors a hardship?" Both she and Lieutenant Awn had settled onto cushions—damp, like everything in Ors, and fungal-smelling. The priest wore a length of yellow cloth twisted around her waist, her shoulders inked with shapes, some curling, some angular, that changed depending on the liturgical significance of the day. In deference to Radchaai propriety, she wore gloves.

"Of course not," said Lieutenant Awn, pleasantly—though, I thought, not entirely truthfully. She had dark brown eyes and close-clipped dark hair. Her skin was dark enough that she wouldn't be considered pale, but not so dark as to be fashionable—she could have changed it, hair and eyes as well, but she never had. Instead of her uniform—long brown coat with its scattering of jeweled pins, shirt and trousers, boots and gloves—

she wore the same sort of skirt the head priest did, and a thin shirt and the lightest of gloves. Still, she was sweating. I stood at the entrance, silent and straight, as a junior priest laid cups and bowls in between Lieutenant Awn and the Divine.

I also stood some forty meters away, in the temple itself—an atypically enclosed space 43.5 meters high, 65.7 meters long, and 29.9 meters wide. At one end were doors nearly as tall as the roof was high, and at the other, towering over the people on the floor below, a representation of a mountainside cliff somewhere else on Shis'urna, worked in painstaking detail. At the foot of this sat a dais, wide steps leading down to a floor of gray-and-green stone. Light streamed in through dozens of green skylights, onto walls painted with scenes from the lives of the saints of the cult of Ikkt. It was unlike any other building in Ors. The architecture, like the cult of Ikkt itself, had been imported from elsewhere on Shis'urna. During pilgrimage season this space would be jammed tight with worshippers. There were other holy sites, but if an Orsian said "pilgrimage" she meant the annual pilgrimage to this place. But that was some weeks away. For now the air of the temple susurrated faintly in one corner with the whispered prayers of a dozen devotees.

The head priest laughed. "You are a diplomat, Lieutenant Awn."

"I am a soldier, Divine," answered Lieutenant Awn. They were speaking Radchaai, and she spoke slowly and precisely, careful of her accent. "I don't find my duty a hardship."

The head priest did not smile in response. In the brief silence that followed, the junior priest set down a lipped bowl of what Shis'urnans call tea, a thick liquid, lukewarm and sweet, that bears almost no relationship to the actual thing.

Outside the doors of the temple I also stood in the

cyanophyte-stained plaza, watching people as they passed. Most wore the same simple, bright-colored skirting the head priest did, though only very small children and the very devout had much in the way of markings, and only a few wore gloves. Some of those passing were transplants, Radchaai assigned to jobs or given property here in Ors after the annexation. Most of them had adopted the simple skirt and added a light, loose shirt, as Lieutenant Awn had. Some stuck stubbornly to trousers and jacket, and sweated their way across the plaza. All wore the jewelry that few Radchaai would ever give up—gifts from friends or lovers, memorials to the dead, marks of family or clientage associations.

To the north, past a rectangular stretch of water called the Fore-Temple after the neighborhood it had once been, Ors rose slightly where the city sat on actual ground during the dry season, an area still called, politely, the upper city. I patrolled there as well. When I walked the edge of the water I could see myself standing in the plaza.

Boats poled slowly across the marshy lake, and up and down channels between groupings of slabs. The water was scummy with swaths of algae, here and there bristling with the tips of water-grasses. Away from the town, east and west, buoys marked prohibited stretches of water, and within their confines the iridescent wings of marshflies shimmered over the water weeds floating thick and tangled there. Around them larger boats floated, and the big dredgers, now silent and still, that before the annexation had hauled up the stinking mud that lay beneath the water.

The view to the south was similar, except for the barest hint on the horizon of the actual sea, past the soggy spit that bounded the swamp. I saw all of this, standing as I did at various points surrounding the temple, and walking the streets of the town itself. It was twenty-seven degrees C, and humid as always.

That accounted for almost half of my twenty bodies. The remainder slept or worked in the house Lieutenant Awn occupied—three-storied and spacious, it had once housed a large extended family and a boat rental. One side opened on a broad, muddy green canal, and the opposite onto the largest of local streets.

Three of the segments in the house were awake, performing administrative duties (I sat on a mat on a low platform in the center of the first floor of the house and listened to an Orsian complain to me about the allocation of fishing rights) and keeping watch. "You should bring this to the district magistrate, citizen," I told the Orsian, in the local dialect. Because I knew everyone here, I knew she was female, and a grandparent, both of which had to be acknowledged if I were to speak to her not only grammatically but also courteously.

"I don't know the district magistrate!" she protested, indignant. The magistrate was in a large, populous city well upriver from Ors and nearby Kould Ves. Far enough upriver that the air was often cool and dry, and things didn't smell of mildew all the time. "What does the district magistrate know about Ors? For all I know the district magistrate doesn't exist!" She continued, explaining to me the long history of her house's association with the buoy-enclosed area, which was off-limits and certainly closed to fishing for the next three years.

And as always, in the back of my mind, a constant awareness of being in orbit overhead.

"Come now, Lieutenant," said the head priest. "No one likes Ors except those of us unfortunate enough to be born here. Most Shis'urnans I know, let alone Radchaai, would rather be in a city, with dry land and actual seasons besides rainy and not rainy."

Lieutenant Awn, still sweating, accepted a cup of so-called tea, and drank without grimacing—a matter of practice and determination. "My superiors are asking for my return."

On the relatively dry northern edge of the town, two brown-uniformed soldiers passing in an open runabout saw me, raised hands in greeting. I raised my own, briefly. "One Esk!" one of them called. They were common soldiers, from *Justice of Ente*'s Seven Issa unit, under Lieutenant Skaaiat. They patrolled the stretch of land between Ors and the far southwestern edge of Kould Ves, the city that had grown up around the river's newer mouth. The *Justice of Ente* Seven Issas were human, and knew I was not. They always treated me with slightly guarded friendliness.

"I would prefer you stay," said the head priest, to Lieutenant Awn. Though Lieutenant Awn had already known that. We'd have been back on *Justice of Toren* two years before, but for the Divine's continued request that we stay.

"You understand," said Lieutenant Awn, "they would much prefer to replace One Esk with a human unit. Ancillaries can stay in suspension indefinitely. Humans . . ." She set down her tea, took a flat, yellow-brown cake. "Humans have families they want to see again, they have lives. They can't stay frozen for centuries, the way ancillaries sometimes do. It doesn't make sense to have ancillaries out of the holds doing work when there are human soldiers who could do it." Though Lieutenant Awn had been here five years, and routinely met with the head priest, it was the first time the topic had been broached so plainly. She frowned, and changes in her respiration and hormone levels told me she'd thought of something dismaying. "You haven't had problems with *Justice of Ente* Seven Issa, have you?"

"No," said the head priest. She looked at Lieutenant Awn with a wry twist to her mouth. "I know you. I know One Esk. Whoever they'll send me—I won't know. Neither will my parishioners."

"Annexations are messy," said Lieutenant Awn. The head priest winced slightly at the word *annexation* and I thought I saw Lieutenant Awn notice, but she continued. "Seven Issa wasn't here for that. The *Justice of Ente* Issa battalions didn't do anything during that time that One Esk didn't also do."

"No, Lieutenant." The priest put down her own cup, seeming disturbed, but I didn't have access to any of her internal data and so could not be certain. "*Justice of Ente* Issa did many things One Esk did not. It's true, One Esk killed as many people as the soldiers of *Justice of Ente*'s Issa. Likely more." She looked at me, still standing silent by the enclosure's entrance. "No offense, but I think it was more."

"I take no offense, Divine," I replied. The head priest frequently spoke to me as though I were a person. "And you are correct."

"Divine," said Lieutenant Awn, worry clear in her voice. "If the soldiers of *Justice of Ente* Seven Issa—or anyone else—have been abusing citizens . . ."

"No, no!" protested the head priest, her voice bitter. "Radchaai are so very careful about how citizens are treated!"

Lieutenant Awn's face heated, her distress and anger plain to me. I couldn't read her mind, but I could read every twitch of her every muscle, so her emotions were as transparent to me as glass.

"Forgive me," said the head priest, though Lieutenant Awn's expression had not changed, and her skin was too dark to show the flush of her anger. "Since the Radchaai have bestowed citizenship on us . . ." She stopped, seemed to reconsider her words.

"Since their arrival, Seven Issa has given me nothing to complain of. But I've seen what your human troops did during what you call *the annexation*. The citizenship you granted may be as easily taken back, and . . ."

"We wouldn't . . ." protested Lieutenant Awn.

The head priest stopped her with a raised hand. "I know what Seven Issa, or at least those like them, do to people they find on the wrong side of a dividing line. Five years ago it was noncitizen. In the future, who knows? Perhaps not-citizen-enough?" She waved a hand, a gesture of surrender. "It won't matter. Such boundaries are too easy to create."

"I can't blame you for thinking in such terms," said Lieutenant Awn. "It was a difficult time."

"And I can't help but think you inexplicably, unexpectedly naive," said the head priest. "One Esk will shoot me if you order it. Without hesitation. But One Esk would never beat me or humiliate me, or rape me, for no purpose but to show its power over me, or to satisfy some sick amusement." She looked at me. "Would you?"

"No, Divine," I said.

"The soldiers of *Justice of Ente* Issa did all of those things. Not to me, it's true, and not to many in Ors itself. But they did them nonetheless. Would Seven Issa have been any different, if it had been them here instead?"

Lieutenant Awn sat, distressed, looking down at her unappetizing tea, unable to answer.

"It's strange. You hear stories about ancillaries, and it seems like the most awful thing, the most viscerally appalling thing the Radchaai have done. Garsedd—well, yes, Garsedd, but that was a thousand years ago. This—to invade and take, what, half the adult population? And turn them into walking corpses, slaved to your ships' AIs. Turned against their own people. If you'd asked me before you . . . *annexed* us, I'd have said it was a fate worse than death." She turned to me. "Is it?"

"None of my bodies is dead, Divine," I said. "And your estimate of the typical percentage of annexed populations who were made into ancillaries is excessive."

"You used to horrify me," said the head priest to me. "The very thought of you near was terrifying, your dead faces, those expressionless voices. But today I am more horrified at the thought of a unit of living human beings who serve voluntarily. Because I don't think I could trust them."

"Divine," said Lieutenant Awn, mouth tight. "I serve voluntarily. I make no excuses for it."

"I believe you are a good person, Lieutenant Awn, despite that." She picked up her cup of tea and sipped it, as though she had not just said what she had said.

Lieutenant Awn's throat tightened, and her lips. She had thought of something she wanted to say, but was unsure if she should. "You've heard about Ime," she said, deciding. Still tense and wary despite having chosen to speak.

The head priest seemed bleakly, bitterly amused. "News from Ime is meant to inspire confidence in Radch administration?"

This is what had happened: Ime Station, and the smaller stations and moons in the system, were the farthest one could be from a provincial palace and still be in Radch space. For years the governor of Ime used this distance to her own advantage—embezzling, collecting bribes and protection fees, selling assignments. Thousands of citizens had been unjustly executed or (what was essentially the same thing) forced into service as ancillary bodies, even though the manufacture of ancillaries was no longer legal. The governor controlled all communications and travel permits, and normally a station AI would report such activity to the authorities, but Ime Station had been somehow prevented from doing so, and the corruption grew, and spread unchecked.

Until a ship entered the system, came out of gate space only a few hundred kilometers from the patrol ship *Mercy of Sarrse*. The strange ship didn't answer demands that it identify itself. When *Mercy of Sarrse*'s crew attacked and boarded it, they found dozens of humans, as well as the alien Rrrrrr. The captain of *Mercy of Sarrse* ordered her soldiers to take captive any humans that seemed suitable for use as ancillaries, and kill the rest, along with all the aliens. The ship would be turned over to the system governor.

Mercy of Sarrse was not the only human-crewed warship in that system. Until that moment human soldiers stationed there had been kept in line by a program of bribes, flattery, and, when those failed, threats and even executions. All very effective, until the moment the soldier *Mercy of Sarrse* One Amaat One decided she wasn't willing to kill those people, or the Rrrrrr. And convinced the rest of her unit to follow her.

That had all happened five years before. The results of it were still playing themselves out.

Lieutenant Awn shifted on her cushion. "That business was all uncovered because a single human soldier refused an order. And led a mutiny. If it hadn't been for her . . . well. Ancillaries won't do that. They can't."

"That business was all uncovered," replied the head priest, "because the ship that human soldier boarded, she and the rest of her unit, had aliens on it. Radchaai have few qualms about killing humans, especially noncitizen humans, but you're very cautious about starting wars with aliens."

Only because wars with aliens might run up against the terms of the treaty with the alien Presger. Violating that agreement would have extremely serious consequences. And even so, plenty of high-ranking Radchaai disagreed on that topic. I saw Lieutenant Awn's desire to argue the point. Instead she said, "The governor of Ime was not cautious about it. And would have started that war, if not for this one person."

"Have they executed that person yet?" the head priest asked, pointedly. It was the summary fate of any soldier who refused an order, let alone mutinied.

"Last I heard," said Lieutenant Awn, breath tight and turning shallow, "the Rrrrrr had agreed to turn her over to Radch authorities." She swallowed. "I don't know what's going to happen." Of course, it had probably already happened, whatever it was. News could take a year or more to reach Shis'urna from as far away as Ime.

The head priest didn't answer for a moment. She poured more tea, and spooned fish paste into a small bowl. "Does my continued request for your presence present any sort of disadvantage for you?"

"No," said Lieutenant Awn. "Actually, the other Esk lieutenants are a bit envious. There's no chance for action on *Justice of Toren*." She picked up her own cup, outwardly calm, inwardly angry. Disturbed. Talking about the news from Ime had increased her unease. "Action means commendations, and possibly promotions." And this was the last annexation. The last chance for an officer to enrich her house through connections to new citizens, or even through outright appropriation.

"Yet another reason I would prefer you," said the head priest.

I followed Lieutenant Awn home. And watched inside the temple, and overlooked the people crisscrossing the plaza as they always did, avoiding the children playing kau in the center of the plaza, kicking the ball back and forth, shouting and laughing. On the edge of the Fore-Temple water, a teenager from the upper city sat sullen and listless watching half a dozen little children hopping from stone to stone, singing:

One, two, my aunt told me
Three, four, the corpse soldier
Five, six, it'll shoot you in the eye
Seven, eight, kill you dead
Nine, ten, break it apart and put it back together.

As I walked the streets people greeted me, and I greeted them in return. Lieutenant Awn was tense and angry, and only nodded absently at the people in the street, who greeted her as she passed.

The person with the fishing-rights complaint left, unsatisfied. Two children rounded the divider after she had gone, and sat cross-legged on the cushion she had vacated. They both wore lengths of fabric wrapped around their waists, clean but faded, though no gloves. The elder was about nine, and the symbols inked on the younger one's chest and shoulders—slightly smudged—indicated she was no more than six. She looked at me, frowning.

In Orsian addressing children properly was easier than addressing adults. One used a simple, ungendered form. "Hello, citizens," I said, in the local dialect. I recognized them both— they lived on the south edge of Ors and I had spoken to them quite frequently, but they had never visited the house before. "How can I help you?"

"You aren't One Esk," said the smaller child, and the older made an abortive motion as if to hush her.

"I am," I said, and pointed to the insignia on my uniform jacket. "See? Only this is my number Fourteen segment."

"I *told* you," said the older child.

The younger considered this for a moment, and then said, "I have a song." I waited in silence, and she took a deep breath, as though about to begin, and then halted, perplexed-seeming. "Do you want to hear it?" she asked, still doubtful of my identity, likely.

"Yes, citizen," I said. I—that is, I–One Esk—first sang to amuse one of my lieutenants, when *Justice of Toren* had hardly been commissioned a hundred years. She enjoyed music, and had brought an instrument with her as part of her luggage allowance. She could never interest the other officers in her hobby and so she taught me the parts to the songs she played. I filed those away and went looking for more, to please her. By the time she was captain of her own ship I had collected a large library of vocal music—no one was going to give me an instrument, but I could sing anytime—and it was a matter of rumor and some indulgent smiles that *Justice of Toren* had an interest in singing. Which it didn't—I—I–*Justice of Toren*—tolerated the habit because it was harmless, and because it was quite possible that one of my captains would appreciate it. Otherwise it would have been prevented.

If these children had stopped me on the street, they would have had no hesitation, but here in the house, seated as though for a formal conference, things were different. And I suspected this was an exploratory visit, that the youngest child meant to eventually ask for a chance to serve in the house's makeshift temple—the prestige of being appointed flower-bearer to Amaat wasn't a question here, in the stronghold of Ikkt, but the customary term-end gift of fruit and clothing was. And this child's best friend was currently a flower-bearer, doubtless making the prospect more interesting.

No Orsian would make such a request immediately or directly, so likely the child had chosen this oblique approach, turning a casual encounter into something formal and intimidating. I reached into my jacket pocket and pulled out a handful of sweets and laid them on the floor between us.

The littler girl made an affirmative gesture, as though I had resolved all her doubts, and then took a breath and began.

My heart is a fish
Hiding in the water-grass
In the green, in the green.

The tune was an odd amalgam of a Radchaai song that played occasionally on broadcast and an Orsian one I already knew. The words were unfamiliar to me. She sang four verses in a clear, slightly wavering voice, and seemed ready to launch into a fifth, but stopped abruptly when Lieutenant Awn's steps sounded outside the divider.

The smaller girl leaned forward and scooped up her payment. Both children bowed, still half-seated, and then rose and ran out the entranceway into the wider house, past Lieutenant Awn, past me following Lieutenant Awn.

"Thank you, citizens," Lieutenant Awn said to their retreating backs, and they started, and then managed with a single movement to both bow slightly in her direction and continue running, out into the street.

"Anything new?" asked Lieutenant Awn, though she didn't pay much attention to music, herself, not beyond what most people do.

"Sort of," I said. Farther down the street I saw the two children, still running as they turned a corner around another house. They slowed to a halt, breathing hard. The littler girl opened her hand to show the older one her fistful of sweets. Surprisingly, she seemed not to have dropped any, small as her hand was, as quick as their flight had been. The older child took a sweet and put it in her mouth.

Five years ago I would have offered something more nutritious, before repairs had begun to the planet's infrastructure, when supplies were chancy. Now every citizen was guaranteed enough to eat, but the rations were not luxurious, and often as not were unappealing.

Inside the temple all was green-lit silence. The head priest did not emerge from behind the screens in the temple residence, though junior priests came and went. Lieutenant Awn went to the second floor of her house and sat brooding on an Ors-style cushion, screened from the street, shirt thrown off. She refused the (genuine) tea I brought her. I transmitted a steady stream of information to her—everything normal, everything routine—and to *Justice of Toren.* "She should take that to the district magistrate," Lieutenant Awn said of the citizen with the fishing dispute, slightly annoyed, eyes closed, the afternoon's reports in her vision. "We don't have jurisdiction over that." I didn't answer. No answer was required, or expected. She approved, with a quick twitch of her fingers, the message I had composed for the district magistrate, and then opened the most recent message from her young sister. Lieutenant Awn sent a percentage of her earnings home to her parents, who used it to buy their younger child poetry lessons. Poetry was a valuable, civilized accomplishment. I couldn't judge if Lieutenant Awn's sister had any particular talent, but then not many did, even among more elevated families. But her work and her letters pleased Lieutenant Awn, and took the edge off her present distress.

The children on the plaza ran away home, laughing. The adolescent sighed, heavily, the way adolescents do, and dropped a pebble in the water and stared at the ripples.

Ancillary units that only ever woke for annexations often wore nothing but a force shield generated by an implant in each body, rank on rank of featureless soldiers that might have been poured from mercury. But I was always out of the holds, and I wore the same uniform human soldiers did, now the fighting was done. My bodies sweated under my uniform jackets, and, bored, I opened three of my mouths, all in close proximity to each other on the temple plaza, and sang with those three voices, "My heart is a fish, hiding in the water-grass . . ." One person walking by looked at me, startled, but everyone else ignored me—they were used to me by now.

3

The next morning the correctives had fallen off, and the bruising on Seivarden's face had faded. She seemed comfortable, but she still seemed high, so that was hardly surprising.

I unrolled the bundle of clothes I had bought for her—insulated underclothes, quilted shirt and trousers, undercoat and hooded overcoat, gloves—and laid them out. Then I took her chin and turned her head toward me. "Can you hear me?"

"Yes." Her dark brown eyes stared somewhere distant over my left shoulder.

"Get up." I tugged on her arm, and she blinked, lazily, and got as far as sitting up before the impulse deserted her. But I managed to dress her, in fits and starts, and then I stowed what few things were still out, shouldered my pack, took Seivarden by the arm, and left.

There was a flier rental at the edge of town, and predictably the proprietor wouldn't rent to me unless I put down twice the advertised deposit. I told her I intended to fly northwest, to visit a herding camp—an outright lie, which she likely knew. "You're an offworlder," she said. "You don't know what it's like away from the towns. Offworlders are always flying out to herding camps and getting lost. Sometimes we find them again, sometimes not." I said nothing. "You'll lose my flier and then where will I be? Out in the snow with my starving children, that's where." Beside me Seivarden stared vaguely off into the distance.

I was forced to put down the money. I had a strong suspicion I would never see it again. Then the proprietor demanded extra because I couldn't display a local pilot certification—something I knew wasn't required. If it had been, I would have forged one before I came.

In the end, though, she gave me the flier. I checked its engine, which seemed clean and in good repair, and made sure of the fuel. When I was satisfied, I put my pack in, seated Seivarden, and then climbed into the pilot's seat.

Two days after the storm, the snowmoss was beginning to show again, sweeps of pale green with darker threads here and there. After two more hours we flew over a line of hills, and the green darkened dramatically, lined and irregularly veined in a dozen shades, like malachite. In some places the moss was smeared and trampled by the creatures that grazed on it, herds of long-haired bov making their way southward as spring advanced. And along those paths, on the edges here and there, ice devils lay in carefully tunneled lairs, waiting for a bov to put a foot wrong so they could drag it down. I saw no trace of them, but even the herders who lived their lives following the bov couldn't always tell when one was near.